The Ultimate Persuasion

CATHY WILLIAMS

MILLS & BOON

First Published in Great Britain 2016
By Mills & Boon, an imprint of HarperCollins*Publishers*
1 London Bridge Street, London, SE1 9GF

THE ULTIMATE PERSUASION © 2016 Harlequin Books S. A.

A Tempestuous Temptation, *The Notorious Gabriel Diaz* and *The Truth Behind His Touch* were first published in Great Britain by Harlequin (UK) Limited.

A Tempestuous Temptation © 2012 Cathy Williams.
The Notorious Gabriel Diaz © 2013 Cathy Williams.
The Truth Behind His Touch © 2012 Cathy Williams.

ISBN: 978-0-263-92056-7

05-0316

Our policy is to use papers that are natural, renewable and recyclable products and made from wood grown in sustainable forests.The logging and manufacturing processes conform to the legal environmental regulations of the country of origin.

Printed and bound in Spain
by CPI, Barcelona

Cathy Williams is originally from Trinidad, but has lived in England for a number of years. She currently has a house in Warwickshire, which she shares with her husband Richard, her three daughters, Charlotte, Olivia and Emma, and their pet cat, Salem. She adores writing romantic fiction, and would love one of her girls to become a writer—although at the moment she is happy enough if they do their homework and agree not to bicker with one another!

A TEMPESTUOUS TEMPTATION

BY
CATHY WILLIAMS

CHAPTER ONE

Luiz Carlos Montes looked down at the slip of paper in his hand, reconfirmed that he was at the correct address and then, from the comfort of his sleek, black sports car, he briefly scanned the house and its surroundings. His immediate thought was that this was not what he had been expecting. His second thought was that it had been a mistake to drive his car here. The impression he was getting was that this was the sort of place where anything of any value that could be stolen, damaged or vandalised just for the hell of it would be.

The small terraced house, lit by the street lamp, fought a losing battle to maintain some level of attractiveness next to its less palatable neighbours. The tidy pocket-sized front garden was flanked on its left side by a cement square on which dustbins were laid out in no particular order, and on its right by a similar cement square where a rusted car languished on blocks, awaiting attention. Further along was a parade of shops comprised of a Chinese takeaway, a sub-post office, a hairdresser, an off-licence and a newsagent which seemed to be a meeting point for just the sort of youths whom Luiz suspected would not hesitate to zero in on his car the second he left it.

Fortunately he felt no apprehension as he glanced at the group of hooded teenagers smoking in a group outside the off-licence. He was six-foot-three with a muscled body that was honed to perfection thanks to a rigorous routine of exercise and sport when he could find the time. He was more than capable of putting the fear of God into any group of indolent cigarette-smoking teenagers.

But, hell, this was still the last thing he needed. On a Friday evening. In December. With the threat of snow in the air and a shedload of emails needing his attention before the whole world went to sleep for the Christmas period.

But family duty was, in the end, family duty and what choice had he had? Having seen this dump for himself, he also had to concede that his mission, inconvenient though it might be, was a necessary one.

He exhaled impatiently and swung out of the car. It was a bitterly cold night, even in London. The past week had been characterised by hard overnight frosts that had barely thawed during the day. There was a glittery coating over the rusting car in the garden next to the house and on the lids of the bins in the garden to the other side. The smell of Chinese food wafted towards him and he frowned with distaste.

This was the sort of district into which Luiz never ventured. He had no need to. The faster he could sort this whole mess out and clear out of the place, the better, as far as he was concerned.

With that in mind, he pressed the doorbell and kept his finger on it until he could hear the sound of footsteps scurrying towards the front door.

On the verge of digging into her dinner, Aggie heard the sound of the doorbell and was tempted to ignore it, not least because she had an inkling of an idea as to whose finger was on it. Mr Cholmsey, her landlord, had been making warning noises about the rent, which was overdue.

'But I always pay on time!' Aggie had protested when he had telephoned her the day before. 'And I'm only overdue by *two days*. It's not my fault that there's a postal strike!'

Apparently, though, it was. He had been kind enough to 'do her the favour' of letting her pay by cheque when *all his other tenants* paid by direct debit... And *look where it got him*...it just *wasn't good enough*... People were queuing for that house...he could rent it to a more reliable tenant *in a minute*...

If the cheque wasn't with him *by the following day*, he would have to have cash from her.

She had never actually met Mr Cholmsey. Eighteen months ago, she had found the house through an agency and everything had been absolutely fine—until Mr Cholmsey had decided that he could cut out the middle man and handle his own properties. Since then, Alfred Cholmsey had been an ongoing headache, prone to ignoring requests for things to be fixed and fond of reminding her how scarce rentable properties were in London.

If she ignored the summons at the door, she had no doubt that he would find some way of breaking the lease and chucking her out.

Keeping the latch on, she cautiously opened the door a crack and peered out into the darkness.

'I'm really sorry, Mr Cholmsey...' She burst into speech, determined to get her point of view across before her disagreeable, hateful landlord could launch his verbal attack. 'The cheque should have arrived by now. I'll cancel it and make sure that I have the cash for you tomorrow. I promise.' She wished the wretched man would do her the courtesy of at least standing in her very reduced line of vision instead of skulking to the side, but there was no way that she was going to pull open the door. You could never be too careful in this neighbourhood.

'Who the hell is Mr Cholmsey, and what are you talking about? Just open the door, Agatha!'

That voice, that distinctive, *loathsome* voice, was so unexpected that Aggie suddenly felt the need to pass out. What was Luiz Montes doing here? On her doorstep? *Invading her privacy?* Wasn't it bad enough that she and her brother had been held up for inspection by him over the past eight months? Verbally poked and prodded under the very thin guise of hospitality and 'just getting to know my niece's boyfriend and his family'. Asked intrusive questions which they had been forced to skirt around and generally treated with the sort of suspicion reserved for criminals out on parole.

'What are *you* doing here?'

'Just open the door! I'm not having a conversation with you on your doorstep!' Luiz didn't have to struggle to imagine what her expression would be. He had met her sufficient times with her brother and his niece to realise that she disapproved of everything he stood for and everything he said. She'd challenged him on every point he made. She was defensive, argumentative and pretty much everything he would have made an effort to avoid in a woman.

As he had told himself on numerous occasions, there was no way he would ever have subjected himself to her company had he not been placed, by his sister who lived in Brazil, in the unenviable position of having to take an interest in his niece and the man she had decided to take up with. The Montes family was worth an untold fortune. Checking out the guy his niece was dating was a simple precaution, Luisa had stressed. And, while Luiz couldn't see the point because the relationship was certain to crash and burn in due course, his sister had insisted. Knowing his sister as well as he did, he had taken the path of least resistance and agreed to keep a watchful eye on Mark Collins, and his sister, who appeared to come as part of the package.

'So who's Mr Cholmsey?' was the first thing he said as he strode past her into the house.

Aggie folded her arms and glared resentfully at him as he looked around at his surroundings with the sort of cool contempt she had come to associate with him.

Yes, he was good-looking, all tall and powerful and darkly sexy. But from the very second she had met him, she had been chilled to the bone by his arrogance, his casual contempt for both her and Mark—which he barely bothered to hide—and his thinly veiled threat that he was watching them both and they'd better not overstep the mark.

'Mr Cholmsey's the landlord—and how did you get this address? Why are you here?'

'I had no idea you rented. Stupid me. I was under the impression that you owned your own house jointly. Now, where did I get that from, I wonder?'

He rested cool, dark eyes on Aggie. 'I was also under the impression that you lived somewhere…slightly less unsavoury. A crashing misconception on my part as well.' However far removed Agatha Collins was from the sort of women Luiz preferred—tall brunettes with legs up to their armpits and amenable, yielding natures—he couldn't deny that she was startlingly pretty. Five-four tops, with pale, curly hair the colour of buttermilk and skin that was satiny smooth. Her eyes were purest aquamarine, offset by dark lashes, as though her creator had been determined to make sure that she stood out from the crowd and had taken one little detail and made it strikingly different.

Aggie flushed and mentally cursed herself for falling in

with her brother and Maria. When Luiz had made his first, unwelcome appearance in their lives, she had agreed that she would downplay their financial circumstances, that she would economise harmlessly on the unadorned truth.

'My mum's insisted that Uncle Luiz check Mark out,' Maria had explained tightly. 'And Uncle Luiz is horribly black-and-white. It'd be better if he thinks that you're… okay… Not exactly rich, but not completely broke either.'

'You still haven't told me what you're doing here,' Aggie dodged.

'Where's your brother?'

'He isn't here and neither is Maria. And when are you going to stop *spying* on us?'

'I'm beginning to think that my *spying* is starting to pay dividends,' Luiz murmured. 'Which one of you told me that you lived in Richmond?' He leaned against the wall and looked down at her with those bottomless dark eyes that always managed to send her nervous system into instant freefall.

'I didn't say that we *lived* in Richmond,' Aggie prevaricated guiltily. 'I probably told you that we go cycling there quite a bit. In the park. It's not my fault that you might have got hold of the wrong end of the stick.'

'I *never* get hold of the wrong end of the stick.' The casual interest which he had seen as an unnecessary chore now blossomed into rampant suspicion. She and her brother had lied about their financial circumstances and had probably persuaded his niece to go along for the ride and back them up. And that, to Luiz, was pointing in only one direction. 'When I got the address of this place, I had to double check because it didn't tally with what I'd been told.' He began removing his coat while Aggie watched in growing dismay.

Every single time she had met Luiz, it had been in one

of London's upmarket restaurants. She, Mark and Maria had been treated over time to the finest Italian food money could buy, the best Thai to be found in the country, the most expensive French in the most exclusive area. Pre-warned by Maria that it was her uncle's way of keeping tabs on them, they had been unforthcoming on personal detail and expansive on polite chitchat.

Aggie had bristled at the mere thought that they were being sized up, and she had bristled even more at the nagging suspicion that they had both been found wanting. But restaurants were one thing. Descending on them here was taking it one step too far.

And now his coat was off, which implied that he wasn't about to do the disappearing act she desperately wanted. Something about him unsettled her and here, in this small space, she was even more unsettled.

'Maybe you could get me something to drink,' he inserted smoothly. 'And we can explore what other little lies might come out in the wash while I wait for your brother to show up.'

'Why is it suddenly so important that you talk to Mark?' Aggie asked uneasily. 'I mean, couldn't you have waited? Maybe invited him out for dinner with Maria so that you could try and get to the bottom of his intentions? Again?'

'Things have moved up a gear, regrettably. But I'll come back to that.' He strolled past her through the open door and into the sitting room. The decor here was no more tasteful than it was in the hall. The walls were the colour of off-cheese, depressing despite the old movie posters that had been tacked on. The furniture was an unappealing mix of old and used and tacky, snap-together modern. In one corner, an old television set was propped on a cheap pine unit.

'What do you mean that *things have moved up a gear*?'

Aggie demanded as he sat on one of the chairs and looked at her with unhurried thoroughness.

'I guess you know why I've been keeping tabs on your brother.'

'Maria mentioned that her mother can be a little over-protective,' Aggie mumbled. She resigned herself to the fact that Luiz wasn't leaving in a hurry and reluctantly sat down on the chair facing him.

As always, she felt dowdy and underdressed. On the occasions when she had been dragged along to those fancy restaurants—none of which she would ever have sampled had it not been for him—she had rooted out the dressiest clothes in her wardrobe and had still managed to feel cheap and mousey. Now, in baggy, thick jogging bottoms and Mark's jumper, several sizes too big, she felt screamingly, ridiculously frumpy. Which made her resent him even more.

Luiz gave an elegant shrug. 'It pays to be careful. Naturally, when my sister asked me to check your brother out, I tried to talk her out of it.'

'You did?'

'Sure. Maria's a kid and kids have relationships that fall by the wayside. It's life. I was convinced that this relationship would be no different but I eventually agreed that I would keep an eye on things.'

'By which,' Aggie inserted bitterly, 'you meant that you would quiz us on every aspect of our lives and try and trip us up.'

'Congratulations. You both provided a touchingly united front. I find that I barely know a single personal thing about either of you and it's dawning on me that the few details you've imparted have probably been a tissue of lies—starting with where you live. It would have saved time and effort if I'd employed a detective to ferret out whatever background information was necessary.'

'Maria thought that—'

'Do me a favour. Keep my niece out of this. You live in a dump, which you rent from an unscrupulous land-lord. You can barely afford the rent. Tell me, do either of you hold down jobs, or were those fabrications as well?'

'I resent you barging into my house.'

'Mr Cholmsey's house—if you can call it a house.'

'Fine! I still resent you barging in here and insulting me.'

'Tough.'

'In fact, I'm asking you to leave!'

At that, Luiz burst out laughing. 'Do you really think that I've come all the way here so that I can leave the sec-ond the questioning gets a little too uncomfortable for you?'

'Well, I don't see the point of you hanging around. Mark and Maria aren't here.'

'I've come because, like I said, things have moved up a gear. It seems that there's now talk of marriage. It's not going to do.'

'Talk of marriage?' Aggie parroted incredulously. 'There's no talk of marriage.'

'At least, none that your brother's told you about. Maybe the touching united front isn't quite as united as you'd like it to be.'

'You...you are just the most *awful* human being I've ever met!'

'I think you've made that glaringly clear on all the oc-casions that we've met,' Luiz remarked coolly. 'You're en-titled to your opinions.'

'So you came here to...what? Warn my brother off?

Warn Maria off? They might be young but they're not under age.'

'Maria comes from one of the richest families in Latin America.'

'I beg your pardon?' Aggie looked at him in confusion. Yes, of course she had known that Maria was not the usual hand-to-mouth starving student working the tills on the weekend to help pay for her tuition fees. But *one of the richest families in Latin America?* No wonder she had not been in favour of either of them letting on that they were just normal people struggling to get by on a day-to-day basis!

'You're kidding, right?'

'When it comes to money, I lose my sense of humour.' Luiz abruptly sat forward, elbows resting on his thighs, and looked at her unsmilingly. 'I hadn't planned on taking a hard line, but I'm beginning to do the maths and I don't like the results I'm coming up with.'

Aggie tried and failed to meet his dark, intimidating stare. Why was it that whenever she was in this man's company her usual unflappability was scattered to the four corners? She was reduced to feeling too tight in her skin, too defensive and too self-conscious. Which meant that she could barely think straight.

'I have no idea what you're talking about,' she muttered, staring at her linked fingers while her heart rate sped up and her mouth went dry.

'Wealthy people are often targets,' Luiz gritted, spelling it out in clear syllables just in case she chose to miss the message. 'My niece is extremely wealthy and will be even wealthier when she turns twenty-one. Now it appears that the dalliance I thought would peter out after a couple of months has turned into a marriage proposal.'

'I still can't believe that. You've got your facts wrong.'

'Believe it! And what I'm seeing are a couple of fortune hunters who have lied about their circumstances to try and throw me off course.'

Aggie blanched and stared at him miserably. Those small white fibs had assumed the proportions of mountains. Her brain felt sluggish but already she could see why he would have arrived at the conclusion that he had.

Honest people didn't lie.

'Tell me…is your brother really a musician? Because I've looked him up online and, strangely enough, I can't find him anywhere.'

'Of course he's a musician! He…he plays in a band.'

'And I'm guessing this band hasn't made it big yet… hence his lack of presence on the Internet.'

'Okay! I give up! So we may have…have…'

'Tampered with the truth? Stretched it? Twisted it to the point where it became unrecognisable?'

'Maria said that you're very black-and-white.' Aggie stuck her chin up and met his frowning stare. Now, as had happened before, she marvelled that such sinful physical beauty, the sort of beauty that made people think of putting paint to canvas, could conceal such a cold, ruthless, brutally dispassionate streak.

'Me? Black-and-white?' Luiz was outraged at this preposterous assumption. 'I've never heard anything so ridiculous in my entire life!'

'She said that you form your opinions and you stick to them. You never look outside the box and allow yourself to be persuaded into another direction.'

'That's called strength of character!'

'Well, that's why we weren't inclined to be one hundred percent truthful. Not that we *lied*…'

'We just didn't reveal as much as we could have.'

'Such as you live in a rented dump, your brother sings

in pubs now and again and you are a teacher—or was that another one of those creative exaggerations?'

'Of course I'm a teacher. I teach primary school. You can check up on me if you like!'

'Well that's now by the by. The fact is, I cannot allow any marriage to take place between my niece and your brother.'

'So you're going to do what, exactly?' Aggie was genuinely bewildered. It was one thing to disapprove of someone else's choices. It was quite another to force them into accepting what you chose to cram down their throat. Luiz, Maria's mother, every single member of their superwealthy family, for that matter, could rant, storm, wring their hands and deliver threatening lectures—but at the end of the day Maria was her own person and would make up her own mind.

She tactfully decided not to impart that point of view. He claimed that he wasn't black-and-white but she had seen enough evidence of that to convince her that he was. He also had no knowledge whatsoever of how the other half lived. In fact, she doubted that he had ever even come into contact with people who weren't exactly like him, until she and Mark had come along.

'Look.' She relented slightly as another point of view pushed its way through her self-righteous anger. 'I can understand that you might harbour one or two reservations about my brother...'

'Can you?' Luiz asked with biting sarcasm.

Right now he was kicking himself for not having taken a harder look at the pair of them. He was usually as sharp as they came when other people and their motivations were involved. He had had to be. So how had they managed to slip through the net?

Her brother was disingenuous, engaging, apparently

open. He looked like the kind of guy who could hold his own with anyone—tall, muscular, with the same shade of blonde hair as his sister but tied back in a ponytail; when he spoke, his voice was low and gentle.

And Agatha—so stunningly pretty that anyone could be forgiven for staring. But, alongside that, she had also been forthright and opinionated. Was that what had taken him in—the combination of two very different personalities? Had they cunningly worked off each other to throw him off-guard? Or had he just failed to take the situation seriously because he hadn't thought the boy's relationship with his niece would ever come to anything? Luisa was famously protective of Maria. Had he just assumed that her request for him to keep an eye out had been more of the same?

At any rate, they had now been caught out in a tangle of lies and that, to his mind, could mean only one thing.

The fact that he'd been a fool for whatever reason was something he would have to live with, but it stuck in his throat.

'And I know how it must look…that we weren't completely open with you. But you have to believe me when I tell you that you have nothing to fear.'

'Point one—fear is an emotion that's alien to me. Point two—I don't have to believe anything you say, which brings me to your question.'

'My question?'

'You wondered what I intended to do about this mess.'

Aggie felt her hackles rise, as they invariably did on the occasions when she had met him, and she made a valiant effort to keep them in check.

'So you intend to warn my brother off,' she said on a sigh.

'Oh, I intend to do much better than that,' Luiz drawled,

watching the faint colour in her cheeks and thinking that she was a damn good actress. 'You look as though you could use some money, and I suspect your brother could as well. You have a landlord baying down your neck for unpaid rent.'

'I paid!' Aggie insisted vigorously. 'It's not my fault that there's a postal strike!'

'And whatever you earn as a teacher,' Luiz continued, not bothering to give her protest house room, 'It obviously isn't enough to scrape by. Face it, if you can't afford the rent for a dump like this, then it's pretty obvious that neither of you has a penny to rub together. So my offer to get your brother off the scene and out of my niece's life should put a big smile on your face. In fact, I would go so far as to say that it should make your Christmas.'

'I don't know what you're talking about.'

Those big blue eyes, Luiz thought sourly. They had done a damn good job of throwing him off the scent.

'I'm going to give you and your brother enough money to clear out of this place. You'll each be able to afford to buy somewhere of your own, live the high life, if that's what takes your fancy. And I suspect it probably is...'

'You're going to *pay us off*? To make us *disappear*?'

'Name your price. And naturally your brother can name his. No one has ever accused me of not being a generous man. And on the subject of your brother...when exactly is he due back?' He looked pointedly at his watch and then raised his eyes to her flushed, angry face. She was perched on the very edge of her chair, ramrod-erect, and her knuckles were white where her fingers were biting into the padded seat. She was the very picture of outrage.

'I can't believe I'm hearing this.'

'I'm sure you'll find it remarkably easy to adjust to the thought.'

'You can't just *buy people off*!'

'No? Care to take a small bet on that?' His eyes were as hard and as cold as the frost gathering outside. 'Doubtless your brother wishes to further his career, if he's even interested in a career. Maybe he'd just like to blow some money on life's little luxuries. Doubtless he ascertained my niece's financial status early on in the relationship and between the two of you you decided that she was your passport to a more lucrative lifestyle. It now appears that he intends to marry her and thereby get his foot through the door, so to speak, but that's not going to happen in a million years. So when you say that I can't *buy people off*? Well, I think you'll find that I can.'

Aggie stared at him open-mouthed. She felt as though she was in the presence of someone from another planet. Was this how the wealthy behaved, as though they owned everything and everyone? As though people were pieces on a chess board to be moved around on a whim and disposed of without scruple? And why was she so surprised when she had always known that he was ruthless, cold-hearted and single-minded?

'Mark and Maria love each other! That must have been obvious to you.'

'I'm sure Maria imagines herself in love. She's young. She doesn't realise that love is an illusion. And we can sit around chatting all evening, but I still need to know when he'll be here. I want to get this situation sorted as soon as possible.'

'He won't.'

'Come again?'

'I mean,' Aggie ventured weakly, because she knew that the bloodless, heartless man in front of her wasn't going to warm to what she was about to tell him, 'he and Maria decided to have a few days away. A spur-of-the-moment thing. A little pre-Christmas break…'

'Tell me I'm not hearing this.'

'They left yesterday morning.'

She started as he vaulted upright without warning and began pacing the room, his movements restless and menacing.

'Left to go where?' It was a question phrased more like a demand. 'And don't even think of using your looks to pull a fast one.'

'Using my looks?' Aggie felt hot colour crawl into her face. While she had been sitting there in those various restaurants, feeling as awkward and as colourless as a sparrow caught up in a parade of peacocks, had he been looking at her, assessing what she looked like? That thought made her feel weirdly unsteady.

'Where have they gone?' He paused to stand in front of her and Aggie's eyes travelled up—up along that magnificent body sheathed in clothes that looked far too expensive and far too hand-made for their surroundings—until they settled on the forbidding angles of his face. She had never met someone who exuded threat and power the way he did, and who used that to his advantage.

'I don't have to give you that information,' she said stoutly and tried not to quail as his expression darkened.

'I really wouldn't play that game with me if I were you, Agatha.'

'Or else what?'

'Or else I'll make sure that your brother finds himself without a job in the foreseeable future. And the money angle? Off the cards.'

'You can't do that. I mean, you can't do anything to ruin his musical career.'

'Oh no? Please don't put that to the test.'

Aggie hesitated. There was such cool certainty in his voice that she had no doubt that he really would make sure her brother lost his job if she didn't comply and tell him what he wanted.

'Okay. They've gone to a little country hotel in the Lake District,' she imparted reluctantly. 'They wanted a romantic, snowed-in few days, and that part of the world has a lot of sentimental significance for us.' Her bag was on the ground next to her. She reached in, rummaged around and extracted a sheet of paper, confirmation of their booking. 'He gave me this, because it's got all the details in case I wanted to get in touch with him.'

'The Lake District. They've gone to the *Lake District*.' He raked his fingers through his hair, snatched the paper from her and wondered if things could get any worse. The Lake District was not exactly a hop and skip away. Nor was it a plane-ride away. He contemplated the prospect of spending hours behind the wheel of his car in bad driving conditions on a search-and-rescue mission for his sister— because if they were thinking of getting married on the sly, what better time or place? Or else doing battle with the public transport system which was breaking under the weight of the bad weather. He eliminated the public-transport option without hesitation. Which brought him back to the prospect of hours behind the wheel of his car.

'You make it sound as though they've taken a trip to the moon. Well, I guess you'll want to give Maria a call... I'm not sure there's any mobile-phone service there, though. In fact, there isn't. You'll have to phone through to the hotel and get them to transfer you. She can reassure you that they're not about to take a walk down the aisle.' Aggie wondered how her brother was going to deal with Luiz when Luiz waved a wad of notes in front of him and told him to clear off or else. Mark, stupidly, actually liked the man, and stuck up for him whenever Aggie happened to mention how much he got on her nerves.

Not her problem. She struggled to squash her instinctive urge to look out for him. She and Mark had been a tight unit since they were children, when their mother had died and, in the absence of any father, or any relatives for that matter, they had been put into care. Younger by four years, he had been a sickly child, debilitated by frequent asthma attacks. Like a surrogate mother hen, she had learnt to take care of him and to put his needs ahead of her own. She had gained strength, allowing him the freedom to be the gentle, dreamy child who had matured into a gentle, dreamy adult—despite his long hair, his earring and the tattoo on his shoulder which seemed to announce a different kind of person.

'Well, now that you know where they are, I guess you'll be leaving.'

Luiz, looking at her down-bent head, pondered this sequence of events. Missing niece. Missing boyfriend. Long trip to locate them.

'I don't know why I didn't see this coming,' he mused. 'Having a few days away would be the perfect opportunity for your brother to seal the deal. Maybe my presence on the scene alerted him to the fact that time wouldn't be on his side when it came to marrying my niece. Maybe he figured that the courtship would have to be curtailed and the main event brought forward...a winter wedding. Very romantic.'

'That's the most ridiculous thing I've ever heard!'

'I'd be surprised if you didn't say that. Well, it's not going to happen. We'll just have to make sure that we get to that romantic hideaway and surprise them before they have time to do anything regrettable.'

'*We?*'

Luiz looked at her with raised eyebrows. 'Well, you don't imagine that I'm going to go there on my own and leave you behind so that you can get on the phone and warn your brother of my impending arrival, do you?'

'You're crazy! I'm not going anywhere with you, Luiz Montes!'

'It's not ideal timing, and I can't say that I haven't got better things to do on a Friday evening, but I can't see a way out of it. I anticipate we'll be there by tomorrow lunchtime, so you'll have to pack enough for a weekend and make it quick. I'll need to get back to my place so that I can throw some things in a bag.'

'You're not hearing what I'm saying!'

'Correction. I am hearing. I'm just choosing to ignore what you're saying because none of it will make any difference to what I intend to do.'

'I refuse to go along with this!'

'Here's the choice. We go, I chat to your brother, I dangle my financial inducement in front of him… A few tears all round to start with but in the end everyone's happy. Plan B is I send my men up to physically bring him back to London, where he'll find that life can be very uncomfortable when all avenues of work are dried up. I'll put the word out in the music industry that he's not to be touched with a barge pole. You'd be surprised if you knew the extent of my connections. One word—*vast*. I'm guessing that as his loyal, devoted sister, option two might be tough to swallow.'

'You are…are…'

'Yes, yes, yes. I know what you think of me. I'll give you ten minutes to be at the front door. If you're not there, I'm coming in to get you. And look on the bright side, Agatha. I'm not even asking you to take time off from your job. You'll be delivered safely back here by Monday morning, in one piece and with a bank account that's stuffed to the rafters. And we'll never have to lay eyes on each other again!'

CHAPTER TWO

'I JUST can't believe that you would blackmail me into this,' was the first thing she said as she joined him at the front door, bag reluctantly in hand.

'Blackmail? I prefer to call it *persuasion*.' Luiz pushed himself off the wall against which he had been lounging, calculating how much work he would be missing and also working out that his date for the following night wasn't going to be overjoyed at this sudden road trip. Not that that unduly bothered him. In fact, to call it a *date* was wildly inappropriate. He had had four dates with Chloe Bern and on the fifth he had broken it gently to her that things between them weren't working out. She hadn't taken it well. This was the sixth time he would be seeing her and it would be to repeat what he had already told her on date five.

Aggie snorted derisively. She had feverishly tried to find a way of backing out, but all exits seemed to have been barred. Luiz was in hunting mode and she knew that the threats he had made hadn't been empty ones. For the sake of her brother, she had no choice but to agree to this trip and she felt like exploding with anger.

Outside, the weather was grimly uninviting, freezing cold and with an ominous stillness in the atmosphere.

She followed him to his fancy car, incongruous between

the battered, old run-arounds on either side, and made another inarticulate noise as he beeped it open.

'You're going to tell me,' Luiz said, settling into the driver's seat and waiting for her as she strapped herself in, 'that this is a pointless toy belonging to someone with more money than sense. Am I right?'

'You must be a mind reader,' Aggie said acidly.

'Not a mind reader. Just astute when it comes to remembering conversations we've had in the past.' He started the engine and the sports car purred to life.

'You can't have remembered everything I've said to you,' Aggie muttered uncomfortably.

'Everything. How do you think I'm so sure that you never mentioned renting this dump here?' He threw her a sidelong glance. 'I'm thinking that your brother doesn't contribute greatly to the family finances?' Which in turn made him wonder who would be footing the bill for the romantic getaway. If Aggie barely earned enough to keep the roof over her head, then it stood to reason that Mark earned even less, singing songs in a pub. His jaw tightened at the certainty that Maria was already the goose laying the golden eggs.

'He can't,' Aggie admitted reluctantly. 'Not that I mind, because I don't.'

'That's big of you. Most people would resent having to take care of their kid brother when he's capable of taking care of himself.' They had both been sketchy on the details of Mark's job and Luiz, impatient with a task that had been foisted onto his shoulders, had not delved deeply enough. He had been content enough to ascertain that his niece wasn't going out with a potential axe-murderer, junkie or criminal on the run. 'So…he works in a bar and plays now and then in a band. You might as well tell me the truth,

Agatha. Considering there's no longer any point in keeping secrets.'

Aggie shrugged. 'Yes, he works in a bar and gets a gig once every few weeks. But his talent is really with songwriting. You'll probably think that I'm spinning you a fairy story, because you're suspicious of everything I say...'

'With good reason, as it turns out.'

'But he's pretty amazing at composing. Often in the evenings, while I'm reading or else going through some of the homework from the kids or preparing for classes, he'll sit on the sofa playing his guitar and working on his latest song over and over until he thinks he's got it just right.'

'And you never thought to mention that to me because...?'

'I'm sure Mark told you that he enjoyed songwriting.'

'He told me that he was a musician. He may have mentioned that he knew people in the entertainment business. The general impression was that he was an established musician with an established career. I don't believe I ever heard you contradict him.'

The guy was charming but broke, and his state of penury was no passing inconvenience. He was broke because he lived in a dreamworld of strumming guitars and dabbling about with music sheets.

Thinking about it now, Luiz could see why Maria had fallen for the guy. She was the product of a fabulously wealthy background. The boys she had met had always had plentiful supplies of money. Many of them either worked in family businesses or were destined to. A musician, with a notebook and a guitar slung over his shoulder, rustling up cocktails in a bar by night? On every level he had been her accident waiting to happen. No wonder they had all seen fit to play around with the truth! Maria was sharp enough to have known that a whiff of the truth would have had alarm bells ringing in his head.

'I happen to be very proud of my brother,' Aggie said stiffly. 'It's important that people find their own way. I know you probably don't have much time for that.'

'I have a lot of time for that, provided it doesn't impact my family.'

The traffic was horrendous but eventually they cleared it and, after a series of back roads, emerged at a square of elegant red-bricked Victorian houses in the centre of which was a gated, private park.

There had been meals out but neither she nor her brother had ever actually been asked over to Luiz's house.

This was evidence of wealth on a shocking scale. Aside from Maria's expensive bags, which she'd laughingly claimed she couldn't resist and could afford because her family was 'not badly off', there had been nothing to suggest that not badly off had actually meant staggeringly rich.

Even though the restaurants had been grand and expensive, Aggie had never envisioned the actual lifestyle that Luiz enjoyed to accompany them. She had no passing acquaintance with money. Lifestyles of the rich and famous were things she occasionally read about in magazines and dismissed without giving it much thought. Getting out of the car, she realised that, between her and her brother and Luiz and his family, there was a chasm so vast that the thought of even daring to cross it gave her a headache.

Once again she was reluctantly forced to see why Maria's mother had asked Luiz to watch the situation.

Once again she backtracked over their glossing over of their circumstances and understood why Luiz was now reacting the way he was. He was so wrong about them both but he was trapped in his own circumstances and had probably been weaned on suspicion from a very young age.

'Are you going to come out?' Luiz bent down to peer at her through the open car door. 'Or are you going to stay there all night gawping?'

'I wasn't gawping!' Aggie slammed the car door behind her and followed him into a house, a four-storey house that took her breath away, from the pale marble flooring to the dramatic paintings on the walls to the sweeping banister that led up to yet more impeccable elegance.

He strode into a room to the right and after a few seconds of dithering Aggie followed him inside. He hadn't glanced at her once. Just shed his coat and headed straight for his answer machine, which he flicked on while loosening his tie.

She took the opportunity to look round her: stately proportions and the same pale marbled flooring, with softly faded silk rugs to break the expanse. The furniture was light leather and the floor-to-ceiling curtains thick velvet, a shade deeper in colour than the light pinks of the rugs.

She was vaguely aware that he was listening to what seemed to be an interminable series of business calls, until the last message, when the breathy voice of a woman reminded him that she would be seeing him tomorrow and that she couldn't wait.

At that, Aggie's ears pricked up. He might very well have accused her of being shady when it came to her and her brother's private lives. She now realised that she actually knew precious little about *him*.

He wasn't married; that much she knew for sure because Maria had confided that the whole family was waiting for him to tie the knot and settle down. Beyond that, of course, he *would* have a girlfriend. No one as eligible as Luiz Montes would be without one. She looked at him surreptitiously and wondered what the owner of that breathy, sexy voice looked like.

'I'm going to have a quick shower. I'll be back down in ten minutes and then we'll get going. No point hanging around.'

Aggie snapped back to the present. She was blushing. She could feel it. Blushing as she speculated on his private life.

'Make yourself at home,' Luiz told her drily. 'Feel free to explore.'

'I'm fine here, thank you very much.' She perched awkwardly on the edge of one of the pristine leather sofas and rested her hands primly on her lap.

'Suit yourself.'

But as soon as he had left the room, she began exploring like a kid in a toyshop, touching some of the clearly priceless *objets d'art* he had randomly scattered around: a beautiful bronze figurine of two cheetahs on the long, low sideboard against the wall; a pair of vases that looked very much like the real thing from a Chinese dynasty; she gazed at the abstract on the wall and tried to decipher the signature.

'Do you like what you see?' Luiz asked from behind her and she started and went bright red.

'I've never been in a place like this before,' Aggie said defensively.

Her mouth went dry as she looked at him. He was dressed in a pair of black jeans and a grey-and-black-striped woollen jumper. She could see the collar of his shirt underneath, soft grey flannel. All the other times she had seen him he had been formally dressed, almost as though he had left work to meet them at whatever mega-expensive restaurant he had booked. But this was casual and he was really and truly drop-dead sexy.

'It's a house, not a museum. Shall we go?' He flicked off the light as she left the sitting room and pulled out his mobile phone to instruct his driver to bring the four-by-four round.

'*My* house is a house.' Aggie was momentarily distracted from her anger at his accusations as she stared back at the mansion behind her and waited with him for the car to be delivered.

'Correction. Your house is a hovel. Your landlord deserves to be shot for charging a tenant for a place like that. You probably haven't noticed, but in the brief time I was there I spotted the kind of cracks that advertise a problem with damp—plaster falling from the walls and patches on the ceiling that probably mean you'll have a leak sooner rather than later.'

The four-by-four, shiny and black, slowed and Luiz's driver got out.

'There's nothing I can do about that,' Aggie huffed, climbing into the passenger seat. 'Anyway, you live in a different world to me...to us. It's almost impossible to find somewhere cheap to rent in London.'

'There's a difference between cheap and hazardous. Just think of what you could buy if you had the money in your bank account...' He manoeuvred the big car away from the kerb. 'Nice house in a smart postcode... Quaint little garden at the back... You like gardening, don't you? I believe it's one of those things you mentioned...although it's open to debate whether you were telling the truth or lying to give the right impression.'

'I wasn't lying! I love gardening.'

'London gardens are generally small but you'd be surprised to discover what you can get for the right price.'

'I would never accept a penny from you, Luiz Montes!'

'You don't mean that.'

That tone of comfortable disbelief enraged her. 'I'm not interested in money!' She turned to him, looked at his aristocratic dark profile, and felt that familiar giddy feeling.

'Call me cynical, but I have yet to meet someone who isn't interested in money. They might make noises about money not being able to buy happiness and the good things in life being free, but they like the things money can do and the freebies go through the window when more expensive ways of being happy enter the equation. Tell me seriously that you didn't enjoy those meals you had out.'

'Yes, I *enjoyed* them, but I wouldn't miss them if they weren't there.'

'And what about your brother? Is he as noble minded as you?'

'Neither of us are materialistic, if that's what you mean. You met him. Did he strike you as the sort of person who… who would lead Maria on because of what he thought he could get out of her? I mean, didn't you like him at all?'

'I liked him, but that's not the point.'

'You mean the point is that Maria can go out with someone from a different background, just so long as there's no danger of getting serious, because the only person she would be allowed to settle down with would be someone of the same social standing as her.'

'You say that as though there's something wrong with it.'

'I don't want to talk about this. It's not going to get us anywhere.' She fell silent and watched the slow-moving traffic around her, a sea of headlights illuminating late-night shoppers, people hurrying towards the tube or to catch a bus. At this rate, it would be midnight before they cleared London.

'Would you tell me something?' she asked to break the silence.

'I'm listening.'

'Why didn't you try and put an end to their relationship from the start? I mean, why did you bother taking us out for all those meals?'

'Not my place to interfere. Not at that point, at any rate. I'd been asked to keep an eye on things, to meet your brother and, as it turns out, you too, because the two of you seem to be joined at the hip.' He didn't add that, having not had very much to do with his niece in the past, he had found that he rather enjoyed their company. He had liked listening to Mark and Maria entertain him with their chat about movies and music. And even more he had liked the way Aggie had argued with him, had liked the way it had challenged him into making an effort to get her to laugh. It had all made a change from the extravagant social events to which he was invited, usually in a bid by a company to impress him.

'We're not joined at the hip! We're close because...' Because of their background of foster care, but that was definitely something they had kept to themselves.

'Because you lost your parents?'

'That's right.' She had told him in passing, almost the first time she had met him, that their parents were dead and had swiftly changed the subject. Just another muddled half-truth that would further make him suspicious of their motives.

'Apart from which, I thought that my sister had been overreacting to the whole thing. Maria is an only child without a father. Luisa is prone to pointless worrying.'

'I can't imagine you taking orders from your sister.'

'You haven't met Luisa or any of my five sisters. If you had, you wouldn't make that observation.' He laughed and Aggie felt the breath catch in her throat because, for once, his laughter stemmed from genuine amusement.

'What are they like?'

'All older than me and all bossy.' He grinned sideways at her. 'It's easier to surrender than to cross them. In a family of six women, my father and I know better than to try and argue. It would be easier staging a land war in Asia.'

That glimpse of his humanity unsettled Aggie. But she had had glimpses of it before, she recalled uneasily. Times when he had managed to make her forget how dislikeable he was, when he had recounted something with such dry wit that she had caught herself trying hard to stifle a laugh. He might be hateful, judgemental and unfair, he might represent a lot of things she disliked, but there was no denying that he was one of the most intelligent men she had ever met—and, when it suited him, one of the most entertaining. She had contrived to forget all of that but, stuck here with him, it was coming back to her fast and she had to fumble her way out of her momentary distraction.

'I couldn't help overhearing those messages earlier on at the house,' she said politely.

'Messages? What are you talking about?'

'Lots of business calls. I guess you're having to sacrifice working time for this…unless you don't work on a weekend.'

'If you're thinking of using a few messages you overheard as a way of trying to talk me out of this trip, then you can forget it.'

'I wasn't thinking of doing that. I was just being polite.'

'In that case, you can rest assured that there's nothing that can't wait until Monday when I'm back in London. I have my mobile and if anything urgent comes up, then I can deal with it on the move. Nice try, though.'

'What about that other message? I gather you'll be missing a date with someone tomorrow night?'

Luiz stiffened. 'Again, nothing that can't be handled.'

'Because I would feel very guilty otherwise.'

'Don't concern yourself with my private life, Aggie.'

'Why not?' Aggie risked. 'You're concerning yourself with mine.'

'Slightly different scenario, wouldn't you agree? To the best of my knowledge, I haven't been caught trying to con anyone recently. My private life isn't the one under the spotlight.'

'You're impossible! You're so...*blinkered*! Did you know that Maria was the one who pursued Mark?'

'Do me a favour.'

'She was,' Aggie persisted. 'Mark was playing at one of the pubs and she and her friends went to hear them. She went to meet him after the gig and she gave him her mobile number, told him to get in touch.'

'I'm finding that hard to believe, but let's suppose you're telling the truth. I don't see what that has to do with anything. Whether she chased your brother or your brother chased her, the end result is the same. An heiress is an extremely lucrative proposition for someone in his position.' He switched on the radio and turned it to the traffic news.

London was crawling. The weather forecasters had been making a big deal of snow to come. There was nothing at the moment but people were still rushing to get back home and the roads were gridlocked.

Aggie wearily closed her eyes and leaned back. She was hungry and exhausted and trying to get through to Luiz was like beating her head against a brick wall.

She came to suddenly to the sound of Luiz's low, urgent voice and she blinked herself out of sleep. She had no idea how long she had been dozing, or even how she could manage to doze at all when her thoughts were all over the place.

He was on his phone, and from the sounds of it not enjoying the conversation he was having.

In fact, sitting up and stifling a yawn, it dawned on her that the voice on the other end of the mobile was the same smoky voice that had left a message on his answer machine earlier on, and the reason Aggie knew that was because the smoky voice had become high-pitched and shrill. Not only could *she* hear every word the other woman was saying, she guessed that if she rolled down her window the people in the car behind them would be able to as well.

'This is not the right time for this conversation...' Luiz was saying in a harried, urgent voice.

'Don't you dare hang up on me! I'll just keep calling! I deserve better than this!'

'Which is why you should be thanking me for putting an end to our relationship, Chloe. You do deserve a hell of a lot better than me.'

Aggie rolled her eyes. Wasn't that the oldest trick in the book? The one men used when they wanted to exit a relationship with their consciences intact? Take the blame for everything, manage to convince their hapless girlfriend that breaking up is all for her own good and then walk away feeling as though they've done their good deed for the day.

She listened while Luiz, obviously resigning himself to a conversation he hadn't initiated and didn't want, explained in various ways why they weren't working as a couple.

She had never seen him other than calm, self-assured, in complete control of himself and everything around him. People jumped to attention when he spoke and he had always had that air of command that was afforded to people of influence and power.

He was not that man when he finally ended the call to the sound of virulent abuse on the other end of the line.

'Well?' he demanded grittily. 'I am sure you have an opinion on the conversation you unfortunately had to over-hear.'

When she had asked him about his private life, this was not what she had been expecting. He had quizzed her about hers, about her brother's; a little retaliation had seemed only fair. But that conversation had been intensely personal.

'You've broken up with someone and I'm sorry about that,' Aggie said quietly. 'I know that it's wretched when a relationship comes to an end, especially if you've in-vested in it, and of course I don't want to talk about that. It's your business.'

'I like that.'

'What?'

'Your kind words of sympathy. Believe me when I tell you that there's nothing that could have snapped me out of my mood as efficiently as that.'

'What are you talking about?' Aggie asked, confused. She looked at him to see him smiling with amusement and when he flicked her a sideways glance his smile broadened.

'I'm not dying of a broken heart,' he assured her. 'In fact, if you'd been listening, I'm the one who instigated the break-up.'

'Yes,' Aggie agreed smartly. 'Which doesn't mean that it didn't hurt.'

'Are you speaking from experience?'

'Well, yes, as a matter of fact!'

'I'm inclined to believe you,' Luiz drawled. 'So why did you dump him? Wasn't he man enough to deal with your wilful, argumentative nature?'

'I'm neither of those things!' Aggie reddened and glared at his averted profile.

'On that point, we're going to have to differ.'

'I'm only argumentative with *you*, Luiz Montes! And perhaps that's because you've accused me of being a liar and an opportunist, plotting with my brother to take advantage of your niece!'

'Give it a rest. You have done nothing but argue with me since the second you met me. You've made telling comments about every restaurant, about the value of money, about people who think they can rule the world from a chequebook… You've covered all the ground when it comes to letting me know that you disapprove of wealth. Course, how was I to know that those were just cleverly positioned comments to downplay what you were all about? But let's leave that aside for the moment. Why did you dump the poor guy?'

'If you must know,' Aggie said, partly because constant arguing was tiring and partly because she wanted to let him know that Stu had not found her in the least bit argumentative, 'he became too jealous and too possessive, and I don't like those traits.'

'Amazing. I think we've discovered common ground.'

'Meaning?'

'Chloe went from obliging to demanding in record time.' They had finally cleared London and Luiz realised that unless they continued driving through the night they would have to take a break at some point along the route. It was also beginning to snow. For the moment, though, that was something he would keep to himself.

'Never a good trait as far as I am concerned.' He glanced at Aggie and was struck again by the extreme ultra-femininity of her looks. He imagined that guys could get sucked in by those looks only to discover a wildcat behind the angelic front. Whatever scam she and her brother had concocted between them, she had definitely been the brains behind it. Hell, he could almost appreciate the sharp, outspoken intelligence there. Under the low-level sniping, she was a woman a guy could have a conversation with and that, Luiz conceded, was something. He didn't have much use for conversation with women, not when there were always so many more entertaining ways of spending time with them.

Generally speaking, the women he had gone out with had never sparked curiosity. Why would they? They had always been a known quantity, wealthy socialites with impeccable pedigrees. He was thirty-three years old and could honestly say that he had never deviated from the expected.

With work always centre-stage, it had been very easy to slide in and out of relationships with women who were socially acceptable. In a world where greed and avarice lurked around every corner, it made sense to eliminate the opportunist by making sure never to date anyone who could fall into that category. He had never questioned it. If none of the women in his past had ever succeeded in capturing his attention for longer than ten seconds, then he wasn't bothered. His sisters, bar two, had all done their duty and reproduced, leaving him free to live his life the way he saw fit.

'So…what do you mean? That the minute a woman wants something committed you back away? Was that what your ex-girlfriend was guilty of?'

'I make it my duty never to make promises I can't keep,' Luiz informed her coolly. 'I'm always straight with women. I'm not in it for the long run. Chloe, unfortunately, began thinking that the rules of the game could be changed somewhere along the line. I should have seen the signs, of course,' he continued half to himself. 'The minute a woman starts making noises about wanting to spend a night in and play happy families is the minute the warning bells should start going off.'

'And they didn't?' Aggie was thinking that wanting to spend the odd night in didn't sound like an impossible dream or an undercover marriage proposal.

'She *was* very beautiful,' Luiz conceded with a laugh.

'Was that why you went out with her? Because of the way she looked?'

'I'm a great believer in the power of sexual attraction.'

'That's very shallow.'

Luiz laughed again and slanted an amused look at her. 'You're not into sex?'

Aggie reddened and her heart started pounding like a drum beat inside her. 'That's none of your business!'

'Some women aren't.' Luiz pushed the boundaries. Unlike the other times he had seen her, he now had her all to himself, undiluted by the presence of Mark and his niece. Naturally he would use the time to find out everything he could about her and her brother, all the better to prepare him for when they finally made it to the Lake District. But for now it was no hardship trying to prise underneath her prickly exterior to find out what made her tick. They were cooped up together in a car. What else was there to do? 'Are you one of those women?' he asked silkily.

'I happen to think that sex isn't the most important thing in a relationship!'

'That's probably because you haven't experienced good sex.'

'That's the most ridiculous thing I've ever heard in my life!' But her face was hot and flushed and she was finding it difficult to breathe properly.

'I hope I'm not embarrassing you...'

'I'm not *embarrassed*. I just think that this is an inappropriate conversation.'

'Because...?'

'Because I don't want to be here. Because you're dragging me off on a trek to find my brother so that you can accuse him of being an opportunist and fling money at him so that he goes away. Because you think that we can be bought off.'

'That aside...' He switched on his wipers as the first flurries of snow began to cloud the glass. 'We're here and we can't maintain hostilities indefinitely. And I hate to break this to you, but it looks as though our trip might end up taking a little longer than originally anticipated.'

'What do you mean?'

'Look ahead of you. The traffic is crawling and the snow's started to fall. I can keep driving for another hour or so but then we're probably going to have to pull in somewhere for the night. In fact, keep your eyes open. I'm going to divert to the nearest town and we're going to find somewhere overnight.'

CHAPTER THREE

IN THE end, she had to look up somewhere on his phone because they appeared to have entered hotel-free territory.

'It's just one reason why I try to never leave London,' Luiz muttered in frustration. 'Wide, empty open spaces with nothing inside them. Not even a halfway decent hotel, from the looks of it.'

'That's what most people love about getting out of London.'

'Repeat—different strokes for different folks. What have you found?' They had left the grinding traffic behind them. Now he had to contend with dangerously icy roads and thickly falling snow that limited his vision. He glanced across but couldn't see her face because of the fall of soft, finely spun golden hair across it.

'You're going to be disappointed because there are no fancy hotels, although there *is* a B and B about five miles away and it's rated very highly. It's a bit of a detour but it's the only thing I've been able to locate.'

'Address.' He punched it into his guidance system and relaxed at the thought that he would be able to take a break. 'Read me what it says about this place.'

'I don't suppose anyone's ever told you this but you talk to people as though they're your servants. You just expect people to do what you want them to do without question.'

'I would be inclined to agree with that,' Luiz drawled. 'But for the fact that you don't slot into that category, so there goes your argument. I ask you to simply tell me about this bed and breakfast, which you'll do but not until you let me know that you resent the request, and you resent the request for no other reason that I happen to be the one making it. The down side of accusing someone of being black-and-white is that you should be very sure that you don't fall into the same category yourself.'

Aggie flushed and scowled. 'Five bedrooms, two *en suite*, a sitting room. And the price includes a full English breakfast. There's also a charming garden area but I don't suppose that's relevant considering the weather. And I'm the least prejudiced person I know. I'm extremely open minded!'

'Five bedrooms. Two *en suite*. Is there nothing a little less basic in the vicinity?'

'We're in the country now,' Aggie informed him tersely, half-annoyed because he hadn't taken her up on what she had said. 'There are no five-star hotels, if that's what you mean.'

'You know,' Luiz murmured softly, straining to see his way forward when the wipers could barely handle the fall of snow on the windscreen, 'I can understand your hostility towards me, but what I find a little more difficult to understand is your hostility towards all displays of wealth. The first time I met you, you made it clear that expensive restaurants were a waste of money when all over the world people were going without food... But hell, I don't want to get into this. It's hard enough trying to concentrate on not going off the road without launching into yet another pointless exchange of words. You're going to have to look out for a sign.'

Of course, he had no interest in her personally, not beyond wanting to protect his family and their wealth from her, so she should be able to disregard everything he said. But he had still managed to make her feel like a hypocrite and Aggie shifted uncomfortably.

'I'm sorry I can't offer to share the driving,' she muttered, to smooth over her sudden confusion at the way he had managed to turn her notions about herself on their head. 'But I don't have my driving licence.'

'I wouldn't ask you to drive even if you did,' Luiz informed her.

'Because women need protecting?' But she was half-smiling when she said that.

'Because I would have a nervous breakdown.'

Aggie stifled a giggle. He had a talent for making her want to laugh when she knew she should be on the defensive. 'That's very chauvinistic.'

'I think you've got the measure of me. I don't make a good back-seat driver.'

'That's probably because you feel that you always have to be in control,' Aggie pointed out. 'And I suppose you really are always in control, aren't you?'

'I like to be.' Luiz had slowed the car right down. Even though it was a powerful four-wheel drive, he knew that the road was treacherous and ungritted. 'Are you going to waste a few minutes trying to analyse me now?'

'I wouldn't dream of it!' But she was feverishly analysing him in her head, eaten up with curiosity as to what made this complex man tick. She didn't care, of course. It was a game generated by the fact that they were in close proximity, but she caught herself wondering whether his need for absolute control wasn't an inherited obligation. He was an only son of a Latin American magnate. Had he been trained to see himself as ruler of all he surveyed? It occurred to her that this wasn't the first time she had found herself wondering about him, and that was an uneasy thought.

'Anyway, we're here.' They were now in a village and she could see that it barely encompassed a handful of shops, in between and around which radiated small houses, the sort of houses found in books depicting the perfect English country village. The bed and breakfast was a tiny semi-detached house, very easily bypassed were it not for the sign swinging outside, barely visible under the snow.

It was very late and the roads were completely deserted. Even the bed and breakfast was plunged in darkness, except for two outside lights which just about managed to illuminate the front of the house and a metre or two of garden in front.

With barely contained resignation, Luiz pulled up outside and killed the engine.

'It looks wonderful,' Aggie breathed, taken with the creamy yellow stone and the perfectly proportioned leaded windows. She could picture the riot of colour in summer with all manner of flowers ablaze in the front garden and the soporific sound of the bees buzzing between them.

'Sorry?' Luiz wondered whether they were looking at the same house.

''Course, I would rather not be here with *you*,' Aggie emphasised. 'But it's beautiful. Especially with the snow on the ground and on the roof. Gosh, it's really deep as well! That's the one thing I really miss about living in the south. Snow.'

On that tantalising statement, she flung open the car door and stepped outside, holding her arms out wide and her head tilted up so that the snow could fall directly onto her face.

In the act of reaching behind him to extract their cases, Luiz paused to stare at her. She had pulled some fingerless gloves out of her coat pocket and stuck them on and standing like that, arms outstretched, she looked young, vulnerable and achingly innocent, a child reacting to the thrill of being out in the snow.

Beside the point what she looks like, he told himself, breaking the momentary spell to get their bags. She was pretty. He knew that. He had known that from the very first second he had set eyes on her. The world was full of pretty women, especially *his* world, which was not only full of pretty women but pretty women willing to throw themselves at him.

Aggie began walking towards the house, her feet sinking into the snow, and only turned to look around when he had slammed shut the car door and was standing in front of it, a bag in either hand—his mega-expensive bag, her forlorn and cheaply made one which had been her companion from the age of fourteen when she had spent her first night at a friend's house.

He looked just so incongruous. She couldn't see his expression because it was dark but she imagined that he would be bewildered, removed from his precious creature comforts and thrown into a world far removed from the expensive one he occupied. A bed and breakfast with just five bedrooms, only two of which were *en suite*! What a horror story for him! Not to mention the fact that he would have to force himself to carry on being polite to the sister of an unscrupulous opportunist who was plotting to milk his niece for her millions. He was lead actor in the middle of his very worst nightmare and as he stood there, watching her, she reached down to scoop up a handful of snow, cold and crisp and begging to be moulded into a ball.

All her anger and frustration towards him and towards herself for reacting to him when she should be able to be cool and dismissive went into that throw, and she held her breath as the snowball arched upwards and travelled with deadly accuracy towards him, hitting him right in the middle of that broad, muscled, arrogant chest.

She didn't know who was more surprised. Her, for having thrown it in the first place, or him for being hit for the first time in his life by a snowball. Before he could react, she turned her back and began plodding to the front door.

He deserved that, she told herself nervously. He was insulting, offensive and dismissive. He had accused her and her brother in the worst possible way of the worst possible things and had not been prepared to nurture any doubts that he might be wrong. Plus he had had the cheek to make her question herself when she hadn't done anything wrong!

Nevertheless, she didn't want to look back over her shoulder for fear of seeing what his reaction might be at her small act of resentful rebellion.

'Nice shot!' she heard him shout, at which she began to turn around when she felt the cold, wet compacted blow of his retaliation. She had launched her missile at his chest and he had done the same, and his shot was even more faultless than hers had been.

Aggie's mouth dropped open and she looked at him incredulously as he began walking towards her.

'Good shot. Bull's eye.' He grinned at her and he was transformed, the harsh, unforgiving lines of his face replaced by a sex appeal that was so powerful that it almost knocked her sideways. The breath caught in her throat and she found that she was staring up at him while her thoughts tumbled around as though they had been tossed into a spin drier turned to full speed.

'You too,' was all she could think of saying. 'Where did you learn to throw a snowball?'

'Boarding school. Captain of the cricket team. I was their fast bowler.' He rang the doorbell but he didn't take his eyes from her face. 'Did you think that I was so pampered that I wouldn't have been able to retaliate?' he taunted softly.

'Yes.' Her mouth felt as though it was stuffed with cotton wool. Pampered? Yes, of course he was…and yet a less pampered man it would have been hard to find. How did that make sense?

'Where did *you* learn to throw a shot like that? You hit me from thirty metres away. Through thick snow and poor visibility.'

Aggie blinked in an attempt to gather her scattered wits, but she still heard herself say, with complete honesty, 'We grew up with snow in winter. We learned to build snowmen and have snowball fights and there were always lots of kids around because we were raised in a children's home.'

Deafening silence greeted this remark. She hadn't planned on saying that, but out it had come, and she could have kicked herself. Thankfully she was spared the agony of his contempt by the door being pulled open and they were ushered inside by a short, jolly woman in her sixties who beamed at them as though they were much expected long-lost friends, even though it was nearly ten and she had probably been sound asleep.

Of course there was room for them! Business was never good in winter…just the one room let to a long-standing resident who worked nearby during the week…not that there was any likelihood that he would be leaving for his home in Yorkshire at the weekend…not in this snow…had they seen anything like it…?

The jovial patter kept Aggie's turbulent thoughts temporarily at bay. Regrettably, one of the *en suite* rooms was occupied by the long-standing resident who wouldn't be able to return to Yorkshire at the weekend. As she looked brightly between them to see who would opt for the remaining *en suite* bedroom, Aggie smiled innocently at Luiz until he was forced to do the expected and concede to sharing a bathroom.

She could feel him simmering next to her as they were proudly shown the sitting room, where there was 'a wide assortment of channels on the telly because they had recently had cable fitted'. And the small breakfast room where they could have the best breakfast in the village, and also dinner if they would like, although because of the hour she could only run to sandwiches just now...

Aggie branched off into her own, generously proportioned and charming bedroom and nodded blandly when Luiz informed her that he would see her in the sitting room in ten minutes. They both needed something to eat.

There was just time to wash her face, no time at all to unpack or have a bath and get into fresh clothes. Downstairs, Luiz was waiting for her. She heard the rumble of his voice and low laughter as he talked to the landlady. Getting closer, she could make out that he was explaining that they were on their way to visit relatives, that the snow had temporarily cut short their journey. That, yes, public transport would have been more sensible but for the fact that the trains had responded to the bad weather by going on strike. However, what a blessing in disguise, because how else would they have discovered this charming part of the world? And perhaps she could bring them a bottle of wine with their sandwiches...whatever she had to hand would do as long as it was cold...

'So...' Luiz drawled as soon as they had the sitting room to themselves. 'The truth is now all coming out in the wash. Were you ever going to tell me about your background or were you intending to keep that little titbit to yourself until it no longer mattered who knew?'

'I didn't think it was relevant.'

'Do me a favour, Aggie.'

'I'm not ashamed of…' She sighed and ran her fingers through her hair. It was cosy in here and beautifully warm, with an open fire at one end. He had removed his jumper and rolled his sleeves up and her eyes strayed to his arms, sprinkled with dark hair. He had an athlete's body and she had to curb the itch to stare at him. She didn't know where that urge was coming from. Or had it been there from the start?

Wine was brought to them and she felt like she needed some. One really big glass to help her through this conversation…

'You're not ashamed of…? Concealing the truth?'

'I didn't think of it as concealing the truth.'

'Well, forgive me, but it seems a glaring omission.'

'It's not something I talk about.'

'Why not?'

'Why do you think?' She glared at him, realised that the big glass of wine had somehow disappeared in record time and didn't refuse when her wine glass was topped up.

Luiz flushed darkly. It wouldn't do to forget that this was not a date. He wasn't politely delving down conversational avenues as a prelude to sex. Omissions like this mattered, given the circumstances. But those huge blue eyes staring at him with a mixture of uncertainty and accusation were getting to him.

'You tell me.'

'People can be judgemental,' Aggie muttered defensively. 'As soon as you say that you grew up in a children's home, people switch off. You wouldn't understand. How could you? You've always led the kind of life people like us dreamt about. A life of luxury, with family all around you. Even if your sisters were bossy and told you what to do when you were growing up. It's a different world.'

'I'm not without imagination,' Luiz said gruffly.

'But this is just something else that you can hold against us…just another nail in the coffin.'

Yes, it was! But he was still curious to find out about that shady background she had kept to herself. He barely noticed when a platter of sandwiches was placed in front of them, accompanied by an enormous salad, along with another bottle of excellent wine.

'You went to a boarding school. I went to the local comprehensive where people sniggered because I was one of those kids from a children's home. Sports days were a nightmare. Everyone else would have their family there, shouting and yelling them on. I just ran and ran and ran and pretended that there were people there cheering *me* on. Sometimes Gordon or Betsy—the couple who ran the home—would try and come but it was difficult. I could deal with all of that but Mark was always a lot more sensitive.'

'Which is why you're so close now. You said that your parents were dead.'

'They are.' She helped herself to a bit more wine, even though she was unaccustomed to alcohol and was dimly aware that she would probably have a crashing headache the following morning. 'Sort of.'

'Sort of? Don't go coy on me, Aggie. How can people be *sort of* dead?'

Stripped bare of all the half-truths that had somehow been told to him over a period of time, Aggie resigned herself to telling him the unvarnished truth now about their background. He could do whatever he liked with the information, she thought recklessly. He could try to buy them off, could shake his head in disgust at being in the company of someone so far removed from himself. She should never have let her brother and Maria talk her into painting a picture that wasn't completely accurate.

A lot of that had stemmed from her instinctive need to protect Mark, to do what was best for him. She had let herself be swayed by her brother being in love for the first time, by Maria's tactful downplaying of just how protective her family was and why... And she also couldn't deny that Luiz had rubbed her up the wrong way from the very beginning. It hadn't been hard to swerve round the truth, pulling out pieces of it here and there, making sure to nimbly skip over the rest. He was so arrogant. He almost deserved it!

'We never knew our father,' she now admitted grudgingly. 'He disappeared after I was born, and continued showing up off and on, but he finally did a runner when Mum became pregnant with Mark.'

'He did a runner...'

'I'll bet you haven't got a clue what I'm talking about, Luiz.'

'It's hard for me to get my head around the concept of a father abandoning his family,' Luiz admitted.

'You're lucky,' Aggie told him bluntly and Luiz looked at her with dry amusement.

'My life was prescribed,' he found himself saying. 'Often it was not altogether ideal. Carry on.'

Aggie wanted to ask him to expand, to tell her what he meant by a 'prescribed life'. From the outside looking in, all she could see was perfection for him: a united, large family, exempt from all the usual financial headaches, with everyone able to do exactly what they wanted in the knowledge that if they failed there would always be a safety net to catch them.

'What else is there to say? I was nine when Mum died.' She looked away and stared off at the open fire. The past was not a place she revisited with people but she found that she was past resenting what he knew about her. He would never change his mind about the sort of person he imagined she was, but that didn't mean that she had to accept all his accusations without a fight.

'How did she die?'

'Do you care?' Aggie asked, although half-heartedly. 'She was killed in an accident returning from work. She had a job at the local supermarket and she was walking home when she was hit by a drunk-driver. There were no relatives, no one to take us in, and we were placed in a children's home. A wonderful place with a wonderful couple running it who saw us both through our bad times; we couldn't have hoped for a happier upbringing, given the circumstances. So please don't feel sorry for either of us.' The sandwiches were delicious but her appetite had nosedived.

'I'm sorry about your mother.'

'Are you?' But she was instantly ashamed of the bitterness in her voice. 'Thank you. It was a long time ago.' She gave a dry, self-deprecating laugh. 'I expect all this information is academic because you've already made your mind up about us. But you can see why it wouldn't have made for a great opening conversation…especially when I knew from the start that the only reason you'd bothered to ask Maria out with us was so that you could check my brother out.'

Normally, Luiz cared very little about what other people thought of him. It was what made him so straightforward in his approach to tackling difficult situations. He never wasted time beating about the bush. Now, he felt an unaccustomed dart of shame when he thought back to how unapologetic he had been on every occasion he had met them, how direct his questions had been. He had made no attempt to conceal the reason for his sudden interest in his niece. He hadn't been overtly hostile but Aggie, certainly, was sharp enough to have known exactly what his motives were. So could he really blame her if she hadn't launched into a sob story about her deprived background?

Strangely, he felt a tug of admiration for the way she had managed to forge a path for herself through difficult circumstances. It certainly demonstrated the sort of strength of personality he had rarely glimpsed in the opposite sex. He grimaced when he thought of the women he dated. Chloe might be beautiful but she was also colourless and unambitious…just another cover girl born with a silver spoon in her mouth, biding her time at a fairly pointless part-time job until a rich man rescued her from the need to pretend to work at all.

'So where was this home?'

'Lake District,' Aggie replied with a little shrug. She looked into those deep, deep, dark eyes and her mouth went dry.

'Hence you said that they went somewhere that had sentimental meaning for you.'

'Do you remember everything that people say to you?' Aggie asked irritably and he shot her one of those amazing, slow smiles that did strange things to her heart rate.

'It's a blessing and a curse. You blush easily. Do you know that?'

'That's probably because I feel awkward here with you,' Aggie retorted, but on cue she could feel her face going red.

'No idea why.' Luiz pushed himself away from the table and stretched out his legs to one side. He noticed that they had managed to work their way through nearly two bottles of wine. 'We're having a perfectly civilised conversation. Tell me why you decided to move to London.'

'Tell me why *you* did.'

'I took over an empire. The London base needed expanding. I was the obvious choice. I went to school here. I understand the way the people think.'

'But did you *want* to settle here? I mean, it must be a far cry from Brazil.'

'It works for me.'

He continued looking at her as what was left of the sandwiches were cleared away and coffee offered to them. Considering the hour, their landlady was remarkably obliging, waving aside Aggie's apologies for arriving at such an inconvenient time, telling them that business was to be welcomed whatever time it happened to arrive. Beggars couldn't be choosers.

But neither of them wanted coffee. Aggie was so tired that she could barely stand. She was also tipsy; too much wine on an empty stomach.

'I'm going to go outside for a bit,' she said. 'I think I need to get some fresh air.'

'You're going outside in *this* weather?'

'I'm used to it. I grew up with snow.' She stood up and had to steady herself and breathe in deeply.

'I don't care if you grew up running wild in the Himalayas, you're not going outside, and not because I don't think that you can handle the weather. You're not going outside because you've had too much to drink and you'll probably pass out.'

Aggie glared at him and gripped the table. God, her head was swimming, and she knew that she really ought to get to bed, do just as he said. But there was no way that she was going to allow him to dictate her movements on top of everything else.

'Don't tell me what I can and can't do, Luiz Montes!'

He looked at her in silence and then shrugged. 'And do

you intend to go out without a coat, because you're used to the snow?'

'Of course not!'

'Well, that's a relief.' He stood up and shoved his hands in the pockets of his trousers. 'Make sure you have a key to get back in,' he told her. 'I think we've caused our obliging landlady enough inconvenience for one night without having to get her out of bed to let you in because you've decided to take a walk in driving snow.'

Out of the corner of his eye, he saw Mrs Bixby, the landlady, heading towards them like a ship in full sail. But when she began expressing concern about Aggie's decision to step outside for a few minutes, Luiz shook his head ever so slightly.

'I'm sure Agatha is more than capable of taking care of herself,' he told Mrs Bixby. 'But she will need a key to get back in.'

'I expect you want me to thank you,' Aggie hissed, once she was in possession of the front-door key and struggling to get her arms into her coat. Now that she was no longer supporting herself against the dining-room table, her light-headedness was accompanied by a feeling of nausea. She also suspected that her words were a little slurred even though she was taking care to enunciate each and every syllable very carefully.

'Thank me for what?' Luiz walked with her to the front door. 'Your coat's not done up properly.' He pointed to the buttons which she had failed to match up properly, and then he leaned against the wall and watched as she fumbled to try and remedy the oversight.

'Stop staring at me!'

'Just making sure that you're well wrapped up. Would you like to borrow my scarf? No bother for me to run upstairs and get it for you.'

'I'm absolutely fine.' A wave of sickness washed over her as she tilted her head to look him squarely in the face.

Very hurriedly, she let herself out of the house while Luiz turned to Mrs Bixby and grinned. 'I intend to take up residence in the dining room. I'll sit by the window and make sure I keep an eye on her. Don't worry; if she's not back inside in under five minutes, I'll forcibly bring her in myself.'

'Coffee while you wait?'

'Strong, black would be perfect.'

He was still grinning as he manoeuvred a chair so that he could relax back and see her as she stood still in the snow for a few seconds, breathing in deeply from the looks of it, before tramping in circles on the front lawn. He couldn't imagine her leaving the protective circle of light and striking out for an amble in the town. The plain truth was that she had had a little too much to drink. She had been distinctly green round the gills when she had stood up after eating a couple of sandwiches, although that was something she would never have admitted to.

Frankly, Luiz had no time for women who drank, but he could hardly blame her. Neither of them had been aware of how much wine had been consumed. She would probably wake up with a headache in the morning, which would be a nuisance, as he wanted to leave at the crack of dawn, weather permitting. But that was life.

He narrowed his eyes and sat forward as she became bored with her circular tramping and began heading towards the little gate that led out towards the street and the town.

Without waiting for the coffee, he headed for the front door, only pausing on the way to tell Mrs Bixby that he'd let himself back in.

She'd vanished from sight and Luiz cursed fluently

under his breath. Without a coat it was freezing and he was half-running when he saw her staggering up the street with purpose before pausing to lean against a lamp post, head buried in the crook of her elbow.

'Bloody woman,' he muttered under his breath. He picked up speed as much as he could and reached her side just in time to scoop her up as she was about to slide to the ground.

Aggie shrieked.

'Do you intend to wake the entire town?' Luiz began walking as quickly as he could back to the bed and breakfast. Which, in snow that was fast settling, wasn't very quickly at all.

'Put me down!' She pummelled ineffectively at his chest but soon gave up because the activity made her feel even more queasy.

'Now, that has to be the most stupid thing ever to have left your lips.'

'I said put me *down*!'

'If I put you down, you wouldn't be able to get back up. You don't honestly think I missed the fact that you were hanging onto that lamp post for dear life, do you?'

'I don't need rescuing by you!'

'And I don't need to be out here in freezing weather playing the knight in shining armour! Now shut up!'

Aggie was so shocked by that insufferably arrogant command that she shut up.

She wouldn't have admitted it in a million years but it felt good to be carried like this, because her legs had been feeling very wobbly. In fact, she really had been on the point of wanting to sink to the ground just to take the weight off them before he had swept her off her feet.

She felt him nudge the front door open with his foot, which meant that it had been left ajar. It was humiliating to think of Mrs Bixby seeing her like this and she buried herself against Luiz, willing herself to disappear.

'Don't worry,' Luiz murmured drily in her ear. 'Our friendly landlady is nowhere to be seen. I told her to go to bed, that I'd make sure I brought you in in one piece.'

Aggie risked a glance at the empty hall and instructed him to put her down.

'That dumb suggestion again. You're drunk and you need to get to bed, which is what I told you before you decided to prove how stubborn you could be by ignoring my very sound advice.'

'I am not *drunk*. I am *never* drunk.' She was alarmed by a sudden need to hiccup, which she thankfully stifled. 'Furthermore, I am *more than* capable of making my own way upstairs.'

'Okay.' He released her fast enough for her to feel the ground rushing up to meet her and she clutched his jumper with both hands and took a few deep breaths. 'Still want to convince me that you're *more than capable* of making your own way upstairs?'

'I hate you!' Aggie muttered as he swept her back up into his arms.

'You have a tendency to be repetitive,' Luiz murmured, and he didn't have to see her face to know that she was glaring at him. 'And I'm surprised and a little offended that you hate me for rescuing you from almost certainly falling flat on your face in the snow and probably going to sleep. As a teacher, you should know that that is the most dangerous thing that could happen, passing out in the snow. While under the influence of alcohol. Tut, tut, tut. You'd be struck off the responsible-teacher register if they ever found out about that. Definitely not a good example to set for impressionable little children, seeing their teacher the worse for wear...'

'Shut up,' Aggie muttered fiercely.

'Now, let's see. Forgotten which room is yours… Oh, it's coming back to me—the only one left with the *en suite*! Fortuitous, because you might be needing that…'

'Oh be quiet,' Aggie moaned. 'And hurry up! I think I'm going to be sick.'

CHAPTER FOUR

She made it to the bathroom in the nick of time and was horribly, shamefully, humiliatingly, wretchedly sick. She hadn't bothered to shut the door and she was too weak to protest when she heard Luiz enter the bathroom behind her.

'Sorry,' she whispered, hearing the flush of the toilet and finding a toothbrush pressed into her hand. While she was busy being sick, he had obviously rummaged through her case and located just the thing she needed.

She shakily cleaned her teeth but lacked the energy to tell him to leave.

Nor could she look at him. She flopped down onto the bed and closed her eyes as he drew the curtains shut, turned off the overhead light and began easing her boots off.

Luiz had never done anything like this before. In fact, he had never been in the presence of a woman quite so violently sick after a bout of excessive drinking and, if someone had told him that one day he would be taking care of such a woman, he would have laughed out loud. Women who were out of control disgusted him. An out-of-control Chloe, shouting hysterically down the phone, sobbing and shrieking and cursing him, had left him cold. He looked at Aggie, who now had her arm covering her face, and wondered why he wasn't disgusted.

He had wet a face cloth; he mopped her forehead and heard her sigh.

'So I guess I should be thanking you,' she said, without moving the hand that lay across her face.

'You could try that,' Luiz agreed.

'How did you know where to find me?'

'I watched you from the dining room. I wasn't going to let you stay out there for longer than five minutes.'

'Because, of course, you know best.'

'Staggering in the dark in driving snow when you've had too much to drink isn't a good idea in anyone's eyes,' Luiz said drily.

'And I don't suppose you'll believe me when I tell you that this is the first time I've ever…ever…done this?'

'I believe you.'

Aggie lowered her protective arm and looked at him. Her eyes felt sore, along with everything else, and she was relieved that the room was only lit by the small lamp on the bedside table.

'You do?'

'It's my fault. I should have said no to that second bottle of wine. In fact, I was barely aware of it being brought.' He shrugged. 'These things happen.'

'But I don't suppose they ever happen to you,' Aggie said with a weak smile. 'I bet you don't drink too much and stagger all over the place and then end up having to be helped up to bed like a baby.'

Luiz laughed. 'No, can't say I remember the last time that happened.'

'And I bet you've never been in the company of a woman who's done that.'

No one would dare behave like that in my presence, was what he could have said, except he was disturbed to find that that would have made him sound like a monster.

'No,' he said flatly. 'And now I'm going to go and get you some painkillers. You're going to need them.'

Aggie yawned and looked at him drowsily. She had a sudden, sharp memory of how it had felt being carried by him. He had lifted her up as though she weighed nothing and his chest against her slight frame had been as hard as steel. He had smelled clean, masculine and woody.

'Yes. Thank you,' she said faintly. 'And once again, I'm so sorry.'

'Stop apologising.' Luiz's tone was abrupt. Was he really so controlling that women edited their personalities just to be with him; sipped their wine but left most of it and said no to dessert because they were afraid that he might pass judgement on them as being greedy or uncontrolled? He had broken off with Chloe and had offered her no explanation other than that she would be 'better off without him'. Strictly speaking, true. But he knew that, in the face of her hysterics, he had been impatient, short-tempered and dismissive. He had always taken it as a given that women would go out of their way to please them, just as he had always taken it as a given that he led a life of moving on; that, however hard they tried, one day it would just be time for him to end it.

Aggie bristled at his obvious displeasure at her repeated apology. God, what must he think of her? The starting point of his opinions had been low enough, but they would be a hundred times lower now—except when the starting point was gold-digger, then how much lower could they get?

She was suddenly too tired to give it any more thought. She half-sat up when he approached with a glass of water. She obediently swallowed two tablets and was reassured that she would be right as rain in the morning. More or less.

'Thanks,' Aggie said glumly. 'And please wake me up first thing.'

'Of course.' Luiz frowned, impatient at the sudden burst of unwelcome introspection which had left him questioning himself.

Aggie fell asleep with that frown imprinted on her brain. It was confusing that someone she didn't care about should have any effect on her whatsoever, but he did.

She vaguely thought that things would be back to normal in the morning. She would dislike him. He would stop being three-dimensional and she would cease to be curious about him.

When she groggily came to, her head was thumping, her mouth tasted of cotton wool and Luiz was slumped in a chair he had pulled and positioned next to her bed. He was fully clothed.

For a few seconds, Aggie didn't take it in, then she struggled up and nudged him.

'What are *you* doing here?'

Belatedly she realised that, although the duvet was tucked around her, she was trouserless and jumperless; searing embarrassment flooded through her.

'I couldn't leave you in the state you were in.' Luiz pressed his eyes with his fingers and then raked both hands through his tousled hair before looking at her.

'I wasn't *in a state*. I…yes…I was…sick but then I fell asleep.'

'You were sick again,' Luiz informed her. 'And that's not taking into account raging thirst and demands for more tablets.'

'Oh God.'

'Sadly, God wasn't available, so it was up to me to find my way down to the kitchen for orange juice because you claimed that any more water would make you feel even more sick. I also had to deal with a half-asleep temper tantrum when I refused to double the dose of painkillers...'

Aggie looked at him in horror.

'Then you said that you were hot.'

'I didn't.'

'You threw off the quilt and started undressing.'

Aggie groaned and covered her face with her hands.

'But, gentleman that I am, I made sure you didn't completely strip naked. I undressed you down to the basics and you fell back asleep.'

Luiz watched her small fingers curl around the quilt cover. He imagined she would be going through mental hell but she was too proud to let it show. Had he ever met anyone like her in his life before? He'd almost forgotten the reason she was with him. She seemed to have a talent for running circles round his formidable single-mindedness and it wasn't just now that they had been thrown together. No, it had happened before. Some passing remark he might have made to which she had taken instant offence, dug her heels in and proceeded to argue with him until he'd forgotten the presence of other people.

'Well...thank you for that. I...I'd like to get changed now.' She addressed the wall and the dressing table in front of her, and heard him slap his thighs with his hands and stand up. 'Did you manage to get any sleep at all?'

'None to speak of,' Luiz admitted.

'You must be exhausted.'

'I don't need much sleep.'

'Well, perhaps you should go and grab a few hours before we start on the last leg of this journey.' It would be nice if the ground could do her a favour and open up and swallow her whole.

'No point.'

Aggie looked at him in consternation. 'What do you

mean that there's no point? It would be downright fool-hardy for you to drive without sleep, and I can't share any of the driving with you.'

'We've covered that. There's no point because it's gone two-thirty in the afternoon, it's already dark and the snow's heavier.' Luiz strode towards the window and pulled back the curtains to reveal never-ending skies the colour of lead, barely visible behind dense, relentlessly falling snow. 'It would be madness to try and get anywhere further in weather like this. I've already booked the rooms for at least another night. Might be more.'

'You can't!' Aggie sat up, dismayed. 'I thought I'd be back at work on Monday! I can't just *disappear*. This is the busiest time of the school year!'

'Too bad,' Luiz told her flatly. 'You're stuck. There's no way I intend to turn around and try and get back to London. And, while you're busy worrying about missing a few classes and the Nativity play, spare a thought for me. I didn't think that I'd be covering half the country in driving snow in an attempt to rescue my niece before she does something stupid.'

'Meaning that your job's more important than mine?' Aggie was more comfortable with this: an argument. Much more comfortable than she was with feverishly thinking about him undressing her, taking care of her, putting her to bed and playing the good guy. 'Typical! Why is it that rich people always think that what they do is more impor-tant than what everyone else does?' She glared at him as he stood by the door, impassively watching her.

For one blinding moment, it occurred to her that she was in danger of seeing beyond the obvious differences between them to the man underneath. If she could list all the things she disliked about him on paper, it would be easy to keep her distance and to fill the spaces between

them with hostility and resentment. But to do that would
be to fall into the trap of being as black-and-white in her
opinions as she had accused him of being.

She paled and her heartbeat picked up in nervous confusion. Had he been working his charm on her from the
very beginning? When he had drawn grudging laughs
from her and held her reluctantly spellbound with stories
of his experiences in foreign countries; when he had engaged her interest in politics and world affairs, while Maria
and Mark had been loved up and whispering to each other,
distracted by some shared joke they couldn't possibly resist. Had she already begun to see beyond the cardboard
cut-out she wanted him to be?

And, stuck together in a car with him, here in this bed
and breakfast. Would an arrogant, pompous, single-minded
creep really have helped her the way he had the night before, not laughing once at her inappropriate behaviour?
Keeping watch over her even though it meant that he hadn't
got a wink of sleep? She had to drag out the recollection
that he had offered her money in return for his niece; that
he was going to offer her brother money to clear off; that
liking or not liking someone was not something that mattered to him because he was like a juggernaut when it
came to getting exactly what he wanted. He had loads of
charm when it suited him, but underneath the charm he
was ruthless, heartless and emotionless.

She felt a lot calmer once that message had got to her
wayward, rebellious brain and imprinted itself there.

'Well?' she persisted scornfully, and Luiz raised his
eyebrows wryly.

'I take it you're angling for a fight. Is this because you
feel embarrassed about what happened last night? If it
is, then there's really no need. Like I said…these things
happen.'

'And, like you also said, you've never had this experience in your life before!' Aggie thought that it would help things considerably if he didn't look so damn gorgeous standing there, even though he hadn't slept and should look a wreck. 'You've never fallen down drunk, and I'll bet that none of your girlfriends have either.'

'You're right. I haven't and they haven't.'

'Is that because none of your girlfriends have ever had too much to drink?'

'Maybe they have.' Luiz shrugged. 'But never in my presence. And, by the way, I don't think that my job is any better or worse than yours. I have a very big deal on the cards which is due to close at the beginning of next week. A takeover. People's jobs are relying on the closure of this deal, hence the reason why it's as inconvenient for me to be delayed with this as it is for you.'

'Oh,' Aggie said, flustered.

'So, if you need to get in touch with your school and ask them for a day or so off, then I'm sure it won't be the end of the world. Now, I'm going to have a shower and head downstairs. Mrs Bixby might be able to rustle you up something to eat.'

He closed the door quietly behind him. At the mention of food, Aggie's stomach had started to rumble, but she made sure not to rush her bath, to take her time washing her hair and using the drier which she found in a drawer in the bedroom. She needed to get her thoughts together. There was no doubt that the fast-falling snow would keep them in this town for another night. It wasn't going to be a case of a few hours on the road and then, whatever the outcome, goodbye to Luiz Montes for ever.

She was going to have his company for longer than she had envisaged and she needed to take care not to fall into the trap of being seduced by his charm. It amazed her that common sense and logic didn't seem to be enough to keep her mind on the straight and narrow.

Rooting through her depleted collection of clothes, she pulled out yet more jeans and a jumper under which she stuck on various layers, a vest, a long-sleeved thermal top, another vest over that…

Looking at her reflection in the mirror, she wondered whether it was possible to look frumpier. Her newly washed hair was uncontrollable, curling in an unruly tumble over her shoulders and down her back. She was bare of make-up because there seemed no point in applying any, and anyway she had only brought her mascara and some lip gloss with her. Her clothes were a dowdy mixture of blues and greys. Her only shoes were the boots she had been wearing because she hadn't foreseen anything more extended than one night somewhere and a meal grabbed on the hop, but now she wished that she had packed a little bit more than a skeleton, functional wardrobe.

Luiz was on the phone when she joined him in the sitting room but he snapped shut the mobile and looked at her as she walked towards him.

With all those thick, drab clothes, anyone could be forgiven for thinking that she was shapeless. She wasn't. He had known that from the times he had seen her out, usually wearing dresses in which she looked ill at ease and uncomfortable. But even those dresses had been designed to cover up. Only last night had he realised just how shapely she was, despite the slightness of her frame.

Startled, he felt the stirrings of an arousal at the memory and he abruptly turned away to beckon Mrs Bixby across for a pot of tea.

'Not for me.' Aggie declined the cup put in front of her. 'I've decided that I'm going to go into town, get some fresh air.'

'Fresh air. You seem to be cursed with a desire for fresh air. Isn't that what got you outside last night?'

But she couldn't get annoyed with him because his voice was lazy and teasing. 'This time I'm not falling over myself. Like I told you, I enjoy snow. I wish it snowed more often in London.'

'The city would grind to a standstill. If you're heading out, then I think I'll accompany you.'

Aggie tried to stifle the flutter of panic his suggestion generated. She needed to clear her mind. However much she lectured herself on all the reasons she had for hating him, there was a pernicious thread of stubbornness that just wanted to go its own merry way, reminding her of his sexiness, his intelligence, that unexpected display of consideration the night before. How was she to deal with that stubbornness if he didn't give her a little bit of peace and privacy?

'I actually intended on going on my own,' she said in a polite let-down. 'For a start, it would give you time to work. You always work. I remember you saying that to us once when your mobile phone rang for the third time over dinner and you took the call. Besides, if you have an important deal to close, then maybe you could get a head start on it.'

'It's Saturday. Besides, it would do me good to stretch my legs. Believe it or not, chairs don't make the most comfortable places to sleep.'

'You're not going to let me forget that in a hurry, are you?'

'Would you if you were in my shoes?'

Aggie had the grace to blush.

'No,' Luiz murmured. 'Thought not. Well, at least you're honest enough not to deny it.' He stood up, towering over her while Aggie stuffed her hands in the pockets of her coat and frantically tried to think of ways of dodging him.

And yet, disturbingly, wasn't she just a little pleased that he would be with her? For good or bad, and she couldn't decide which, her senses were heightened whenever he was around. Her heart beat faster, her skin tingled more, her pulse raced faster and every nerve ending in her seemed to vibrate.

Was that nature's way of keeping her on her toes in the face of the enemy?

'You'll need to have something to eat,' was the first thing he said when they were outside, where the brutal cold was like a stinging slap on the face. The snow falling and collecting on the already thick banks on the pavements turned the winter-wonderland scene into a nightmare of having to walk at a snail's pace.

Her coat was not made for this depth of cold and she could feel herself shivering, while in his padded Barbour, fashioned for arctic conditions, he was doubtless as snug as a bug in a rug.

'Stop telling me what to do.'

'And stop being so damned mulish.' Luiz looked down at her. She had rammed her woolly hat low down over her ears and she was cold. He could tell from the way she had hunched up and the way her hands were balled into fists in the pockets of the coat. 'You're cold.'

'It's a cold day. I like it. It felt stuffy inside.'

'I mean, your coat is inadequate. You need something warmer.'

'You're doing it again.' Aggie looked up at him and her breath caught in her throat as their eyes tangled and he didn't look away. 'Behaving,' she said a little breathlessly, 'as though you have all the answers to everything.' She was dismayed to find that, although she was saying

the right thing, it was as if she was simply going through
the motions while her body was responding in a different manner. 'I've been meaning to buy another coat, but
there's hardly ever any need for it in London.'

'You can buy one here.'

'It's a bad time of the year for me,' Aggie muttered.
'Christmas always is.' She eyed the small town approaching with some relief. 'We exchange presents at school…
then there's the tree and the food…it all adds up. You
wouldn't understand.'

'Try me.'

Aggie hesitated. She wasn't used to confiding. She just
wasn't built that way and she especially couldn't see the
point in confiding in someone like Luiz Montes, a man
who had placed her in an impossible situation, who was
merciless in pursuit, who probably didn't have a sympathetic bone in his body.

Except, a little voice said in her head, *he took care of
you last night, didn't he? Without a hint of impatience or
rancour.*

'When you grow up in a children's home,' she heard
herself say, 'even in a great children's home like the one
I grew up in, you don't really have any money. Ever. And
you don't get brand-new things given to you. Well, not
often. On birthdays and at Christmas, Betsy and Gordon
did their best to make sure that we all had something new,
but most of the time you just make do. Most of my clothes
had been worn by someone else before. The toys were all
shared. You get into the habit of being very careful with
the small amounts of money you get given or earn by doing
chores. I still have that habit. We both do. You'll think it
silly, but I've had this coat since I was seventeen. It only
occurs to me now and again that I should replace it.'

Luiz thought of the women he had wined and dined

over the years. He had never hesitated in spending money on them. None of those relationships might have lasted, but all the women had certainly profited financially from them: jewellery, fur coats, in one instance a car. The memory of it repulsed him.

'That must have been very limiting, being a teenager and not being able to keep up with the latest fashion.'

'You get used to it.' Aggie shrugged. 'Life could have been a lot worse. Look, there's a café. You're right. I should have something to eat. I'm ravenous.' It also felt a little weird to be having this conversation with him.

'You're changing the subject,' he drawled as they began mingling with the shoppers who were out in numbers, undeterred by the snow. 'Is that something else you picked up growing up in a children's home?'

'I don't want to be cross-examined by you.' They were inside the café which was small and warm and busy, but there were spare seats and they grabbed two towards the back. When Aggie removed her gloves, her fingers were pink with cold and she had to keep the coat on for a little longer, just until she warmed up, while two waitresses gravitated, goggle-eyed, to Luiz and towards their table to take their order.

'I could eat everything on the menu.' Aggie sighed, settling for a chicken baguette and a very large coffee. 'That's what having too much to drink does for a girl. I can't apologise enough.'

'And I can't tell you how tedious it is hearing you continually apologise,' Luiz replied irritably. He glanced around him and sprawled back in the chair. 'I thought women enjoyed nothing more than talking about themselves.'

Aggie shot him a jaundiced look and sat back while her baguette, stuffed to bursting, was placed in front of her. Luiz was having nothing; it should have been a little embarrassing, diving into a foot-long baguette while he watched her eat, but she didn't care. Her stomach was rumbling with hunger. And stranded in awful conditions away from her home turf was having a lowering effect on her defences.

'I'll bet that really gets on your nerves,' Aggie said between mouthfuls, and Luiz had the grace to flush.

'I tend to go out with women whose conversations fall a little short of riveting.'

'Then why do you go out with them? Oh yes, I forgot. Because of the way they look.' She licked some tarragon mayonnaise from her finger and dipped her eyes, missing the way he watched, with apparent fascination, that small, unconsciously sensual gesture. Also missing the way he sat forward and shifted awkwardly in the chair. 'Why do you bother to go out with women if they're boring? Don't you want to settle down and get married? Would you marry someone who bored you?'

Luiz frowned. 'I'm a busy man. I don't have the time to complicate my life with a relationship.'

'Relationships don't have to complicate lives. Actually, I thought they were supposed to make life easier and more enjoyable. This baguette is delicious; thank you for getting it for me. I suppose we should discuss my contribution to this…this…'

'Why? You wouldn't be here if it weren't for me.'

He drummed his fingers on the table and continued to look at her. Her hair kept falling across her face as she leant forward to eat the baguette and, as fast as it fell, she tucked it behind her ear. There were crumbs by her mouth and she licked them off as delicately as a cat.

'True.' Aggie sat back, pleasantly full having demolished the baguette, and she sipped some of her coffee, holding the mug between both her hands. 'So.' She tossed him a challenging look. 'I guess your parents must want you to get married. At least, that's...'

'At least that's what?'

'None of my business.'

'Just say what you were going to say, Aggie. I've seen you half-undressed and ordering me to fetch you orange juice. It's fair to say that we've gone past the usual pleasantries.'

'Maria may have mentioned that everyone's waiting for you to tie the knot.' Aggie stuck her chin up defiantly because if he could pry into her life, whatever his reasons, then why shouldn't she pry into his?

'That's absurd!'

'We don't have to talk about this.'

'There's nothing *to* talk about!' But wasn't that why he found living in London preferable to returning to Brazil—because his mother had a talent for cornering him and pestering him about his private life? He loved his mother very much, but after three futile attempts to match-make him with the daughters of family friends he had had to draw her to one side and tell her that she was wasting her time.

'My parents have their grandchildren, thanks to three of my sisters, and that's just as well, as I have no intention of tying any knots any time soon.' He waited for her response and frowned when none was forthcoming. 'In our family,' he said abruptly, 'the onus of running the business, expanding it, taking it out of Brazil and into the rest of the world, fell on my shoulders. That's just the way it is. It doesn't leave a lot of time for pandering to a woman's needs. Aside from the physical.' He elaborated with a sudden, wolfish smile.

Aggie didn't smile back. It didn't sound like that great a trade-off to her. Yes, lots of power, status, influence and money, but if you didn't have time to enjoy any of that with someone you cared about then what was the point?

She suddenly saw a man whose life had been prescribed from birth. He had inherited an empire and he had never had any choice but to submit to his responsibility. Which, she conceded, wasn't to say that he didn't enjoy what he did. But she imagined that being stuck up there at the very top, where everyone else's hopes and dreams rested on your shoulders, might become a lonely and isolated place.

'Spare me the look of sympathy.' Luiz scowled and looked around for a waitress to bring the bill.

'So what happens when you marry?' she asked in genuine bewilderment, even though she was sensing that the conversation was not one he had any particular desire to continue. In fact, judging from the dark expression on his face, she suspected that he might be annoyed with himself for having said more than he wanted to.

'I have no idea what you mean by that.'

'Will you give over the running of your…er…company to someone else?'

'Why would I do that? It's a family business. No one outside the family will ever have direct control.'

'You're not going to have much time to be a husband, in that case. I mean, if you carry on working all the hours God made.'

'You talk too much.' The bill had arrived. He paid it, leaving a massive tip, and didn't take his eyes from Aggie's face.

She, in turn, could feel her temples begin to throb and her head begin to swim. His eyes drifted down to her full mouth, taking in the perfect, delicate arrangement of her features. Yes, he had looked at her before, had sized her up the first time they had met. But had he looked at her in the past like *this*? There was a powerful, sexual element to his lazy perusal of her face. Or was she imagining it? Was it just his way of avoiding the conversation?

Her breasts were tingling and her thoughts were in turmoil. Aside from the obvious reasons, this man was not her type at all. She might appreciate his spectacular good looks in a detached way but on every other level she had never had time for men who belonged to the striped-suit brigade, whose *raison d'être* was to live and die for the sake of work. She liked them carefree and unconventional and creative, so why had her body reacted like that just then—with the unwelcome frisson of a teenager getting randy on her first date with the guy of her dreams? God, even worse, was it the first time she had reacted like that? Or had she contrived to ignore all those tell-tale signs of a woman looking at a man and imagining?

'Yes. You're right. I do.' Her breathing was shallow, her pupils dilated.

On a subliminal level, Luiz registered these reactions. He was intensely physical, and if he didn't engage in soul searching relationships with women he made up for that in his capacity to read them and just know when they were affected by him.

Usually, it was a simple game with a foregone conclusion, and the women who ended up in his bed were women who understood the rules of the game. He played fair, as far as he was concerned. He never promised anything, but he was a lavish and generous lover.

So what, he wondered, was *this* all about? What the hell was going on?

She was standing up, brushing some crumbs off her jumper and slinging back on the worn, too-thin coat, pulling the woolly hat low down on her head, wriggling her fingers into her gloves. She wasn't looking at him. In fact, she was doing a good job of making sure that she didn't look at him.

Like a predator suddenly on the alert, Luiz could feel something inside him shift gear. He fell in beside her once they were outside and Aggie, nervous for no apparent reason, did what she always did when she was nervous. She began talking, barely pausing to draw breath. She admired the Christmas lights a little too enthusiastically and paused to stand in front of the first shop they came to, apparently lost in wonder at the splendid display of household items and hardware appliances. Her heart was thumping so hard that she was finding it difficult to hold on to her thoughts.

How had they ended up having such an intensely personal conversation? When had she stopped keeping him at a distance? Why had it become so easy to forget all the things she should be hating about him? Was that the power of lust? Did it turn your world on its head and make you lose track of everything that was sensible?

Just admitting to being attracted to him made her feel giddy, and when he told her that they should be getting back because she looked a little white she quickly agreed.

Suddenly this trip seemed a lot more dangerous than it had done before. It was no longer a case of trying to avoid constant sniping. It was a case of trying to maintain it.

CHAPTER FIVE

BY THE Monday morning—after two evenings spent by Aggie trying to avoid all personal conversation, frantically aware of the way her body was ambushing all her good intentions—the relentless snow was beginning to abate, although not sufficiently for them to begin the last leg of their journey.

The first thing Aggie did was to telephone the school. As luck would have it, it was shut, with just a recorded message informing her that, due to the weather, it would remain shut until further notice. She didn't know if it was still snowing in London, but the temperatures across the country were still sub-zero and she knew from experience that, even if the snow had stopped, sub-zero temperatures would result in frozen roads and pavements, as well as a dangerously frozen playground. This routinely happened once or twice a year, although usually only for a couple of days at most, and Health and Safety were always quick to step in and advise closures.

Then she looked at the pitiful supply of clothes remaining in her bag and said goodbye to all thoughts of saving any money at all for the New Year.

'I need to go back into town,' she told Luiz as soon as she had joined him in the dining room, where Mrs Bixby was busy chatting to the errant guest who had returned the evening before and was complaining bitterly about his chances of doing anything of any use. Salesmen rarely appreciated dire weather.

'More fresh air?'

'I need to buy some stuff.'

'Ah. New coat, by any chance?' Luiz sat back, tilting his chair away from the table so that he could cross his legs.

'I should get another jumper…some jeans, maybe. I didn't think that we would be snowed in when we're not even halfway through this trip.'

Luiz nodded thoughtfully. 'Nor had I. I expect I'll be forced to get some as well.'

'And you're missing your…meetings. You mentioned that deal you needed to get done.'

'I've telephoned my guys in London. They'll cover me in my absence. It's not perfect, but it'll have to do. This evening I'll have a conference call and give them my input. I take it you've called the school?'

'Closed anyway.' She sat back as coffee was brought for them, and chatted for a few minutes with their landlady, who was extremely cheerful at the prospect of having them there longer than anticipated.

'So your school's closed. How fortuitous,' Luiz murmured. 'I've tried calling the hotel where your brother is supposed to be holed up with Maria and the lines are down.'

'So is there any point in continuing?' Aggie looked at him and licked her lips. 'They were only going to be there for a few days. We could get up there and find they've already caught the train back to London.'

'It's a possibility.'

'Is that all you have to say?' Aggie cried in an urgent undertone. '*It's a possibility?* Neither of us can afford to spend time away from our jobs on a possibility!' The thought of her cold, uncomfortable, Luiz-free house beckoned like a port in a storm. She didn't understand why she was feeling what she was, and the sooner she was removed from the discomfort of her situation the better, as far as she was concerned. 'You have important meetings to go to. You told me so yourself. Just think of all those poor people whose livelihoods depend on you closing whatever deal it is you have to close!'

'Why, Aggie, I hadn't appreciated how concerned you were.'

'Don't be sarcastic, Luiz. You're a workaholic. It must be driving you crazy being caught out like this. It would take us the same length of time to return to London as it would to get to the Lake District.'

'Less.'

'Even better!'

'Furthermore, we would probably be driving away from the worst of the weather, rather than into it.'

'Exactly!'

'Which isn't to say that I have any intention of returning to London without having accomplished what I've set out to do. When I start something, I finish it.'

'Even if finishing it makes no sense?'

'This is a pointless conversation,' Luiz said coolly. 'And why the sudden desperation to jump ship?'

'Like I said, I thought I would be away for one night, two at most. I have things to do in London.'

'Tell me what. Your school's closed.'

'There's much more to teaching than standing in front of the children and teaching them. There are lessons to prepare, homework to mark.'

'And naturally you have no computer with you.'

'Of course I haven't.' He wasn't going to give way. She hadn't really expected that he would. She had known that he was the type of man who, once embarked on a certain course, saw it through to the finish. 'I have an old computer. There's no way I could lug that anywhere with me. Not that I thought I'd need it.'

'I'll buy you a laptop.' To Luiz's surprise, it was out before he had had time to think over the suggestion.

'I beg your pardon?'

'Everyone needs a laptop, something they can take with them on the move.' He flushed darkly and raked his fingers through his hair. 'I'm surprised you haven't got one. Surely the school would subsidise you?'

'I have a school computer but I don't take it out of the house. It's not my property.' Aggie was in a daze at his suggestion, but underneath, a slow anger was beginning to build. 'And would the money spent on this act of generosity be deducted from my full and final payment when you throw cash at me and my brother to get us out of the way? Are you keeping a mental tally?'

'Don't be absurd,' Luiz grated. He barely glanced at the food that had been placed in front of him by Mrs Bixby who, sensing an atmosphere, tactfully withdrew.

'Thanks, but I think I'll turn down your kind offer to buy me a computer.' This was how far apart their lives were, Aggie thought. Her body might play tricks on her, make her forget the reality of their situation, but this was the reality. They weren't on a romantic magical-mystery tour and he wasn't the man of her dreams. She was here because he had virtually blackmailed her into going with him and, far from being the man of her dreams, he was cold, single-minded and so warped by his privileged background that it was second nature to him to buy people. He could, so why not? His dealings with the human race were all based on financial transactions. He had girlfriends because they were beautiful and amused him for a while. But what else was there in his life? And did he imagine that there was nothing money couldn't buy?

'Too proud, Aggie?'

'I have no idea what you're talking about.'

'You think I've insulted you by offering to buy you something you need. You're here because of me. You'll probably end up missing work because of me. You'll need to buy clothes because of me.'

'So are you saying that you made a mistake in dragging me along with you?'

'I'm saying nothing of the sort.' Luiz looked at her, frowning with impatience. More and more he was finding it impossible to believe that she could be any kind of gold-digger. What sane opportunist would argue herself out of a free wardrobe? A top-of-the-range laptop computer? 'Of course you had to come with me.' But his voice lacked conviction. 'It's possible you weren't involved in trying to set your brother up with my niece,' he conceded.

'So you *did* make a mistake dragging me along with you.'

'I still intend to make sure that your brother stays away from Maria.'

'Even though you must know that he had no agenda when he got involved with her?'

Luiz didn't say anything and his silence spoke louder than words. Of course, he would never allow Mark to marry his niece. None of his family would. The wealthy remained wealthy because they protected their wealth. They married other wealthy people. That was his world and it was the only world he understood.

It was despicable, so why couldn't she look at him with indifference and contempt? Why did she feel this tremendous physical pull towards him however much her head argued that she shouldn't? It was bewildering and enraging at the same time and Aggie had never felt anything like it before. It was as if a whole set of brand-new emotions had been taken out of a box and now she had no idea how to deal with them.

'You really do come from a completely different world,' Aggie said. 'I think it's very sad that you can't trust anyone.'

'There's a little more to it than that,' Luiz told her, irritated. 'Maria's mother fell in love with an American twenty years ago. That American was Maria's father. There was a shotgun wedding. My sister went straight from her marriage vows to the hospital to deliver her baby. Of course, my parents were concerned, but they knew better than to say anything.'

'Why were they concerned? Because he was an American?'

'Because he was a drifter. Luisa met him when she was on holiday in Mexico. He was a lifeguard at one of the beaches. She was young and he swept her off her feet, or so the story goes. The minute they were married, the demands began. It turned out that Brad James had very expensive tastes. The rolling estate and the cars weren't enough; he wanted a private jet, and then he needed to be bankrolled for ventures that were destined for disaster. Maria knows nothing of this. She only knows that her father was killed in a light-aeroplane crash during one of his flying lessons. Luisa never forgot the mistakes she made.'

'Well, I'm sorry about that. It must have been hard growing up without a father.' She bit into a slice of toast that tasted like cardboard. 'But I don't want anything from you and neither does my brother.'

'You don't want anything from anyone. Am I right?'

Aggie flushed and looked away from those dark, piercing eyes. 'That's right.'

'But I'm afraid I insist on buying you some replacement clothes. Accept the offer in the spirit in which it was intended. If you dislike accepting them to such an extent, you can chuck them in a black bin-bag when you return to London and donate them all to charity.'

'Fine.' Her proud refusal now seemed hollow and churlish. He was being practical. She needed more clothes through no fault of her own. He could afford to buy them for her, so why shouldn't she accept the offer? It made sense. He wasn't to know that she wasn't given to accepting anything from anyone and certainly not charitable donations. Or maybe he had an idea.

At any rate, if he wanted to buy her stuff, then not only would she accept but she would accept with alacrity. It was better, wasn't it, than picking away at generosity, finding fault with it, tearing it to shreds?

With Christmas not far away, the town was once again bustling with shoppers, even though the snow continued falling. There was no convenient department-store but a series of small boutiques.

'I don't usually shop in places like this.' Aggie dithered outside one of the boutiques as Luiz waited for her, his hand resting on the door, ready to push it open. 'It looks expensive. Surely there must be somewhere cheaper?' He dropped his hand and stood back to lean against the shop front.

They had walked into town in silence. It had irritated the hell out of Luiz. Women loved shopping. So what if she had accepted his offer to buy her clothes under duress? The fact was, she was going to be kitted out, and surely she must be just a little bit pleased? If she was, then she was doing a damned good job of hiding it.

'And I've never stayed in a bed and breakfast before the

one we're in now,' Luiz said shortly. 'You're fond of reminding me of all the things I'm ignorant of because I've been insulated by my background. Well, I'm happy to try them out. Have you heard me complain once about where we're staying? Even though you've passed sufficient acid remarks about me being unable to deal with it because the only thing I can deal with are five-star hotels.'

'No,' Aggie admitted with painful honesty, while her face burned. She wanted to cover her ears with her hands because everything he was saying had a ring of truth about it.

'So I'm taking it that there are two sets of rules here. You're allowed to typecast me, whilst making damned sure that you don't get yourself typecast.'

'I can't help it,' Aggie muttered uncomfortably.

'Well, I suggest you try. So we're going to go into that shop and you're going to try on whatever clothes you want and you're going to let me buy whatever clothes you want. The whole damned shop if it takes your fancy!'

Aggie smiled and then giggled and slanted an upwards look at him. 'You're crazy.'

In return, Luiz smiled lazily back at her. She didn't smile enough. At least, not with him. When she did, her face became radiantly appealing. 'Compliment or not?' he murmured softly, and Aggie felt the ground sway under her feet.

'I'm not prepared to commit on that,' she told him sternly, but the corners of her mouth were still twitching.

'Come on.'

It was just the sort of boutique where the assistants were trained to be scary. They catered for rich locals and passing tourists. Aggie was sure that, had she strolled in, clad in her worn clothes and tired boots, they would have followed her around the shop, rearranging anything she happened to take from the shelves and keeping a close eye just in case she was tempted to make off with something.

With Luiz, however, shopping in an over-priced boutique was something of a different experience. The young girl who had greeted them at the door, as bug-eyed in Luiz's presence as the waitress had been on Saturday in the café, was sidelined and they were personally taken care of by an older woman who confided that she was the owner of the shop. Aggie was made to sit on the *chaise longe*, with Luiz sprawled next to her, as relaxed as if he owned the place. Items of clothing were brought out and most were immediately dismissed by him with a casual wave of the hand.

'I thought *I* was supposed to be choosing my own outfits,' Aggie whispered at one point, guiltily thrilled to death by this take on the shopping experience.

'I know what would look good on you.'

'I should get some jeans…' She worried her lower lip and inwardly fretted at the price of the designer jeans which had been draped over a chair, awaiting inspection. Belatedly, she added, 'And you don't know what would look good on me.'

'I know there's room for improvement, judging from the dismal blacks and greys I've seen you wear in the past.'

Aggie turned to him, hot under the collar and ready to be self-righteous. And she just didn't know what happened. Rather, she knew *exactly* what happened. Their eyes clashed. His, dark and amused… Hers, blue and sparking. Sitting so close to each other on the sofa, she could breathe him in and she gave a little half-gasp.

She knew he was going to kiss her even before she felt his cool lips touch hers, and it was as if she had been waiting for this for much longer than a couple of days. It was as if she had been waiting ever since the very first time they had met.

It was brief, over before it had begun, although when he drew back she found that she was still leaning into him, her mouth parted and her eyes half-closed.

'Bad manners to launch into an argument in a shop,' he murmured, which snapped her out of her trance, though her heart was beating so hard that she could scarcely breathe.

'You kissed me to shut me up?'

'It's one way of stopping an argument in the making.'

Aggie tried and failed to be enraged. Her lips were still tingling and her whole body felt as though it was on fire. That five-second kiss had been as potent as a red-hot branding iron. While she tried hard to conceal how affected she had been by it, he now looked away, the moment already forgotten, his attention back to the shop owner who had emerged with more handfuls of clothing, special items from the stock room at the back.

'Jeans—those three pairs. Those jumpers and that dress...not that one, the one hanging at the back.' He turned to Aggie, whose lips were tightly compressed. 'You look as though you've swallowed a lemon whole.'

'I would appreciate it if you would keep your hands to yourself!' she muttered, flinty-eyed, and Luiz grinned, unperturbed by this show of anger.

'I hadn't realised that my hands had made contact with your body,' he said silkily. 'If they had, you would certainly know about it. Now, be a good girl and try on that lot. Oh, and I want to see how you look in them.'

Aggie, the very last person on earth anyone could label an exhibitionist, decided that she hated parading in front of Luiz. Nevertheless, she couldn't deny the low-level buzz of unsettling excitement threading through her as she walked out in the jeans, the jumpers and various T-shirts in bright colours. He told her to slow down and not run as though she was trying out for a marathon. When she finally arrived at the dress, she held it up and looked at him quizzically.

'A dress?'

'Humour me.'

'I don't wear bright blues.' Nor did she wear silky dresses with plunging necklines that clung to her body like a second skin, lovingly outlining every single curve.

'This is a crazy dress for me to try on in the middle of winter,' she complained, walking towards him in the high heels which the sales assistant had slipped under the door for her. 'When it's snowing outside…'

Luiz could count on the fingers of one hand the times when he had ever been lost for words. He was lost for words now. He had been slouching on the low sofa, his hands lightly clasped on his lap, his long legs stretched out in front of him. Now he sat up straight and ran his eyes slowly up and down the length of her small but incredibly sexy body.

The colour of the dress brought out the amazing aquamarine of her eyes, and the cut of the stretchy, silky fabric left very little to the imagination when it came to revealing the surprising fullness of her breasts, the slenderness of her legs and the flatness of her stomach. He wanted to tell her to go back inside the dressing room and remove her bra so that he could see how the dress looked without two white bra-straps visible on her narrow shoulders.

'We'll have the lot.' His arousal was sudden, fierce and painful and he was damned thankful that he could reach for his coat which he had draped over the back of the chair and position it on his lap. He couldn't take his eyes off her but he knew that the longer he looked, the more uncomfortable he was going to get.

'And we'd better get a move on,' he continued roughly. 'I don't want to be stuck out here in town for much longer.' He watched, mesmerised, at the sway of her rounded bottom as she walked back towards the changing room. 'And we'll have those shoes as well,' he told the shop owner, who couldn't do enough for a customer who had practically bought half the shop, including a summer dress which she had foreseen having to hold in the store room until better weather came along.

'Thank you,' Aggie said once they were outside and holding four bags each. A coat had been one of the purchases. She was wearing it now and, much as she hated to admit it, it felt absolutely great. She hadn't felt a twinge of conscience as she had bid farewell to her old threadbare one in the shop, where it had been left for the shop owner to dispose of.

'Was it as gruelling an experience as you had imagined?' He glanced down and immediately thought of those succulent, rounded breasts and the way the dress had clung to them.

'It was pretty amazing,' Aggie admitted. 'But we were in there way too long. You want to get back. I understand that. I just…have one or two small things I need to get. Maybe we could branch off now? You could go and buy yourself some stuff.'

'You mean you don't want me to parade in front of you?' Luiz murmured, and watched with satisfaction the hectic flush that coloured her cheeks.

He hadn't expected this powerful sexual attraction. He had no idea where it was coming from. He wasn't sure when, exactly, it had been born and it made no sense, because she was no more his type than he, apparently, was hers. She was too argumentative, too mouthy and, hell, hadn't he started this trip with her in the starring role of gold-digger? Yet there was something strangely erotic and forbidden about his attraction, something wildly exciting about the way he knew she looked at him from under her lashes. He got horny just thinking about it.

Problem was…what was he to do with this? Where was he going to go with it?

He surfaced from his uncustomary lapse in concentration to find her telling him something about a detour she wanted him to make.

'Seven…what? What are you talking about?'

'I said that I'd like to stop off at Sevenoaks. It'll be a minor detour and I haven't been back there in over eighteen months.'

'What's Sevenoaks?'

'Haven't you been listening to a word I've been saying?' She assumed that, after the little jaunt in the clothes shop, his mind had now switched back to its primary preoccupation, which was work, and in that mode she might just as well have been saying 'blah, blah, blah'.

'In one ear, out the other,' Luiz drawled, marvelling that he could become so lost in his imagination that he literally hadn't heard a word she had been saying to him.

'Sevenoaks is the home we grew up in,' Aggie repeated. 'Perhaps we could stop off there? It's only a slight detour and it would mean a lot to me. I know you're in a rush to get to Mark's hotel, but a couple of hours wouldn't make a huge difference, would it?'

'We could do that.'

'Right…well…thanks.' Suddenly she felt as though she wouldn't have minded spending the rest of their time in the town with him. In response to that crazy thought, she took a couple of small steps back, just to get out of that spellbinding circle he seemed to project around him, the one which, once entered, wreaked havoc with her thought processes. 'And I'll head off now and see you back at the bed and breakfast.'

'What are you going to buy?' Luiz frowned as he continued to stare down at her. 'I thought we'd covered all essential purchases. Unless there are some slightly less essential ones outstanding? There must be a lingerie shop of sorts somewhere...'

Aggie reacted to that suggestion as though she had been stung. She imagined parading in front of him wearing nothing but a lacy bra and pants and she almost gasped aloud.

'I can get my own underwear—thank you.' She stumbled over the words in her rush to get them out. 'And, no, I wasn't talking about that!'

'What, then?'

'Luiz, it's getting colder out here and I'd really like to get back to the bed and breakfast so...' She took a few more steps back, although her eyes remained locked with his, like stupid, helpless prey mesmerised by an approaching predator.

Luiz nodded, breaking the spell. 'I'll see you back there in...' he glanced at his watch. '...a couple of hours. I have some work to do. Let's make it six-thirty in the dining room. If we're to have any kind of detour, then we're going to have to leave very early in the morning, barring any overnight fall of snow that makes it impossible. So we'll get an early night.'

'Of course,' Aggie returned politely. She was gauging from the tone of his voice that, whatever temporary truces came into effect, nothing would deflect him from his mission. It suddenly seemed wildly inappropriate that she had thrilled to his eyes on her only moments before as she had provided him with his very own fashion show, purchased at great expense. She might have made a great song and dance about her scorn for money, her lack of materialism but, thinking about how she had strutted her stuff to those lazy, watchful eyes, she suddenly felt as though without even realising it she had been bought somehow. And not only that, she had enjoyed the experience.

'And I just want you to know…' Her voice was cooler by several degrees. 'That once we're back in London, I shall make sure that all the stuff you bought for me is returned to you.'

'Not this rubbish again!' Luiz dismissed impatiently. 'I thought we'd gone over all that old ground and you'd finally accepted that it wasn't a mortal insult to allow me to buy you a few essential items of clothing, considering we've been delayed on this trip?'

'Since when is a summer dress *an essential item of clothing*?'

'Climb out of the box, Aggie. So the dress isn't essential. Big deal. Try a little frivolity now and again.' He couldn't help himself. His gaze drifted down to her full lips. It seemed that even when she was getting on his nerves she still contrived to turn him on.

'You think I'm dull!'

'I think this is a ridiculous place to have an ongoing conversation about matters that have already been sorted. Standing in the snow. The last thing either of us need is to succumb to an attack of winter flu.'

With her concerns casually swatted away, and her pride not too gently and very firmly put in its place, Aggie spun round on her heels without a backward glance.

She could imagine his amusement at her contradictory behaviour. One minute she was gracefully accepting his largesse, the next minute she was ranting and railing against it. It made no sense. It was the very opposite of the determined, cool, always sensible person she considered herself to be.

But then, she was realising that in his presence that determined, cool and always sensible person went into hiding.

Annoyed with herself, she did what she had to do in town, including purchasing some very functional underwear, and once back at the bed and breakfast she retreated up to her bedroom with a pot of tea. The landline at the hotel to which they were heading was still down and neither could she make contact with her brother on his mobile.

At this juncture, she should have been wringing her hands in worry at the prospect of the scene that would imminently unfold. She should have been depressed at the thought of Luiz doing his worst and bracing herself for a showdown that might result in her having to pick up the pieces. Her fierce protectiveness of her brother should have kicked in.

Instead, as she settled in the chair by the window with her cup of tea, she found herself thinking of Luiz and remembering the brush of his lips on hers. One fleeting kiss that had galvanised all the nerve-endings in her body.

She found herself looking forward to seeing him downstairs, even though she knew that it was entirely wrong to do so. Fighting the urge to bathe and change as quickly as possible, she took her time instead and arrived in the dining room half an hour after their agreed time.

She paused by the door and gathered herself. Luiz was in the clothes he had presumably bought after they had parted company, a pair of black jeans and a black, round-necked jumper. He had pushed his chair back and in front of him was his laptop, at which he was staring with a slight frown.

He looked every inch the tycoon, controlling his empire from a distance. He was a man who could have any woman he wanted. To look at him was to know that beyond a shadow of a doubt. So why was she getting into such a tizzy at the sight of him? He had kissed her to shut her up, and here she was, reacting as though he had swept her off her feet and transported her to his bed.

Luiz looked up and caught her in the act of staring. He shut his computer and in the space of a few seconds had clocked the new jeans, tighter than her previous ones, and one of the new, more brightly coloured long-sleeved T-shirts that clung in a way she probably hadn't noticed. It was warm in the dining room. No need for a thick jumper.

'I hope I'm not interrupting your work,' Aggie said, settling in the chair opposite him. There was a bottle of wine chilling in a bucket next to the table and she eyed it suspiciously. Now was definitely not the time to over-indulge.

'All finished, and you'll be pleased to know that the deal is more or less done and dusted. Jobs saved. Happy employees. A few lucky ones might even get pay rises. What did you buy in town after you left me?'

He poured her some wine and she fiddled with the stem of the glass.

'A few toys,' Aggie confessed. 'Things to take to the home. The children don't get a lot of treats. I thought it would be nice if I brought some with me. I shall wrap them; it'll be hugely exciting for them. 'Course, I couldn't really splash out, but I managed to find a shop with nothing in it over a fiver.'

Luiz watched the animation on her face. This was what the women he dated lacked. They had all been beautiful. In some cases, they had graced the covers of magazines. But, compared to Aggie's mobile, expressive face, theirs seemed in recollection lifeless and empty. Like mannequins. Was it any wonder that he had tired of them so quickly?

'Nothing over a fiver,' he murmured, transfixed by her absorption in what she was saying.

Having pondered the mystery of why he found her so compellingly attractive, Luiz now concluded that it was because she offered more than a pretty face and a sexy body. He had always tired easily of the women he had gone out with. No problem there; he didn't want any of them hanging around for ever. But the fact that Chloe, who had hardly been long-term, could be classified as one of his more enduring relationships was saying to him that his jaded palate needed a change of scene.

Aggie might not conform to what he usually looked for but she certainly represented a change of scene. In every possible way.

'Why are you looking at me like that?' Aggie asked suspiciously.

'I was just thinking about my own excessive Christmases.' He spread his hands in a self-deprecating gesture. 'I am beginning to see why you think I might live in an ivory tower.'

Aggie smiled. 'Coming from you, that's a big admission.'

'Perhaps it's one of the down sides of being born into money.' As admissions went, this was one of his biggest, and he meant it.

'Well, if I'm being perfectly honest…' Aggie leaned towards him, her face warm and appreciative, her defence system instantly defused by a glimpse of the man who could admit to shortcomings. 'I've always thought that pursuing money was a waste of time. 'Course, it's not the be-all and end-all, but I really enjoyed myself in that boutique today.'

'Which bit of it did you enjoy the most?'

'I've never actually sat on a chair and had anyone bring clothes to me for my inspection. Is that how it works with you?'

'I don't have time to sit on chairs while people bring me clothes to inspect,' Luiz said wryly. 'I have a tailor. He has my measurements and will make suits whenever I want them. I also have accounts at the major high-end shops. If I need anything, I just have to ask. There are people there who know the kind of things I want. Did you enjoy modelling the clothes for me?'

'Well…um…' Aggie went bright red. 'That was a first for me as well. I mean, I guess you wanted to see what you were paying for. That sounds awful. It's not what I meant.'

'I know what you meant.' He sipped some of his wine and regarded her thoughtfully over the rim of his glass. 'I would gladly have paid for the privilege of seeing you model those clothes for me,' he murmured. 'Although my guess is that you would have been outraged at any such suggestion. Frankly, it was a bit of a shame that there was any audience at all. Aside from myself, naturally. If it had been just the two of us, I would have insisted you remove your bra when you tried that dress on, for starters.'

Aggie's mouth fell open and she stared at him in disbelieving shock.

'You don't mean that,' she said faintly.

'Of course I do.' He looked surprised that she should disbelieve him.

'Why are you saying these things?'

'I'm saying what I mean. I don't know how it's happened, but I find myself violently attracted to you, and the reason I feel I can tell you this is because I know you feel the same towards me.'

'I do not!'

'Allow me to put that to the test, Aggie.'

This time there was nothing fleeting or gentle about his kiss. It wasn't designed to distract her. It was designed to prove a point, and she was as defenceless against its urgent power as she would have been against a meteor hurtling towards her at full tilt.

There was no rhyme or reason behind her reaction, which was driven purely on blind craving.

With a soft moan of surrender, she reached further towards him and allowed herself to drown in sensations she had never felt before.

'Point proved.' Luiz finally drew back but his hand remained on the side of her face, caressing her hot cheek. 'So the only remaining question is what we intend to do about this…'

CHAPTER SIX

AGGIE couldn't get to sleep. Luiz's softly spoken words kept rolling around in her mind. He had completely dropped the subject over dinner but the electricity had crackled between them and the atmosphere had been thick with unspoken thoughts of them in bed together.

Had she been that transparent all along? When had he realised that she was attracted to him? She had been at pains to keep that shameful truth to herself and she cringed to think how casually he had dropped it into the conversation as a given.

He was a highly sexual man and he would have no trouble in seeing sex between them as just the natural outcome of mutual attraction. He wouldn't be riddled with anxiety and he wouldn't feel as though he was abandoning his self-respect. For him, whatever the reasons for their trip, a sexual relationship between them would always be a separate issue which he would be able to compartmentalise. He was accustomed to relationships that didn't overlap into other areas of his life.

At a little after one, she realised that it was pointless trying to force herself to go to sleep.

She pulled on the dressing gown that had been supplied and was hanging on a hook on the bathroom door, shoved her feet in her bedroom slippers and headed for the door.

One big disadvantage of somewhere as small as this was that there was no room-service for those times when sleep was elusive and a glass of milk was urgently needed. Mrs Bixby had kindly pointed out where drinks could be made after hours and had told them both that they were free to use the kitchen as their own.

Aggie took her time pottering in the kitchen. A cup of hot chocolate seemed a better idea than a glass of milk and it was a diversion to turn her mind to something other than turbulent thoughts of Luiz.

She tried without success to stifle her flush of pleasure at his admission that he had been looking at her.

Caught up between the stern lectures she was giving herself about the craziness of his proposal, like uninvited guests at a birthday party were all sorts of troublesome questions, such as when exactly had he been looking at her and how often…?

None of that mattered, she told herself as she headed back up the stairs with the cup of hot chocolate. What mattered, what was *really* important, was that they get this trip over with as soon as possible and, whatever the outcome, she would then be able to get back to her normal life with its safe, normal routine. One thing that had been gained in the process was that he no longer suspected her of profiteering and she thought that he had probably dropped his suspicions of her brother as well. He still saw it as his duty to intervene in a relationship he thought was unacceptable, but at least there would be no accusations of opportunism.

However, when Aggie tried to remember her safe, normal routine before all these complications had arisen, she found herself thinking about Luiz. His dark, sexy face superimposed itself and squashed her attempts to find comfort in thinking about the kids at the school and what they would be getting up to in the run up to Christmas.

She didn't expect to see the object of her fevered thoughts at the top of the stairs. She was staring down into the mug of hot chocolate, willing it not to spill, when she looked up and there he was. Not exactly at the top of the stairs, but in the shadowy half-light on the landing, just outside one of the bedrooms, with just a towel round his waist and another hand towel slung over his neck.

Aggie blinked furiously to clear her vision and when the vision remained intact she made a strangled, inarticulate noise and froze as he strolled towards her.

'What are you doing here?' she asked in an accusing gasp as he reached to relieve her of the mug, which threatened to fall because her hands were trembling so much.

'I could ask *you* the same question.'

'I…I was thirsty.'

Luiz didn't answer. There were only five rooms on the floor and, if he hadn't known already, it wouldn't have been hard to guess which was hers because it was the only one with a light on. It shone through the gap under the door like a beacon and he beelined towards it so that she found herself with no choice but to follow him on unsteady legs.

The sight of his broad, bronzed back, those wide, powerful shoulders, made her feel faint. Her breasts ached. Her whole body was in the process of reminding her of the futility of denying the sexual attraction he had coolly pointed out hours earlier, the one she had spent the last few restless hours shooting down in flames.

He was in no rush. While her nerves continued to shred and unravel, he seemed as cool as a cucumber, standing back with a little bow to allow her to brush past him into the bedroom, where she abruptly came to a halt and stopped before he could infiltrate himself any further.

'Good night.'

Her cheeks were burning and she couldn't look him in

the eye but she could imagine the little mocking smile on his mouth at her hoarse dismissal.

'So you couldn't sleep. I'm not sure if a hot drink helps with that. I have a feeling that's an old wives' tale…' Luiz ignored her good-night, although he didn't proceed into the bedroom. It was sheer coincidence that he had bumped into her on the landing, *pure bloody coincidence,* but didn't fate work in mysterious ways? The laws of attraction… wasn't that what they called it? He remembered some girl-friend waffling on about that years ago while he had listened politely and wondered whether she had taken leave of her senses. Yet here it was at work, because he had been thinking about the woman standing wide-eyed in front of him and had decided to cool his thoughts down with a shower, only to find her practically outside his bedroom door. Never did he imagine that he would thank providence for the basic provisions of a bed and breakfast with only two *en suites.*

'I was thirsty, I told you.'

'I was having trouble sleeping too,' Luiz said frankly, his dark eyes roving over her slight frame. Even at this ungodly hour, she still managed to look good. No make-up, hair all over the place but still bloody good. Good enough to ravish. Good enough to lift and carry straight off to that king-sized bed behind her.

He felt his erection push up, hard as steel, and his breath quickened.

Aggie cleared her throat and said something polite along the lines of, 'oh dear, that's a shame,' at which Luiz grinned and held out the mug so that she could take it.

'Would you like to know why?'

'I'm not really interested.'

'Aren't you?' Whatever she might say, Luiz had his answer in that fractional pause before she predictably shook her head.

He hadn't been off the mark with her. She wanted him as much as he wanted her. He could always tell these things. His mouth curved in lazy satisfaction as he played with the idea of eliminating the talking and just…kissing her. Just plunging his hands into that tangled blonde hair, pulling her towards him so that she could have proof of just how much he was turned on, kissing her until she begged him not to stop. He could feel her alertness and it hit him that he hadn't been turned on by any woman to this extent before in his life.

He had spent the past couple of hours with his computer discarded next to him on the bed while he had stared up at the ceiling, hands folded behind his head, thinking of her. He had made his intentions clear and then dropped the matter in the expectation that, once the seed was planted, it would take root and grow.

'I want you,' he murmured huskily. 'I can't make myself any clearer, and if you want to touch you can feel the proof for yourself.'

Aggie's heart was thudding so hard that she could barely think straight.

'And I suppose you always get what you want?' She stuck her disobedient hands behind her back.

'You tell me. Will I?'

Aggie took a deep breath and risked looking at him even though those dark, fabulous eyes brought on a drowning sensation.

'No.'

For a few seconds, Luiz thought that he had heard incorrectly. Had she just turned him down? Women never said no to him. Why would they? Without a trace of vanity, he knew exactly what he brought to the table when it came to the opposite sex.

'No,' he tried out that monosyllable and watched as she glanced down with a little nod.

'What do you mean, *no*?' he asked in genuine bafflement.

Aggie's whole body strained to be touched by him and the power of that yearning shocked and frightened her.

'I mean you've got it wrong,' she mumbled.

'I can feel what you're feeling,' he said roughly. 'There's something between us. A chemistry. Neither of us was asking for this but it's there.'

'Yes, well, that doesn't matter.' Aggie looked at him with clear-eyed resolve.

'What do you mean, *that doesn't matter*?'

'We're on opposite sides of the fence, Luiz.'

'How many times do I have to reassure you that I have conceded that you were innocent of the accusations I originally made?'

'That's an important fence but there are others. You belong to a dynasty. You might think it's fun to step outside the line for a while, but I'm not a toy that you can pick up and then discard when you're through with it.'

'I never implied that you were.' Luiz thought that, as toys went, she was one he would dearly love to play with.

'I may not be rich and I may have come from a foster home, but it doesn't mean that I don't have principles.'

'And if I implied that you didn't, then I apologise.'

'And it doesn't mean that I'm weak either!' Aggie barrelled through his apology because, now that she had gathered momentum, she knew that it was in her interests to capitalise on it.

'Where are you going with that?' Luiz had the strangest feeling of having lost control.

'I'm not going to just *give in* to the fact that, yes, you're an attractive enough man and we happen to be sharing the same space...'

'I honestly can't believe I'm hearing this.'

'Yes, well, it's not my fault that you've lived such a charmed life that you've always got everything you wanted at the snap of a finger.'

Luiz looked down into those aquamarine eyes that could make a grown man go weak at the knees and shook his head in genuine incomprehension. Yes, okay, so maybe he had had a charmed life and maybe he had always got what he wanted, but this was crazy! The atmosphere between them was tangible and electric... What was wrong with two consenting adults giving in to what they both clearly wanted, whether she was brave enough to admit that or not?

'So...' Aggie took a couple of steps towards the door and placed her hand firmly on the door knob. As a support, it was wonderful because her legs felt like jelly. 'If you don't mind, I'm very tired and I really would like to get to bed now.'

She didn't dare meet his eyes, not quite, but lowering them was equally hazardous because she was then forced to stare at his chest with its dark hair that looked so aggressively, dangerously *un-English*; at his flat, brown nipples and at the clearly defined ripple of muscle and sinew.

Luiz realised that he was being dismissed and he straightened, all the time telling himself that the woman, as far as he was concerned, was now history. He had never been rejected before, at least not that he could remember, and he would naturally accept the reality that he was being rejected now, very politely but very firmly rejected. He had never chased any woman and he should have stuck with that format.

'Of course,' he said coldly, reaching to hold both ends of the towel over his shoulders with either hand.

Immediately, Aggie felt his cool withdrawal and hated it.

'I'll…er…see you tomorrow morning. What time do you want to leave?' This time she did look him squarely in the face. 'And will you still be taking that detour to…you know? I'd understand if you just want to get to our destination as quickly as possible…' But she would miss seeing Gordon and Betsy and all the kids; would miss seeing how everything was. Opportunities to visit like this were so rare. Frankly non-existent.

'And you question *my* motives?'

'What are you talking about?' It was Aggie's turn to be puzzled and taken aback at the harsh, scathing contempt in his voice.

'You have just made me out to be a guy who can't control his baser instincts—yet I have to question your choice of men because you seem to lump me into the category as the sort of man who gives his word on something only to retract it if it's no longer convenient!'

Hot colour flared in her cheeks and her mouth fell open.

'I never said…'

'Of course you did! Well, I told you that I would make that detour so that you could visit your friends at your foster home and I intend to keep my promise. I may be many things, but I am honourable.'

With that he left, and Aggie fell against the closed door, like a puppet whose strings had been suddenly severed. Every bone in her body was limp and she remained there for a few minutes, breathing heavily and trying not to think about what had just taken place. Which, of course, was impossible. She could still breathe in his scent and feel his disturbing presence around her.

So he had made a pass at her, she thought, trying desperately to reduce it to terms she could grasp. Men had made passes at her before. She was choosy, accustomed to brushing them aside without a second thought.

But this man…

He got to her. He roused her. He made her aware of her sexuality and made her curious to have it explored. Even with all those drawbacks, all those huge, gaping differences between them…

But it was good that she had turned him down, she told herself. He had been open and upfront with her, which naturally she appreciated. Fall into bed because they were attracted to one another? Lots of other women would have grabbed the opportunity; Aggie knew that. Not only was he drop-dead gorgeous, but there was something innately persuasive and unbearably sexy about him. His arrogance, on the one hand, left her cold but on the other it was mesmeric.

Fortunately, she reasoned as she slipped back between the sheets and closed her eyes, she was strong enough to maintain her wits! That strength was something of which she could justifiably be proud. Yes, she might very well be attracted to him, but she had resisted the temptation to just give in.

With the lights out, the cup of hot chocolate forgotten and sleep even more elusive than it had been before she had headed down to the kitchen, Aggie wondered about those other women who had given in. He always got what he wanted. What had he wanted? And why on earth would he be attracted to a woman like her? She was pretty enough, but he could certainly get far prettier without the hassle of having any of them question him or argue with him or stubbornly refuse to back down.

Aggie was forced to conclude that there might be truth in the saying that a change was as good as a rest.

She was different, and he had assumed that he could just reach out and pluck her like fruit from a tree, so that he could sample her before tossing her aside to return to the other varieties of fruit with which he was familiar.

It was more troubling to think of her own motivations, because she was far more serious when it came to relationships. So why was she attracted to him? Was there some part of her, hitherto undiscovered, that really was all about the physical? Some hidden part of her, free of restraint, principles and good judgement, that she had never known existed?

More to the point, how on earth were they going to get along now that this disturbing ingredient had been placed in the mix? Would he be cool and distant towards her because she had turned him down?

Aggie knew that she shouldn't really care but she found that she did. Having seen glimpses of his charm, his intelligence, his sense of humour, she couldn't bear the thought of having to deal with his coolness.

She found that she need not have worried. At least, not as much as she had. She arrived for breakfast the following morning to find him chatting to Mrs Bixby. Although his expression was unreadable when he looked across to where she was standing a little nervously by the door, he greeted her without any rancour or hostility, drawing her into the conversation he had been having with the older woman. Something about the sights they could take in *en route*, which also involved convoluted anecdotes about Mrs Bixby's various relatives who lived there. She seemed to have hordes of family members.

Luiz looked at her not looking at him, deliberately keeping her face turned away so that she could pour all her energy into focusing on Mrs Bixby.

He had managed to staunch his immediate reaction to her dismissal of him. He had left her room enraged and baffled at the unpleasant novelty of having been beaten back. The rage and bafflement had been contained, as he had known they would be, because however uncharacteristic his behaviour had been in that moment, he was still a man who was capable of extreme self-control. He would have to shrug her off with the philosophical approach of you win a few, you lose a few. And, if he had never lost any, then this was as good a time as any to discover what it felt like. With a woman who was, in the bigger picture, an insignificant and temporary visitor to his life.

Outside, the snow had abated. Aggie had called the school, vaguely explained and then apologised for her absence. She hadn't felt all that much better when she had been told that there was nothing to rush back for because the term was nearly over.

'You know what it's like here,' the principal had chuckled. 'All play and not much work with just a week to go before the holidays. If you have family problems, then don't feel guilty about taking some time off to sort them out.'

Aggie did feel guilty, though, because the 'family problems' were a sluggish mix of her own problems which she was trying to fight a way through and it felt deceitful to give the impression that they were any more widespread than that.

She looked surreptitiously at Luiz and wondered what was going through his head. His deep, sexy voice wafted around her and made her feel a little giddy, as though she was standing on a high wire, looking a long way down.

Eventually, Mrs Bixby left and Luiz asked politely in a friendly voice whether she was packed and ready to go.

'We might as well take advantage of the break in the weather,' he said, tossing his serviette onto his plate and pushing his chair back. 'It's not going to last. If you go and bring your bag down, I'll settle up and meet you by reception.'

So this was how it was going to be, Aggie thought. She knew that she should have been pleased. Pleased that he was being normal. Pleased that there would not be an atmosphere between them. Almost as though nothing had happened at all, as though in the early hours of the morning she hadn't bumped into him on the landing, he hadn't strolled into her room wearing nothing but a couple of towels and he certainly hadn't told her that he wanted her. It could all have been a dream because there was nothing in his expression or in the tone of his voice to suggest otherwise.

There was genuine warmth in Mrs Bixby's hugs as she waved them off, and finally Aggie twisted back around in her seat and waited for something. Something to be said. Some indication that they had crossed a line. But nothing.

He asked for the address to the foster home and allowed her to programme the satnav, although her fingers fumbled and it took ages before the address was keyed in and their course plotted.

It would take roughly a few hours. Conditions were going to worsen slightly the further north they went. They had been lucky to have found such a pleasant place to stay a couple of nights but they couldn't risk having to stop again and make do.

Luiz chatted amiably and Aggie was horrified to find that she hated it. Only now was she aware of that spark of electricity that had sizzled between them because it was gone.

When the conversation faltered, he eventually tuned in to the local radio station and they drove without speaking, which gave her plenty of time alone with her thoughts.

In fact, she was barely aware of the motorway giving way to roads, then to streets, and she was shocked when he switched off the radio, stopped the car and said,

'We seem to be here.'

For the first time since they had started on this uncomfortable trip, Luiz was treated to a smile of such spontaneous delight and pleasure that it took his breath away. He grimly wondered whether there was relief in that smile, relief that she was to be spared more of his company. Whether she was attracted to him or not, she had made it perfectly clear that her fundamental antipathy towards him rendered any physical attraction null and void.

'It's been *such* a long time since I was here,' she breathed fervently, hands clasped on her lap. 'I just want to sit here for a little while and breathe it in.'

Luiz thought that anyone would be forgiven for thinking that she was a prodigal daughter, returned to her rightful palatial home. Instead, what he saw was an averagely spacious pebble-dashed house with neat gardens on either side of a gravel drive. There was an assortment of outside toys on the grass and the windows of one of the rooms downstairs appeared to have drawings tacked to them. There were trees at the back but the foliage was sparse and unexciting.

'Same bus,' she said fondly, drawing his attention to a battered vehicle parked at the side. 'Betsy's always complained about it but I think she likes its unpredictability.'

'It's not what I imagined.'

'What did you imagine?'

'It seems small to house a tribe of children and teenagers.'

'There are only ever ten children at any one time and it's bigger at the back. You'll see. There's a conservatory—a double conservatory, where Betsy and Gordon can relax in the evenings while the older ones do their homework. They were always very hot on us doing our homework.' She turned to him and rested her hand on his forearm. 'You don't have to come in if you don't want to. I mean, the village is only a short drive away, and you can always go there for a coffee or something. You have my mobile number. You can call me when you get fed up and I'll come.'

'Not ashamed of me, by any chance, are you?' His voice was mild but there was an edge to it that took her aback.

'Of course I'm not! I was…just thinking of you. I know you're not used to this…er…sort of thing.'

'Stop stereotyping me!' Luiz gritted his teeth and she recoiled as though she had been slapped.

He hadn't complained once when they had been at the bed and breakfast. In fact, he had seemed sincerely impressed with everything about it, and had been the soul of charm to Mrs Bixby. Aggie was suddenly ashamed at the label she had casually dropped on his shoulders and she knew that, whatever his circumstances of birth, and however little he was accustomed to roughing it, he didn't deserve to be shoved in a box. If she did that, then it was about *her* hang-ups and not his.

'I'm sorry,' she said quickly, and he acknowledged the apology with a curt nod.

'Take your time,' he told her. 'I'll bring that bag in and don't rush. I'll watch from the sidelines. I've just spent the last few hours driving. I can do without another bout of it so that I can while away some time in a café.'

But he allowed her half an hour to relax in familiar surroundings without him around. He turned his mind to work, although it was difficult to concentrate when he was half-thinking of the drive ahead, half-thinking of her, wondering what it must feel like to be reunited with her pseudo-family. He had thought that she had stopped seeing him as a one-dimensional cardboard cut-out, but she hadn't, and could he blame her? He had stormed into her life like a bull in a china shop, had made his agenda clear from the beginning, had pronounced upon the problem and produced his financial solution for sorting it out. In short, he had lived down to all her expectations of someone with money and privilege.

He had never given a passing thought in the past as to how he dealt with other people. He had always been supremely confident of his abilities, his power and the reach of his influence. As the only son from a family whose wealth was bottomless, he had accepted the weight of responsibility for taking over his family's vast business concerns, adding to them with his own. Alongside that, however, were all the advantages that came with money—including, he reluctantly conceded, an attitude that might or might not be interpreted as arrogant and overbearing.

It was something that had never been brought to his notice, but then again he was surrounded by people who feared and respected him. Would they ever point out anything that might be seen as criticism?

Agatha Collins had no such qualms. She was in a league of her own. She didn't hold back when it came to pointing out the things she disliked about him although, he mused, she was as quick to apologise if she thought she had been unfair as she was to heap criticism when she thought she had a point. He had found himself in the company of someone who spoke her mind and damned the consequences.

On that thought, he slung his long body out of the car, collected the bag of presents which she had bought the day before and which he could see, as he idly peered into the bag, she had wrapped in very bright, jolly Christmas paper.

The door was pulled open before he had time to hit the

buzzer and he experienced a few seconds of complete disorientation. Sensory overload.

Noise; chaos; children; lots of laughter; the smell of food; colour everywhere in the form of paintings on the walls; coats hanging along the wall; shoes and wellies stacked by the side of the door. Somewhere roundabout mid-thigh area, a small dark-haired boy with enormous brown eyes, an earnest face and chocolate smeared round his mouth stared up at him, announced his name—and also announced that he knew who *he* was, because Aggie had said it would be him, which was why Betsy had allowed him to open the door, because they were *never* allowed to open the door. All of this was said without pause while the noise died down and various other children of varying sizes approached and stared at him.

Luiz had never felt so scrutinised in his life before, nor so lost for something to say. Being the focus of attention of a dozen, unblinking children's eyes induced immediate seizure of his vocal chords. Always ready with words, he cleared his throat and was immensely relieved when Aggie emerged from a room at the back, accompanied by a woman in her early seventies, tall, stern-looking with grey hair pulled back in a bun. When she smiled, though, her face radiated warmth and he could see from the reaction of the kids that they adored her.

'You look hassled,' Aggie whispered when introductions had been made. He was assured by Betsy that pandemonium was not usual in the house but she was being lenient, as it was Christmas, and that he must come and have something to eat, and he needn't fear that there would be any food throwing at the table.

'Hassled? I'm never hassled.' He slid his eyes across to her and raised his eyebrows. 'Overwhelmed might be a better word.'

Aggie laughed, relaxed and happy. 'It's healthy to be overwhelmed every so often.'

'Thanks. I'll bear that in mind.' He was finding it difficult to drag his eyes away from her laughing face. 'Busy place.'

'Always. And Betsy is going to insist on showing you around, I'm afraid. She's very proud of what she's done with the house.'

They had passed several rooms and were heading towards the back of the house where he could see a huge conservatory that opened out onto masses of land with a small copse at the back, which he imagined would be heaven for the kids here when it was summer and they could go outside.

'We won't be here long,' she promised. 'There's a little present-giving Christmas party. It's been brought forward as I'm here. I hope you don't mind.'

'Why should I?' Luiz asked shortly. It irked him immensely that, even though he had mentally decided to write her off, he still couldn't manage to kill off what she did to his libido. It was also intensely frustrating that he was engaging in an unhealthy tussle with feelings of jealousy. Everyone and everything in this place had the power to put a smile on her face. The kind of smile which she had shown him on rare occasions only.

He didn't understand this confused flux of emotion and he didn't like it. He enjoyed being in control of his life and of everything that happened around him. Agatha Collins was very firmly out of his control. If she were any other woman, she would have been flattered at his interest in her, and she wouldn't have hesitated to come to bed with him. It had been a simple, and in his eyes foolproof, proposition.

To have been knocked back was galling enough, but to have been knocked back only to find himself getting back to his feet and bracing himself for another onslaught on her defences bordered on unacceptable.

'I thought you might be bored,' Aggie admitted, flushing guiltily as his face darkened. 'Also...'

'Also what?'

'I know you're angry with me.'

'Why would I be angry with you?' Luiz asked coldly.

'Because I turned you down and I know I must have... You must have found that... Well, I guess I dented your ego.'

'You want me. I want you. I proposed we do something about that and you decided that you didn't want to. There's no question of my pride being dented.'

'I just can't approach sex in such a cold-blooded way.' Aggie was ashamed that after her show of will power she was now backtracking to a place from which she could offer up an explanation. 'You move in and out of women and...'

'And you're not a toy to be picked up and discarded when the novelty's worn off. I think you already made that clear.'

'So that's the only reason why I feel a little uncomfortable about asking you to put yourself out now.'

'Well, don't. Enjoy yourself. The end of the journey is just round the corner.'

CHAPTER SEVEN

'WE'RE never going to make it to Sharrow Bay tonight.'

They had been driving for a little under an hour and Luiz looked across to Aggie with a frown.

'Depends on how much more the weather deteriorates.'

'Yes, well, I don't see the point of taking risks on the roads. I mean, it's not as though Mark and Maria are going anywhere. Not in these conditions. We spent a lot longer than I anticipated at Sevenoaks and I apologise about that.'

Aggie didn't know how to get through the impenetrable barrier that Luiz had erected around himself. He had smiled, charmed and chatted with everyone at the home and had done so without a flicker of tension, but underneath she could feel his coolness towards her. It was like an invisible force field keeping her out and she hated it.

'I hope you didn't find it too much of a chore.' She tried again to revive a conversation that threatened to go in the same direction as the last few she had initiated—slap, bang into a brick wall of Luiz's disinterest.

Her pride, her dignity and her sense of moral self-righteousness at having rightly turned down a proposal for no-strings sex for a day or two had disintegrated, leaving in its wake the disturbing realisation that she had made a terrible mistake. Why hadn't she taken what was on offer? Since when did sex have to lead to a serious commitment? There was no tenderness, and he would never whisper sweet nothings in her ear, but the power of the sexual pull he had over her cut right through all of those shortcomings.

Why shouldn't she be greedy for once in her life and just take without bothering about consequences and without asking herself whether she was doing the wrong thing or the right thing?

She had had three relationships in her life and on paper they had all looked as though they would go somewhere. They had been free-spirited, fun-loving, creative guys, nothing at all like Luiz. They had enjoyed going to clubs, attending protest marches and doing things on impulse.

And what had come of them? She had grown bored with behaviour that had ended up seeming juvenile and irresponsible. She had become fed up with the fact that plans were never made, with Saturdays spent lying in bed because none of them had ever shown any restraint when it came to drinking—and if she had tried to intervene she had been shouted down as a bore. With all of them, she had come to dread the aimlessness that she had initially found appealing. There had always come a point when hopping on the back of a motorbike and just riding where the wind took them had felt like a waste of time.

Luiz was so much the opposite. His self-control was formidable. She wondered whether he had ever done anything spontaneous in his life. Probably not. But despite that, or maybe because of it, her desire for him was liberated from the usual considerations. Why hadn't she seen that at the time? She had shot him down as the sort of person who could have relationships with women purely for sex, as if the only relationships worth considering were ones where you spent your time plumbing each other's depths. Except she had tried those and none of them had worked out.

'The kids loved you,' she persevered. 'And so did Betsy and Gordon. I guess it must have been quite an eye-opener, visiting a place like that. I'm thinking that your background couldn't have been more different.'

Like a jigsaw puzzle where the pieces slowly began to fit together, Luiz was seeing the background picture that had made Aggie the woman she had become. It was frustrating and novel to find himself in a position of wanting to chip away at the surface of a woman and dig deeper. She was suspicious, proud, defensive and fiercely independent. She had had to be.

'There's a hotel up ahead, by the way, just in case you agree with me that we need to stop. Next town along…' With every passing minute of silence from him, Aggie could feel her chances of breaking through that barrier slipping further and further out of reach.

'Is there? How do you know?' With her childhood home behind them, she was no longer the laughing, carefree person she had been there. Luiz could feel the tension radiating out of her, and if it were up to him he would risk the snow and plough on. The mission he had undertaken obviously had to reach a conclusion, but the cold-blooded determination that had initially fuelled him had gone. In its place was weary resignation for an unpleasant task ahead.

Aggie's heart picked up speed. How did she know about the hotel? Because she had checked it on the computer Betsy kept in the office. Because she had looked at Luiz as he had stood with his arms folded at the back of the room, watching Christmas presents being given out, and she had known that, however arrogant and ruthless he could be, he was also capable of generosity and understanding. He could easily have turned down her request for that detour. He was missing work, and the faster he could wrap up the business with Mark and his niece, the better for him. Yet not only had he put himself out but he had taken the experience in his stride. He had shown interest in everything Betsy and Gordon had had to say and had interacted with the kids who had been fascinated by the handsome, sophisticated stranger in their midst.

She had been proud of him and had wanted him so intensely that it physically hurt.

'I saw a sign for it a little way back.' She crossed her fingers behind her back at that excusable white lie. 'And I vaguely remember Betsy mentioning ages ago that there was a new fancy hotel being built near here, to capture the tourist trade. It's booming in this part of the world, you know.'

'I didn't see any sign.'

'It was small. You probably missed it. You're concentrating on driving.'

'Wouldn't you rather just plough on? Get where we're heading? If we stick it out for another hour, we should be there, more or less.'

'I'd rather not, if you don't mind.' It suddenly occurred to her that the offer he had extended had now been withdrawn. He wasn't the sort of man who chased women. Having done so with her, he wasn't the sort of man who would carry on in the face of rejection. Did she want to risk her pride by throwing herself at him, when he now just wanted to get this whole trip over and done with so that he could return to his life?

'I have a bit of a headache coming on, actually. I think it must be all the excitement of today—seeing Gordon and Betsy, the children. Gordon isn't well. She only told me when we were about to leave. He's had some heart problems. I worry about what Betsy will do if something happens to him.'

'Okay. Where's the turning?'

'Are you sure? You've already put yourself out enough as it is.' Aggie held her breath. If he showed even a second's reluctance, then she would abandon her stupid plan; she would just accept that she had missed her chance; she would tell herself that it was for the best and squash any inclination to wonder...

'The turning?'

'I'll direct you.'

He didn't ask how she just happened to know the full address of the hotel, including the post code, in case they got lost and needed to use his satnav. After fifteen minutes of slow driving, they finally saw a sign—a real sign this time—and Aggie breathed a sigh of relief when they swung into the courtyard of a small but very elegant country house. Under the falling snow, it was a picture-postcard scene.

A few cars were in the courtyard, but it was obvious that business was as quiet here as it had been at Mrs Bixby's bed and breakfast. How many other people were slowly wending their way north by car in disastrous driving conditions? Only a few lunatics.

Her nerves gathered pace as they were checked in.

'Since this was my suggestion...' She turned to him as they walked towards the winding staircase that led to the first floor and up to their bedrooms. 'I insist on picking up the tab.'

'Have you got the money to pick up the tab?' Luiz asked. 'There's no point suggesting something if you can't carry it out.'

'I might not be rich but I'm not completely broke!' Nerves made her lash out at him. It wasn't the best strategy for enticing him into her bed. 'I'm doing this all wrong,' she muttered, half to herself.

'Doing what all wrong?' Luiz stopped and looked down at her.

'You're nothing like the guys I've been out with.'

'I don't think that standing halfway up the stairs in a hotel is the place for a soul-searching conversation about the men you've slept with.' He turned on his heels and began heading upstairs.

'I don't like you being like this with me!' Aggie caught up with him and tugged the sleeve of his jumper until he turned around and looked at her with impatience.

'Aggie, why don't we just go to our rooms, take some time out and meet in an hour for dinner? This has already turned into a never-ending journey. I've been away from work for too long. I have things on my mind. I don't feel inclined to get wrapped up in a hysterical, emotional conversation with you now.'

Luiz was finding it impossible to deal with his crazy obsession with her. He wondered if he was going stir crazy. Was being cooped up with her doing something to his self-control? It had not even crossed his mind, when he had made a pass at her, that she would turn him down. Was that why he had watched her with Betsy and Gordon and all those kids and the only thing he could think was how much he wanted to get her into his bed? Was he so arrogant, in the end, that he couldn't accept that any woman should say no to him?

The uneasy swirl of unfamiliar emotions had left him edgy and short-tempered. He would have liked to dismiss her from his mind the way he had always been able to dismiss all the inconveniences that life had occasionally thrown at him. He had always been good at that. Ruthlessness had always served him well. That and the knowledge that it was pointless getting sidetracked by things that were out of your control. Aggie sidetracked him and the last thing he needed was an involved conversation that would get neither of them anywhere. Womanly chats were things he avoided like the plague.

'I'm not being hysterical.' Aggie took a deep breath. If she backed away now, she would never do what she felt she had to do. Falling into bed with Luiz might be something she would never have contemplated in a month of Sundays, but then again she had never had to cope with a sexual attraction that was ripping her principles to shreds.

She had come to the conclusion that, whilst she knew it was crazy to sleep with a guy whose attitude towards women she found unnerving and amoral, not to sleep with him would leave her with regrets she would never be able to put behind her. And, if she was going to sleep with him, then she intended to have some control over the whole messy situation.

A lifetime of independence would not be washed away in a five-minute decision.

'I just want to talk to you. I want to clear the air.'

'There's nothing to clear, Aggie. I've done what you asked me to do, and I'm pleased you seemed to have had a good time seeing all your old friends, but now it's time to move on.'

'I may have made a mistake.'

'What are you talking about?'

'Can we discuss this upstairs? In your room? Or we could always go back downstairs to the sitting room. It's quiet there.'

'If you don't mind me changing while you speak, then follow me to my room, by all means.' He turned his back on her and headed up.

'So…' Once inside the bedroom, Luiz began pulling off his sweater which he flung on a chair by the window. Their bags had been brought up and deposited in their separate rooms and he began rummaging through his for some clothes.

'I never wanted to make this trip with you,' Aggie began falteringly, and Luiz stilled and turned to look at her.

'If this is going to be another twenty minutes of recriminations, then let me tell you straight away that I'm not in the mood.' But, even as he spoke, he was seeing her tumble of fair hair and the slender contours of her body encased in a pair of the new jeans and deep burgundy jumper that was close-fitted and a lot sexier than the baggy jumpers she seemed to have stockpiled. Once again, his unruly lack of physical control made him grit his teeth in frustration. 'I'm also not in the mood to hear you make a song and dance about paying your own way.'

'I wasn't going to.' She pressed her back against the closed door.

'Then what was it you wanted to tell me?'

'I've never met anyone like you before.'

'I think,' Luiz said drily, 'you may have mentioned that to me in the past—and not in a good way—so unless you have something else to add to the mix then I suggest you go and freshen up.'

'What I mean is, I never thought I could be attracted to someone like you.'

'I don't do these kinds of conversations, Aggie. Post mortems on a relationship are bad enough; post mortems on a non-relationship are a complete non-starter. Now, I'm going to have a shower.' He began unbuttoning his shirt.

Aggie felt the thrill of sudden, reckless excitement and a desperate urgency to get through to him. Despite or maybe because of her background she had never been a risk taker. From a young age, she had felt responsible for Mark and she had also gathered, very early on, that the road to success wasn't about taking risks. It was about putting in the hard work; risk taking was for people who had safety nets to fall into. She had never had one.

Even in her relationships, she had never strayed from what her head told her she should be drawn to. So they hadn't worked out. At no point, she now realised, had she ever concluded that maybe she should have sat back and taken stock of what her head had been telling her.

Luiz, so different from anyone she had ever known, who had entered her life in the most dubious of circumstances, had sent her into a crazy tailspin. She had found herself in terrifying new territory where nothing made sense and she had reacted by lashing out.

Before he could become completely bored with her circuitous conversation, Aggie drew in a deep breath. 'You made a pass at me and I'm sorry I turned you down.'

Luiz, about to pull off his shirt, allowed his arms to drop to his sides and looked at her through narrowed eyes. 'I'm not with you,' he said slowly.

Aggie propelled herself away from the safety of the door and walked towards him. Every step closer set up a tempo in her body that made her perspire with nervous tension.

'I always thought,' she told him huskily, 'that I could never make love to a guy unless I really liked him.'

'And the boyfriends you've had?'

'I really liked them. To start with. And please don't make it sound as though I've slept around; I haven't. I've just always placed a lot of importance on compatibility.'

'We all make mistakes.' At no point did it occur to Luiz that he would turn her away. The strength of his attraction was too overwhelming. He didn't get it, but he knew himself well enough to realise that it was something that needed sating. 'But the compatibility angle obviously didn't play out with you,' he couldn't help adding with some satisfaction.

'No, it didn't,' Aggie admitted ruefully. She sneaked a glance at him and shivered. He was just so gorgeous. Was it any wonder her will power was sapped? She would never have made a play for him. She would never have considered herself to be in the category of women he might be attracted to. It occurred to her that he only wanted her because she was different from the women he dated, but none of that seemed to matter, and she wasn't going to try and fight it.

'What happened?' Luiz strolled towards the king-sized four-poster bed and flopped down on it, his hands linked behind his head. His unbuttoned shirt opened to reveal a tantalising expanse of bronzed, muscular chest. This was the pose of the conqueror waiting for his concubine, and it thrilled her.

Aggie shrugged. 'They were free spirits. I liked it to start with. But I guess I'm not much of a free spirit.'

'No. You're not.' He gave her a slow, lingering smile that made her toes curl. 'Are you going to continue standing there or are you going to join me?' He patted the space next to him on the bed and Aggie's heart descended very rapidly in the direction of her feet.

She inched her way towards the bed and laughed when he sat forward and yanked her towards him. Her laughter felt like an unspoken release of all her defences. She was letting go of her resentment in the face of something bigger.

'What do you mean?' Heart beating a mile a minute, she collapsed next to him and felt the warmth of his body next to her. It generated a series of intensely physical reactions that left her breathless and gasping.

'So you're not impressed by money. But a free spirit would have taken what I offered—the computer, the extensive wardrobe; would have factored them in as gifts to be appreciated and moved on. You rejected the computer out of hand and agonised over the wardrobe. The only reason you accepted was because you had no more clothes and I had to talk you into seeing the sense behind the offer. And you still tell me you're going to return them all to me when we get back to London. You criticise me for wanting control but you fall victim to the very same tendency.'

'We're not alike at all.' They were both on their sides, fully clothed, staring at one another. There was something very erotic about the experience, because underneath the excitement of discovery lurked like a thrilling present concealed with wrapping paper.

'Money separates us,' Luiz said wryly. 'But in some areas I've discovered that we're remarkably similar. Would this conversation benefit from us being naked, do you think?'

Aggie released a small, treacherous moan and he delivered a rampantly satisfied smile in response. Then he stood up and held out one hand. 'I'm going to run a bath,' he murmured. 'Your room's next to mine. Why don't you go and get some clothes…?'

'It feels weird,' Aggie confided. 'I've never approached an intimate situation like this.'

'But then this is an intimate situation neither of us expected,' Luiz murmured. 'And that in itself is a first for me.'

'What do you mean?'

'It never fails to surprise me just how turned on I get for you.'

'Because I'm nothing like the women you've gone out with?'

'Because you're nothing like the women I've gone out with,' Luiz agreed.

Aggie knew that she should be offended by that, but

then who would she be kidding? He was nothing like the guys she had gone out with. Mutual physical attraction had barrelled through everything and changed the parameters. Maybe that was why it felt so dangerously exciting.

'You're a lot more independent and I find that a turn on.' He softly ran his fingers along her side. He couldn't wait for her to be naked but this leisurely approach was intoxicating. 'You're not a slave to fashion and you're fond of arguing.'

Aggie conceded privately that all three of those things represented a change for him, but a change that he would rapidly tire of. Since she wasn't in it for the long haul, since she too was stepping outside the box, there was no harm in that, although she was uneasily aware of a barely acknowledged disappointment floating aimlessly inside her.

'You like your women submissive,' she said with a little laugh.

'Generally speaking, it's worked in the past.'

'And I like my guys to be creative, not to be ruled by money.'

'And yet, mysteriously, your creative paupers have all bitten the dust.' Luiz found, to his bemusement, that he didn't care for the thought of any other man in her life. It was puzzling, because he had never been the possessive type. In fact, in the past women who had tried to stir up a non-existent jealousy gene by referring to past lovers had succeeded in doing the opposite.

'They haven't been paupers,' Aggie laughed. 'Neither of them. They've just been indifferent to money.'

'And in the end they bored you.'

'I'm beginning to wish I'd never mentioned that,' Aggie said, though only half-joking. 'And if they bored me,' she felt obliged to elaborate, 'it was because they turned out to be boring people, not because they were indifferent to money.' She wriggled off the bed and stood up. 'Perhaps I'll have a bath in my own bathroom…'

Luiz frowned, propping himself up on one elbow. 'Second thoughts?' His voice was neutral but his eyes had cooled.

'No.' Aggie tilted her chin to look at him. 'I don't play games like that.'

'Good.' He felt himself relax. To have been rejected once bordered on the unthinkable. To be rejected twice would have been beyond the pale. 'Then what games do you play? Because I think I can help you out there…'

The promise behind those softly spoken words sent a shiver up her spine and it was still there when she returned to his bedroom a few minutes later. She had not been lying when she had confessed that she had never approached sex like this before. Stripped of all romantic mystique and airy-fairy expectations that it would lead somewhere, this was physical contact reduced to its most concentrated form.

The bath had been run. Aggie could smell the fragrance of jasmine bath oil. The steam in the enormous bathroom did nothing whatsoever to diminish the impact of Luiz, who had stripped out of his clothes and was wearing a towel around his waist.

Outside, the snow continued to fall. In her room, she had taken a few seconds to stare out of the window and absorb the fact that Mark and Maria, and the mission upon which they had embarked only a few days previously, couldn't have been further from her mind. When exactly had she lost track of the reason why she was here in the first place? It was as though she had opened the wardrobe door to find herself stepping into Narnia, reality left behind for a brief window in time.

She could barely remember the routine of her day-today existence. The school, the staff room, the kids getting ready for their Nativity play.

Was Luiz right? She had always fancied herself as a free-spirited person and yet she felt as though this was the first impulsive thing she had ever done in her life. She had thought him freakishly controlled, a power-hungry tycoon addicted to mastering everything and everyone around him, while she—well, she was completely different. Maybe the only difference really was the fact that he was rich and she wasn't, that he had grown up with privilege while she had had to fight her way out of her background, burying herself in studies that could provide her with opportunities.

'Now, what I'd like…' Luiz drawled, and Aggie blinked herself back to the present, 'is to do what I was fantasising about when you did your little catwalk in that shop for me. Instead of showing me how you look with clothes on, show me how you look with them off.'

He sauntered out of the bathroom and lay back down on the bed, just as he had before.

Aggie realised in some part of her that, whilst this should not feel right, it did. She would never have believed it possible for either of them to set aside their personal differences and meet on this plane. Certainly, she would never have believed it of herself, but before she could begin nurturing any doubts about the radical decision she had made she told herself that everyone deserves some time out, and this was her time out. In a day or two, it would be nothing more than a wicked memory of the one and only time she had truly strayed from the path she had laid out for herself.

She watched, fascinated and tingling all over, shocked as he drew back the towel which had been modestly covering him, and revealed his arousal. She nearly fainted when he gently held it in one hand.

Luiz grinned at her. 'So easy to make you blush,' he murmured. Then he fell silent and watched as she began removing her clothes, at first with self-conscious, fumbling fingers, then with more confidence as she revelled in the sight of his darkened, openly appreciative gaze.

'Come here,' he rasped roughly, before she could remove the final strips of clothing. 'I'm finding it hard to wait.'

Aggie sighed and flung her head back as his big hands curved over her breasts, thinly sheathed in a lacy bra. Their mouths met in an explosive kiss, a greedy, hungry kiss, so that they gasped as they surfaced for air and then resumed their kissing as if neither could get enough of the other. Her nipples were tender and sensitive and she moaned when he rolled his thumb over one stiffened peak, seeking and finding it through the lacy gaps in the bra.

She was melting. Freeing a hand from the tangle of his black hair, she shakily pulled off the panties which were damp, proof of her own out-of-control libido.

Luiz was going crazy with *wanting* her. He could hardly bear the brief separation of their bodies as she unclasped her bra from the back and pulled it off.

Her nipples were big, circular discs, clearly defined, pouting temptingly at him. He realised that he had been fantasising about this moment perhaps from the very first time he had laid eyes on her. He had not allowed himself to see her in a sexual way, not when he had been busy working out how to disengage her and her brother from his niece and the family fortune. But enforced time together had whittled away his self-control. It had allowed the seeds of attraction to take root and flourish.

'You have the face of an angel,' he breathed huskily as he rolled her on top of him. 'And the body of a siren.'

'I'm not sure about that.' Aggie gazed down at him. 'Aren't sirens supposed to be voluptuous?'

'God, you're beautiful…' His hands could almost span her waist and he eased her down so that he could take one of those delicate breasts to his mouth and suckle on the hot, throbbing tip. He loved the way she arched her body back, offering herself to him—and even more he loved the way he could sense her spiralling out of control, her fists clenched as she tried to control the waves of sensation washing over her.

He smoothed his hand along the inside of her thigh and she wriggled to accommodate his questing finger. She shuddered when that finger dipped into her honeyed moistness and began stroking her. With her body under sensual attack on two fronts as he continued to worship her breast with his mouth and tease the wet, receptive bud of her femininity with his finger, she could bear it no longer. She flipped off him and lay on her back, breathing heavily and then curling onto her side as he laughed softly next to her.

'Too much?' he asked, and she sighed on a moan.

'Not fair. It's your turn now to feel like you're about to fall off the edge.'

'What makes you think I'm not already there?'

It transpired that he wasn't. In fact, it transpired that he didn't have a clue what being close to the edge was all about. He had foolishly been confusing it with simply *being turned on*.

For an excruciatingly long period of time, she demonstrated what being close to the edge was all about. She touched him and tasted him until he thought he had died and gone to heaven.

Their bodies seemed to merge and become one. She touched him and he touched her, from her breasts, down to her flat belly with its little mole just above her belly button, and then at last to the most intimate part of her.

He peeled apart her delicate folds and dipped his tongue just there until she squirmed with pleasure, her fingers tangled in his hair, her eyes shut and her whole body thrust back to receive the ministrations of his mouth.

He lazily feasted on her silky-sweet moistness until she was begging him to stop. Lost in the moment, he could have stayed there for ever with her legs around him and her body bucking under his mouth.

He finally thrust into her only after he was wearing protection. Putting it on, he found that his hands were shaking. He kicked off the last slither of duvet that remained on the bed and she opened up to him like a flower, her rhythm and movements matching his so that they were moving as one.

Aggie didn't think that she had ever felt so united and in tune with another human being in her life before. Her body was slippery, coated in a fine film of perspiration. His was too.

They climaxed and it was like soaring high above the earth. And then, quietening, they subsided gently back down. She rolled onto her side and looked at him with pleasure.

'That was...'

'Momentous? Beyond description?' God, this was nothing like what he had felt before! Could good sex do this to a man? Make him feel like he could fly? They had only just finished making love and he couldn't wait to take her again. Did that make sense? He had made love to any number of beautiful women before but he had never felt like this. He had never felt as though he was in possession of an insatiable appetite, had never wanted to switch the light on so that he could just *look*...

'I want to take you again, but first...' Luiz felt an urgent need to set a few facts straight, to reassure himself that this feeling of being out of control, carried away by a current against which he seemed to be powerless, was just a temporary situation. 'You know this isn't going to go anywhere, don't you?' He brushed her hair away from her face so that he could look her directly in the eye. So this might be the wrong time and the wrong place to say this, but it had to be said. He had to clear the air. 'I wouldn't want you to think...'

'Shh. I don't think anything.' Aggie smiled bravely while a series of pathways began connecting in her brain. This man she loathed, to whom she was desperately attracted, was a man who could make her laugh even though she had found him overbearing and arrogant, the same man who had slowly filled her head and her heart. It was why she was here now. In bed with him. She hadn't suddenly become a woman with no morals who thought it was fine to jump into bed on the basis of sexual attraction. No. That had been a little piece of fiction she had sold herself because the truth staring her in the face had been unacceptable.

'I'm not about to start making demands. You and I, we're not suited and we never will be. But we're attracted to one another. That's all. So, why don't we just have some fun? Because we both know that tomorrow it all comes to an end.'

CHAPTER EIGHT

AGGIE spent the night in her own bedroom. Drunk with love-making, she had made sure to tiptoe along the corridor at a little after two in the morning. It was important to remind herself that this was not a normal relationship. It had boundaries and Luiz had made sure to remind her of that the night before. She wasn't about to over step any of them.

She heard the beeping of her phone the following morning and woke to find a series of messages from her brother, all asking her to give him a call.

Panicked, Aggie sat up and dialled his mobile with shaking fingers. She was ashamed to admit that her brother had barely registered on her radar over the past few hours. In fact, she guiltily realised that she had been too focused on herself for longer than that to spare much thought for Mark.

She got through to him almost immediately. The conversation, on her end, barely covered a sentence or two. Down the other end of the line, Mark did all the talking and at the end of ten minutes Aggie ended the call, shell-shocked.

Everything was about to change now, and for a few seconds she resented her brother's intrusion into the little bubble she had built for herself. She checked the time on her phone. Luiz had tried to pull her back into bed with him before she had left in the early hours of the morning, but Aggie had resisted. Luiz was a man who always got what he wanted and rarely paused to consider the costs. He wanted her and would see nothing wrong in having her, whenever and wherever. He was good when it came to detaching and, once their time together was over, he would instantly break off and walk away. Aggie knew that she would not be able to, so putting some distance between them, if not sharing a room for the night could be termed putting distance between them, was essential.

So they had agreed to meet for breakfast at nine. Plenty of time to check the weather and for Luiz to catch up with emails. It was now a little after eight, and Aggie was glad for the time in which she could have a bath and think about what her brother had told her.

Luiz was waiting for her in the dining room, where a pot of coffee was already on the table and two menus, one of which he was scanning, although he put it down as she hovered for a few seconds in the doorway.

She was in a pair of faded jeans and a blue jumper, her hair tied back. She looked like a very sexy schoolgirl, and all at once he felt himself stir into lusty arousal. He hadn't been able to get enough of her the night before. In fact, he recalled asking her at one point whether she was too sore for him to touch her again down there. He leaned back in the chair and shot her a sexy half-smile as she walked towards him.

'You should have stayed with me,' were his first words of greeting. 'You would have made an unbeatable wake-up call.'

Aggie slipped into the chair opposite and helped herself to some coffee. Mark and his news were at the top of her mind but it was something she would lead up to carefully.

'You said you wanted to get some work done before you came down to breakfast. I wouldn't have wanted to interrupt you.'

'I'm good at multi-tasking. You'd be surprised how much work I can get through when there's someone between my legs paying attention to...'

'Shh!' She went bright red and Luiz laughed, entertained at her prurience.

'You get my drift, though?'

'Is that the kind of wake-up call you're accustomed to?' She held the cup between her hands and looked at him over the rim. She had kept her voice light but underneath she could feel jealousy swirling through her veins, unwelcome and inappropriate.

'The only wake-up calls I'm accustomed to are the ones that come from alarm clocks.' He hadn't thought about it, but women sleeping in his bed didn't happen.

'You mean you've never had a night with a woman in your bed? What about holidays?'

'I don't do holidays with women.'

Aggie gazed at him in surprise.

'It's not that unusual,' Luiz muttered, shooting her a brooding look from under his lashes. 'I'm a busy man. I don't have time for the demands of a woman on holiday.'

'How on earth do you ever relax?'

'I return to Brazil. My holidays are there.' He shrugged. 'I used to go on holidays with a couple of my pals. The occasional weekend. Usually skiing. Those have dried up over the past few years.'

'Your holidays were with your guy friends?'

'How did we end up having this conversation?' He raked his fingers through his dark hair in a gesture that she had come to recognise as one of frustration.

If this was about sex and nothing more—and he had

made it clear that for him it was—then Aggie knew she should steer clear of in-depth conversations. He wouldn't welcome them. She fancied that it had always been his way of avoiding the commitment of a full-blown relationship, his way of keeping women at a safe distance. If you didn't have any kind of revealing conversation with someone, then it was unlikely that anyone would ever get close to you. Her curiosity felt like a treacherous step in dangerous waters.

'There's nothing wrong with talking to one another.' She glanced down at the menu and made noises about scrambled eggs and toast.

'Guys don't need attention to be lavished on them,' Luiz said abruptly. 'We're all experienced skiers. We do the black runs, relax for a couple of hours in the evening. Good exercise. No one complaining about not being entertained.'

'I can't imagine anyone having the nerve to complain to you,' Aggie remarked, and Luiz relaxed.

'You'd be surprised, although women complaining fades into insignificance when set alongside your remarkable talent for arguing with me. Not that I don't like it. It's your passionate nature. Your *extremely* passionate nature.'

'Plus those chalet girls can be very attractive if you decide you miss the entertainment of females...'

Luiz laughed, his dark eyes roaming appreciatively over her face. 'When I go skiing, I ski. The last thing I've ever wanted is any kind of involvement in those brief windows of leisure time I get round to snatching for myself.'

'And those brief windows have dried up?'

'My father hasn't been well,' Luiz heard himself say. It was a surprising admission and not one he could remember making to anyone. Only he and his mother knew the real state of his father's health. Like him, his father didn't appreciate fuss and he knew that his daughters would fuss around him. He was also the primary figurehead for the family's vast empire. Many of the older clients would react badly to any hint that Alfredo Montes was not in the prime of good health. Whilst for years Luiz had concentrated on his own business concerns, he had been obliged to take a much more active role in his father's various companies over the past few years, slowly building confidence for the day when his father could fully retire.

'I'm sorry.' She reached out and covered his hand with hers. 'What's wrong with him?'

'Forget I said anything.'

'Why? Is it...terminal?'

Luiz hesitated. 'He had a stroke a few years ago and never made a full recovery. He can still function, but not in the way he used to. His memory isn't what it used to be, nor are his levels of concentration. He's been forced into semi-retirement. No one is aware of his health issues aside from me and my mother.'

'So...you've been overseeing his affairs so that he can slow down?'

'It's not a big deal.' He beckoned across a waitress, closing down the conversation while Aggie fitted that background information about him into the bigger picture she was unconsciously building.

Luiz Montes was a workaholic who had found himself in a situation where he couldn't afford to stand still. He had no time for holidays and even less for the clutter of a relationship. But, even into that relentless lifestyle, he had managed to fit in this tortuous trip on behalf of his sister. It proclaimed family loyalty and a generosity of spirit that she had not given him credit for.

'There's something you need to know,' she said, changing the subject. 'Mark finally got through to me this morning. In fact, last night. I left my phone in the bedroom and didn't check it before I went to sleep. I woke up this morning to find missed calls and text messages for me to call him.'

'And?'

'They're not in the Lake District after all. They're in Las Vegas.'

'So they did it. They tied the knot, the bloody fools.' Luiz didn't feel the rage he had expected. He was still dwelling on the uncustomary lapse in judgement that had allowed him to confide in her. He had never felt the need to pour his heart and soul out to anyone. Indeed, he had always viewed such tendencies as weaknesses, but strangely sharing that secret had had a liberating effect. Enough to smooth over any anger he knew he should have been feeling at his niece doing something as stupid as getting married when she was still a child herself.

'I never said that.' Aggie grinned and he raised his eyebrows enquiringly.

'Share the joke? Because I'm not seeing anything funny from where I'm sitting.' But he could feel himself just going through the motions.

'Well, for a start, they haven't got married.'

Luiz looked at her in silence. 'Come again?'

'Your sister was obviously worried for no good reason. Okay, maybe Maria confided that she loved my brother. Maybe she indulged in a bit of girlish wishful thinking, but that was as far as it went. There was never any plan to run away and get married in the dead of night.'

'So we've spent the past few days on a fool's errand? What the hell are they doing in *Las Vegas*?' Less than a week ago, he would have made a sarcastic comment about the funding for such a trip, but then less than a week ago he hadn't been marooned with this woman in the middle of nowhere. Right at this moment in time, he really couldn't give a damn who had paid for what or who was ripping whom off.

He found himself thinking of that foster home—the atmosphere of cheeriness despite the old furnishings and the obvious lack of luxuries. He thought of Aggie's dingy rented house. Both those things should have hit him as evidence of people not out to take what they could get.

'Mark's over the moon.' Aggie rested her chin in the palm of her hand and looked at Luiz with shining eyes. 'He got a call when they'd only just left London. He said that he was going to call me but then he knew that he wasn't expected back for a few days and he didn't want to say anything just in case nothing came of it. But through a friend of a friend of a friend, a record producer got to hear one of his demos and flew them both over so that they could hear some more. He's got a recording contract!'

'Well, I'll be damned.'

'So…' Aggie sat back to allow a plate of eggs and toast to be put in front of her. 'There's no point carrying on any further.'

'No, there isn't.'

'You'll be relieved, I bet. You can get back to your work, although I'm going to preach at you now and tell you that it's not healthy to work the hours you do, even if you feel you have no choice.'

'You're probably right.'

'I mean, you need to be able to enjoy leisure time as much as you enjoy working time. Sorry? What did you say?'

Luiz shrugged. 'When we get back to London.' He hadn't intended on having any kind of relationship with her, but after last night he couldn't foresee relinquishing it just yet. 'A slight reduction in the workload wouldn't hurt. It's the Christmas season. People are kicking back. It's not as frenetic in the business world as it usually is.'

'So you're going to take a holiday?' Aggie's heart did a sudden, painful flip. 'Will you be going to Brazil, then?'

'I can't leave the country just yet.'

'I thought you said that you were going to have a break.'

'Which isn't to say that I'm suddenly going to drop out of sight. There are a couple of deals that need work, meetings I can't get out of.' He pushed his plate away and sat back to look at her steadily. 'We need to talk about… us. This.'

'I know. It wasn't the wisest move in the world. Neither of us anticipated that…that…'

'That we wouldn't be able to keep our hands off one another?'

How easy it was for him to think about it purely in terms of sex, Aggie thought. While *she* could only think of it in terms of falling in love. She wondered how many women before her had made the same mistake of bucking the guidelines he set and falling in love with him. Had his last girlfriend been guilty of that sin?

'The circumstances were peculiar,' Aggie said, keen to be as light-hearted about what happened between them as he was. 'It's a fact that people can behave out of character when they're thrown into a situation they're not accustomed to. I mean, none of this would have happened if we hadn't…found ourselves snowbound on this trip.'

'Wouldn't it?' His dark eyes swept thoughtfully over her flushed face.

'What do you mean?'

'I like to think I'm honest enough not to underestimate this attraction I feel for you. I noticed you the first time I saw you and it wasn't just as a potential gold-digger. I think I was sexually attracted to you from the beginning.

Maybe I would never have done anything about it but I wouldn't bet on that.'

'*I* didn't notice you!'

'Liar.'

'I didn't,' Aggie insisted with a touch of desperation. 'I mean, I just thought you were Maria's arrogant uncle who had only appeared on the scene to warn us off. I didn't even like you!'

'Who's talking about like or dislike? That's quite different from sexual attraction. Which brings me back to my starting point. We'll head back down to London as soon as we've finished breakfast, and when we get to London I want to know what your plans are. Because I'm not ready to give this up just yet. In fact, I would say that I'm just getting started...'

Just yet. Didn't that say it all? But at least he wasn't trying to disguise the full extent of his interest in her; at least he wasn't pretending that they were anything but two ships passing in the night, dropping anchor for a while before moving on their separate journeys.

When Aggie thought of her last boyfriend, he had been fond of planning ahead, discussing where they would go on holiday in five years' time. She had fancied herself in love, but like an illness it had passed quickly and soon after she had realised that what she had really loved was the feeling of permanence that had been promised.

Luiz wasn't promising permanence. In fact, he wasn't even promising anything longer than a couple of weeks or a couple of months.

'You're looking for another notch on your bedpost?' Aggie said lightly and he frowned at her.

'I'm not that kind of man and if you don't think I've been honest with you, then I can only repeat what I've said. I'm not looking for a committed relationship, but neither do I work my way through women because I have a little black book I want to fill. If you really think that, then we're not on the same page, and whatever we did last night will remain a one-time memory.'

'I shouldn't have said that, but Luiz, you can't really blame me, can you? I mean, have you ever had a relationship that you thought might be going somewhere?'

'I've never sought it. On the other hand, I don't use women. Why are we discussing this, Aggie? Neither of us sees any kind of future in this. I thought we'd covered that.' He looked at her narrowly. 'We *have* covered that, haven't we? I mean, you haven't suddenly decided that you're looking for a long-term relationship, have you? Because, I repeat, it's never going to happen.'

'I'm aware of that,' Aggie snapped. 'And, believe me, I'm not on the hunt for anything permanent either.'

'Then what's the problem? Why the sudden atmosphere?' He allowed a few seconds of thoughtful silence during which time she tried to think of something suitably dismissive to say. 'I never asked,' he said slowly. 'But I assumed that when you slept with me there was no one else in your life…'

Aggie's blue eyes were wide with confusion as she returned his gaze, then comprehension filtered through and confusion turned to anger.

'That's a horrible thing to say.' She felt tears prick the back of her eyes and she hurriedly stared down at her plate.

Luiz shook his head, shame-faced and yet wanting to tell her that, horrible it might be, but it wouldn't be the first time a woman had slept with him while still involved with another man. Some women enjoyed hedging their bets. Naturally, once he was involved, all other men were instantly dropped, but from instances like that he had developed a healthy dose of suspicion when it came to the opposite sex.

But, hell, he couldn't lump Aggie into the same category as other women. She was in a league of her own.

Cheeks flushed, Aggie flung down her napkin and stood up. 'If we're leaving, I need to go upstairs and get my packing done.'

'Aggie...' Luiz vaulted to his feet and followed her as she stormed out of the dining room towards the staircase. He grabbed her by her arm and pulled her towards him.

'It doesn't matter.'

'It *matters*. I...I apologise for what I said.'

'You're so suspicious of everyone! What kind of world do you live in, Luiz Montes? You're suspicious of gold-diggers, opportunists, women who want to take advantage of you...'

'It's ingrained, and I'm not saying that it's a good thing.' But it was something he had never questioned before. He looked at her, confused, frowning. 'I want to carry on seeing you when we get back to London,' he said roughly.

'And you've laid down so many guidelines about what that entails!' Aggie sighed and shook her head. This was so bad for her, yet even while one part of her brain acknowledged that there was another part that couldn't contemplate giving him up without a backward glance. Even standing this close to him was already doing things to her, making her heart beat faster and turning her bones to jelly.

'I'm just attempting to be as honest as I can.'

'And you don't have to worry that I'm going to do anything stupid!' She looked at him fiercely. If only he knew how stupid she had already been, he would run a mile. But, just as she had jumped in feet first to sleep with him and damn the consequences, she was going to carry on sleeping with him, taking what she could get like an addict too scared of quitting until it was forced upon them.

She wasn't proud of herself but, like him, she was honest.

Luiz half-closed his eyes with relief. He only realised that he had been holding his breath when he expelled it slowly. 'The drive back will be a lot easier,' he said briskly. His hand on her arm turned to a soft caress that sent shivers racing up and down her spine.

'And are you still going to…talk to Mark when they get back from London? Warn him off Maria?'

Luiz realised that he hadn't given that any thought at all. 'They're not getting married. Crisis defused.' He looked at her and grinned reluctantly. 'Okay. I've had other things on my mind. I hadn't given any thought to what was going to happen next in this little saga. Now I'm thinking about it and realising that Luisa can have whatever mother-to-daughter chat she thinks she needs to have. I'm removing myself from the situation.'

'I'm glad.'

She smiled and all Luiz could think was that he was chuffed that he had been responsible for putting that smile on her face.

Once, he would not have been able to see beyond the fact that any relationship where the levels of wealth were so disproportionately unbalanced was doomed to failure, if not worse. Once the financial inequality would have been enough for him to continue his pursuit, to do everything within his power to remove Aggie's brother from any position from which he could exert influence over his niece. Things had subtly changed.

'So,' she said softly. 'I'm going to go and pack and I'll see you back here in half an hour or so?'

Luiz nodded and she didn't ask for any details of what

would happen next. Of course, they would return to her house, but then what? Would they date one another or was that too romantic a notion for him? Would he wine and dine her, the way he wined and dined the other women he went out with? She was sure that he was generous when it came to the materialistic side of any relationship he was in. What he lacked in emotional giving, he would more than make up for in financial generosity. He was, after all, the man who had suggested buying her a laptop computer because she happened not to possess one. And this before they had become lovers.

But, if he had his ground rules, then she had hers. She would not allow him to buy anything for her nor would she expect any lavish meals out or expensive seats at the opera or the theatre. If his approach to what they had was to put all his cards on the table, then she would have to make sure that she put some of her own cards on the table as well.

As if predicating for a quick journey back to London, as opposed to the tortuous one they had embarked upon when they had set off, the snow had finally dwindled to no more than some soft, light flurries.

The atmosphere was heavy with the thrill of what lay ahead. Aggie was conscious of every movement of his hands on the steering wheel. She sneaked glances at his profile and marvelled at the sexy perfection of his face. When she closed her eyes, she imagined being alone with him in a room, submitting to his caresses.

Making small talk just felt like part of an elaborate dance between them. He was planning on visiting his family in Brazil over the Christmas period. She asked him about where he lived. She found that she had an insatiable appetite for finding out all the details of his background. Having broken ground with his confidences about his father, he talked about him, about the stroke and the effect it had had on him. He described his country in ways that brought it alive. She felt as though there were a million things she wanted to hear about him.

Mark and Maria would not be returning to the country for a few days yet, and as they approached the outskirts of London he said in a lazy drawl that already expected agreement to his proposal, 'I don't think you should carry on living in that dump.'

Aggie laughed, amused.

'I'm not kidding. I can't have you living there.'

'Where would you have me living, Luiz?'

'Kensington has some decent property. I could get you somewhere.'

'Thanks, but I think we've already covered the problem of rent in London and how expensive it is.'

'You misunderstand me. When I say that I could get you somewhere, I mean I could *buy* you somewhere.'

Aggie's mouth dropped open and she looked at him in astonishment and disbelief.

'Well?' Luiz prompted, when there was silence following this remark.

'You can't just go and *buy somewhere* for a woman you happen to be sleeping with, Luiz.'

'Why not?'

'Because it's not right.'

'I want you to live somewhere halfway decent. I have the money to turn that wish into reality. What could be more right?'

'And just for the sake of argument, what would happen with this halfway decent house when we broke up?'

Luiz frowned, not liking the way that sounded. He knew he was the one who'd laid down that rule, but was there really any need to underline it and stick three exclamation marks after it for good measure?

'You'd keep it, naturally. I never give a woman gifts and then take them away from her when the relationship goes sour.'

'You've had way too much your own way for too long,' Aggie told him. It was hardly surprising. He had grown up with money and it had always been second nature to indulge his women with gifts. 'I'm not going to accept a house from you. Or a flat, or whatever. I'm perfectly happy where I am.'

'You're not,' Luiz contradicted bluntly. 'No one could be perfectly happy in that hovel. The closest anyone could get to feeling anything about that place is that it's a roof over your head.'

'I don't want anything from you.' After the great open spaces of up north, the business of London felt like four walls pressing down on her.

That was not what Luiz wanted to hear, because for once he *wanted* to give her things. He wanted to see that smile on her face and know that he was responsible for putting it there.

'Actually,' Aggie continued thoughtfully, 'I think we should just enjoy whatever we have. I don't want you giving me any presents or taking me to expensive places.'

'I don't do home-cooked meals in front of the television.'

'And I don't do lavish meals out. Now and again, it's nice to go somewhere for dinner, but it's nice not to as well.' Aggie knew that she was treading on thin ice here. Any threat of domesticity would have him running a mile, but how much should she sacrifice for the sake of love and lust?

'I'm not into all that stuff,' she said. 'I don't wear jewels and I don't have expensive tastes.'

'Why are you so difficult?'

'I didn't realise I was.'

'From a practical point of view, your house is going to be a little cramped with your brother there and my niece popping her head in every three minutes. I'm not spending time at your place with the four of us sitting on a sagging sofa, watching television while my car gets broken into outside.'

Aggie laughed aloud. 'That's a very weak argument for getting your own way.'

'Well, you can't blame a guy for trying.'

But he wished to God he had tried a little harder when they finally arrived back at her dismal house in west London. Snow had turned to slush and seemed to have infused the area with a layer of unappealing grey.

Aggie looked at him as he reviewed the house with an expression of thinly concealed disgust and she smiled. He was so spoiled, so used to getting everything he wanted. It was true that he had not complained once at any of the discomforts he had had to endure on their little trip, at least at any of the things which in his rarefied world would have counted as discomforts. But it would be getting on his nerves that he couldn't sort this one out. Especially when he had a point. Mr Cholmsey couldn't have created a less appealing abode to rent if he had tried.

She wondered how she could have forgotten the state of disrepair it was in.

'You could at least come back with me to my apartment,' Luiz said, lounging against the wall in the hallway as Aggie dumped her bag on the ground. 'Indulge yourself, Aggie.' His voice was as smooth as chocolate and as tempting. 'There's nothing wrong with wanting to relax in a place where the central heating doesn't sound like a car backfiring every two minutes.'

Aggie looked helplessly at him, caught up in a moment of indecision. He bent to kiss her, a sweet, delicate kiss as he tasted her mouth, not touching her anywhere else, in fact hardly moving from his indolent pose against the wall.

'Not fair,' she murmured.

'I want to get you into my bath,' Luiz murmured softly. 'My very big, very clean bath, a bath that can easily fit the both of us. And then afterwards I want you in my bed, my extra-wide and extra-long king-sized bed with clean linen. And if you're really intent on us doing the telly thing, you can switch on the television in my bedroom; it's as big as a cinema screen. But before that, I want to make love to you in comfort, and then when we're both spent I want to send out for a meal from my guy at the Savoy. No need for you to dress up or go out, just the two of us. He does an excellent chocolate mousse for dessert. I'd really like to have it flavoured with a bit of you…'

'You win,' Aggie said on a sigh of pure pleasure. She reached up and pulled him down to her and in the end they found themselves clinging to one another as they wended an unsteady path up to her bedroom.

Despite Luiz's adamant proclamations that he wanted to have her in his house, she was so damned delectable that he couldn't resist.

Her top was off by the time they hit the top of the stairs. By the bedroom door, her bra was draped over the banister and she had wriggled out of her jeans just as they both collapsed onto the bed which, far from being king-sized, was only slightly bigger than a single.

'I've been wanting to do this from the second we got into my car to drive back to London,' Luiz growled, in a manner that was decidedly un-cool. 'In fact, I was very tempted to book us into a room in the first hotel we came to just so that I could do this. I don't know what it is about you, but the second I'm near you I turn into a caveman.'

Aggie decided that she liked the sound of that. She lay back and watched as he rid himself of his clothes. This was frantic sex, two slippery bodies entwined. Leisurely foreplay would have to wait, he told her, he just needed to feel himself inside her, hot and wet and waiting for him.

Luiz could say things that drove her wild, and he drove her wild now as he huskily told her just how she made him feel when they were having sex.

Every graphic description made her wetter and more turned on and when he entered her she was so close to the edge that she had to grit her teeth together to hold herself back.

His movements were deep, his shaft big and power-ful, taking her higher and higher until she cried out as she climaxed. Her nails dug into his shoulder blades and she arched back, her head tilted back, her eyes closed, her nostrils slightly flared.

She was the most beautiful creature Luiz had ever laid eyes on. He felt himself explode inside her and by then it was too late. He couldn't hold it back. He certainly couldn't retrieve the results of his ferocious orgasm and he col-lapsed next to her with a groan.

'I didn't use protection.' He was still coming down from a high but his voice was harshly self-admonishing, bitterly angry for his oversight. He looked at her, then sat up, legs over the side of the bed, head in his hands, and cursed si-lently under his breath.

'It's okay,' Aggie said quickly. Well, if she hadn't got the message that this was a man who didn't want to set-tle down, then she was getting it now loud and clear. Not only did he not want to settle down, but the mere thought of a pregnancy was enough to turn him white with horror.

'I'm safe.'

Luiz exhaled with relief and lay back down next to her. 'Hell, I've never made that mistake in my life before. I don't know what happened.' But he did. He had lost control. This was not the man he was. He didn't lose control.

Looking at him, Aggie could see the disgust on his face that he could ever have been stupid enough, *human* enough to make a slip-up.

For all the ways he could get under her skin, she reminded herself that Luiz Montes was not available for anything other than a casual affair. She might love him but she should look for nothing more than unrequited love.

CHAPTER NINE

'WHAT'S wrong?' Luiz looked at Aggie across the width of the table in the small chain restaurant where he had just been subjected to a distinctly mediocre pizza and some even more mediocre wine.

'Nothing's wrong.' But Aggie couldn't meet his eyes. He had a way of looking at her. It made her feel as though he could see down to the bottom of her soul, as though he could dredge up things she wanted to keep to herself.

The past month had been the most amazing time of her life. She had had the last week at school, where the snow had lingered for a few days until finally all that had been left were the remains of two snowmen which the children had built.

Luiz had visited her twice at school. The first time he had just shown up. All the other teachers had been agog. The children had stared. Aggie had felt embarrassed, but embarrassed in a proud way. Everyone, all her friends at the school, would be wondering how she had managed to grab the attention of someone like Luiz, even if they didn't come right out and say it. And, frankly, Aggie still wondered how she had managed to achieve that. She didn't think that she could ever fail to get a kick just looking at him and when those dark, fabulous eyes rested on her she didn't think that she could ever fail to melt.

He had returned to Brazil for a few days over Christmas. Aggie had decided that it would be a good time to get her act together and use his absence to start building a protective shell around her, but the very second she had seen him again she had fallen straight back into the bottomless hole from which she had intended to start climbing out.

She felt as though she was on a rollercoaster. Her whole system was fired up when he was around and there wasn't a single second when she didn't want to be in his company, although at the back of her mind she knew that the rollercoaster ride would end and when it did she would be left dazed and shaken and turned inside out.

'It's this place!' Luiz flung his napkin on his half-eaten pizza and sat back in his chair.

'What?'

'Why are you too proud to accept my invitations to restaurants where the food is at least edible?'

Aggie looked at him, momentarily distracted by the brooding sulkiness on his dark face. He looked ridiculously out of place here. So tall, striking and exotic, surrounded by families with chattering kids and teenagers. But she hadn't wanted to go anywhere intimate with him. She had wanted somewhere bright, loud and impersonal.

'You've taken me to loads of expensive restaurants,' she reminded him. 'I could start listing them if you'd like.'

Luiz waved his hand dismissively. Something was wrong and he didn't like it. He had grown accustomed to her effervescence, to her teasing, to the way she made him feel as though the only satisfactory end to his day was when he saw her. Right now she was subdued, her bright-blue eyes clouded, and he didn't like the fact that he couldn't reach her.

'We need to get the bill and clear out of here,' he growled, signalling to a waitress, who appeared so quickly that Aggie thought she might have been hanging around waiting for him to call her across. 'I can think of better things to do than sit here with cold, congealing food on our plates, waiting for our tempers to deteriorate.'

'No!'

'What do you mean, *no?*' Luiz narrowed his eyes on her flushed face. Her gaze skittered away and she licked her lips nervously. The thought of her not wanting to head back to his place as fast as they could suddenly filled him with a sense of cold dread.

'I mean, it's still early.' Aggie dragged the sentence out while she frantically tried to think of how she would say what she had to say. 'Plus it's a Saturday. Everyone's out having fun.'

'Well, let's go have some fun somewhere else.' He leaned towards her and shot her a wolfish grin. 'Making love doesn't have to be confined to a bedroom. A change of scenery would work for me too...'

'A change of scenery?' Aggie asked faintly. She giddily lost herself in his persuasive, sexy, slow smile. He had come directly to her house, straight from the office, and he was still in his work clothes: a dark grey, hand-tailored suit. The tie would be bunched up in the pocket of his jacket, which he had slung over the back of the chair along with his coat, and he had rolled up the sleeves of his shirt. He looked every inch the billionaire businessman and once again she was swept away on an incredulous wave of not knowing how he could possibly be attracted to her.

And yet there were times, and lots of them, when they seemed like two halves of the same coin. Aggie had grown fond of recalling those times. Half of her knew that it was just wishful thinking on her part, a burning desire to see him relating to her in more than just an insatiably sexual capacity, but there was no harm in dreaming, was there?

'I'm losing you again.' Luiz ran his fingers through his hair and looked at her with an impatient shake of his head. 'Come on. We're getting out of here. I've had enough of this cheap and cheerful family eaterie. There's more to a Saturday night than this.'

He stood up and waited as she scrambled to her feet. It was still cold outside, but without the bite of before Christmas, when it had hurt just being outdoors. Aggie knew she should have stayed put inside the warm, noisy, crowded restaurant but coward that she was, she wanted to leave as much as he did.

Once she would have been more than satisfied with a meal out at the local pizzeria but now she could see that it could hardly be called a dining experience. It was a place to grab something or to bring kids where they could make as much mess as they wanted without staff getting annoyed.

'We could go back to my house,' Aggie said reluctantly as Luiz swung his arm over her shoulders and reached out to hail a cab with the other.

He touched her as though it was the most natural thing in the world. It was just something else she had relegated to her wishful-thinking cupboard. *If he can be so relaxed with me, surely there's more to what we have than sex...?*

Except not once had he ever hinted at what that something else might be. He never spoke of a future and she knew that he was careful not to give her any ideas. He had warned her at the beginning of their relationship that he wasn't into permanence and he had assumed that the warning held good.

He didn't love her. She was a temporary part of his life and he enjoyed her and she had given him no indication that it was any different for her.

'And where's your brother?'

'He might be there with Maria. I don't know. As you

know, he leaves for America on Monday. I think he was planning on cooking something special for them.'

'So your suggestion is we return to that dump where we'll be fighting for space alongside your brother and my niece, interrupting their final, presumably romantic meal together. Unless, of course, we hurry up to your unheated bedroom where we can squash into your tiny bed and make love as noiselessly as possible.'

Luiz loathed her house but he had given up trying to persuade her to move out to something bigger, more comfortable and paid for by him. She had dug her heels in and refused to budge, but the upshot was that they spent very little time there. In fact, the more Aggie saw her house through his eyes, the more dissatisfied she was with it.

'There's no need to be difficult!' Aggie snapped, pulling away to stare up at him. 'Why do you always have to get your own way?'

'If I always got my own way then explain why we've just spent an hour and a half in a place where the food is average and the noise levels are high enough to give people migraines. What the hell is going on, Aggie? I didn't meet you so that I could battle my way through a bad mood!'

'I can't always be sunshine and light, Luiz!'

They stared at each other. Aggie was hardly aware of the approach of a black cab until she was being hustled into it. She heard Luiz curtly give his address and sighed with frustration, because the last place she wanted to be with him was at his apartment.

'Now…' He turned to face her and extended his arm along the back of the seat. 'Talk to me. Tell me what's going on.' His eyes drifted to the mutinous set of her mouth and he wanted to do nothing more than kiss it back into smiling submission. He wasn't normally given to issuing invitations to women to talk. He was a man of action and his preferred choice, when faced with a woman who clearly *wanted to talk*, was to bury all chat between the sheets. But Aggie, he had to concede, was different. If he suggested burying the chat between the sheets, she would probably round on him with the full force of her feisty, outspoken, brazenly argumentative personality.

'We do need to talk,' she admitted quietly, and she felt him go still next to her.

'Well, I'm all ears.'

'Not here. We might as well wait till we get to your place, although I would have preferred to have this conversation in the restaurant.'

'You mean where we would hardly have been able to hear one another?'

'What I have to say…people around would have made it easier.'

Luiz was getting a nasty, unsettled feeling in the pit of his stomach. She had turned him down once. It was something he hadn't forgotten. This sounded very much like a second let-down and he wasn't about to let that happen. Pride slammed into him with the force of a sledgehammer.

'I'm getting the message that this *talk* of yours has to do with us?'

Aggie nodded miserably. This *talk* was something she had rehearsed in her head for the past four hours and yet she was no closer to knowing where she would begin.

'What's there to talk about?' Luiz drawled grimly. 'We've already covered this subject. I'm not looking for commitment. Nor, you told me, were you. We understand one another. We're on the same page.'

'Sometimes things change.'

'Are you telling me that you're no longer satisfied with what we've got? That after a handful of weeks you're looking for something more?' Luiz refused to contemplate having his wings clipped. He especially didn't care for the thought of having anyone try to clip them on his behalf. Was she about to issue him with some kind of ultimatum? Promise more if he wanted to carry on seeing her, sleeping with her? Just thinking about it outraged him. Other women might have dropped hints—grown misty-eyed in front of jewellers, introduced him to friends with babies— but none of them had ever actually given him a stark choice and he was getting the feeling that that was precisely what Aggie was thinking of doing.

Aggie clenched her fists on her lap. The tone of his voice was like a slap in the face. Did he really think that she had been stupid enough to misunderstand his very clear ground rules?

'What if I were?' she asked, curious to see where this conversation would take them, already predicting its final, painful destination and willing it masochistically on herself.

'Then I'd question whether you weren't wondering if being married to a rich man might be more financially lucrative than dating him!'

Every muscle in Aggie's body tensed and she looked at him astounded, hurt and horrified.

'How could you *say* that?'

Luiz scowled and looked away. He fully deserved that reprimand. He could scarcely credit that he had actually accused her of having a financial agenda. She had proved to be one of the least materialistic women he had ever met. But, hell, the thought of her walking out on him had sparked something in him he could barely understand.

'I apologise,' he said roughly. 'That was below the belt.'

'But do you honestly believe it?' Aggie was driven to know whether this man she loved so much could think so little of her that he actually thought she might try and con him into commitment.

'No. I don't.'

She breathed a sigh of relief because she would never have been able to live with that.

'Then why did you say it?'

'Look, I don't know what this is about, but I'm not interested in playing games. And I won't have my hand forced. Not by you. Not by anybody.'

'Because you don't need anyone? The great Luiz Montes doesn't need anything or anyone!'

'And tell me, what's wrong with that?' He was baffled by her. Why the hell was she spoiling for a fight? And why had she suddenly decided that she wanted more than what they had? Things had been pretty damn good between them. Better than good. He fought down the temptation to explode.

'I don't want to have this argument with you,' Aggie said, glancing towards the taxi driver who was maintaining a discreet disinterest. He probably heard this kind of thing all the time.

'And I don't want to argue with you,' Luiz confirmed smoothly. 'So why don't we pretend none of it happened?' There was one way of stalling any further confrontation. He pulled her towards him and curled his hands into her soft hair.

Aggie's protesting hands against his chest curved into an aching caress. As his tongue delved to explore her mouth, she felt her body come alive. Her nipples tightened in the lace bra, pushing forward in a painful need to be suckled and touched. Her skin burned and the wetness between her legs was an agonising reminder of how this man could get to her. No matter that there was talking to be done. No matter that making love was not what she wanted to do.

'Now, isn't that better?' he murmured with satisfaction. 'I'd carry on, my darling, but I wouldn't want to shock our cab driver.'

As if to undermine that statement, he curved his hand over one full breast and slowly massaged it until she had to stop herself from crying out.

Ever since they had begun seeing one another, her wardrobe had undergone a subtle transformation. The uninspiring clothes she had worn had been replaced by a selection of brighter, more figure-hugging outfits.

'You're wearing a bra,' he chided softly into her ear. 'You know I hate that.'

'You can't always get what you want, Luiz.'

'But it's what we *both* want, isn't it? I get to touch you without the boring business of having to get rid of a bra and you get to be touched without the boring business of having to get rid of a bra. It's a win-win situation. Still, I guess sometimes it adds a little spice to the mix if I have to work my way through layers of clothes…'

'Stop it, Luiz!'

'Tell me you don't like what I'm doing.' He had shimmied his hand underneath the tight, striped jumper and had pulled down her bra to free one plump mound.

This was the way to stifle an argument, he thought. Maybe he had misread the whole thing. Maybe she hadn't been upping the ante. Maybe what she wanted to talk about had been altogether more prosaic. Luiz didn't know and he had no intention of revisiting the topic.

With a rueful sigh, he released her as the taxi slowed, moving into the crescent. He neatly pulled down the jumper, straightening it. 'Perhaps just as well that we're here,' he confessed with a wicked glint in his dark eyes.

'Going all the way in the back seat of a black cab would really be taking things a step too far. I think when we get round to public performing we'll have to think carefully where to begin...'

Aggie had had no intention of performing with him on any level, never mind in public. She shifted in the seat. When she should have been as cool as she could, she was hot and flustered and having to push thoughts of him taking her in his hallway out of her head.

The house which had once filled her with awe she now appreciated in a distinctly less gob-smacked way. She still loved the beautiful *objets d'art*, but there were few personal touches which made her think that money could buy some things, but not others. It could buy beauty but not necessarily atmosphere. In fact, going out with Luiz had made her distinctly less cowed at the impressive things money could buy and a lot less daunted by the people who possessed it.

'So.' Luiz discarded his coat and jacket as soon as they were through the door. 'Shall we finish what we started? No need to go upstairs. If you go right into the kitchen and sit on one of the stools, I'll demonstrate how handy I can be with food. I guarantee I'll be a damn sight more imaginative with ingredients than that restaurant tonight was.'

'Luiz.' She was shaking as she placed her hand firmly on his chest. No giving in this time.

'Good God, woman! Tell me you don't want to start talking again.' He pushed his hands under her coat to cup her rounded buttocks, pulling her against him so that she could feel his arousal pushing through his trousers, as hard as a rod of iron. 'And, if you want to talk, then let's talk in bed.'

'Bed's not a good idea,' Aggie said shakily.

'Who says I want good ideas?'

'I'd like a cup of coffee.'

Luiz gave in with a groan of pure frustration. He banged his fist on the wall, shielded his head in the crook of his arm and then glanced at her with rueful resignation.

'Okay. You win. But take it from me, talking is never a very good idea.'

How true, Aggie thought. From his point of view, it would certainly not herald anything he wanted to hear.

She marvelled that in a few hours life could change so dramatically.

She had been poring over the school calendar and working out what lessons she should think about setting when something in her head had suddenly clicked.

She had seen the calendar and the concept of dates had begun to flicker. Dates of when she had last seen her period. She had never paid a great deal of attention to her menstrual cycle. It happened roughly on time. What more was there to say about it?

Her hands had been shaking when, a little over an hour later, she had taken that home-pregnancy test. She had already thought of a thousand reasons why she was silly to be concerned. For a start, Luiz was obsessive about contraception. Aside from that one little slip-up, he had been scrupulous.

Within minutes she had discovered how one little slip-up could change the course of someone's life.

She was pregnant by a man who didn't love her, had warned her off involvement and had certainly never expressed any desire to have children. In the face of all those stark realities, she had briefly contemplated not telling him. Just breaking off the relationship; disappearing. Disappearing, she had reasoned for a few wild, disoriented moments, would not be difficult to do. She hated the house and her brother was soon to leave London to embark upon the next exciting phase of his life. She could ditch everything and return up north, find something there. Luiz would not pursue her and he would never know that he had fathered a child.

The thought didn't last long. He would find out; of course he would. Maria would tell him. And, aside from that, how could she deprive a man of his own child? Even a child he hadn't wanted?

'What I'm going to say will shock you,' Aggie told him as soon as they were sitting down in his living room, with a respectable distance between them.

Luiz, for the first time in his life, was prey to fear. It ripped through him, strangling his vocal chords, making him break out in a fine film of perspiration.

'You're not…ill, are you?'

Aggie looked at him with surprise. 'No. I'm not,' she asserted firmly. He had visibly blanched and she knew why. Of course, he would be remembering his own father's illness, which he had spoken to her about in more depth over the time they had been together.

'Then what is it?'

'There's no easy way to tell you so I'm going to come right out and say it. I'm pregnant.'

Luiz froze. For a few seconds, he wondered whether he had heard correctly but he was not a man given to flights of imagination and the expression on her face was sufficient to tell him that she wasn't joking.

'You can't be,' he said eventually.

Aggie's eyes slid away from his. Whenever she had thought of being pregnant, it had been within a rosy scenario involving a man she loved who loved her back. Never had she envisaged breaking the news to a man who looked as though she had detonated a bomb in his front room.

'I'm afraid I can be, and I am.'

'I was careful!'

'There was that one time.' Against her better judgement—for she had hardly expected her news to be met
with whoops of joy—she could feel a slow anger begin to
burn inside her.

'You told me that there was no risk.'

'I'm sorry. I made a mistake.'

Luiz didn't say anything. He stood up and walked restively towards the floor-to-ceiling window to stare outside.
The possibility of fatherhood was not one that had ever
occurred to him. It was something that lay in the future.
Way down the line. Possibly never. But she was carrying
his baby inside her.

Aggie miserably looked at him, turned away from her
and staring out of the window. Doubtless he was thinking
about his life which now lay in ruins. If ever there was a
man who was crushed under the weight of bad news, then
he was that man.

'You decided to tell me this in a *pizzeria*?' Luiz spun
round and walked towards her. He leaned over, bracing
himself on either side of her, and Aggie shrank back into
the chair.

'I didn't want…*this*!' she cried.

'This *what*?'

'I knew how you'd react and I thought it would be
more…more…civilised if I told you somewhere out in
the open!'

'What did you think I would do?'

'We need to discuss this like adults and we're not going
to get anywhere when you're standing over me like this,
threatening me!'

'God, how the hell did this happen?' Luiz returned to
the sofa and collapsed onto it.

It felt to Aggie as though everything they had shared

had shattered under the blow of this pregnancy. Which just went to show how fragile it had all been from the very start. Not made to last and not fashioned to withstand any knocks—although, in fairness, a pregnancy couldn't really be called a knock. More like an earthquake, shaking everything from the foundations up.

'Stupid question.' He pressed his thumbs to his eyes and then leaned forward to look at her, his hands resting loosely on his thighs. 'Of course I know how it happened, and you're right. We have to talk about it. Hell, what's there to talk about? We'll have to get married. What choice do we have?'

'Get married? That's not what I want!' she threw at him, fighting to contain her anger because he was just doing what, in his misguided way, he construed as the decent thing. 'Do you really think I told you about this because I wanted you to marry me?'

'What does it matter? My family would be bitterly disappointed to think I had fathered a child and allowed it to be born out of wedlock.'

What a wonderful marriage proposal, Aggie thought with a touch of hysteria: *you're pregnant; we'd better get married or risk the wrath of my traditional family.*

'I don't think so,' Aggie said gently.

'What does that mean?'

'It means that I can't accept your generous marriage proposal.'

'Don't be crazy. Of course you can!'

'I have no intention of marrying someone just because I happen to be having his baby. Luiz, a pregnancy is not the right reason to be married to someone.' She could tell from the expression on his face that he was utterly taken aback that his offer had been rejected. 'I'm sorry if your parents would find it unacceptable for you to have a child out of wedlock, but I'm not going to marry you so that your parents can avoid disappointment.'

'That's not the only reason!'

'Well, what are the others?' She could quell the faint hope that he would say those three words she wanted to hear. That he loved her. He could expand on that. She wouldn't stop him. He could tell her that he couldn't live without her.

'It's better for a child to have both parents on hand. I am a rich man. I don't intend that any child of mine will go wanting. Two reasons and there's more!' Why, Luiz thought, was she being difficult? She had just brought his entire world crashing down around him and he had risen admirably to the occasion! Couldn't she see that?

'A child can have both parents on hand without them being married,' Aggie pointed out. 'I'm not going to deprive you of the opportunity to see him or her whenever you want, and of course I understand that you will want to assist financially. I would never dream of stopping you from doing that.' She lowered her eyes and nervously fiddled with her fingers.

There was something else that would have to be discussed. Would they continue to see one another? Part of her craved their ongoing relationship and the strength and support she would get from it. Another part realised that it would be foolhardy to carry on as though nothing had happened, as though a rapidly expanding stomach wasn't proof that their lives had changed for ever. She wouldn't marry him. She couldn't allow him to ruin his life for the sake of a gesture born from obligation. She hated the thought of what would happen as cold reality set in and he realised that he was stuck with her for good. He would end up hating and resenting her. He would seek solace in the arms of other women. He might even, one day, find a woman to truly love.

'And there's something else,' she said quietly. 'I don't think it's appropriate that we continue…seeing one another.'

'What?' Luiz exploded, his body alive with anger and bewilderment.

'Stop shouting!'

'Then don't give me a reason to shout!'

They stared at each other in silence. Aggie's heart was pounding inside her. 'What we have was never going to go the full distance. We both knew that. You were very clear on that.'

'Whoa! Before you get carried away with the preaching, answer me this one thing. Do we or do we not have fun when we're together?' Luiz felt as though he had started the evening with clear skies and calm seas, only to discover that a force-ten hurricane had been waiting just over the horizon. Not only had he found himself with a baby on the way, but on top of that here she was, informing him that she no longer wanted to have anything to do with him. A growing sense of panicked desperation made him feel slightly ill.

'That's not the point!'

'Then what the hell is? You're not making any sense, Aggie! I've offered to do the right thing by you and you act as though I've insulted you. You rumble on about a child not being a good enough reason for us to be married. I don't get it! Not only is a child a bloody good reason to get married, but here's the added bonus—we're good together! But that's not enough for you! Now, you're talking about walking away from this relationship!'

'We're friends at the moment and that's how I'd like our relationship to stay for the sake of our child, Luiz.'

'We're more than just friends, damn it!'

'We're friends with benefits.'

'I can't believe I'm hearing this!' He slashed the air with his hand in a gesture of frustration, incredulity and impatience. His face was dark with anger and those beautiful eyes that could turn her hot and cold were flat with accusation.

In this sort of mood, withstanding him was like trying to swim up a waterfall. Aggie wanted to fly to him and just let him decide what happened next. She knew it would be a mistake. If they carried on seeing one another and reached the point where, inevitably, he became fed up and bored, their relationship thereafter would be one of bitterness and discomfort. Couldn't he see long-term? For a man who could predict trends and work out the bigger picture when it came to business, he was hopelessly inadequate in doing the same when it came to his private life. He lived purely for the moment. Right now he was living purely for the moment with her and he wasn't quite ready for it to end. Right now, his solution to their situation was to put a ring on her finger, thereby appeasing family and promoting his sense of responsibility. He just didn't think ahead.

Aggie knew, deep down, that if she didn't love him she would have accepted that marriage proposal. She would not have invested her emotions in a hopeless situation. She would have been able to see their union as an arrangement that made sense and would have been thankful that he was standing by her. Was it any wonder that he was now looking at her as though she had taken leave of her senses?

'I don't want us to carry on, waiting until the physical side of things runs out of steam and you start looking somewhere else,' she told him bluntly. 'I don't want to become so disillusioned with you that I resent you being in my life. It wouldn't be a good background for a child.'

'Who says the physical side would run out of steam?'

'It always has for you! Hasn't it? Unless…I'm different? Unless what you feel for me is…different?'

Suddenly feeling cornered, Luiz fell back on the habits of a lifetime of not yielding to leading questions. 'You're having my baby. Of course you're different.'

'I'm beginning to feel tired, Luiz.' Aggie wondered why she continued to hope for words that weren't going to come. 'And you've had a shock. I think we both need to take a little time out to think about things, and when we next meet we can discuss the practicalities.'

'The practicalities…?' Luiz was finding it hard to get a grip on events.

'You've been nagging me to move out of that house.' Aggie smiled wryly. 'I guess that might be something on the list to discuss.' She stood up to head for her coat and he stilled her with his hand.

'I don't want you going back to that place tonight. Or ever. It's disgusting. You have my baby to consider now.'

'And that's the word, Luiz—*discuss*. Which doesn't mean you tell me what you want me to do and I obey.'

She began putting on her coat while Luiz watched with the feeling that she was slipping through his fingers.

'You're making a mistake,' he ground out, barring her exit and staring down at her.

'I think,' Aggie said sadly, 'the mistakes have already been made.'

CHAPTER TEN

LUIZ looked at the pile of reports lying on his desk eagerly awaiting his attention and swivelled his chair round to face the expanse of glass that overlooked the busy London streets several stories below.

It was another one of those amazing spring days: blue, cloudless skies, a hint of a breeze. It did nothing to improve his concentration levels. Or his mood, for that matter. Frankly, his mood was in urgent need of improvement ever since Aggie had announced her pregnancy over two months ago.

For the first week, he had remained convinced that she would come to her senses and accept his offer of marriage. He had argued for it from a number of fronts. He had demanded that she give him more good reasons why she couldn't see it from his point of view. It had been as successful as beating his head against a brick wall. It had seemed to him, in his ever-increasing frustration, that the harder he tried to push the faster she retreated, so he had dropped the subject and they had discussed all those practicalities she had talked about.

At least there she had listened to what he had to say and agreed with pretty much everything. At least her pride wasn't going to let her get in the way of accepting the massively generous financial help he had insisted on providing, although she had stopped short of letting him buy her the house of her dreams.

'When I move into my dream house,' she had told him, her mouth set in a stubborn line, 'I don't want to know that it's been bought for me as part of a package deal because I happen to be pregnant.'

But she had moved out of the hovel two weeks previously, into a small, modern box in a pleasant part of London close to her job. The job which she insisted she would carry on doing until she no longer could, despite his protests that there was no need, that she had to look after herself.

'I'm more than happy to accept financial help as far as the baby is concerned,' she had told him firmly. 'But there's no need for you to lump me in the same bracket.'

'You're the mother of my child. Of course I'm going to make sure that you get all the money you need.'

'I'm not going to be dependent on you, Luiz. I intend to carry on working until I have the baby and then I shall take it up again as soon as I feel the baby is old enough for a nursery. The hours are good at the school and there are all the holidays. It's a brilliant job to have if you've got a family.'

Luiz loathed the thought of that just as he loathed the fact that she had managed to shut him out of her life. They communicated, and there were no raised voices, but she had withdrawn from him and it grated on him, made him ill-tempered at work, incapable of concentrating.

And now something else had descended to prey on his mind. It was a thought that had formulated a week ago when she had mentioned in passing that she would be going to the spring party which all the teachers had every year.

Somehow, he had contrived to ignore the fact that she had a social life outside him. Reminded of it, he had quizzed her on what her fellow teachers were like, and had discovered that they weren't all female and they weren't all middle-aged. They enjoyed an active social life. The teaching community was close-knit, with many teachers from different schools socialising out of work.

'You're pregnant,' he had informed her. 'Parties are a no-go area.'

'Don't worry. I won't be drinking,' she had laughed, and right then he had had a worrying thought.

She had turned down his marriage proposal, had put their relationship on a formal basis, and was this because she just wanted to make sure that she wasn't tied down? Had he been sidelined because at the back of her mind, baby or no baby, she wanted to make sure that she could return to an active social life? One that involved other men, the sort of men she was normally drawn to? He had been an aberration. Was she eager to resume relationships with one of those creative types who weren't mired in work and driven by ambition?

Luiz thought of the reports waiting on his desk and smiled sardonically. If only she knew… No one could accuse him of being mired in work now, or driven by ambition. Having a bomb detonate in his life had certainly compelled him to discover the invaluable art of delegation! If only his mother could see him now, she would be overjoyed that work was no longer the centre of his universe.

A call interrupted the familiar downward trend of his thoughts and he took it on the second ring.

He listened, scribbled something on a piece of paper and stood up.

For the first time in weeks, he felt as though he was finally doing something; finally, for better or for worse, trying to stop a runaway train, which was what his life had become.

Over the weeks, his secretary had grown so accustomed to her boss's moody unpredictability—a change from the man whose life had previously been so highly organised—that she nodded without question when he told her that he would be going out and wasn't sure when he would be back. She had stopped pointing out meetings that required his presence. Her brain now moved into another gear, the one which had her immediately working out who would replace him.

Luiz called his driver on his way down. Aggie would be at school. He tried to picture her expression when he showed up. It distracted him from more tumultuous thoughts—thoughts of her having his child and then re-discovering a single life; thoughts of her getting involved with another man; thoughts of that other man bringing up his, Luiz's, child as his own while Luiz was relegated to playing second fiddle. The occasional father.

Having never suffered the trials and tribulations of a fertile imagination, he found that he had more than made up for the lifelong omission. Now, his imagination seemed to be a monstrous thing released from a holding pen in which it had been imprisoned for its entire life, and now it was making up for lost time.

It was a situation that Luiz could not allow to continue but, as the car wound its way through traffic that was as dense as treacle, he was gripped by a strange sense of panic. He had spent all of his adult life knowing where he was going, knowing how he was going to get there. Recently, the signposts had been removed and the road was no longer a straight one forward. Instead, it curved in all directions and he had no idea where he would end up. He just knew the person he wanted to find at its destination.

'Can't you go a little faster?' he demanded, and cursed silently when his driver shot him a jaundiced look in the rear-view mirror before pointing out that they hadn't yet invented a car that could fly—although, when and if they ever did, he was sure that Mr Montes would be the first to own one.

They made it to the school just as the bell sounded for lunch and Aggie was heading to the staff room. She had been blessed with an absence of morning sickness but she felt tired a lot of the time.

And it was such a struggle maintaining a distance from Luiz. Whenever she heard that deep, dark drawl down the end of the telephone, asking her how her day had been, insisting she tell him everything she had done, telling her about what he had done, she wanted nothing more than to take back everything she had said about not wanting him in her life. He phoned a lot. He visited a lot. He treated her like a piece of delicate china, and when she told him not to he shrugged his shoulders ruefully and informed her that he couldn't help being a dinosaur when it came to stuff like that.

She had thought when she had delivered her speech to him all those weeks ago that he would quickly come to terms with the fact that he would not be shackled to her for the wrong reasons. She had thought that he would soon begin to thank her for letting him off the hook, that he would begin to relish his freedom. An over-developed sense of responsibility was something that wouldn't last very long. He didn't love her. It would be easy for him to cut the strings once he had been given permission to do so.

But he wasn't making it easy for her to get over him. Or to move on.

She had now moved from the dump, as he had continued to call it, and was happy enough in the small, modern house he had provided for her. She was still in her job and had insisted that she would carry on working before and after the baby was born, but there were times when she longed to be away from London with its noise, pollution and traffic.

And, aside from those natural doubts, she was plagued by worries about how things would unravel over time.

She couldn't envisage ever seeing him without being affected. Having been so convinced that she was doing the right thing in refusing to marry him, having prided herself on her cool ability to look at the bigger picture, she found herself riddled with angst that she might have made the wrong decision.

She stared with desolation at the sandwich she had brought in with her and was about to bite into it when… there he was.

Amid the chaos of children running in the corridors and teachers moving around the school stopping to tell them off, Luiz was suddenly in front of her, lounging against the door to the staff room.

'I know you don't like me coming here,' Luiz greeted her as he strolled towards her desk. He wondered whether she should be eating more than just a sandwich for her lunch but refrained from asking.

'You always cause such a commotion,' Aggie said honestly. 'What do you want, anyway? I have a lot of work to do during my lunch hour. I can't take time out.'

As always, she had to fight the temptation to touch him. It was as though, whenever she saw him, her brain sent signals to her fingers, making them restive at remembered pleasures. He always looked so good! Too good. His hair had grown and he hadn't bothered to cut it and the slight extra length suited him, made him even more outrageously sexy. Now he had perched on the side of her table and she had to drag her eyes away from the taut pull of his trousers over his muscular thighs.

Luiz watched as she looked away, eager for him to leave, annoyed that he had shown up at her workplace. Tough. He couldn't carry on as he had. He was going crazy. There were things he needed to say to her and, the further she floated away from him, the more redundant his words would become.

Teachers were drifting in now, released from their classes by the bell, and Luiz couldn't stop himself from glancing at them, trying to see whether any of the men might be contenders for Aggie. There were three guys so far, all in their thirties from the looks of it, but surely none of them would appeal to her?

Once, he would have been arrogantly certain of his seductive power over her. Unfortunately, he was a lot less confident on that score, and he scowled at the thought that some skinny guy with ginger hair might become his replacement.

'You look tired,' Luiz said abruptly.

'Have you come here to do a spot check on me? I wish you'd stop clucking over me like a mother hen, Luiz. I told you I can take care of myself and I can.'

'I haven't come here to do a spot check on you.'

'Then why are you here?' She risked a look at him and was surprised at the hesitation on his face.

'I want to take you somewhere. I… There are things I need to…talk to you about.'

Instinctively, Aggie knew that whatever he wanted to talk about would not involve finances, the baby or her health—all of which were subjects he covered in great detail in his frequent visits—whilst, without even being aware of it, continuing to charm her with witty anecdotes of what he was up to and the people he met. So what, she wondered nervously, could be important enough for him to interrupt her working day and to put such a hesitant expression on his usually confident face?

All at once her imagination took flight. There was no doubt that he was getting over her. He had completely stopped mentioning marriage. In fact, she hadn't heard a word on the subject for weeks. He visited a lot and phoned a lot but she knew that that was because of the baby she was carrying. He was an 'all or nothing' man. Having never contemplated the thought of fatherhood, he had had it foisted upon him and had reacted by embracing it with an enthusiasm that was so typical of his personality. He did nothing in half-measures.

As the woman who happened to be carrying his child, she was swept up in the tidal wave of his enthusiasm. But already she could see the signs of a man who no longer viewed her with the untrammelled lust he once had. He could see her so often and speak to her so often because she had become *a friend*. She no longer stirred his passion.

Aggie knew that she should have been happy about this because it was precisely what she had told him, at the beginning, was necessary for their relationship to survive on a long-term basis. Friendship and not lust would be the key to the sort of amicable union they would need to be good parents to their child.

Where he had taken that on board, however, she was still struggling and now she couldn't think what he might want to talk to her about that had necessitated a random visit to the school.

Could it be that he had found someone else? That would account for the shadow of uncertainty on his face. Luiz was not an uncertain man. Fear gripped her, turning her complexion chalky white. She could think of no other reason for him to be here and to want to *have a talk* with her. A talk that was so urgent it couldn't wait. He intended to brace her for the news before she heard about it via the grapevine, for her brother would surely find out and impart the information to her.

'Is it about…financial stuff?' she asked, clinging to the hope that he would say yes.

'It's nothing to do with money, or with any practicalities, Aggie. My car's outside.'

Aggie nodded but her body was numb all over as she gathered her things, her bag, her lightweight jacket and followed him to where his car was parked on a single yellow line outside the school.

'Where are we going? I have to be back at school by one-thirty.'

'You might have to call and tell them that you'll be later.'

'Why? What can you have to say that can't be said closer to the school? There's a café just down that street ahead. Let's go there and get this little talk of yours over and done with.'

'It's not that easy, I'm afraid.'

She noticed that the hesitation was back and it chilled her once again to the core.

'I'm stronger than you think,' she said, bracing herself. 'I can handle whatever you have to tell me. You don't need to get me to some fancy restaurant to break the news.'

'We're not going to a fancy restaurant. I know you well enough by now not to make the mistake of taking you somewhere fancy unless you have at least an hour to get ready in advance.'

'It's not my fault I still get a little nervous at some of those places you've taken me to. I don't feel comfortable being surrounded by celebrities!'

'And it's what I like about you,' Luiz murmured. That, along with all the thousands of other little quirks which should have shown him by now the significance of what he felt for her. He had always counted himself as a pretty shrewd guy and yet, with her, he had been as thick as the village idiot.

'It is?' Aggie shamefully grasped that barely audible compliment.

'I want to show you something.' The traffic was free-flowing and they were driving quickly out of London now, heading towards the motorway. For a while, Aggie's mind went into freefall as she recollected the last time she had been in a car heading out of London. His car. Except then, the snow had been falling thick and fast and little had she known that she had been heading towards a life-changing destiny. If, at the time, she had been in possession of a crystal ball, would she have looked into it and backed away from sleeping with him? The answer, of course, was no. For better or for worse she had thought at the time, and she still thought so now, even though the better had lasted for precious little time.

'What?' Aggie pressed anxiously.

'You'll have to wait and see.'

'Where are we going?'

'Berkshire. Close enough. We'll be there shortly.'

Aggie fell silent but her mind continued playing with a range of ever-changing worst-case scenarios, yet she couldn't imagine what he could possibly have to show her outside London. She hadn't thought there was much out-side the city that interested him although, to be fair, when-ever he spoke of his time spent on that fateful journey, his voice held a certain affection for the places they had seen.

She was still trying to work things out when the car eventually pulled up in front of a sprawling field and he reached across to push open the door for her.

'What…what are we doing here?' She looked at him in

bewilderment and he urged her out, leading her across the grass verge and into the field which, having been reached via a series of twisting, small lanes, seemed to be surrounded by nothing. It was amazing, considering they were still so close to London.

'Do you like it?' Luiz gazed down at her as she mulled over his question.

'It's a field, Luiz. It's peaceful.'

'You don't like me buying you things,' he murmured roughly. 'You have no idea how hard it is for me to resist it but you've made me see that there are other ways of expressing…what I feel for you. Hell, Aggie. I don't know if I'm telling you this the way I should. I'm no good at… things like this—talking about feelings.'

Aggie stared up at his perfect face, shadowed with doubt and strangely vulnerable. 'What are you trying to say?'

'Something I should have said a long time ago.' He looked down at her and shuffled awkwardly. 'Except I barely recognised it myself, until you turned me away. Aggie, I've been going crazy. Thinking about you. Wanting you. Wondering how I'm going to get through life without you. I don't know if I've left it too late, but I can't live without you. I need you.'

Buffeted in all directions by wonderful waves of hope, Aggie could only continue to stare. She was finding it hard to make the necessary connections. Caution was pleading with her not to jump to conclusions but the look in his eyes was filling her with burgeoning, breathless excitement.

Luiz stared into those perfect blue eyes and took strength from them.

'I don't know what you feel for me,' he said huskily. 'I turned you on but that wasn't enough. When it came to women, I wasn't used to dealing in any other currency aside from sex. How was I to know that what I felt for you went far beyond lust?'

'When you say *far beyond...*'

'I don't know when I fell in love with you, but I did and, fool that I am, it's been a realisation that's been long in coming. I can only hope not too long. Look, Aggie...' He raked long fingers through his hair and shook his head in the manner of someone trying hard to marshal his thoughts into coherent sentences. 'I'm taking the biggest gamble of my life here, and hoping that I haven't blown all my chances with you. I love you and...I want to marry you. We were happy once, we had fun. You may not love me now, but I swear to God I have enough love for the two of us and one day you'll come to...'

'Shh.' She placed a finger over his beautiful mouth. 'Don't say another word.' Tears trembled, glazing over her eyes. 'I turned down your marriage proposal because I couldn't cope with the thought that the man I was...*am*... desperately in love with had only proposed because he thought it was the thing he should do. I couldn't face the thought of a reluctant, resentful husband. It would have meant my heart breaking every day we were together and that's why I turned you down.' She removed her finger and tiptoed to lightly kiss his lips.

'You'll marry me?'

Aggie smiled broadly and fell into him, reaching up to link her hands behind his neck. 'It's been agony seeing you and talking to you,' she confessed. 'I kept wondering if I had done the right thing.'

'Well, it's good to hear that I wasn't the only one suffering.'

'So you brought me all the way out here to tell me that you love me?'

'To show you this field and hope that it could be my strongest argument to win you back.'

'What do you mean?'

'Like I said.' Luiz, with his arm around her shoulders, turned her so that they were both looking at the same sprawling vista of grass and trees. 'I know you don't like me buying you things so I bought this for us. Both of us.'

'You bought…this field?'

'Thirty acres of land with planning permission to build. There are strict guidelines on what we can build but we can design it together. This was going to be my last attempt to prove to you that I was no longer the arrogant guy you once couldn't stand, that I could think out of the box, that I was worth the gamble.'

'My darling.' Aggie turned to him. 'I love you so much.' There was so much more she wanted to say but she was so happy, so filled with joy that she could hardly speak.

* * * * *

THE NOTORIOUS
GABRIEL DIAZ

BY
CATHY WILLIAMS

CHAPTER ONE

'WHAT DO YOU *mean*? Explain again. I'm not getting it.'
Lucy Robins looked between her parents, buying time
while her brain tried to catch up with what she had just
been told. Running round and round at her feet, Freddy,
the pug she had adopted three years ago, now made a stab
at grabbing her attention by flipping over on his back and
playing dead.

'Not now, Freddy!' she said, patting her lap. With that
small show of encouragement, the brown and black dog
scrambled onto her lap and proceeded to gaze adoringly
up at her.

The second Lucy had got her mother's phone call she
had known something was wrong. Celia Robins never
called her daughter at work, even though Lucy had repeatedly told her that it really didn't matter—that it wasn't
as though she worked in an office where there was a big,
bad boss keeping a watchful eye over employees and pun-
ishing anyone caught using their mobile.

The huge garden centre, set within the grounds of bo-
tanical gardens, which drew visitors from the across the
country, was the most relaxed of environments. There,
Lucy was part-gardener, helping with the landscaping
team, and part-artist, using her newly gained degree in
graphic art to draw exquisite detailed illustrations of flow-

ers for a comprehensive book of the flora and fauna at the centre.

Her mother's call had come just as she had been about to start replanting a batch of delicate orchids that had been meticulously cared for since their arrival at the centre six months previously. She had heard the words, *'Honey, could you possibly come home? There's something of an emergency...'* and had flown to her car, pausing only to tell Victor where she was going and to scoop up Freddy, who was allowed free rein in the outdoor space.

Now she stared in dismay at her father's drooping figure. 'What do you mean you're in trouble with the company finances?'

Nicholas Robins, as small and round as his wife was tall and slender, raised apologetic eyes to his daughter. 'I borrowed some money a few years ago, Luce. Not much. When your mother had her stroke...things just got a little crazy... I thought we were going to lose her... I wanted to give her her dream of a cruise... I wasn't thinking rationally...'

On her lap, Freddy had nodded off and was snoring. Lucy stroked his fat tummy. Her skin was clammy. When her father had announced that he and her mother were going on a cruise—a lifetime dream, a wonderful opportunity that might be their last—he had told her he had received an unexpected bonus at work. The company had just been taken over by an electronics giant and Lucy had believed him—had been over the moon at his unexpected good luck.

'When she recovered—' her father's voice was laboured, heavy '—I wanted to take her somewhere special. I thought if I borrowed a little bit more I could repay it before it was missed. I can't believe I was that stupid.'

Lucy glanced worriedly towards her mother. Celia Robins was a frail woman who would be unable to cope with the distressing catastrophe unfolding in front of her. The stroke she had suffered had sapped her of her energy, and both Lucy and her father lived in constant fear that she would suffer another.

'I didn't think that anything would change after GGD took us over,' her father continued in a shaking voice. 'Before the takeover, I was the only bookkeeper there. They brought in a team of financial whiz kids. I managed to keep things under wraps for as long as I could, and I'd started repaying the money, but this morning I was called in and told they had found some discrepancies and that it might be an idea if I took a little leave until it gets sorted out....'

Appalled, Lucy didn't know what to say. Her father was by no means a crook, and yet she knew with a sinking heart that no lawyer in the land would see it that way. He had helped himself to company funds and that was where the story would end. There would be no room for sob stories or excuses. That wasn't how big organisations operated. Especially that would not be how GGD would operate.

Gabriel Garcia Diaz was the guy who had founded GGD. Ruthless, cold and brilliant, he had risen to dominate the field of electronics in the space of a mere eight years, consuming smaller companies and growing more and more powerful in the process. Gabriel Garcia Diaz was the shark in the pond, and a shark wouldn't look at small minnows like her father and weep tears of sympathy for his plight.

A wash of nervous perspiration broke out over her. For the past two years she had contrived to put Gabriel Diaz out of her mind, but now the past galloped towards her, stampeding into the present and crashing through the flimsy defences she had erected to keep the unsettling memory of him at bay.

She had met him quite by accident. For weeks the talk of the town had been the takeover of Sims Electronics by GGD. The big guns were rolling into town and would be rescuing the ailing company where her father worked, transforming it into a mega-sized giant and in the process creating hundreds of jobs.

Lucy hadn't been able to get worked up over it. She'd been pleased that the rampant unemployment that afflicted their little slice of Somerset would be brought to an end, but big business didn't interest her. She had just got her job at the garden centre and all her excitement had been saved for that. She loved plants, she loved working outdoors, and she'd also had something else to celebrate. She had been called in and offered the task of illustrating the centre's first documented book of all the rare and exotic species of flowers being cultivated in the massive greenhouses.

Indeed, she had forgotten that the big boss of GGD would be rolling into town. Excited to tell her father about her new area of responsibility, for both her parents knew how keen she was to utilise her art degree, she had hopped on her bike in her lunch hour and cycled like the wind to where he worked.

It had only been when she had spotted the sleek black limo and the convoy of similarly grand cars in the parking lot that she'd belatedly remembered that it was the big day.

In the glittering summer sun, all the employees of Sims had gathered outside the building while, dominating the space in the centre, and surrounded by an alarming circle of threatening men in dark suits, one man had stood literally head and shoulders above the rest.

Lucy's eyes had been drawn to him, and even from a safe distance she'd been able to feel the power of his personality radiating out with shocking force. Everyone's attention had been glued to his face. Some of them had had their mouths half open, in thrall to whatever he was saying. She hadn't been able to hear. She'd been too far away. However, she'd understood what it was about the man that commanded their attention. Beyond the aura of power he was just the most incredible human being she had ever clapped eyes on. Tall, with raven-black hair, harsh, beautifully chiselled features and a bronzed colouring that lent him the air of someone breathtakingly exotic, he was as spectacularly beautiful as a lovingly carved statue of a Greek god.

Her father had been in the inner circle, dressed in his best suit, but as the tall man had headed to the open doors of the company, surrounded by his entourage, her father had fallen back and she'd taken the chance to race towards him on her bike so that she could tell him her good news.

Mr VIP had been heading off to inspect the building and the components centre. Later, Lucy hadn't understood how it was that he had managed to notice her amidst the excited commotion surrounding him. Had he spotted her cycling away? Had he radioed one of his lackeys who had remained outside with the fleet of cars, primed for a hasty departure? Nor, at the time, had she thought anything of the beefy guy in the suit who'd asked her who she was and what she was doing on the premises.

Anxious not to mention any connection with her father, for she didn't know if it was against rules for employees to speak when their attention should be one hundred percent focused on their leader, Lucy had instead vaguely told him that she worked at the garden centre and had been checking to make sure all the plants they'd installed for the visit were okay.

Later, packing up for the day, she had had her first real contact with Gabriel Garcia Diaz. About to cycle home, she had been bending down to the wheel lock on the bike.

When she'd stood up, there he'd been. At a distance, two bodyguards had lounged by a shiny black car.

He had literally taken her breath away. Never had she felt such a strange compulsion to stare and stare and stare—as though her eyes couldn't get their fill of his bronzed, exotic beauty. Up close he'd been so much more breathtaking, and when he'd spoken, his voice had been a low, dark, lazy drawl…asking her to tell him her name… telling her that he had noticed her…informing her that he hadn't planned on staying over but he would now make an exception to take her out….

Lucy had been speechless, flustered and vaguely terrified. What sort of man approached a woman he didn't know and informed her that she would be taken out to dinner? In a tone of voice that denied any negative response?

His urbane sophistication, his staggering good looks, and the lazy, sexual appreciation in those dark, dark eyes had made her head swim. Backing away, she had turned him down. She hadn't been able to imagine what a man like him would want with someone like her, but as soon as she'd asked herself the question she'd come up with the answer. *Sex.*

She had virtually run for cover and had continued to turn him down for the remainder of that week, which had seen deliveries of flowers—terrifically expensive flowers, the centre of attention at the garden centre—and one express delivery of a gold bracelet that she had refused to accept. He hadn't approached her again in person, but the sustained bombardment, designed to erode her defences, had confused her and sent her further into hiding. In the end she had left a text message on the cell number he had given her. She had told him to go away, that she had a boyfriend…

And he had.

Curiously, the abrupt cessation of all that attention had left her feeling deflated for weeks afterwards. Then, gradually, she had gathered herself and put the memory of him behind her as just one of those weird things.

Working at the garden centre left her no time to question the disturbing impact he had had on her. Nor had he returned to visit the offices where her father continued to work. Huge though the modernisations and expansions had been to Sims, it remained, or so she had been told, just a very small tentacle of one mammoth conglomerate.

Now, as Lucy looked at her parents, who seemed frightened and diminished by the rapidity with which everything they knew seemed to be unravelling, the image of Gabriel Diaz rose up in her head like a dark, avenging angel.

'Perhaps I could help,' she offered, her heart beating nervously. 'I mean, I get a good salary at the garden centre, and I could always ask whether they would advance me some of the money for the illustrations I've already done for their second volume. I'm nearly through with them. I'm sure they wouldn't mind.... Plus Kew Gardens are interested in commissioning me to do some work for them....'

'It's no good, honey.' Nicholas Robins shook his head with something approaching despair. 'I tried to talk to them...to explain the circumstances. I offered to have my salary cut by as much as it took to pay the debt off but they weren't interested. They said that's not how they run their organisation. One strike and you're out.'

'And you spoke to...to...Mr Diaz himself?' His name passing her lips sent a shiver through her, and again she recalled those glittering, mesmerising dark eyes and the way they had looked at her.

'Oh, no.' Her father sighed. 'I asked if I could see him but this matter isn't important enough for *him* to get involved. The man's hardly in the country as it is.'

'So what's going to happen?' Lucy could barely phrase the question because she was so scared of the answer, but ducking reality was never a good idea. Her voice was thick with tears but she wouldn't let herself cry. Her parents were both distressed enough as it was. She was an only child, and they had had her late in life and always protected her. Her unhappiness would be as wounding to them as their own.

'At best,' her father confessed, 'we'll lose the roof over our heads. At worst…'

That dreadful worst-case scenario remained unspoken, but it hovered in the air like a malignant cloud. At worst he could go to jail. Embezzlement was an offence that the courts took very seriously.

Lucy opened her mouth to suggest that they could both always come and live with her, sell their house and beg to pay off the debt with the proceeds, but practically how on earth would that work? She rented a small one-bedroomed cottage on the edge of the village. It suited her needs ideally, with its big, rambling garden and a tiny studio off the kitchen, where she often worked at her illustrations at night, but at best it was only good to house one girl and her dog. Stick two more human beings in and there wouldn't be room to move.

The options were running out fast. Her mother rose to make them all another pot of tea, and in her absence Lucy leaned forward and hurriedly asked how her mother was doing. *Really*.

'I'm worried,' her father said unhappily. 'She's being supportive but she has to be scared stiff. And we both know her health isn't good. If I get put away you'll have to look after her, Luce. She can't look after herself….'

'You won't get put away!' But the sound of options running out was the sound of jail doors being clanged shut. 'I could have a word....' she said finally.

'With who, my darling? Believe me, I've tried my damnedest and they're not interested. I even offered to show them receipts for how the money was spent...the holiday Mum and I took after she had the stroke.... They don't care. They're there to do a job and there's no appealing to them....'

'I could see Mr Diaz...'

'My love, he'll be a hundred times worse. He's a money-making machine without an emotional bone in his body. Sims went from being a small, friendly family firm to being part of a giant company where profits get made but there's a price to be paid. There's no such thing as compassionate leave. He has his minions there to make sure no one leaves early or even makes personal calls....'

Lucy thought back to that broodingly arrogant face and could well believe that anyone daring to disobey Gabriel Diaz would be hung, drawn and quartered without trial.

And yet he had sought her out two years ago, had made his intentions perfectly clear. He had wanted her. She hadn't understood why at the time, and she was no nearer to understanding now, but couldn't that brief flare of attraction help her out now? Perhaps encourage him to be more sympathetic to her parents' plight than he might normally have been under the circumstances?

Glancing up, Lucy caught sight of herself in the long oval mirror over the fireplace. What she saw was a slender girl with waist-length fair hair the colour of vanilla ice cream streaked with toffee, at the moment swept back into a haphazard ponytail, a heart-shaped face and green eyes. There was nothing there to get excited about as far as she was concerned, and chances were that the man wouldn't even remember who she was, but wasn't it worth the risk of approaching him?

'Let me think about things, Dad,' she told him, moving to where he was slumped on the sofa to give him a hug. 'I'll see what I can do. I'll try and get to Mr Diaz... you can never tell...'

She was thankful that her parents knew nothing of that peculiar little episode two years ago. Had they known that the devil in disguise had made a pass at her they would have immediately forbidden any contact. They were deeply traditional and would have been appalled to think that she might be allowed entry to Gabriel Diaz's hallowed walls simply because he had once fancied her for a week.

As it was, they did their best over the next hour to drop the conversation, to talk about less contentious topics, but by the time Lucy left later that evening she was drained, and so scared on behalf of her parents that she almost couldn't think clearly.

Not even the soothing act of drawing could calm her tumultuous thoughts and Freddy, sensing her mood, trotted behind her with a forlorn look on his squashy little face, the very picture of a depressed mutt.

The following morning she didn't give herself a chance to argue her way out of what she knew she had to do. Instead she phoned the garden centre first thing and explained that she wouldn't be coming in. She didn't anticipate being in London longer than a couple of hours, but Freddy would have to be deprived of his day dashing around the gardens, chasing insects. He gazed at her reproachfully as she closed the front door on him, immune to her promises of a treat when she returned.

It was warm outside. Summer had arrived with a bounce, delivering blue, cloudless skies for the past three weeks, and today was no exception.

It was a shame that she had no attractive dresses to wear to a meeting she suspected would be grueling—if it even took place at all. As her father had said, Gabriel Diaz was out of the country most of the time. Working at the garden centre had made her lazy when it came to her wardrobe. There was no need for her to wear anything dressy, so she had a cupboard that was full to bursting with faded jeans, combat trousers, jumpers, T-shirts and overalls.

She chose the least worn of her jeans, one of the few T-shirts that didn't advertise a rock band, and the most respectable of her shoes—a pair of black flats.

The mirror reflected back to her a picture of a girl, five foot eight, slender to the point of skinny, with long blond hair, which she personally considered her best feature. As a last resort, to add glamour to the package, but feeling tainted by the very act of aiming to appeal to someone via her looks, she dabbed on a little lip gloss. That, however, was as far as she was prepared to go.

In the middle of concluding a distasteful conversation with a certain tall, sexy brunette model he had been seeing for the past four months, and whose presence in his life had now outstayed its welcome, Gabriel Diaz was interrupted by his secretary poking her head into his office to tell him that he had a visitor.

'Name?'

'She refused to say,' Nicolette said apologetically. 'She said it's personal. I could tell her that you're not in…'

In receipt of information like that, Gabriel's first response would usually have been to assume that the woman in question was a lover. Despite his dislike of any woman intruding in his workspace, it had been known to happen. Women had an irritating tendency to think that sex bought them leniency in certain areas—to imagine that sleeping with him entitled them to pop into his office for nothing more than a quick chat. Gabriel could have told them that such behaviour only guaranteed an early exit from his life.

But having just come off the phone with Imogen, he knew that his mood was not conducive to completing the report that was blinking at him on his computer.

He berated himself for not taking action sooner to terminate his relationship with Imogen. Glamorous she might very well be, but she had displayed sufficient signs of clinginess early on for him to have realised that whatever they had would end in tears. Sure enough, the fifteen-minute telephone conversation he had just had with her had been ample proof that her expectations had far exceeded what had been on offer.

This was the third woman Gabriel had had in eight months. Even for him that was a record. What was it about women who just never seemed to get the message that he wasn't in it for the long haul? It wasn't as though he didn't make it clear to them from the very beginning that he was not a man who was on the lookout for commitment. No one could ever accuse him of not being scrupulously fair on that front. He never, *ever* made promises he had no intention of keeping. And yet time and again what started out as something light-hearted and fun ended up with him having to wriggle away from a woman who'd begun taking an unhealthy interest in domestic life and an even more unhealthy interest in diamond rings and friends with babies.

He scowled at the memory of Imogen shrieking down the phone that he had led her on. Such behaviour disgusted Gabriel. And he found it particularly annoying that she had seen fit to call him at work.

Faced with the prospect of being distracted from his report or seeing a mystery woman for ten minutes, he decided that bit of light relief might do the trick.

'Show her up.' He sat back and braced himself for someone on a begging mission. 'But make sure you tell her that I have ten minutes to spare and no more. Oh, and Nicolette? Remind her that I already contribute heavily to a number of charities. The money pit isn't bottomless....'

Hovering on the ground floor, where all the marble and glass and chrome and well-groomed artificial plants were combining to send her blood pressure shooting through the roof, Lucy was trying hard not to panic.

A surprise visit to Gabriel Diaz had seemed such a good idea at the time. In fact, it had seemed like the *only* idea at the time. But now a serious case of nerves was threatening to make her turn tail and flee.

The building, which she had located in the labyrinth of office buildings in the heart of the City, was terrifyingly impressive. Everyone at Sims had been thrilled to death when their small two-storeyed brick-clad office block had been expanded and turned into a high-tech glasshouse. Her father had related numerous tales of clean tiled floors and brand-new top-of-the-range desks. Lucy thought that he would be rendered speechless were he to see the opulence of DGG headquarters.

She had almost expected to be told that Gabriel wasn't in the country, and she told herself that it was a *sign* that he *was* in the country, *was* in his office and *would* see her.

She kept her eyes peeled as she walked past the bank of snobby girls at the circular reception desk in the middle, with its sleek, wafer-thin computer terminals, and breathed a sigh of relief when she spotted a middle-aged woman striding towards her.

This must be Gabriel's secretary. Or one of them. At least the woman heading in her direction, unlike the girls at the reception desk, wasn't looking at her as though she were something dragged in by the cat after a night on the tiles.

'You're…?'

'Lucy. I'm sorry I didn't give…er…Gabriel my name, but I thought it might be nice to surprise him….' Lucy was open by nature, and subterfuge made her cheeks pinken.

'He can't allot you much time, I'm afraid. Mr Diaz is on a very tight schedule.'

Nicolette was well-versed in the sort of women her boss dated. This girl was not at all built in the same mould. Nor had Nicolette ever seen anyone quite so stunningly pretty and, judging from the clothes and the lack of make-up, quite so ignorant of her looks.

As they took the lift up to the directors' floor she made sure to keep the conversation light.

Lucy was grateful for that. She was awed and impossibly daunted by her surroundings. Every slab of marble and sheet of glass in the building breathed money and power. The employees were all decked out in designer suits and looked as though they were dashing off to very important, life-changing meetings.

In her jeans and T-shirt and flat black ballet shoes she felt as conspicuous as a bull in a china shop. She knew that people were staring as the lift disgorged them into a vast, elegant space, thickly carpeted, with a central circular sunken area in which various other besuited people were doing clever things in front of computers.

Her skin literally crawled with nerves, and her legs were so wobbly that it was a challenge to move one in front of the other.

Beyond the central atrium, a wide corridor was flanked on either side by private offices the likes of which could only, surely, be found in a company with profits to burn.

She found that she was lagging behind as Nicolette

strode briskly towards the office at the very end of the corridor. Noiseless air-conditioning meant that it was much cooler inside the building than it had been outside, and it felt positively chilly up here on the eighth floor. She clamped her teeth together to stop them from chattering.

'If you'd wait here…?'

Nicolette's smile was kindly but Lucy hardly noticed. Her pink mouth, lip gloss long since gone, had fallen open at the opulence of her surroundings. Light grey smoked glass concealed this outer office from prying eyes. The walls were white, and dominated on one side by a huge abstract painting and on the other by smoked ash doors behind which lay heaven only knew what. Another office? A wardrobe stuffed full of designer suits? A bathroom? Or maybe a torture chamber into which recalcitrant employees could be marched and taught valuable life lessons?

Nicolette's desk was bigger than the studio room in her house where Lucy did her meticulous drawings. At a push it could be converted into a dining table to seat ten.

She was staring at it, fighting the sensation that she had somehow been transported into a parallel universe, when she was told that Mr Diaz would see her now.

Lucy had thought she hadn't forgotten what Gabriel looked like. As she entered his office and the door behind her clicked softly closed she realised she actually had. The man slowly turning from the window where he had been standing, looking out, was so much taller than she remembered. She was pinned to the spot by eyes the colour of bitter chocolate. Time had done nothing to dim the staggering force of his personality—the same force she had felt the first time she had seen him, surrounded by his minions. It swept over her, strangling her vocal cords and scrambling her ability to think.

* * *

This was not what Gabriel had expected. He had expected a middle-aged harpy with a begging bowl and pictures of unfortunate children.

But this was the woman whose image he had never quite been able to eradicate from his head. She had been stunning then and she was even more stunning now—although he would have been hard pressed to put his finger on what, exactly, it was about her that held his gaze with such ferocious intensity.

Her skin was pale gold and smooth as satin, and that amazing hair, pulled back into a long plait that ran down the length of her narrow spine, had the same effect on him now as it had two years ago. Confronted by the one and only woman who had ever said no to him, Gabriel schooled his features into polite curiosity. He didn't know what she wanted, but the residue of his frustration and annoyance suddenly lifted.

'Thank you for seeing me.' Lucy hovered by the door, not having been invited to take one of the leather chairs that were ranged in front of a desk that was even bigger than the one belonging to his secretary. His silence was unnerving. It propelled her into hurried speech. 'You probably don't remember me. We met a couple of years ago. When you…ah…came to Somerset…Sims Electronics? It was one of the companies you took over…. I'm sorry. I didn't even introduce myself. Lucy…ah…Robins. I'm sorry. You won't have a clue who I am….'

Regret at her hasty decision to descend on him unannounced rushed over her, making her want to stumble back out of the door and as far away from this intimidating building as she could get. She didn't know if she should walk towards him and extend her hand in a gesture of politeness, but just the thought of touching him sent her nerves into further debilitating freefall.

Not have a clue who she was? Gabriel wanted to laugh aloud at that one. One look at her face and he was realising that her polite rejection still rankled a lot more than he had suspected. He was not a man who had his advances spurned. The experience had burnt a hole in his memory. But what the hell was she doing here? Had she turned up two years ago he would have assumed that it was because she'd had a rethink about her incomprehensible decision to turn him away—but now...? All this time later...? No, something was at play here, and intense curiosity kicked into gear. It felt great. Invigorating. Especially after his ludicrous phone call with Imogen.

'Are you going to say anything?' she asked, her nerves making her stumble over the question.

At that, Gabriel pushed himself away from the window and indicated one of the chairs in front of his desk.

'I remember you,' he drawled, resuming his seat and watching every detail of the emotions flitting across her face. 'The girl from the garden centre. You returned an item of jewellery. What did you do with the flowers? Introduce them to the incinerator?'

Lucy lowered her eyes and fumbled her way to the chair, not knowing whether he expected an answer to that deliberately provocative question. Her skin was burning, as though someone had shoved her to stand in front of an open flame, and although she wasn't looking at him the harsh, perfect angles of his face were imprinted in her head with the forcefulness of a branding iron.

Staring down uncomfortably at her entwined fingers, she literally could see nothing else but his dark-as-midnight eyes, the curl of his sensuous mouth, the coolly arrogant inclination of his head. But she was glad to be sitting. At least it gave her legs some reprieve from the threat of collapsing under her.

'So what do you want?' Gabriel asked with studied indifference. 'You have ten minutes of my time and counting.'

Lucy balled her hands into fists. She understood that they had parted company on less than ideal terms. Perhaps his pride had been wounded because she had turned him down. But was that any reason for him to make this even more difficult for her than it already was? Two years ago she had been offered a glimpse of his arrogance. Now she could see that in no way had it diminished over time.

'I've come about my father.' She took a deep breath and forced herself to meet his mildly enquiring gaze. 'I don't know if you've heard, but there's been a bit of a situation… at the company…'

Gabriel frowned. His business interests were so extensive that entire companies that sheltered under his umbrella were practically self-accounting. Now he rapidly clicked his computer and began scrolling through all the details of Sims. It took him no time at all to unearth what her mystery trip to his office was all about.

'By *situation*,' he said coldly, 'I take it that you're referring to your father's embezzlement?'

'Please don't call it that.'

'You're here because your father's been caught out with his hand in the till. I'm hoping you're not going to ask me to turn a blind eye to his thieving just because once upon a time I gave you a second look…?'

Mortification ripped through her, making her slight frame tremble. 'You don't understand! My father's not *a thief.*'

'No? Then we have a different take on what constitutes a thief. In my view, it's someone who has been caught trying to rip a company off…dipping into the coffers…taking money…' He leant forward and placed the palms of his hands flat on his desk. 'Taking money without permission, presumably to enjoy the high life!'

'He… Look, he knows that what he did was wrong.…'

'Good! Then perhaps the courts will look on him favourably and not make the sentence too harsh! Alternatively, they might just want to flex their muscles and demonstrate that fraud isn't something to be taken lightly! Now…'

He stood up and cursed himself for the impact she still seemed to have on him—even when she was sitting in *his* chair, in *his* office, bleating on about her father and trying to pull the sympathy card. All of which added up to a situation with which he had less than zero tolerance.

'If that's all, Nicolette will show you out.…'

CHAPTER TWO

LUCY'S SPINE STIFFENED in stubborn, angry refusal to see this as the conclusion of her expedition to London. He had treated her with contempt and hadn't even bothered to hear her out. Of course he had every good reason to dismiss her, but the thought of her father being chucked into a prison cell like a common criminal…. He would never survive that, and neither would her mother.

She could feel his eyes burning into her downturned head and she fought down the sickening wave of pride that made her want to leave with her head held high. Right now pride was a commodity she couldn't afford.

'Please…please hear me out,' she whispered, daunted beyond belief by the cold hostility emanating from him.

'Whatever for?' Gabriel's voice was harshly blunt. 'Embezzlement in my company is not accepted on any level. It's as simple as that. It's outrageous to think that you came here to parade your wares in front of me in the hope that I might bend the rules. Hell, you haven't even bothered to wear something decent!'

'Parade my wares?' Lucy looked at him with bewilderment.

'I wasn't born yesterday. I know the way women operate. Fair means or foul pretty much sums it up. You thought that you could use your sexy little body to score a few

points. Big mistake. I've seen a lot of sexy bodies in my
time, and I'm inured to *any* woman who tries to use hers
for any kind of profit.'

Sexy little body. Those three words, uttered so casually,
brought a hectic colour to her cheeks. Having never considered herself in terms of how she looked, it was somehow
shocking to hear him refer to her appearance so bluntly.

She was also uncomfortable with the brief surge of pleasure she'd felt at hearing herself described as *sexy*. She had
never felt like a sexy woman. Sexy women had attitude.
They flashed their eyes and swayed their hips and pouted
and flirted. She had never done any of those things, and
wouldn't have been able to do them even if she had spent
a lifetime reading books on how to achieve it. She just
wasn't sexy, and that was why she had shied away from
relationships with boys at college.

She was conservative, traditional—one of those boring
types who had never slept around and was saving herself
for the guy she eventually fell in love with. Her parents
had done a good job in instilling values that had long been
left by the wayside by most girls over the age of seventeen.

And yet he had called her *sexy*. She thought that perhaps he needed his eyes checked, but now was hardly the
time to point that out. Not when he was staring at her as
though she was something that had crawled out of a dust-
bin into his immaculate office with the sole intention of
making a mess.

'I didn't come here to...to...'

Watching the rise and fall of her chest, and inwardly
remarking on a repertoire of facial expressions he hadn't
seen in a very long time in any woman, Gabriel caught
himself wondering whether it was that wide-eyed innocence that he found so appealing. Appealing against his
better judgement.

She had a face that would make any man go crazy, and yet it was coupled with a transparency that could only be dangerous.

'To…to…?' He parroted her stammer mockingly.

'You're horrible,' Lucy uttered on a desperate cry, 'and I'm really sorry I came here in the first place. I shouldn't have. Dad said that he'd tried to explain to your people at the company but none of them would listen. I might have guessed that you wouldn't listen either. I'm sorry I took up your precious time!' She began to stand up.

His order to *'Sit!'* took her so much by surprise that she practically fell back into the chair.

'You mean you're going to listen to…?'

Gabriel raised one imperious hand to cut her off mid-sentence. 'You can forget about any sob stories. Your father stole money from my company and that's the end of it. I'm not interested in listening to a long, tedious and fabricated list of extenuating circumstances. There *are* no extenuating circumstances when it comes to theft.'

He swung his long, lean body out of the chair and moved with economical grace to perch on the edge of his desk, his hands loosely clasped together. Nicolette knocked and popped into the office to remind him of a meeting due to be held in the conference room in fifteen minutes. Gabriel waved her aside.

'Let Davis cover for me,' he said, not taking his eyes off Lucy's downbent fair head. Her entire posture spoke of weary, despairing resignation. She had come to try and save her father's skin, and he supposed he could award her one or two brownie points for that, but he was pleased that she had got the essential message—which was that he was no sucker. Spinning him hard luck stories was a non-starter.

He knew that at this juncture he should send her away

and let her father try and convince the long arm of the law that it had all been a terrible mistake. But why hide from the truth? She was the one who'd got away and he still found her curiously attractive. Even dressed in clothes no woman should wear, and with a begging bowl in her hands.

His last abortive relationship with Imogen...the line of beautiful bodies and beautiful faces and easy availability... he was bored with them all. He was tired of women who simpered whenever they were with him, sick of the certain knowledge that they would all do whatever he wanted, however outrageous his request might be.

At the age of thirty-two, he found his palate was lamentably jaded. Looking at the woman in front of him made him feel as though he had been injected with youth serum. Everything about her fascinated him—from her naïveté in showing up at his office with a sob story right down to the novelty of being in the company of a woman who didn't ask *How high?* the second he told her to jump.

It was almost *challenging* to think that what he had missed first time round could now be his.

Dark, speculative eyes drifted down to the shape of her small, high breasts and his arousal was as fierce as it was sudden. She chose that very moment to raise moss-green eyes to him and he smiled a slow, satisfied smile—the smile of someone anticipating victory in a battle that had yet to commence.

'How was your trip to London?' Gabriel asked, maintaining eye contact.

'I beg your pardon?'

'Good trip? It must have been a wrench leaving the plants behind....'

'Why are you asking me these questions? I thought you were in a rush. I thought you could only spare me a few minutes. What's the point wasting the few minutes I have telling you about my trip?'

'Well, it's more worthwhile than wasting them telling me about what a sterling character your father is....'

Lucy fell silent, although he continued to stare at her. She didn't know where his weird turn in the conversation was going, but she clung to the slender hope that whilst he was talking he might still be prepared to listen. Surely he couldn't be *so* lacking in emotion that he wouldn't even hear her out?

His dark, watchful eyes set up a series of stirring reactions inside her until she could feel her temples begin to throb. She just didn't know what he wanted her to say and confusion brought a flush of colour to her cheeks. 'I...the journey was fine....'

'And your job? How's that going?'

'Good. Great. I...' She was gripped by a sudden idea and her eyes brightened. 'Better than great, in fact. I...I don't only work in the garden centre—I do quite a bit of illustrative work as well. I...I did a degree in graphic art and I was commissioned two years ago to do some drawings of the rare plants and flowers for a compendium the centre was putting together....'

Gabriel made a non-committal sound that was neither encouraging nor discouraging. Frankly he couldn't care less about whatever drawings she had been commissioned to do, but he was enjoying the genuine enthusiasm on her face. He toyed with the pleasant thought that *he* might be able to generate that same enthusiasm. Once more he was subjected to a wildly pressing urge to release her hair so that he could tangle his fingers in its rippling length.

Any woman in possession of looks like hers should not have been caught dead in a pair of faded jeans and a T-shirt—least of all in *his* presence. He had expressed disgust that she might come to him with a view to using her body to get what she wanted without even bothering to dress for the occasion, but now he realised that he would have been disappointed had she done so.

Hadn't he had his fill of Barbie dolls? Wasn't he sick to his back teeth of women who were perfectly manicured, perfectly groomed and perfectly dressed in the most expensive and revealing clothes that money could buy?

Lucy was disconcerted by that lazy appraisal in his roving dark eyes. It made her feel uncomfortable. She suppressed the crazy notion that buried beneath her discomfort a slow swirl of excitement was eddying in her veins, making her breasts tingle and sending a shooting, melting warmth between her legs.

She pressed her legs firmly together and leaned forward, gripping the soft leather of the chair. 'What I'm trying to say,' she said quickly, because he struck her as a man who lost interest fast and she needed to grab his attention before that happened, 'is that I get paid well for my art work. I've been putting money aside for the past couple of years. I've been trying to save so that I can afford to buy the little cottage I rent at the moment. Mrs Hardy, who owns it, says that she'll continue renting it to me until I can afford to put down a deposit and get a mortgage from the bank....'

'Where are you going with this?'

'Right. Well...would you be amenable to *me* paying you back the money that Dad...er...borrowed from your company? You can take all the money I've saved. It's a little over four thousand pounds. And I'm willing and happy to give you everything I earn. I mean, I'd have to keep a little aside for bills and food, but you could have the rest....'

'First, your father didn't *borrow* the money. Second, I'm afraid your savings and some of your monthly earnings wouldn't begin to put a dent in his debt. Frankly, you'd be paying me until the day you died and beyond. So you can scrap that suggestion straight away.'

'In other words there's no point to me being here at all, is there?'

Lucy watched her bright idea disappear over the horizon, taking with it all hope that she might appeal to Gabriel's better side. It was clear that he didn't have one of those. Not only that, but he was deriving great enjoyment from watching her squirm. Perhaps this was his way of exacting revenge for having been turned down by her two years ago. A man like Gabriel Diaz, blessed with drop-dead good looks and the trappings of wealth, would not be used to *any* woman turning him down. She was now paying the high price for being one of that rare breed of woman who had.

'Call me crazy—because anyone else in my situation would have thrown you out on your ear the second you walked into this office and opened your mouth—but you might have a way out of this....'

'Really?' Hope flared and she looked at him with nervous, wary anticipation.

Gabriel noted that she had amazing eyes. They were a peculiar shade of green—deep green, the colour of the sea in certain lights.

'Really. But before I get to what I have in mind let me ask you this: what happened to the boyfriend?'

'Sorry?' Lucy frowned, at a loss to understand where this reference to a boyfriend had come from. She didn't *have* a boyfriend.

'The boyfriend,' Gabriel said impatiently. 'The one you told me you had when you sent me your Dear John text.'

'I really offended you back then, didn't I?'

Gabriel laughed with caustic amusement. '*Offended* me?'

'I—I didn't mean to...' Lucy continued in an anxious stammer. 'I'm not used to...'

'Spare me the involved explanation. Just tell me the fate of the boyfriend.'

Lucy had no idea what this had to do with the matter in hand. She had to cast her mind back even to remember that small white lie. At the time the presence of a man in her life had seemed the only way of wriggling out of the situation. Gabriel Diaz had oozed sex, and there was no way she would have accepted his proposition. He had also oozed persistence. Added together, she had felt it perfectly acceptable to produce a fictitious other half, and afterwards she'd been very glad she had done so—because a quick trip on the internet had shown her what she had already suspected. Gabriel Diaz was a player—a man who, from everything she had read, worked his way through women without conscience. There were pictures of him with various beauties, none of whom had stayed the course of time.

'He...ah...it didn't work out,' Lucy mumbled, dropping her gaze and staring with furious concentration at the tips of her very unflattering black pumps.

'No? What went wrong?'

'I don't really want to talk about it,' she muttered, licking her lips and frantically trying to imagine what the fate of this made up guy might have been. One tiny and necessary white lie was one thing. A series of follow-on lies was not going to do. But his continuing silence was already telling her that she was expected to expand. And yet, she thought with a rare spark of defiance, why should she? He had been horrible to her. Arrogant, sneering and dismissive. Why should she tell him anything she didn't want to?

But that sliver of hope he had dangled in front of her was an effective gag on her rebellious thoughts. If nothing else she owed it to her parents to take advantage of any crumb of mercy he was prepared to throw her way. Perhaps he could arrange for her father to be let go, but for his reputation to remain intact and any prison sentence to be waived. That would certainly be a worthwhile result. Her parents played an active part in the community. It would be hard if her father's situation were to become public knowledge. Fortunately the two men who had uncovered the problem were both Londoners and would not be hanging around.

'He…um…broke up with me,' Lucy imparted reluctantly. 'And then, shortly afterwards, he went away. To… to New Zealand… To live with the woman he dumped me for…' This seemed the best way to ensure that her fictitious boyfriend was well and truly out of the way. 'But I still don't understand what this has to do with anything….'

'A boyfriend on the scene would have been a nuisance when it comes to what I have in mind….' Gabriel didn't *do* women with husbands, and he didn't do women who had boyfriends either. Why would he? The world was full of beautiful, single, willing women. Why go to the trouble of courting someone who came with baggage?

'And what *do* you have in mind?'

'You. I have *you* in mind.' Gabriel watched with wonderment a face that expressed absolutely no comprehension of what he was getting at.

She was literally at a loss. Any other woman would have followed the thread of this conversation, and certainly by now would have got the message loud and clear. This woman was staring at him with a frown, as though he had produced a complicated maths problem from under a hat and demanded she provide a solution immediately.

'May I do something?' he asked with silken assurance, and then, just in case she was *still* away with the fairies and not getting where he was going, he strolled behind her. Before she could react he was pulling free her hair, releasing it from its constricting braid.

Lucy swivelled round and stood up, faltering backwards until she bumped into the edge of his desk.

'What are you doing?' With one hand she clasped her loosed hair, pulling it over one shoulder. She couldn't peel her eyes away from his face, and her heart was pounding so fiercely in her chest that she could scarcely breathe. She gave a little squeak of horror as he very slowly strolled towards her.

'I wanted to do that the first time I laid eyes on you,' Gabriel murmured.

He smiled, and that smile had the effect of making her feel as though she was falling through the air with no safety net beneath her. Her stomach lurched and every nerve in her body was at screaming pitch.

'I saw you on that bike and I wanted you. Simple as that. You were like a gazelle—all beauty and grace. And, mysteriously, I find that I *still* want you....'

'But you *can't*...' Lucy breathed jerkily. 'You...you date supermodels....'

'How do you know that?'

'Because I looked you up on the internet!' She went bright red. He was standing so close to her that she could feel his heat. He must be able to feel hers, because she was certainly burning up.

'You did, did you?' Gabriel was intensely satisfied that he had made more of an impression on her than he had given himself credit for—boyfriend or no boyfriend. An indifferent woman would never have looked him up on the internet. More to the point, an indifferent woman wouldn't be looking at him now with lurking excitement in her eyes. Even if she *was* strenuously trying to conceal it. An expert when it came to the opposite sex, he could sense her response to him as clearly as if it had been emblazoned on her forehead in neon lettering.

'I was curious….' Lucy defended.

'Curiosity is good.' He leant forward to brace himself on the desk, his hands on either side of her, caging her in.

The fantasy of taking her here—in his office, on his desk—was so powerful that he hardened, his erection painful as it pressed thickly against the zipper of his trousers. Gone was the jaded, world-weary feeling that had settled over him for what seemed like years. For that alone she would be worth every penny.

'So here's my proposal…'

Regretfully, he straightened, because being so close to her, breathing in that refreshing innocence, the clean, minty smell of her fabulous hair, was doing all sorts of things to his body. Much as he enjoyed the sensation, he had to acknowledge that they *were* in his office, and Nicolette *was* just one door away. Having his secretary accidentally burst in on a scene of rampant lovemaking on his desk would not be good for her dodgy blood pressure.

At no point did it occur to him that Lucy might reject his advances the way she had rejected them two years ago. This time he held the trump card, and he had every intention of using it.

As he strolled back towards his chair he could feel her eyes on him, and he knew with every primitive instinct in his body that she had not been immune to that brief moment of contact when he had touched her hair.

'I won't try to wrap it up in any fancy packaging. I want you, and in return for having you in my bed I'm willing to let your father off the hook. All the stolen money will be replaced. Orders issued to my two finance guys that with the debt owing to me cleared the matter is to be buried, never again to resurface. Of course your father won't be able to return to his job. That would be taking the joke a step too far. After all, a thief is a thief is a thief. But he will be retired with a generous package, and hopefully a salutary lesson in never dipping his fingers in the till of any company again....'

Lucy couldn't help staring at him. Here was the same man who had shown up at the garden centre with his lackeys in tow and a dinner invitation he'd expected to be accepted. Now he was offering her an invitation of another sort, and this time he was calling the shots. She was truly appalled at his lack of morality. Was this how *all* rich people operated? Did they assume that they just needed to snap their fingers and the rest of the world would dance to their tune?

'That's ridiculous...' She edged away from the desk and began backing unsteadily towards the door. She eyed the backpack she had brought with her. It was on the ground, next to the chair she had fallen into when she had first entered his office. Her unravelled hair fell in a long, thick blond curtain over one shoulder, but she was hardly aware of it as she took small steps towards the bag.

'What's so ridiculous about it?'

His words halted her, and she jerked up to stare at him with an expression of disbelief. 'You're asking me to be... to...'

'Sleep with me...make love...have sex—at times and places of my choosing... No need to tiptoe over the details.'

'But that's utterly immoral!'

'So's stealing—and on the plus side sex *isn't* a criminal offence punishable with a jail sentence....' He was incredulous that she was even quibbling over his generous offer. As rescue packages went, he didn't think she could have landed herself a better one.

And yet she was still staring at him as though he had

asked if she wouldn't mind stripping off and running naked down the street. What exactly, he wondered, was the problem here? If she was playing hard to get in an attempt to up the ante then she was definitely barking up the wrong tree. He would never have dreamt of doing a deal like this with any other woman. Perhaps that had something to do with the fact that she was the only woman ever to have turned him down. But, although she might be the exception, her window of opportunity was small.

'I'm sorry. I couldn't.'

Lucy retrieved her backpack and clutched it in front of her like a shield. She wondered whether there was anything else she could say that would buy her father some clemency, but in her heart she knew that the offer on the table was the only one this man would be making. She also knew that by turning it down she was condemning her parent to swift retribution.

But how could she possibly do what he wanted? Sex, for him, was clearly no more than a physical transaction. It was irrelevant that there was no emotion involved. She had always promised herself that sex for her would have lots of emotion involved. How could she abandon the moral principles she had been weaned on?

Gabriel shrugged. He strolled towards her and received the impression that she was holding her ground only by the skin of her teeth. Given half a chance she would have hightailed it through the door at speed.

'Your choice,' he told her with casual indifference.

'Isn't there something else you want?' Lucy asked desperately.

'No.' Gabriel refused to mince words. 'That's the only deal on the table.'

'And so…my dad…'

'Goodbye freedom. Hello Cell Block H….'

'You're the most heartless, unsympathetic man I've ever met in my entire life!'

'But I have many other things to offer....' Gabriel's voice was low and husky. She had a dusting of freckles on her nose and her eyelashes were so thick and dark that anyone would think she had laid on the mascara with a trowel were it not for the fact that she radiated a natural glow that had nothing to do with make-up.

He had always found that a certain element of surprise worked when it came to disarming his opponents. He used it now.

Lucy, staring at him with the dazed expression of someone suddenly subjected to a whiplash rollercoaster of events they had been least expecting, was not prepared for his lean brown hand as he reached to curl his fingers in her hair. She was certainly not prepared for his cool mouth as it descended to meet hers, and she was even less prepared for the way her body was galvanised into a reaction that was so strong it deprived her of the ability to breathe.

She had been kissed before, but never like this. As his tongue gently parted her lips she felt scorching heat race through her. Her breasts were heavy, sensitive to the slight brush of his chest against hers. Her nipples tingled in a way that shot signals to every other part of her body. Like wax subjected to open flame, she was melting. She heard a low moan and was shocked to realise that it was coming from *her*.

With a push, she separated her treacherous body from his and found no opposition. Indeed, he released her immediately and stood back with a slight smile curving his beautiful mouth.

'How *could* you?'

'Take advantage of you? You enjoyed it...'

'I did *not*!' Lucy cried fiercely. 'I'm *not* like that! I'm *not* like those women you go out with!' But she was mortified, and ashamed of her body—which was loudly protesting her virtuous words. 'I'm going!'

She took a couple of panicky steps to remove herself from the stranglehold of his proximity and he didn't follow her. He reached for something on his desk, scribbled on it.

'Here's my card. I'll give you twenty-four hours, and after that my offer expires. Word of advice? It's a generous offer. Think very carefully before you decide to put your principles ahead of common sense. And don't kid yourself that you would be disgusted by the deal. You came alive for me just then, and there's plenty more where that came from....'

'Don't *say* those things!' But already she was reacting to his words, her mind flashing erotic images through her head—images that made her squirm because they were so new, so unexpected, so horribly, frighteningly different from anything she had ever experienced before.

She was barely aware of leaving his office. She couldn't have said how she managed to make it to the train station or get on the train. Several times she looked at the card he had given her and was tempted to rip it into shreds and chuck it in the nearest bin.

So why didn't she? He had offered her a devil's contract. She should have thrown that card away the second she left his office. She should never have accepted it in the first place!

Her thoughts were all over the place. Scenery flashed past and she saw none of it. When she tried to recall the conversation they had had all she could see was his sinfully handsome face, all she could hear was the velvety persuasiveness of his low, sexy drawl. He hadn't touched her, but she felt as though he had. Her body tingled as though he had run those lean brown fingers over it.

She was determined that he couldn't *buy* her, but even as she stood self-righteously on her podium and declared that as an absolute certainty a little voice in her head was reminding her of how he had made her feel, how that kiss had cut through all her fine words and blown them apart into smithereens.

Once home, she briefly dropped in to make sure Freddy was all right, and then drove to her parents' house—to find neither of them there and the house in darkness.

On top of everything that had been going on this could only mean bad news—which was confirmed when she called her father on his mobile to be told that they were at the hospital.

'Your mother had a turn.'

He was holding it together, but with difficulty. Lucy could hear that down the phone line.

'I didn't want to worry you. You've been worried enough already. At any rate, they're doing tests, but they think she may have had a mild panic attack. They'll keep her in overnight. There's no need to get yourself into a tizzy about it....'

But that was easier said than done.

In the space of a couple of days her world had shifted on its axis. Her comfortable routine had been blown apart.

At the hospital, exhausted after a day's worth of travelling, Lucy was cheered to hear that her mother had indeed suffered only a mild panic attack, but when the doctor took her aside, with her father, and gravely told them that they should make sure that Celia was kept as stress-free as possible, she could only think of that offer Gabriel had made.

What price high-minded principles when her mother was lying on a hospital bed and her father was staring down the barrel of a gun?

Would it be the end of the world for *her*? Was she *re-*

ally prepared to sacrifice her parents for the wonderful prize of her virginity?

It was dark by the time she eventually made it back to her cottage. After a day cooped up indoors Freddy was raring for some fun and she spent half an hour outside with him. Her mind was clouded with anxiety as she threw his ball and watched as he fetched it, romping back to her triumphantly and waiting so that the exercise could be repeated.

Lucy knew what she had to do, but it wasn't going to be easy.

And yet the memory of that searing kiss leapt into her head and her heart began to pound.

The palms of her hands were clammy when, an hour later, after she had tried and failed to have something to eat, she tapped Gabriel's number into her telephone.

The business card he had given her displayed a dizzying array of numbers but he had handwritten his cell number, which probably meant that it was a number only released to a small number of privileged people. She figured that the women who had that number probably thought they had won the lottery.

He picked up on the third ring and immediately she wondered where he was. At the office? In his house or apartment, or whatever expensive pad he called home? It certainly wouldn't be a quaint little house in the suburbs!

'It's me. It's Lucy. Lucy Robins. I came to see you at your off—'

'My memory is in perfect working order,' Gabriel said drily. He had literally just stepped through the front door of his sprawling house in Kensington. It was the one of the most prestigious houses in one of the most prestigious roads in London.

He began removing his tie, heading to the kitchen to

pour himself a whisky. Amazing. Even the sound of her voice had an invigorating effect on his libido.

'I'm taking it you've had a little think about the conversation we had today...?' he encouraged, when her awkward, stammering introduction was followed by complete silence.

'Yes, I have.'

'And you've come to what conclusion? That your father is to face those cruel, unforgiving and heartless scales of justice and reap his due rewards?'

'No...'

That single monosyllable sounded as though it had been dragged out of her, but Gabriel was unperturbed by that. Had she really been as repulsed by him as she had tried to convince him then the offer would have been withdrawn. But she wasn't. Reaching for a glass, he smiled to himself—the satisfied smile of a predator that has successfully corralled its prey and can look forward to enjoying the catch.

'Maybe we can talk,' she muttered.

'Count on it. I'll be with you tomorrow.' Some meetings would have to be rearranged, but she was a prize that would be worth that small inconvenience.

'No!' Lucy was alone in the cottage, but she still looked guiltily around her—as though at any moment the walls might decide to spout ears. Have Gabriel swan down to Somerset? She could think of nothing worse! There was no way she would ever let her parents suspect that she had struck this deal. They would be horrified. It would be her shameful secret and would have to be kept exclusively in London. A shameful weekend secret. It was the only way. 'I...I can come to London at the weekend...'

'Not sure I can wait that long.'

'Please. It's only two days away. If you give me your

address…or better still we could meet at…a restaurant…
or something…'

'I'll text you my address.' Anticipation roared through
him as it never had before. 'When I see you I don't want
anyone around.' He was already thinking of that slender,
loose-limbed body, as graceful as a dancer's. He would
definitely have to have a cold shower tonight. 'I can't
wait….'

CHAPTER THREE

TWO DAYS LATER Lucy was back on the train, speeding up to London. On the one hand she was a nervous wreck. Gabriel was no longer someone she could shove to the back of her mind and forget because he wasn't physically around.

He had phoned her twice since her decision to give him what he wanted. She felt as if he was keeping tabs on her, making sure his quarry wasn't allowed any second thoughts, although his conversations were not at all threatening. He asked her about her day and expressed interest in the details. Lucy didn't believe for a minute that he really cared one way or the other about successfully transplanted orchids or the large order the garden centre had taken from a chain of hotels in the north. She knew that he was trying to put her at her ease, but instead of feeling relieved she just felt increasingly as if she had been bought and was now being primed for consumption.

On the other hand the wheels were in motion for her father's reprieve.

She had told her dad haltingly, because lying didn't come easy—especially lying to her parent—that she had managed to get in touch with Gabriel and the meeting had been a good one.

'I think he might be prepared to let you off,' she had said only the morning before.

A more suspicious parent would have immediately jumped to the right conclusion that any favour granted from someone like Gabriel Diaz would require a hefty payback, but suspicion didn't run deep in Nicholas Robins's bones. He was a man who saw the good in people, and he had had no trouble accepting that Gabriel Diaz had been open to persuasion.

'It's a first-time offence,' she had offered by way of explanation for a decision that made no sense, 'and I don't know—maybe he doesn't want to get on the wrong side of the local people by dragging you through the courts. I… er…told him how sorry you were, and how affected everyone in the community would be if you were to be punished…how they close ranks against outsiders…'

'And did you tell him that I will be willing to sacrifice all my pay until the debt's cleared? I could get a second job…something to bring a little money in… The bulk of my earnings could go towards paying him back…. Did you mention that I had already started making repayments?'

Lucy hadn't had the heart to tell her father that the likelihood of him returning to his old job was about as likely as a trip to the moon. Instead she had waxed lyrical about Gabriel's wonderfully sympathetic nature…the vast reserves of wealth that had enabled him to write off her father's debt as a mere bagatelle that could be swept under the carpet…his empathy for a man who had borrowed money, misguidedly, for a very worthwhile cause…

She'd had to stop herself from laughing out loud at the one hundred percent inaccurate and ridiculous picture she had painted of a man who was just the opposite of the one she had so feverishly described to her father.

The main thing was that her father no longer faced the threat of being thrown into prison. Also, her mother had been released from the hospital and was cheered by this change in their fortunes.

They were both so naive that Lucy could have wept, but she'd kept up the optimistic front and only sagged when she'd got to the station and bade farewell to her village for the weekend.

Details to finalise, she had told them, and then, to add credence to her story, she had hinted that she liked Gabriel more than she was letting on.

All in all she had given an award-winning performance. She hated herself for it, but her hands were tied.

Now she stared down at the overnight bag that was on the seat next to her. She was travelling first class at Gabriel's insistence. Well, it was preferable to the car he had offered to send for her, or the helicopter that he'd assured her would be no great trouble. She had explained a lot to her parents, but there was no way she could have explained a helicopter landing in the village square to collect her.

As soon as her eyes alighted on the overnight bag her pulses began to race and she had to lean back and briefly close her eyes. Tonight she should have been going to the movies with two of her girlfriends, who had now also been on the receiving end of a few white lies. Her life, which had been so uncomplicated before, now seemed to be comprised of a string of half-truths. She was an innocent little insect that had inadvertently strayed into a spider's web, and her every move ensured greater entrapment.

Gabriel had told her that a driver would be sent to collect her from the station. But she walked out into the blinding sunshine to see immediately that any prolonged period of reprieve was at an end—because Gabriel himself was there, casually dressed and looking ludicrously out of place amidst the banks of stressed-out, tired passengers leaving the station.

She couldn't fail to notice how many women looked at him. He, with arrogant indifference, appeared not to notice the attention he was getting. He was lounging against the railings, his eyes hidden behind dark sunglasses. Across the street she could see his black limo, parked and waiting.

Gabriel spotted her as soon as she walked out of the station and noted with dissatisfaction that she seemed to have gone to great pains to dress in the least flattering outfit conceivable. Not jeans this time, but combat trousers the colour of sludge and yet another T-shirt. The flat shoes had been replaced with trainers. He didn't think that he had ever gone out with or even personally known *any* woman who possessed a pair of trainers. As far as he was concerned that kind of footwear was suitable only for the gym.

Even disadvantaged by her poor choice of clothing, though, her beauty was still a source of radiance. Her impossibly long hair was back in its habitual braid, and once more his fingers itched to undo it. He smiled in pleasant anticipation of that event and headed in her direction.

Watching him approach, his body language a textbook lesson in cool self-assurance, Lucy resisted the temptation to turn tail and flee. He was truly breathtakingly sexy, and the closer he got to her the more he took her breath away.

The enormity of what lay ahead made her want to faint, but she kept moving forward, propelled by the meaning of the relief on her parents' faces when she had told them that their troubles might be over.

'Good trip?' Gabriel relieved her of her overnight bag and wondered whether it would be rude to ferry her immediately to Harrods so that everything she possessed—overnight bag included—could be replaced. He felt he might enjoy a ceremonial burning of her entire wardrobe.

'I didn't think you would be here to meet me. You said you'd be sending your driver....'

'I found that I couldn't wait…. You should be flattered.'

Lucy was making sure not to walk too close to him. She didn't want to be here at all, had been put in a position of having no choice, and she hated the strange effect he had on her. She would be facing bigger problems soon enough. Her nervous system deserved as much rest as it could get before those problems arose.

'Where are we going now?' she asked anxiously, stepping back as he opened the door of the car for her.

'I expect you're in need of a bath.' Gabriel waited until he was sitting next to her before he went on. 'Train journeys always have that effect on me.'

'Do you take many?'

She pressed herself against the door and Gabriel suppressed a stab of sheer annoyance. This wasn't what he was used to. Women didn't act disappointed when they saw him, and they didn't try to put distance between them. It was going to be a challenging weekend if she intended to scuttle around him like a terrified rabbit. He cheered up when he reminded himself that he had never been one to shy away from a challenge.

'Admittedly, no,' Gabriel conceded with an elegant shrug. 'I don't do delays, timetables or discomfort. We'll be going back to my place. You can have a bath. Freshen up…'

Lucy didn't want to dwell on any of those disconcerting things and rushed into hasty speech. 'I want to thank you for calling your people off Dad. He said that he's been told by them that charges aren't going to be pressed and he's very relieved.'

'I'm sure he is,' Gabriel responded smoothly. 'I would be, too, were I in his position. There can be nothing so worrying as a trip to a police station followed by a prison sentence. How did he take our little deal? I suppose, given the alternative, he wasn't overly bothered....'

'I didn't go into the details.' Lucy shot him a look of simmering resentment from under her lashes.

'That must have been difficult, given the circumstances. How many employers would have consent to overlook fraud?'

'I wish you'd stop calling it that.'

'If the cap fits... So, tell me how you managed to explain the terms of our arrangement...?'

Lucy guiltily thought of the way she had tiptoed around any difficult explanation through a mixture of practically turning Gabriel into some sort of earthly saint, filled with the milk of human kindness, and implying that she was girlishly attracted to him, thereby excusing any trips to London, should this crazy situation go past a single weekend.

'I...er...they were just so pleased that...er...'

'Getting the picture. Neither of them wanted to ask too many questions. Sometimes it's easier for people to skim over the details—especially when those details might force them to take a stand. I don't like you tying your hair back like that.'

'Sorry?'

'And I'm not entirely taken with your choice of clothing either....'

'These are the kind of clothes I wear....'

'And that's great when you're surrounded by plants, mud and soil, but when you're with me the surroundings will be vastly different and you'll be expected to look the part.'

'I've been meaning to have a little chat with you about... about that...' Lucy had never been so insulted before. Nor was she turned on by the prospect of being moulded into someone who *looked the part.* But staging an argument in her defence would require a lot of tact, because the inescapable truth *was* that he had bought her. And now he presumed that he had rights.

'About what?'

'This arrangement...how long do you think it's going to take?'

Once again Gabriel fought down his annoyance. Her dewy smooth skin, light gold from time spent outdoors in the summer months, was flushed. She looked like someone who, knowing that they had to stomach a dose of vile medicine, was keen to ascertain how much, *exactly*, they would be required to swallow. Did she have any idea of how insulting her evident reluctance was?

'How long is a piece of string?' He threw the unanswerable question back at her. 'And what makes you think,' he drawled, 'that you're going to be in a hurry for it to end?'

'Of course I am! I don't even want to *be* here. I'm only here because I have no choice! Why would I want this situation to last longer than necessary?'

'I can think of one or two scenarios...'

'That's because you're egotistical and you're accustomed to women fawning over you and wanting to be in your company!' She almost wept in frustration at the slow smile he gave her. She modulated her voice and tried to infuse calm into her overwrought body. 'I'm just asking because I can't keep taking weekends off. For starters I have a dog, and I can't fob him off on Mum and Dad every weekend. They're old. They don't want the responsibility. Plus I have friends, *a life*....'

'Too bad.' There was no point humouring her on this score, Gabriel reasoned. He wondered what this *life* that she was talking about consisted of. There was no boyfriend on the scene. Or was there? Had she said what she had wanted him to hear to save her skin? Or rather the skin of her parents? 'What's this *life* you're talking about?'

'Friends…'

'Any in particular? The boyfriend from two years ago may be happily shearing sheep in New Zealand, but I'm not going to be impressed if he's been replaced by someone else and you've diplomatically decided to keep him under wraps….'

Lucy wondered how many lies she had told so far. She was losing count. Very soon she would need a calculator to keep abreast.

'I'm referring to my girlfriends. We have an active social life back home.'

'Doing what?'

'Cinema…and we have supper at each other's houses… I just need to have some sort of idea of when my life will get back to normal!'

'I think it's best to work on the assumption that "normal" for you stopped the day your father got caught stealing from me,' Gabriel remarked drily.

Without her even noticing they had left the crowded streets around the station behind and were now in an exclusive residential area. For several long minutes she could only stare at the massive elegant houses set in a street unlike any she had ever seen in all her trips to London. There were no inconvenient pedestrians cluttering the pavements, no cars bumper to bumper, impatient to get to destinations unknown. These houses were clearly owned by people wealthy enough to ensure that serenity in the middle of one of the most vibrant cities in the world was guaranteed.

When his limo pulled up in front of the most impressive of the lot—a huge, white-fronted Georgian mansion nestled at the end of a peaceful, tree-lined street that ended in a cul-de-sac—it took Lucy a while to collect her thoughts and respond to the door that was being held open for her by his driver.

There surely could not have been a more effective way of underlining what he had said about her normal life being temporarily on hold.

No wonder he had made such a song and dance about her clothes! No wonder he had told her that in his world she would have to *look the part*! She felt as though she had gone from being in *Little House on the Prairie* to *Dallas*.

Her mouth went dry as they entered the mansion. There was a lot of marble. Cream marble shot with very pale pink on which sat silk rugs in muted colours with elaborate patterns. The paintings on the walls all looked vaguely familiar. If she didn't recognise some of them, she felt she ought to.

The door shut behind her and Lucy fell back in sheer terror.

'I don't belong here,' she said quickly, staring around and clutching her backpack in both her hands.

'Interestingly, that's not the reaction my house usually generates in women.'

Gabriel moved to stand in front of her with an amused expression softening the harsh contours of his face. Lucy stared up at him, her eyes huge and round.

'Generally speaking,' he expanded, shoving his hands in his pockets and grinning, 'there's a lot of *wow...what an incredible place...I can't believe this...*'

Lucy was held captive by that grin. There was so much unconscious charm in it that she felt she could understand why women fell at his feet. Naturally she was at pains to remind herself she was immune to anything like that, given the horror of the situation in which she found herself, but still...

'Why do you need something as big as this when there's only one of you…?' she asked inanely.

He seemed to find that even more hilarious.

'I don't need to. I choose to. There's a difference.'

The tone of his voice said it all. He was a man who got what he wanted. He might not *need* something, but if he *wanted* it then he got it. He didn't *need* her, but he *wanted* her—and he had found at his disposal the perfect means to achieve that. She was a commodity that he had procured through blackmail.

'You're spoiled rotten—do you know that?' she said, turning away and fumbling with her backpack, because a sudden wave of self-pity was bringing tears to her eyes and she would not allow herself to cry about this predicament.

'Come again?'

'You're like a *kid*!' Lucy shouted, staring him down. 'An over-indulged rich kid who points his finger and knows that he can have whatever he points at—even if it's not necessary, even if the thing he wants now, *right now*, will probably be tossed aside in a day's time!'

Gabriel was enraged that she should dare to say something like that to him. But her slender frame was trembling, and if she weren't clutching her backpack she would almost certainly have been throwing it at him. And all because he had thrown her thieving father a lifeline and brought her back to a house that had twice received offers to be placed in a glossy magazine!

'You've got me here! And you won't even have the decency to tell me when I'll be released!' she practically sobbed.

Gabriel fought to control his spiralling temper. He had never been a man to lose control. He also hated hysterics.

'I'll show you to the bathroom,' he gritted.

Lucy continued to look at him with unalloyed hostility.

Her hair was unravelling from its braid and her sea-green eyes were spitting fire. How was it that she was still managing to get to him? On the one hand there was a gentleness to her that was almost childlike. On the other he had never been in the presence of such a little hellcat in his life before. Her every emotion was swept to the surface and emerged undiluted by artifice. Was that why she had such an effect on him? Because she was so incredibly different from all the other women he had been with?

He spun round and began heading up the stairs. Lucy, for want of any other option, began following him. Her backpack was slung over one shoulder. Ahead, he was carrying her overnight bag.

The majestic staircase opened onto an exquisite landing. Here, the marble gave way to rich wooden flooring, and as they passed room after room she was privy to the sight of shutters, billowing voile, deep, rich drapes and yet more of those amazing silk rugs that were to be found on the ground floor.

He turned left and she almost collided into the back of him as she came to an abrupt halt in a bedroom. Like everything else in the house the scale of this room was eye-wateringly grand. Two enormous windows overlooked a large garden and they were dressed with deep burgundy drapes. The furniture was built in, so there were no bits of furniture to interrupt the open sweep of the room or to distract the attention from the massive, aggressively masculine bed that now stared at her with mocking triumph.

Lucy croaked and stared back at it. *His room.* The room she would be sharing. With him. The bed was big, but not so big that she would be able to partition herself away from his daunting body.

She wouldn't think about that yet. She would cross that bridge when she came to it.

'Is this the room I'll be sleeping in?' she asked, on the off-chance that this was a spare bedroom—one that coincidentally looked lived-in. By him.

'I'll run you a bath.'

Gabriel pushed open a concealed door and Lucy followed him towards a bathroom that was as big as the ground floor of her cottage. The bath was huge. To Lucy's dazed eyes it looked as though it could hold a football team. Big, fluffy towels hung on a heated towel rail and she stared at him as her mouth went dry.

'Thank you,' she squeaked. 'I can take things from here.'

'Relax,' Gabriel urged. 'Admittedly these circumstances are a bit on the unusual side, but let's not kid ourselves. We're attracted to one another. There's no reason why we shouldn't have fun....'

He curved his hand to the side of her head and Lucy stopped breathing altogether as he began stroking her face, running his thumb along her cheekbone.

'I'm *not* attracted to you. You've got it all wrong....'

Her voice faltered as he ran his thumb over her mouth. Of their own accord her lips parted and she found that she could barely catch her breath. Her breasts swelled, became sensitive. She was scarcely aware of him undoing her hair, and she was even less aware of him propelling her gently back until she was against the cool tiled wall.

'Don't talk,' Gabriel murmured. He slipped his hand under her T-shirt and those dangerously long, lean fingers travelled upwards until they found the soft cotton of her bra.

Lucy had felt nothing like this in her life before. She wasn't a prude. At college there had been boys interested in her. She had even gone out with two of them. But neither had tempted her beyond the stage of kissing and some fondling.

How did any of this make sense? her mind was screaming. How had those two boys at college she had really liked not been able to get past the starting post and yet Gabriel Diaz—a man she *disliked*, a man who had *blackmailed* her into his bedroom—was now having this electrifying effect on her, sending her body into terrifying, excited freefall?

When he unclasped her bra she moaned, and she moaned more as his big hand cupped her breast, as his fingers played with her erect nipple.

Gabriel felt the conflict in her. Her face was flushed, her eyes half closed. God, her body was setting him on fire. He was so aroused that it was painful. He pushed up the T-shirt and groaned in appreciation of her small breasts, their nipples two big, rosy discs, begging to be sucked.

He had never been one to lose control when it came to sex. However beautiful and desirable a woman, he had always been able to wait. Having sex up against a wall was for horny teenagers with libidos that needed to be brought into line.

God, where was his formidable self-control now? He hoisted her up in one easy movement, marvelling at how light she was, and there her nipples were, where they should be—by his mouth.

She straddled him, her arms loosely linked behind his head and her body as hot as a piece of toast. He blindly sought out those tempting peaks, clamping his mouth over one and suckling hard so that she was gasping and wriggling and moaning in his arms.

Crazy with sensation, and barely able to get her head round what was happening, Lucy was lost. The T-shirt had completely ridden up, as had her unclasped bra, and the sight of his dark head at her breasts was an amazing turn-on. Her body was alive. It had never felt so alive. Her jeans were a cumbersome hindrance that she wanted to kick off. Her underwear, the same sensible cotton as the bra, was damp, and through her jeans the pressure of his body between her legs was sending delicate but insistent shivers through her. She had an urgent need to move against him, harder and harder, until those shivers picked up pace.

She arched back and her eyes opened, looking past his head.

In a mirror that dominated the sand-coloured tiles on the wall opposite the face that stared back at her was a face she didn't recognise. Long blond hair hung in a tangled mane over her shoulders, her lips were swollen, her skin was flushed, as though she was in the grip of a terrible fever, and her eyes glittered with an excitement she had never seen in them in her life before.

It was a truly terrifying sight, and she began wriggling to be put down.

'Wha—?'

'Put me down! What are you *doing*?'

'What am *I* doing?'

It took a few seconds for her protests to get through to him. As soon as she was out of his arms she wrenched down the T-shirt and glared at him.

'You…you…' Lucy spluttered, and tried to think of some fitting put-down. But all she could see in her mind's eye was that disturbing vision of herself in the mirror. 'I want you to leave this bathroom *immediately*!'

'Stop playing games.' Gabriel caught her hand, forcing her to look up at him with glaring accusation. 'And stop kidding yourself that you want me to leave you alone.'

'I *do* want you to leave me alone! I'm not happy to be here and the last thing I need is for you to…to…think that you can just…*assault* me!'

'Be *very* careful how you use your words....'

Lucy stared at him mutely. She didn't understand what was going on. Her heart was thumping so hard she could feel it banging against her ribcage and her body was still throbbing from where it had been touched.

'This isn't me,' she whispered. 'I know what you want from me, but I'm not that kind of person....'

'You don't *think* you are.' He dropped her hand and stood back. 'I'll be waiting in the bedroom for you.'

Gabriel spun round on his heels and heard her lock the door behind him. *Assault?* Her use of that word was highly incendiary, and he was outraged that she could throw herself into the role of victim when not only was he doing her a favour but she had come to him with a smile on her face and a body that was giving off all the right signals.

His arousal was taking a long time to subside. He flung himself on the bed and watched the closed bathroom door with scowling intensity, waiting for it to open and giving himself time to cool down.

This was *not* the sort of situation he had envisaged. When he had tendered his offer he had imagined that she would be relieved—grateful and eager to do whatever he wanted. He had sidestepped her professed hesitation, barely giving it the time of day because he had known underneath all the wide eyes and the um-ing and ah-ing that she found him attractive. He had looked forward to a relationship in which there was mutual understanding and no unreasonable expectations of a happy-ever-after. They would have sex, and it would be an arrangement in which there would be profit on both sides.

For her, her father would walk free. For him, he would finally net the one woman who had escaped him, and the terms would not involve any fear on his part of her wanting any more than she was going to get.

He would never conceive of actually *buying* any woman. Why would he? But in this one instance he had been prepared to make an exception—and how was she reacting? With a ridiculous temper tantrum, insults, and a locked bathroom door. It made no sense to him. He was tempted to break down the door and physically show her just how self-deluded she was in imagining that her response just then had been the response of a woman who didn't want to be where she was. But breaking down bathroom doors would be taking things several steps too far.

He was beginning to rethink that decision when she eventually emerged, draped in his dressing gown that had been hanging on a hook behind the bathroom door. It swamped her. She had tried to keep her hair dry, but damp tendrils hung over her shoulders.

'My bag is on the bed,' Lucy muttered, going hot and cold and averting her eyes from the sight of him splayed with masculine abandon on the giant bed.

'If you're thinking of another pair of jeans, or more of those hideous trousers you were wearing earlier, then you might as well forget it.'

Quick as that, he had forgotten the foul mood into which he had been plunged by her incomprehensible behaviour. She looked good enough to eat, but he was going to make sure that she came to him now. *Begging.* Her pupils were dilated and her trembling hesitancy spoke volumes about a woman who was scared to get too close just in case she went up in flames again.

He liked the thought of being the man who could incite such contradictory responses in her. She could bare her claws all she wanted, and rant and rail about his terrible behaviour in taking advantage of the perilous situation with her father—but, hell, she *still* wanted him…she *still* couldn't help herself.

He felt himself stir as he continued to gaze at her rosy-cheeked face. He patted the space on the bed next to him and smiled.

'I want to get changed.'

'Feel free.' Gabriel relaxed a little more, folded his hands behind his head and followed with interest her reluctance to take him up on his offer.

Her bag was next to him. Lucy tentatively approached it, but as she was about to reach for it he got to her first and pulled her down towards him.

The robe fell open as she flopped on the bed next to him and he hissed long and low under his breath at the sight of those succulent little breasts with their rosy tips. His mind was galvanised into such graphic images that he clenched his jaw to stave off his erection getting out of hand.

There was a lot to be said for variety, he was discovering. His palate was a lot more jaded than he had originally thought!

'Gabriel…no!' Lucy scuttled away from him and clutched the robe around her tightly.

Gabriel sat up. 'I don't go for women who play games.'

'I'm *not* playing games. I *know* why I'm here. I *know* we have a deal and my half of the bargain is to…is to…'

'Lucy, it's no use coming over all girlish and pretending that I'm forcing you to do something you don't want to do.' Gabriel was determined to drag her kicking and screaming towards reality if it killed him. 'And I'm not going to be accused of *assaulting* you.'

'I'm sorry. It was wrong of me to say that.' Much as she might want to stick to that handy description, which would absolve her of all culpability in what had happened earlier in the bathroom, driving honesty compelled her to tell the truth—at least on that front. She closed her eyes briefly and drew in a deep, stabilising breath.

'Ah. So we're inching our way towards an understanding of what's going on here, are we? Slowly but surely you're beginning to wake up to the fact that our trade-off isn't the nightmare you keep telling yourself it is….'

He vaulted off the bed and paced the room. Lucy followed his prowling progress with feverish eyes. He dragged a stool from the window to the bed and settled on it.

'For as long as we're in a relationship you'll enjoy the fruits of my money, and it's not going to be torture. You're burning up for me—so get over your conscience and relax and enjoy what's on the table. You won't even be at my beck and call. You work with your plants during the week and I make sure that my weekends are kept free for you and you alone…suits me down to the ground…'

'I can't give you what you want….'

'You're already giving it to me. I haven't been so turned on by a woman in years…. In fact, I can't remember the last time I wanted to have a woman the second I laid eyes on her—but that's what you do to me. I took one look at you at the station and I would have had you in the back seat of my car if the windows had been blacked out….'

'You're just turned on because I didn't fall at your feet!'

'Who cares about the whys and wherefores?'

'*You* will. Because I'm a virgin….'

CHAPTER FOUR

GABRIEL LOOKED AT her for a few silent seconds, then he burst out laughing.

'Give me a break! Who are you trying to kid? And what leverage do you think a lie like that will give you? You've already got me to settle your father's debt…and I've already told you that while you're with me, you'll enjoy all the things money can buy…so why hold out for further prizes by telling me that you're a virgin?'

Lucy stared furiously at his smirking face. His entire speech made her feel cheap, but there was nothing else she could expect. Nor could she labour the point about it being hateful—not when she had willingly allowed him to touch her; not when her body had responded to that touch with the speed of dry tinder combusting.

'I'm not kidding.'

Gabriel's laughter died in his throat. His eyes skimmed her mutinous closed face and took in the earnestness of her expression. It was beyond belief, but *could* she be telling the truth?

'Of course you are. You're in your twenties…'

'I'm twenty-four—and don't tell me that I'm not telling the truth!' She shied away from the open incredulity in those fabulous, knowing dark eyes. She couldn't have picked a less worthy recipient of this incredibly personal truth, but it was something she couldn't hide from him. Sooner or later he would discover that she wasn't like those sophisticated, experienced women he had dated in the past.

'But how is this possible?' Gabriel was genuinely mystified and shocked to his core. 'You had a boyfriend...'

The mysterious and fictitious boyfriend! How many more times was he going to rear his ugly head? Lucy was sorely tempted to tell him the truth about that, but what would she say? That two years ago she had been so alarmed at Gabriel's aggressive approach that she had fabricated a boyfriend to get rid of him? How flattering was that going to be for a man like Gabriel? A man who enjoyed adulation and was accustomed to the world obeying his commands?

Furthermore, if he became angry enough would he withdraw the terms of his deal? Would her father be back where he had started?

'Er...'

'Don't tell me that the two of you just made do with holding hands and looking longingly into each other's eyes!' He gave a derisive bark of laughter.

'I know a man like you would never understand people who don't put sex at the top of the agenda....'

Gabriel could tell from the embarrassed blush spreading across her cheeks that she was telling the truth—and yet how could that be so? In an age where sex was everywhere, where no holds were barred, how could she have slipped through the net? Especially looking the way she did? Was it her background? He had no idea what her mother was like, or even if she *had* a mother. Had an unstable background with a con man for a father turned her into some kind of buttoned-up prude? And yet she had writhed and squirmed in his arms, had *wanted* to be touched and licked and teased....

'Stop looking at me like that.' Lucy was mortified. 'I'm going to get dressed.' She gathered her overnight back with a jerky movement and scuttled off the bed, still keeping her eyes firmly averted from his incredulous face.

Having just spent the better part of forty-five minutes in the bath, she didn't feel she could justify another forty-five minutes getting into jeans and a T-shirt—and what would be the point anyway? She would still emerge having to face the music....

He was standing by the window when she opened the bathroom door to the bedroom. His first words were, 'I think we should go downstairs...get something to drink...' Even as his mind was playing with the conundrum of a woman of twenty-four who was still a virgin, his eyes were absorbing the terrific sight of her with her hair hanging loose, framing her heart-shaped face in a way that made her look like a living, breathing doll.

Untouched. The thought of being the first man to have her was like a shot of adrenaline, firing his rampant libido. It was a turn-on like nothing in his life before.

'Yes. Of course.' Lucy couldn't look at him. What was he thinking? Maybe that he had purchased sub-standard wares? At great financial cost?

She followed him in subdued silence back down the impressive staircase and into a kitchen that was as expensive as the rest of the house. But she paid little attention to the gleaming speckled black counters and the range of high-tech gadgets and the massive American-style fridge that he was now opening to fetch a jug of fresh orange juice so that he could pour them both a glass.

'Aren't you going to say anything?' she asked eventually. She sat at the kitchen table—a marvel of slate and chrome—and finally stole a look at him from under her lashes.

'What I'd really like is to explore this relationship you had with your boyfriend…because it's not making sense. What kind of guy *was* he?'

'I honestly don't see the point of going into that.' Especially, she thought with a guilty flush, considering he had never even existed. He was now supposed to be in New Zealand. Would she be forced to concoct more information about when he had been living in England? Give him a name? An age? Hobbies?

'It was obviously a relationship that was doomed for disaster if you weren't attracted to one another.'

'I don't want to analyse that…it's over and done with… he's…er…living on the other side of the world now… with…from all accounts…a brand-new wife and a brand-new baby…'

'If you'd accepted my dinner date two years ago I guarantee you wouldn't now be a virgin.'

'You are *so* egotistical!' And yet she knew that he was right. Five seconds in his company was enough to convince her that he had what it took to blow any woman's firmly held principles sky-high. The man should come with a health warning attached.

'Maybe the guy got fed up waiting….' Gabriel didn't know why he was labouring the point. It irked him to imagine that she was perhaps pining for someone who had obviously not cared much for her if he had disappeared across the Atlantic and immediately hitched up with another woman.

'Maybe he did,' Lucy muttered.

'And it still bothers you…?'

She looked up at him, startled. Tempting though it was to expand further on a tale of lost love and broken hearts, she just couldn't do it. 'No,' she told him abruptly. 'What bothers me is not knowing what happens now.'

'What do you *think* happens now?'

'I wouldn't be asking if I knew. I just thought... I just felt it was fair...'

'I get that.' He was looking at her very carefully. Her shy withdrawals and blushing maidenly outrage now seemed to make more sense. He had come on strong and it was no wonder her instinct had been to take flight. 'What if I told you that I can be a very gentle, very tender lover.... I can touch you in a way that will make you open up to me like a flower....'

All those dormant feelings that he had awakened in the bathroom now began stirring back into life at his low, velvety drawl. Her body, once in physical deep freeze, held in storage for the right guy to come along and bring it to life, was making her question the value of preserving herself for someone she hadn't even met yet. Someone she might *never* meet—because who was to say there was a guarantee that there would *be* a Mr Right? She didn't know, and couldn't understand how it was that Mr Wrong could sabotage all her good intentions like this—but he could. Was it his experience? Did he just *know* how to touch a woman so that she stopped being able to think? Was it some special ability of his?

She allowed herself to think about him making love to her and excitement swelled with sudden explosive vigour inside her. The burning memory of his mouth clasped to her nipple sent her body into overdrive.

It would be the very opposite of everything she had ever believed in! Sex without love...in fact, sex without friendship or even passing affection! Did it get any worse? And yet...

She looked at him and his dark, lazy eyes consumed her. Her heart picked up speed.

'But of course I won't.'

'Huh?' Lucy snapped out of her erotic daydream and her mouth fell open in surprise.

'I need something a little stronger than a glass of orange juice.'

Gabriel strolled to the fridge to withdraw a bottle of wine and pour himself a glass. Lucy followed his every small movement with shameful, compulsive fascination. The elegant way he walked, as though he owned the space around him…the flex of muscle beneath his shirt…the strength of his forearms…the powerful width of his shoulders…

She hurriedly looked away as he resumed his seat opposite her. 'Um…you were saying…?' What *had* he been saying? It was impossible to register much when she had been so busy feasting her eyes on him.

'It's off.'

It took a few seconds for his words to sink in. 'What do you mean…? Are you telling me that the deal's off?'

'Regrettably. However tempting I find the notion of sleeping with a virgin…it wouldn't work for me…'

'But we made a deal…we had an arrangement…'

'Deals get broken. It's the way of the world.' Gabriel sipped his wine. His head was still cluttered with images of her underneath him. He would have to do something about that, and quickly.

Lucy sprang to her feet and began pacing the kitchen. She swept her hair back with one hand and finally stood in front of him.

Her body was supple and coltish, and Gabriel cursed himself for not having been able to see that it was also *untouched*. But, hell, how was he to have known?

Should he have explored that weird attraction she had held for him two years ago? How it was that she had lingered in his head long after she had so politely turned him down? And how it was that the notion of having her now, at all costs, had been so irresistible?

Should he somehow have concluded that, for a man as experienced and worldly-wise as he was, the only thing that could have made her stand out was her virginity? No. No sane man would ever have joined the dots and arrived at that conclusion. Virgins over eighteen were as rare as sightings of the dodo bird!

'And what does that mean for my dad?' she asked in a tight voice. 'I told him...' Her lower lip trembled and she bit on it.

'I am a man of honour,' Gabriel said wryly. 'Sit down. You look as though you're about to shatter into a million fragments.' He waited until she was seated, but she was still as tense as a bowstring, with her hands on her thighs and her back ramrod-straight. 'I told you that I would bail your father out and I will. I have already instructed my people to fill in the hole from my own private finances and to close the matter. There will be no record of what your father did. He's in the clear. I also told you that I would pay him off and I still intend to. All things considered, you might say that you've done damn well out of this. Your thieving father lives to steal another day and you don't even have to warm my bed for the favour....'

Lucy's mind had gone a complete blank. The only thing she was aware of was a searing sense of disappointment. It was crazy, but she felt *rejected*.

'You don't look overjoyed. I would expect you to be doing cartwheels round the kitchen at this point.'

'That's very...generous of you...' she said faintly.

'Isn't it?'

'But I don't understand...' She took a deep breath, wiped her clammy hands on her jeans. 'I never realised that being...inexperienced was so awful...'

As conversations went, this was not one for which Gabriel had ever rehearsed. He flushed darkly and wondered how it was that, despite being out of pocket, and with no means of recouping his lost funds, he was reduced to feeling *bad*. Her huge sea-green eyes were staring at him with such honest appeal that he just wanted to scoop her into his arms and show her that being a virgin counted for pretty much everything, that it was a prize for which any red-blooded male would give his eye teeth. Any red-blooded male except him, as it happened.

'This isn't about you,' he told her abruptly.

'If it's not about me, then who on earth is it about?'

'You should be happy. I've just let you off the hook. If you get your things together, I would be more than happy for my driver to return you to the station.'

'My ticket's for tomorrow.' Lucy said the first thing that came to her head. 'And, by the way, I'm very happy. I just wondered… I'm just curious…'

Gabriel vaulted out of his chair, debated whether to have another glass of fortifying wine, decided against it. Instead he helped himself to some water and drank the glass down in one gulp while he kept an eye on her.

'Look…' He sat back down but he felt uncomfortable in his own skin—restless, as though his body couldn't contain the levels of energy leaping through it.

He didn't do soul-searching conversations. There were some men who were good at that sort of thing. He wasn't one of them. But she was still staring at him with those big green eyes and there was no way that he could tell her that a woman just shouldn't ask that sort of question. It wasn't cool. Or maybe there were women who would. How would he know? He had never been in this position before.

'In case you haven't got the message yet, I'm not the kind of guy who's into commitment. I treat my women well…better than well…but I never encourage them to think that there's any more than what I'm prepared to give. You're inexperienced, Lucy. I may be many things, but I'm not into callously hurting girls just because I happen to be attracted to them and just because I can have them. Although…' he allowed himself a self-denigrating smile '…don't think you would be here now if, as you say, I hadn't used unnecessary coercion…'

'No.'

'I firmly believe that all's fair in love and war—but you're a virgin and you're therefore vulnerable. I don't need you getting in over your head.'

'I don't even *like* you. How would I be getting in over my head?'

'If you disliked me that much you would be running for the front door right now with your bags in your hand. I turn you on, and maybe you're a little curious to see where that leads, but there's too much scope for it to lead to places I have no intention of going.'

Lucy was distracted sufficiently to ask, 'You intend to stay a bachelor forever?'

'I prefer to think of it as the foreseeable future.' He shrugged, and a lifetime of cynicism was in that casual gesture. 'This is not something I share with very many people….' *None.* 'My father was married six times. He was the very opposite of a commitment-phobe. He embraced the institution of marriage with whole-hearted enthusiasm. It would have been commendable were it not for the fact that he also embraced infidelity with equal enthusiasm. He once tried to tell me that it was because *he loved women*….'

Gabriel gave a short, derisive, humourless laugh. 'I tend to see it rather differently. It's hard for that argument to carry weight when a man is compelled to marry his latest squeeze, only for that squeeze to be superceded by another model, all in the name of *love*. The marriages became hum-drum and routine…my father began getting itchy feet.' He hadn't meant to launch into a prolonged explanation along these lines, but she was listening so damn well, and the past was rushing up at him with such speed…

Well, what was the big deal in telling her this? he asked himself. It wasn't as though she was going to get any ideas…she wasn't going to see one confidence as a sign of greater things to come…

Moreover, he might not have instigated this situation from the purest of motives, but he *could* have just told her to leave without explanation. He could have sent her on her very fortunate, merry way with all those unanswered questions in her head. But had he? No. And wasn't that an indication of his upstanding nature?

'I suppose, on the plus side, I was the only child from all his careless philandering. Maybe somewhere the old man had a conscience after all.'

'You hated him?'

Gabriel looked at her with some surprise. 'Not at all. In his own way he was a very good father. He simply had no self-control. He was clever enough to set up a trust fund for me that he couldn't get into in his weaker moments. It enabled me to be educated abroad. It was a blessing, con-sidering the rest of his earnings invariably went on ali-mony. He had a good brain, and was a good entrepreneur, but he was always in a situation of *making ends meet* be-cause ex-wives can be costly.'

'And your mother?'

'My mother was one of his victims. Wife number three, as a matter of fact. It broke her heart when he went off her and began seeing wife-to-be number four. She never recovered from him and she died when I was eight, miserable and bitter.'

Lucy gasped and instinctively reached out to him.

'How awful.'

'It was a long time ago.'

'And what happened to you?'

'Oh, I lived with my father until he died, and I was subjected to three more stepmothers and intermittent spells of marital bliss followed by bitter wrangling. I should have hated the old man but I didn't. I learned from him. And here's the moral of what I'm telling you: you're vulnerable. You'll inevitably end up getting hurt. I won't be the one responsible. I learnt pretty young that if you want sex it's better to have it without any unrealistic expectations on either side.'

Lucy had the feeling that she was staring at someone who came from a different planet from hers. Her parents could not be more in love with one another. She cherished the dream of that happy-ever-after relationship while he derided it.

'Go and get your bag, Lucy.'

'My parents are expecting me to be in London for the weekend,' Lucy mumbled.

Plus, they were under the impression that she was *dating* Gabriel. They hadn't asked her whether she would be *sleeping* with him—they would trust her to be holding true to the principles they had instilled in her. Her friends also thought that she was on a date, of sorts. She couldn't face getting the evening train back… There would be humiliating questions that she would have to answer. She would be forced to say that they had broken up after only one date because…what…? He didn't like her? He found her company boring? Backward? Too rough around the edges?

At least if she stuck this weekend out she could maybe

do a couple more—visit London and stay somewhere cheap—at the end of which she would vaguely suggest that they hadn't hit it off after all.

But to return home after only a few hours...

'Well, I'm pretty sure they won't be disappointed to have you back home without having had to endure the un-savoury business of sleeping with their benefactor.'

'I...I think, actually, I might go and have a look around London. After all the effort to get here it seems a shame to waste my trip.'

'I would have thought it was anything *but* a wasted trip.'

'You know, I'd really like to explain about my fath—'

'Drop it. That's all history. I wasn't interested in hear-ing excuses then and I'm even less interested now.'

'It doesn't feel right to accept money from you—'

'Are you telling me that you would rather I held you captive here with no "release date", as you put it?'

'No, of course not!'

Gabriel was right. She had been given her ticket out, so why wasn't she running? Did it *matter* that her friends might ask a few questions about her early return? That her mother might wonder aloud why her so-called date had gone wrong? Her father had been bailed out and she had her precious virginity intact.

So why wasn't she shrieking with joy? Why was she harking back to those weird, wonderful things she had felt when he had touched her? Could it be that she had psyched herself up to sleeping with him and she was now in the grip of a puzzling anticlimax? Had she spent so much time being angry with him for making her pay a price that was so high for the favour he was bestowing on her that she had failed to recognise the very simple truth—which was that she was actually *turned on* by him? Against all odds? He was sexy beyond belief, and she was only human, after all.

Not to mention the fact that her lack of experience hadn't equipped her with the necessary weapons to withstand the onslaught of his blazing personality...

Now he was writing her off as an ill-judged mistake. He was a predator who had sized up his prey and homed in for the kill only to realise that the prey in question wasn't what he had had in mind after all. He was letting her go. She still had no idea what it was about her that had provoked him into giving her a second glance, but she did know that for Gabriel Diaz the sea was replete with fish. Lose one and there would be plenty others.

'Perhaps we could...do something...?' she suggested timidly. 'I mean...I don't suppose you made any plans for today...'

'You want to *do something*?' Gabriel raised his eyebrows disbelievingly. She was priceless. He had just dismissed her, having kindly pointed out her glaring limitations when it came to the role of mistress, and yet here she was, hesitantly asking if they could *do something*! 'Do what?'

'I've never really been to any of the sights in London...'

'Hang on a minute. I'm the arrogant bastard who blackmailed you into a position you supposedly hated, and yet now that you've been released from that position, you want to *hang around*? *Go sightseeing*? You have no idea what you're dealing with...'

'What *am* I dealing with?'

She couldn't control a wicked shiver of anticipation. She had been raised with all her moral values in place, raised on Sunday school and thank-you notes and Girl Guides. She had been raised to fall in love with one of life's good guys, get married, have babies and live in a cottage in the country. Gabriel Diaz was *not* a good guy. His values were all in the wrong places. He was unapologetically dangerous and he was warning her off him. She wasn't just playing with fire…she was walking into an open flame.

'I… It's okay… I'll get my stuff…'

She stood up, but he caught her wrist before she could turn away. 'I'll take you sightseeing.' Gabriel could feel the rapid beating of her pulse. This was not what he should be doing, but that hesitancy in her eyes, at war with the delicacy of her body and the innocence of her come-on, excited him. 'But make no mistake. If you find yourself out of your depth the time for rescue rafts will be over.'

'I've always wanted to go to Madame Tussauds.…'

At a little after six the perfect weather finally broke. They had had their fill of Madame Tussauds, but Lucy had barely taken anything in. All the time they had traipsed through the crowds she had been hyper-sensitive to the man next to her. She wondered what she was doing. She wasn't a *dangerous* kind of girl. The first time she had met him she had been confused and intimidated by the directness of his approach and had ducked for cover. So what was going on now?

She just knew that whenever she looked at him and saw the brooding intensity in his dark, fathomless eyes she couldn't contain the thrill of excitement that threaded its way through her veins like a toxic drug.

Apparently he had never taken a woman sightseeing before. But while she'd nervously chattered her way through the exhibitions, he'd drily provided historical detail to some of the wax figures. He seemed to know a vast amount of information. However successful he was when it came to making money, he was also obviously amazingly well read.

She'd asked him why he didn't enjoy just walking around London. He'd told her that it wasn't his thing. Every time they'd touched on anything remotely personal he'd made sure to send her a guarded warning that she should be careful.

Lucy's brain refused to register any of those warnings. She heard his voice and something in her melted. It was almost as if, under threat, she had responded with anger at his arrogance in bargaining with her body, but with the threat removed something strange, weirdly exciting and entirely unexpected had been allowed to rise to the surface.

After Madame Tussauds they'd had a very late lunch at a very expensive restaurant close to his house. She imagined that it was the sort of place he always took his women. Her jeans had not been remarked upon, but she knew that his wealth would allow him to go anywhere with anyone without question. He was someone to whom normal rules did not apply and he accepted that as his due.

They were leaving the restaurant when the heavens opened and the rain bucketed down with such unexpected force that there was no time to find shelter.

'How far are we from your house?' Lucy had to shout over the clatter of the raindrops slamming against the pavement and the buildings.

'Too far.' He held up one hand to hail a taxi and she impulsively reached across to stop him.

'It's warm. It's summer rain. We could make a dash for it....'

'Not going to happen.'

'Why? Is getting wet something you don't do either?'

Gabriel stared down into her green eyes. He hadn't always been wealthy beyond most people's wildest dreams. He hadn't always been able to snap his fingers and see the world drop at his feet. He'd had an uncomfortable child-hood, watching his mother get too fond of the bottle and then, later, before he was packed off to boarding school at the age of thirteen, hiding out in his bedroom, where the sounds of his father's latest disintegrating marriage couldn't be heard through headphones and loud music.

He had witnessed firsthand the effects of a marital break-up. The constant house-moves because ex-wives needed accommodating. Possessions that were there one minute and gone the next. He had determined that he would live his life differently. For starters, no addiction to walking down the aisle with anyone. For another thing, no fluctuating finances. Total control would be his driving force. He had become inured to the things he had striven to avoid, thanks to his considerable wealth, but now Lucy was staring up at him with just a hint of laughter in her eyes.

'You could always get your clothes dry-cleaned. Or you could get one of your lackeys to take them to the dry cleaner for you, if you don't do trips to dry cleaners...'

The rain continued to pour down on them. Gabriel conceded defeat. He nodded in the direction of his house. He had no intention of running, and he wished to God he had had the foresight to carry an umbrella with him, but still he got a kick watching her as she ran ahead of him, happily getting soaked to the skin.

She was waiting in front of the house when he got there, hopping from one foot to the other. Her hair hung around her in wet blond strands, clinging to her neck and back and arms. There was a flash of lightning and a crack of sharp, sudden thunder and he unlocked the front door and pushed it open to let her precede him.

She smelled of the rain. Even in London it was a clean, fresh smell that filled his nostrils like powerful incense.

Lucy felt goosebumps on her arms as he shut the heavy door behind them, sealing off the noisy clamour of the rain, which now became a muted background sound. It was cooler inside than it had been outside. She turned to him to find his dark eyes fastened on her—but he broke the spell by walking away, telling her over his shoulder that she would have to get changed.

Lucy felt wild and giddy, and her head was full to bursting with thoughts of Gabriel. He had no morals and was bitter beyond his years…he had an unshakeable belief that the only thing that mattered was money, that it was the currency for buying anything and anyone he wanted… He had tried to buy *her* and used the threat of prison for her father as leverage, and he had done it without a shadow of guilt or discomfort…. He was arrogant, and unapologetic about it….

On the other hand there was an integrity in his not assuming a right to her body when he had discovered that she had never slept with a man before…and there was decency in the fact that he had not reneged on his promise to bail her father out even though he had failed to get the exchange he had anticipated. Although his moral codes left a lot to be desired, and his aims in life were far removed from hers, weren't there extenuating circumstances? Hadn't his background made him the man he was? He was emotionally cold, and would never engage fully with a woman…but there had been humour when he had filled in the gaps in her knowledge of history, a spellbinding intelligence, and weren't those engaging qualities in themselves?

As long-term partners went, winning the lottery was a surer bet—but who wanted a long-term partner…?

And when had anyone ever made her feel like this in her life before?

She knew that was the million-dollar question that had been nagging away at the back of her mind. When she stopped telling herself how ridiculous it was to be attracted to a man like him there was a space in her head that was immediately filled with the memory of him holding her in the bathroom, kissing her, running his hands underneath her T-shirt while her body throbbed and vibrated like an engine revving to go.

'Why are you still standing out here?'

Lucy started and swivelled round to look at him. He was holding a mug of something hot and had removed his wet clothes. He was now in an old T-shirt and a pair of low-slung chinos and barefoot. There must be a laundry room nestled somewhere behind the kitchen, she thought, her heart beating fast.

'I…I was just about to go and get changed. I don't want to drip all over your expensive flooring…the rugs…I don't want to ruin them…'

'I think the expensive flooring and the soft furnishings will survive the experience,' Gabriel said drily.

She was looking at him the way a starving man might look at a banquet. Women looked at him. He was used to that. But he wasn't used to women looking at him as though they would give anything in the world *not* to. Lucy's gauche responses set alarm bells ringing in his head, but for once he was finding himself powerless to exercise the self-control on which he prided himself. Instead he was staring back at her—a long, lazy, assessing stare, his eyes roving with bold appreciation over the way her wet clothes were clinging to her body. He could see the definition of her bra underneath the T-shirt and he was overcome with craving—primitive, uncontrollable craving.

'You can look at me all you want,' Gabriel drawled, moving to lean idly against the doorframe, 'but the second you touch all bets are off.…'

'What do you mean?'

'You've had your freedom card. There are no more where that came from. I can only do Mr Nice Guy for a limited period of time, and the window on that is now closed. So stare all you want, but if you want more then you're going to have to play by my rules—and my rules don't apply to anyone who's looking for a safe harbour....'

He turned on his heel and headed back to the kitchen, and Lucy was left to consider what he had said—and to try and work out where the girl who had left her village and her safe life had disappeared to.

CHAPTER FIVE

'So, AM I going to get my driver to take you to the station? Ditch your ticket. It's easy enough for me to buy you a new one....'

Lucy had finally managed to locate Gabriel. He had migrated from the kitchen and his hot drink to the sitting room and a glass of deep red wine. She'd had to search a number of rooms before she found him, and now knew every room was decorated to the same high standard. It was an enormous house. She had no idea how many bathrooms and bedrooms were scattered over the top three floors, but on the ground floor alone there appeared to be a number of sitting areas, a vast conservatory overlooking a garden, and a study—and all this in addition to the kitchen and whatever else lay beyond it. Certainly the laundry room from which he had earlier extracted his change of clothing.

He was sprawled on a leather sofa, nursing his drink, with his laptop flipped open on the low glass coffee table in front of him. He looked cool, composed, effortlessly elegant.

Lucy, who had planned on coming to London with the least flattering clothes she possessed—because why on earth should she make an effort when she was obeying orders under duress?—felt instantly inadequate. He had mentioned disliking her combat trousers, so those had been priority items when she had packed. Her T-shirts were loose and faded, and her trainers, she had fondly imagined, would be handy should she feel the need to run very fast in the opposite direction.

She hadn't banked on getting here and finding all her preconceived notions turned on their head.

'Well?' Gabriel sipped his wine and looked at her over the rim of his glass. He had no intention of helping her out on this score. He wasn't going to ease her into his bed, he wasn't going to tempt her, and he certainly wasn't going to give her any excuse for turning on him and accusing him, for a second time, of assaulting her. That gross exaggeration still stuck in his throat. But with unerring instinct he knew that to someone like Lucy freedom of choice would be the most difficult path. He also knew that it would get him what he wanted—and he wanted *her*.

With all his conditional clauses in place, and his provisos, warnings and barriers in full working order, he looked forward to the sweetest of conquests.

So he didn't rush her into a decision. He just kept his eyes on her, noting her fluctuations of colour and her awkward, hovering stance by the door.

'Perhaps I could stay the night.' Lucy wondered whether she had committed to sleeping with him by saying that and felt inclined to backtrack, but she held her ground.

This was all so crazy, but once she had taken it on board—once she had given house room to the reality that she was violently, helplessly attracted to him—she had squashed all her girlish ideals and succumbed to the most wonderful feeling of liberation.

'In that case let me get you a drink.'

'I don't usually…'

'I'm getting the picture that there are a lot of things that you *don't usually…*' There was a concealed drinks cabinet in the sitting room and he poured her some wine and then sat back down. 'And you can stop standing by the door like a scared rabbit….'

'What did you see in me?'

'Come again?'

'What did you see in me? I mean…two years ago…and now…what did you see in me?'

'You have a habit of asking the most unnerving questions,' Gabriel murmured, watching as she primly sat on one of the chairs facing him and wondering when she would get up the courage to actually enter his radius. She was so unlike the confident, pushy women he associated with—women who would have removed his drink from his hand a long time ago and walked him up the stairs, making it perfectly clear where they wanted the evening to end.

'I'm just curious. I know you don't like the stuff I wear…'

'What man would? I like to see my women in dresses.' He pictured that slender, eye-catching, lightly tanned body in something small and revealing and decided that the thought didn't appeal. 'Floaty affairs. Long.'

'Really? Because those pictures on the internet of you with your dates…well, they were all incredibly…er…underdressed…'

'How long did you spend gazing at me on your computer?'

'Not long!'

Gabriel shrugged, but he was smiling. 'I was attracted to your lack of artifice. I spotted that as soon as I laid eyes on you on that bike. No make-up, wind in your hair, glowing. I liked that trait then and I like it now. I don't meet many women who are natural and straightforward…'

He had a way of looking at her that was as erotic as a physical caress.

'I mean,' he expanded, 'you ask questions other women would shy away from. And you blush. That rates as a virtually extinct art form.'

'So you're attracted to me because I'm a novelty...?'

Gabriel frowned. 'Where are you going with this line of questioning?'

'It's important for me to know how the ground lies.'

'Does it matter why I'm attracted to you? I just am. In fact, I'd much rather you were sitting here next to me instead of over there, but I'm not about to push you into anything. Believe me, if I thought you could handle me then we wouldn't be having this conversation, and we wouldn't be sitting on two chairs like a couple of strangers making small talk.'

'But we *are* a couple of strangers...'

'That's a situation I would have remedied the second you got off the train.'

Gabriel's way of thinking was clearly alien to Lucy. He had no interest in getting to know her. He would chat to her, but his primary interest was making love. Everything else around that main event would be of little concern to him. He was drawn to her because she was different from what he was used to. How different he had only just discovered. Had he known at the time, he wouldn't have made the mistake of pursuing her. No make-up and wind in her hair was very different from *virginal*.

'Someone doesn't stop being a stranger because you sleep with them....'

'Possibly not, but it's a start....'

He sent her a slow, wolfish grin that made her tummy flip over and turned her even breathing into a sharp, breathless pant.

'And when do you start getting bored?'

Lucy felt as though she was tiptoeing round him, trying to find a way into that complex mind that thought so differently from hers. He had explained his reasons for avoiding commitment, but he had spoken so dispassionately that he might have been talking about someone else and not himself. She wondered whether she would really and truly be able to take on a man as impenetrable as Gabriel, but even as she was asking herself the question her responsive body was supplying the answer.

'You sound like an interviewer. I know you're in new terrain here, but loosen up. I can't tell you when I start getting bored with a woman! How would any man be able to answer a question like that? All I can do is repeat what I've told you before. I have ground rules, and I suppose when a woman—any woman—starts thinking that she can stray over the boundaries I usually see fit to call it a day.'

Looking at him, Lucy felt that it was important for her to hear all this. Sleeping around was nothing for Gabriel, and he sought out women who shared his approach. But for Lucy sleeping with Gabriel would be a big deal. She would be acting completely out of character, allowing a physical side to her she had never suspected existed to take precedence over logic and reason. If he had his ground and his boundary lines then it was important for her to recognise that—just as it was important for her to let him know her feelings on the matter.

She couldn't believe that she was thinking like this. She had always assumed that she would only ever be attracted to a man for whom she had strong feelings; and it was unsettling to accept that attraction could have laws of its own that had little or nothing to do with feelings and emotions. It was just pure luck that it was a discovery that she hadn't made earlier.

'And too many women do,' Gabriel admitted heavily. 'Despite the fact that I'm perfectly honest at the onset of any relationship. Sooner or later there's a tendency for them to become clingy and demanding.'

'How awful for you.'

Gabriel looked at her narrowly. 'Am I detecting some sarcasm there?'

'Not at all. It must be difficult when you're so clear about what you *don't* want a woman to be....'

Gabriel threw her a slashing smile that reminded her why she was in this position now, helplessly treading water in the face of his potent masculine charisma.

'Amongst other things, this is part of your appeal,' he continued huskily, watching her carefully with those clever dark eyes.

'What do you mean?'

'You don't have any pointless girlish fantasies about me. You've seen me for what I am since the very second I made you that offer you couldn't refuse. There's no chance that you're going to go romantic on me. There's no chance that you're going to suddenly decide that you want to hear the sound of wedding bells. You're not going to be tempted into thinking that you can change me. Call me selfish, but I like all of that.'

Lucy barely recognised herself in his description. She had *always* had dreams of wedding bells, and she was a fully signed-up member of the romantic club, but she could see where he was going. He had approached her in a manner that left no illusions, and she had made it clear to him that she didn't like him—so if they ended up in bed together it would literally be a case of sexual attraction minus anything else. It would be the ultimate no-strings-attached affair.

She was shocked at the heady sense of power that simple

recognition invested her with. In a very brief space of time his powerful sex appeal and the open invitation in his lazy, assessing eyes had combined to chip away at her resolve.

'You're right. I don't like you....' Although with some confusion she recalled that there had been times during their day spent sightseeing when he had made her laugh and she had completely forgotten the angst that had been her companion on the train to London. She sidelined that thought with a little frown.

'It's so refreshing the way you speak your mind,' Gabriel drawled. 'I've never been in the company of a woman who doesn't think twice about being offensive.'

Sitting on the sofa while she occupied the chair opposite was getting to him. Especially when he knew where they would be ending up. It was like being invited to sit at a table groaning with food and knowing that you couldn't touch a thing... *yet*. The anticipation was killing him. He was a man who took what he wanted and had never been made to wait. Patience was not his middle name, and that had served him well in all his dealings to strike while the iron was hot.

'I don't see myself as an offensive person,' Lucy said slowly.

Gabriel drummed his fingers restlessly on his thigh and toyed with the idea of putting an end to the chat by hauling her over his shoulder and carrying her upstairs to his bedroom.

'Why don't you like me?' he heard himself ask, and winced at the crassness of the question—because other people's opinions of him were irrelevant as far as he was concerned. Instead of prolonging the conversation he should be moving up a gear and heading the chat in the right direction.

'Why do you think?'

'My approach may have been a little unorthodox, but that aside…'

Lucy looked at his perfectly serious face and wanted to burst out laughing. She had noticed during the course of the day that he had a unique way of dealing with people and with situations. He didn't analyse them and nor did he see any failings in his direct approach to getting what he wanted. He had told her in passing that he had once gone to see a movie—which seemed to be a rare event for him—and, not wanting to share the theatre with anyone else, had simply solved the problem by buying all the seats and ensuring complete privacy for himself and whatever woman he had on his arm at the time.

When she had told him that normal people didn't do stuff like that, he had shrugged and said, 'Why not? Makes sense as far as I'm concerned.'

'You're too cold,' Lucy explained, thinking hard, her brow pleated into a small frown. 'Too removed, too insensitive to other people…'

'Enough! I disagree with you on all fronts, but I'm not about to have an argument. Was your ex-boyfriend warm and engaging? A good cook? He couldn't have been that exciting if you never managed to make it past the bedroom door.'

Colour flooded Lucy's cheeks but she held her ground. The ex-boyfriend might not have existed, but *no one* had made it past her bedroom door. 'That's why I don't understand how…why I'm still here,' she confessed honestly. 'I mean…'

Gabriel held up one hand, because he had a feeling where this was going. 'I think I'm about to be treated to another rambling description of everything you dislike about me and I'm tired of talking.' He sat back and stretched his arm along the back of the sofa.

'What do you want to do?'

'I think we both know what I want to do—just like we both know what *you* want to do. So instead of spending the next three hours trying to work out the *whys* let's just cut to the chase.'

He didn't make a move towards her. He just kept her pinned to the spot until she forged a trembling path towards him.

'Don't forget,' Gabriel murmured softly, 'you leave your overactive conscience behind the second you enter my bedroom....'

Lucy nodded.

'And relax.' He smiled crookedly. 'Trust me.'

He reached out and ran one lean finger along her clenched fist. A series of mini-explosions detonated in her. Arousal as fierce as it was sudden slammed into her with the terrifying force of a runaway train.

She followed him in a trance up the stairs to his bedroom—the very same bedroom that she had earlier regarded with such trepidation, when she had thought that she might be sharing that king-sized bed with him, a prisoner of circumstance.

'You're doing that scared rabbit thing again....' Gabriel edged her away from the bedroom door and led her very gently towards a big window that overlooked his back garden. 'What do you think?' He could feel the slight but unmistakable tremor running through her slender body like quicksilver and he raised his hand to massage the back of her neck gently, underneath the thick sweep of her hair.

Lucy stared down at a small but impressive garden, beautifully landscaped and not overlooked. The warmth of his hand on her neck was just right, putting her at ease. 'I prefer the garden to the house.'

'I have no idea what plants are out there. I handed the

whole job over to professionals when I moved here five years ago.'

'That's very lazy.'

'Maybe if I'd known you at the time you could have come and sorted it all out for me. I would have enjoyed watching you in a little pair of shorts and a T-shirt out there....'

He turned her to face him and her heart skipped a beat as she looked up into his dark, beautiful face.

'I wouldn't have enjoyed being watched.' She had never been drawn to dressing up to attract the attention of men. She had always left that to her more flamboyant friends. She enjoyed hearing about their escapades but it wasn't for her. She wondered if that was a legacy of having much older, quieter parents.

Gabriel wondered whether that accounted for the boyfriend running to New Zealand to bond with sheep. He relished the challenge of teaching her to enjoy *him* watching her.

He circled her waist under the T-shirt, and as his hands drifted higher he could feel the rapid beat of her heart under her ribcage. There was nothing voluptuous or overt about her, and her slim body was a joy to touch. The thought of some of his thrusting, busty girlfriends, with their smouldering mascara-heavy eyes and their lacy leave-nothing-to-the-imagination underwear, was vaguely distasteful.

He kept his eyes fixed on her spectacularly pretty, fresh face as his fingers came into contact with her bra. He skimmed two fingers under the top of each cup, tracing a delicate line down to her nipples, and his groin was aching as her eyes fluttered and she breathed in sharply.

Without moving away, he slowly unclasped the bra. Lucy moaned softly and allowed him to strip her gently of the T-shirt and then of her bra. She closed her eyes when she was half undressed, her breasts bared for his inspection.

'You have beautiful breasts,' Gabriel rasped huskily.

'They're too small.'

'They're perfect.' He cupped them and massaged them gently. He wasn't going to rush. 'It would be nice if you opened your eyes.'

Lucy peeped at him. This wasn't the arrogant, super-rich, super-confident guy who had so alarmed her two years ago, and nor was he the manipulative tyrant who had so angered her when he had thrown down his gauntlet and forced her into a deal she resented. This was someone smiling and putting her at ease, keeping his eyes pinned to hers while he continued to caress her breasts until she began finding it difficult to catch her breath.

He edged her towards his bed and then stood back so that he could remove his shirt. Lucy teetered back a few steps, bumped into the base of the bed and fell onto the soft, silky duvet. She looked compulsively at the broad, hard expanse of his chest—not smooth and hairless, like the boys she had known, but roughened with dark hair. A man's chest. She propped herself up on her elbows. So what if she was staring? She couldn't help herself. He was magnificent. How could she restrain herself from greedily devouring the sight?

He hooked his fingers over the waistband of his chinos and tugged them slightly down, so that she could see the defined muscles of his pelvis, the narrowness of his waist. He must work out like a demon, she thought in a daze, and if he didn't then he had been unfairly blessed.

She looked as if she'd forgotten that she was half clothed, her breasts pointed up at him. Her rosebud nipples were a massive turn-on, and Gabriel hesitated to strip completely naked. He was not in the slightest self-conscious of his body, but would his erection spook her?

'I enjoy you watching me like this,' he murmured, moving towards her on the bed.

Lucy smiled. His eyes glittered with dark, rampant appreciation and she felt a sudden sense of heady power. It was nothing like she had ever felt in her life before. She *wanted* to throw off the rest of her clothes and let him touch her all over. She remembered how she had burned for him in the bathroom, before she had backed away, and she wanted that burning again.

Had she really been saving herself for the right guy? Or had she just never been turned on enough actually to make it to bed with anyone? That was the question playing at the back of her mind as he loomed over her before bending down to unzip her trousers.

'I hate these trousers....'

'I know.' Lucy shot him a sheepish smile and lowered her eyes. 'That's why I brought them with me.'

'Did you think that if you dressed badly enough I might be put off wanting to haul you into my arms and carry you off to my bed like a caveman?'

'Something like that.'

'It wouldn't have worked. Unfortunately there's nothing you could ever wear that would have that effect on me. But I'd still like to see you in a dress....'

The trousers were now off, and Gabriel's mouth twitched in amusement at her functional cotton underwear—the sort of underwear that was sold in packets of six from a department store and definitely not the kind that any woman he had dated would have been caught dead wearing.

She was so damned fresh and innocent that he felt a moment of passionate wanting to lock her away in a tower, where no one could lay eyes on her but him. That sudden rush of unexpected possessiveness took him by surprise and he quickly shoved it away, ruthlessly stamping on feelings he neither wanted nor needed.

Lucy lay back. She had released her very long hair and it fanned out around her in a blaze of golden blond, startling against the backdrop of the dark silk duvet cover.

She knew she should be feeling shy, rushing to cover her body, but she wasn't. The opposite. She felt wonderfully brazen. It was something to do with the way he was looking at her—as if she was a delicate morsel he wanted to devour. It was the most amazing experience, and she smiled drowsily at him.

She had no idea how beautiful she was, Gabriel thought. His keen eyes noted the dusting of freckles on her collarbone, the tiny mole by her left breast, the perfect delineation of her nipples. Her stomach was flat and smooth and he could see her hip bones. Once again he wondered what he had ever found appealing in heavy, big breasts and sultry, rounded curves. Lucy's body was slender, but strong from all the outdoor work she did. She led a healthy lifestyle and it showed in her toned, graceful physique.

He gently began pulling down the unappealing underwear and his breathing became unusually laboured as he took in the dark blond, downy curls slanting between her thighs.

'Look at me when I touch you,' he commanded gruffly, then gave her a crooked smile that could have melted a block of ice. 'I want to find out what you like….'

Lucy imagined that she might like everything he did to her. She was loving the way he was simply looking at her now. She desperately wanted him to be as naked as she was, and yet something deep inside her was telling her that he had deliberately left his trousers on so that he could continue to put her at her ease.

She sighed as he moved over her, propping himself up on his hands so that he could stare down at her flushed face. When she raised her arms to wind them around his neck he gently but firmly laid them back at her sides, before bending so that he could lavish his attention on her breasts.

He had died and gone to heaven. Every twitch of her body was an indication of her arousal. It took fierce concentration to keep to what he was doing when he wanted to thrust into her and satisfy the growing ache in his groin.

He clasped her hands in his and licked the stiffened buds of her nipples, teasing them alternately with his tongue. He was getting more and more turned on by her cries and moans and the way she writhed under him, begging for more, and then gasping that she couldn't stand it any longer.

Her nipples were shiny and wet from his mouth and his tongue. Her eyes flickered open as he drew back, and then widened when he reached behind him and gently cupped the feminine mound between her legs before easing his fingers into the slippery moistness that was eagerly awaiting his touch.

'Do you like this?' He found the aroused bud and teased it with his finger, watched the rosy blush that invaded her cheeks.

'Gabriel...' she moaned.

'Have you been touched like this before?' Crazy question, but he really wanted to know—and when she shook her head he couldn't contain the soaring triumph that ripped through him. On and on he continued to rub that small throbbing peak. He knew just when to ease the maddening caress of his fingers and when to pick up the tempo so that her body began to spasm.

She could have wept with frustration when he stopped

so that he could kiss her stomach, move down to her belly button and then…down to that most intimate of places. She was well beyond any inhibition. She let him ease her legs apart and arched back to accommodate his darting, exploring tongue, which was finding the place that turned her on and lathering attention on it.

She curled her fingers into his hair and loosened her legs wider. She had never thought her body was capable of being so exquisitely tortured. His tongue against her was sending her spiralling higher and higher, and yet still he wouldn't let her reach the final climax. She was completely at his mercy, wanting him to take her wholly. She wanted him to fill her and she was shocked at her own driving need.

She was not at all intimidated when he eventually pulled back and removed the rest of his clothes. She wanted to touch his impressive arousal. She watched as he donned protection, but she hardly had time to scramble onto her elbows before he had resumed his position over her. He nudged at her gently, edging himself into her dampness, telling her not to tense and smoothing over her natural inclination to stiffen up.

He was unbelievably tender, moving slowly, letting her relax. Only when he began pushing harder into her did she cry out, but the instant was lost as sensations began driving through her—wonderful sensations as his manhood pressed into her. He thrust deeper and harder and she melted, abandoning herself to wave upon wave of pleasure until she was exhausted.

Gabriel was on a high such as he had never known before. He had had lovers who were experienced in the art of doing anything in any position, and yet he couldn't recall ever having this feeling of soaring satisfaction as he climaxed.

'Bloody hell,' he growled, subsiding against her on the bed. 'That was…incredible…'

Lucy sighed and curled against him. She still couldn't quite believe that she had jumped from one extreme to the other in the blink of an eye. The girl who had so resentfully left Somerset was not the girl on this bed now. How had that happened? How could sexual attraction be so persuasive and so instant? How could it drive you in one direction even though your mind was telling you to run fast in the other?

She rested her hand on his chest and he covered her hand with his, turned onto his side so that he was facing her.

'So…' Gabriel couldn't get enough of her smooth, soft, supple body. Her nipple was peeping out at him beneath the crook of her arm and he knew he could have made love to her all over again. But it seemed inappropriate, given the circumstances. Was she sore? Tender down there? His hand itched to tease her slowly back into a state of readiness for him.

'So…?'

'You took a circuitous route to get where I wanted you to be from the start….'

Lucy blushed. 'I…I'm not sure how all this has happened…' she confessed. 'When I got on that train I thought that if we ended up in bed it would be…'

'A nightmare?'

'Something like that.'

'You underestimate the power of sex.'

Lucy opened her mouth to protest but decided that she didn't have a leg to stand on.

'So what happens now?' she asked with a little frown. 'I mean…now that we've slept together…does that mean…?'

'That the debt's been paid?'

Lucy nodded. She felt a sense of clammy dismay that he might now get rid of her, having had his fill. She suspected that at the back of his mind the challenge of having a woman who had once turned him down had been irresistible. With that challenge no longer there, would he still be driven to sleep with her? It would pay her to remind herself that he could have anyone—why would he choose *her* when her novelty value had already been lost?

Her body was already missing the feel of his in anticipation of being told that she had fulfilled her part of the contract.

'Your father *did* embezzle from my company…and he most certainly *would* have served jail time—so, no… You might have a little way to go with that deal we made…'

He ran his hand along her waist and then over her thigh, where his lazy, circular, feathery light touch had the intended effect of making her body liquefy.

'Sorry to disappoint you…but you're *not* disappointed, are you? You had your chance to bolt and you turned it down…' It was a richly satisfying thought.

'You're very egotistical,' Lucy said truthfully.

'I just enjoy getting what I want—and what I still want for the foreseeable future is…*you*…' He slipped two fingers into the dampness between her thighs and kept his eyes firmly glued to hers. 'It's gratifying to know that the feeling's mutual.…'

Lucy knew that she should feel degraded and angry—but she didn't. In fact, the only thing she felt was turned on. She closed her eyes and parted her mouth as he began to stroke the tight raised bud of her clitoris.

She was so wonderfully responsive! Gabriel couldn't conceive that she might consider one night full and final payment!

She climaxed with soft moans and was embarrassed

when she opened her eyes to find him looking at her with a half-smile.

'Sorry,' she mumbled. 'That wasn't satisfying for you.'

'You'd be surprised… I'm a generous kind of guy. I like giving pleasure. But right now I think it might be a good idea for us to get showered, and then we can do a little more sightseeing before we have dinner somewhere.'

'I haven't brought any clothes to wear out.'

'In which case, we can do our sightseeing at Selfridges. Lots of clothes there. I don't do shopping with women, but I feel I could get a kick out of buying clothes for you.'

'I'm sorry, I can't accept that.'

'Come again?'

'I don't want you buying anything for me.' Was that because she wanted to kid herself that she hadn't been bought? Lucy thought with consternation. Did she want to read more into this than there really was because that way she could make sense of her inability to control her rebellious body?

'There's not a woman on this planet who doesn't like having things bought for them.' He traced the outline of one pert nipple and watched as it tightened and reacted to his touch. 'You'll find me a generous lover in more ways than one. For as long as we're together, whatever you want will be yours.'

At that moment Lucy imagined that he could have talked her into anything. He had taken her body to places of unimaginable delight. He had made her aware of lust as something wildly beyond control. But somehow the thought of having clothes and jewellery and *whatever she wanted* bought for her made her feel sick.

'No, Gabriel.'

Gabriel looked at her, startled.

'When this is all…finished…I don't want to think that I owe you anything.'

'That's not what it would be about—'

'It would be—for me. The only time I would ever accept gifts from a guy is from a guy I love.'

Her mouth was a stubborn line and he shook his head with incomprehension and impatience. From the very start he had seen the advantages of bedding a woman he fancied without any of the complications that usually arose. He had envisaged a relationship based on sex alone, and here she was offering him just the no-strings-attached liaison he wanted. So why was he feeling annoyed?

He reminded himself that she was his, that she had come to him of her own free will, and he relaxed.

'We'll see…' he murmured. 'Now, let's go have a shower—or else I'm going to have to do a bit more than pleasure you with my fingers, and right now I don't think you're up to taking me…are you?'

'Maybe not *right* now.'

'Shame. But by tonight I think we'll both be ready.'

'Yes.' She blushed fiery pink, but why pretend otherwise? She might be a little tender now, but already she couldn't wait for them to be back in this bedroom—for him to be making love to her again…and again…and again…

CHAPTER SIX

LUCY WASN'T ENTIRELY sure when lust started becoming something much more dangerously significant.

She had entered Gabriel's exotic and rarefied world a little over four months ago. After that first weekend they had established a pattern of weekend visits. On her insistence, she was always the one who made the trip up to London to see him.

Several times he had asked her to stay over on the Sunday night, and it had taken real effort on her part not to cave in. But she knew, with gut instinct that caving in was something *all* his women would have done. It was what he would expect of them. She had stood firm, however, because she had her job to consider, and she wasn't about to start fooling around with that just because Gabriel Diaz crooked his finger and worked his magic.

Twice he had unexpectedly phoned her at work and told her that he had to see her—that he would drive down, that he couldn't focus when all he could think about was getting rid of her clothes and taking her....

She had stood firm on that as well, even though just hearing the urgency in his deep, dark voice had filled her body with a wild, throbbing need.

'I hope you're not doing this because you think that playing hard to get will hold my interest,' he had drawled just a couple of weeks ago, when yet again she had antagonised him by telling him that she didn't want him visiting her.

Lucy had vigorously denied any such thing. Did he really think she was that silly? There were so many ways he had of reminding her that he wasn't in it for the long haul. He wasn't even aware of how glaringly clear he was on the subject.

On more than one occasion he had told her that he never, ever forgot to use protection because the last thing he would want was to find himself trapped in the unwanted role of father. He had firmly closed the door on all discussion to do with her family. He wasn't interested in any personal baggage she might be carrying—especially if it involved something as distasteful as a crooked father. That was a side to her of which he wanted no reminders. For him, she existed exclusively in the realms of sex and desire. Anything else was a distraction and an annoyance.

And yet over time they'd laughed, they'd talked, they'd shared opinions. She teased him about his inability to do anything in the kitchen and he kept trying to buy her clothes—which she refused. She now had a couple more dresses to call her own, and even a pair of boots that were not, strictly speaking, functional. They protected her feet from the cold—and it was certainly getting cold now, as winter began to replace what had been a mild autumn—but with heels at over three inches high walking was often a challenge.

Should she have been more aware of the signs that what she was feeling went beyond sex? When should it have occurred to her that she was living from Monday to Friday afternoon in a state of barely suppressed excitement at the prospect of seeing him? That this was not healthy? When should she have stopped pretending that good sex was something non-addictive and that it never led anywhere? How could she have been so stupid as not to realise that making love and falling in love were two sides of the same coin? At least for the sort of person *she* was?

And now here she was, with the train pulling in to London and a magazine in front of her that was a cruel reminder of how stupid she had been.

Lucy had picked the magazine up at the newsstand at the station because she had got there way too early and had forgotten to pack her usual reading fodder for the journey. It was one of those weekly glossies that she never usually read, but she had found herself leafing through it with considerable enjoyment until she came to the centre spread, which was essentially a series of photos taken at the latest prominent society do—in this case the glitzy opening of an art gallery in Canary Wharf. Everyone in the pictures seemed to have a drink in their hand, and were schmoozing with other well-known personalities.

She hadn't expected to see Gabriel in those pictures. He wasn't just in one picture. He was in eight pictures. It was as if the cameraman hadn't been able to get enough of him.

As the train stopped and everyone began the unsteady process of gathering their belongings, eager to clear off, Lucy cast a fulminating glance at the magazine she had stuffed in the netting on the back of the seat in front of her. The instant she had seen those photos she had determined to put them out of her mind. She and Gabriel were not tied to one another. He was a free man and could do whatever he wanted to do!

And yet…

She fetched the magazine back from the resting place to which it had been consigned, hating herself for her masochistic weakness.

It was cold outside.

Gabriel had been remarkably consistent in making sure never to arrange anything that might interrupt one of their weekends. Lucy took a pull-along case with her clothes inside and returned to her house with every stitch of clothing still in it. Few women had ever stayed the night with him, he had admitted early in their relationship. She was the exception. Lucy knew better than to take advantage of that by leaving a wardrobe of clothes behind her, and nor did she want to. She had changed from the young innocent he had first met. Now she had a much more highly developed sense of self-protection.

She glanced at the magazine in her hand and winced. Clearly not *that* developed, or she wouldn't now be feeling as though her heart was forcibly being ripped from her body.

Usually Gabriel accompanied his driver to meet her at the station, and the thrill she felt whenever she laid eyes on him lounging against his car, waiting for her, had not diminished over time. Right now she needed to give herself a few moments to get her thoughts together, so she headed for the nearest bench and sat on it while the crowds surged around her. Against her will, she flattened out that horrid page on her lap and stared.

Gabriel, with the obligatory champagne flute in one hand and a sultry, sexy brunette laughing up at him. The same sultry, sexy brunette was in all the pictures with him, in a tight, tight dress and high, high heels. She had lots and lots of rippling dark hair, and what really shook Lucy was how *good* they looked together. Dark, arresting beauty matching dark, arresting beauty. The camera loved them both.

Had Gabriel complied so willingly to her insistence that they only meet at weekends because it suited him that way? She couldn't get her head round the thought that there might be another woman in his life. Surely she couldn't be so mistaken about someone's personality? She hated herself for even thinking that she was sharing him with someone else, that she couldn't trust him, and yet…

He didn't care about her. Not really. He certainly didn't envisage any sort of long-term relationship. He had made it clear from the very beginning that he wasn't a man into commitment, that he was repulsed by needy, clingy women….

And for a man who was not emotionally tied in any way wouldn't it be easy and tempting to take what was on offer and see no problem in it? Wouldn't exclusivity be something that just didn't exist in his world the way it did in hers?

He was waiting impatiently for her outside, but as soon as he spotted her slight figure emerging from the station Gabriel felt himself relax. He had to suppress a smile at the sight of her waterproof jacket flapping in the wind.

She had indulged in a couple of new items of clothing over the months they had been seeing each other, but she never looked truly comfortable in anything that was fancy. She had proudly donned this new jacket for him a couple of weeks ago, and he had refrained from telling her that the fashionable length and the very attractive belt that she could pull tight to accentuate a waist that was a handspan were sadly diminished by the multitude of pockets—most of which were unnecessary—that turned the jacket into a fashion disaster. When she told him where she bought it he had tried not to wince.

The truth was that the more he saw her, the less he could picture her in anything but clothes in which she felt comfortable—although that didn't mean that he intended giving up on trying to buy her a new wardrobe. The most she would allow him to buy for her was a meal, and even then he always got the feeling that she would rather be staying put or, when it had been warmer, dragging him to picnics in the park, where she'd insisted on getting him on a bike before enjoying lunches she'd enthusiastically prepared herself, despite his protests that he could have the whole thing fully catered—right down to bringing a butler to help.

'You're late. I was beginning to get worried.'

Lucy looked vaguely up at him and saw a laughing man with a champagne flute in his hand and a sexy brunette at his side.

'I…I thought I'd forgotten something on the train and I had to dash back inside to have a look.'

'And had you?' He couldn't wait. He tipped her face up and kissed her with a distinctly uncool lack of restraint.

Every single thought instantly flew out of Lucy's head. Her body reacted as it always did—with a surge of pure, undiluted longing.

'You have no idea how much I've been wanting to do that,' Gabriel said gruffly.

And have you done that? was Lucy's thought. *With another woman? A dark-haired curvy woman with huge breasts and big hair…?*

She didn't want to be thinking these thoughts. She desperately wanted to be the liberated, carefree woman he thought she was—a woman who was as uninvolved as he was, apart from the sex angle—but the thoughts still kept filtering through her brain.

'I'd planned on taking you to one of the top restaurants in the country.' He opened the door and then settled down in the back seat alongside her, leaving his driver to deal with her overnight bag. 'But I'm thinking that a night in might be altogether more enjoyable.'

He couldn't keep his hands off her. Once or twice he

had paused to ponder this interesting phenomenon, because no woman had had that effect on him before, but his pondering never lasted longer than a few seconds. He was well trained in only accepting the facts that fitted in with his life plan.

'I think I'd prefer to eat out,' Lucy told him with a forced smile. 'But not at one of those restaurants with fancy menus and dishes with names I have to ask the head waiter to translate.'

'It's their job. They don't mind.' He grinned at her. 'In fact, it probably makes their day when someone asks them to explain in English what there's no need to say in French.'

'Except no one does, do they?' Lucy muttered, trying and failing to drag herself out of the gloomy vortex into which her thoughts were heading. She laboured the point, her face averted because one look at him and she would be reduced to drowning all over again. 'I mean the people who go to restaurants like those all *know* what the stuff on the menu means. They're well travelled. They don't have to ask for help.'

'What's got into you?'

'Nothing's got into me. I'm just saying.'

'Where would you like to go?'

'Oh, let's just stay in,' she conceded in an abrupt turn-around, because even though she was busily lecturing herself on the stupidity of saying anything—anything *at all*—about those pictures in the trashy magazine she had only glimpsed *accidentally*, in her heart she knew that she would. And a scene in a restaurant would be much more embarrassing than a scene inside his house.

Although restaurants weren't furnished with king-sized beds and baths that could comfortably hold two...

Restaurants also didn't come with scope for her falling into his arms at the slightest opportunity.

Like right now, when he was lightly tickling her wrist on that very sensitive bit that he knew she loved. She couldn't move her hand any more than a chained man could run a marathon.

'Good,' Gabriel said with satisfaction. 'It's been a long week, and I'm in urgent need of just the kind of relaxation only you can provide.'

'It's always sex with you, isn't it, Gabriel?'

'Okay. So now I'm thinking that there's something wrong. Did that fool deliver the wrong plant order?'

'No, that was all fine.' It was brought home to her just how much he knew about the daily workings of her life. He often telephoned, and she would chatter merrily away. She loved the sound of his voice, and yet…how much did *she* know about the daily workings of *his* life? She definitely hadn't known about any openings of art galleries!

'Then do you want to tell me what's bugging you, or shall we go round and round in circles till we get to my place?' Whatever was on her mind, Gabriel was supremely confident that he would be able to sort it out. She had a gratifying respect for what he said, just so long as he didn't touch on the subject of her attire.

'I'm just tired.'

'Easily sorted. I have just the remedy for that.' He shut the partition between himself and his driver and turned to her.

'Gabriel, no! You can't…people can see right in!'

'It's dark outside. An advantage of the days getting shorter. And we're not stuck in traffic.'

God, he wanted her. It was the same every weekend. He just couldn't wait. But never before had he felt the overwhelming need to touch her before they'd even made it to the house. He peeled aside the lapels of her coat and slipped his hand underneath the various layers of thermal vest and jumper to tease his way under the stretchy bra.

'I loathe it when you wear a bra,' he growled softly.

'I thought you loathed it when I went without one....' She curled her fingers into his dark hair and rested back as he pushed up her clothes and the bra in one easy movement, so that one breast offered itself to his searching mouth. When he latched onto her nipple with a low moan of contentment she couldn't stop herself from wriggling lower in the seat.

It was mind-blowingly erotic to watch him through lowered lashes as he suckled hard on her nipple, drawing it into his mouth and sending piercing arrows of pleasure through her. As always, just with one touch, her body was screaming out for more.

As the car purred into the cul de sac he reluctantly detached himself from her breast, neatly pulled her clothes back down and grinned.

'You taste like heaven....' This was so much more effective than talking sometimes.... 'One of these days we're going to go on a drive, park in an isolated lay-by somewhere and I'm going to make love to you very thoroughly in the back seat of this car.... I'm going to start with your mouth, and then I'm going to move to your breasts, and by the time I get to...'

'Shh!' Her face was bright red, and the worrying thoughts that had been her companions on the train were temporarily displaced by images of him doing those things to her in the back seat of his car.

'Let's get you inside. I'll order something for us to eat later.'

He was an irresistible force, and she was as powerless in the face of it as a matchstick being swept along on a wild, torrential river.

By now she was familiar with his house and no longer over-awed at its size and opulence. She knew its layout intimately, and so she knew where they were going as soon as he branched off to the left.

His study was one of the rooms in his house that she loved the most. Unlike the rest of the rooms, most of which she privately found lacking in soul, the study was warm and decorated in deep colours. The Persian carpet was all faded rich reds and burgundies, the velvet drapes that pooled on the ground were of a similarly dark maroon colour, and the desk was a huge mahogany antique. To one side a low, comfortable sofa had been positioned for those times, Gabriel had told her, when he wanted to work through the night with only occasional interruptions for sleep.

They made it to the sofa in a state of semi-undress, having left a trail of discarded clothing *en route*.

'We'll have to dispense with the foreplay just this once,' Gabriel husked. 'I can't wait.'

His impressive steel erection pressed against her thigh as he quickly disposed of her pants.

Lucy moaned her assent. These were the only times when she saw him stripped of his self-control and she loved it. She loved the heady feeling of knowing that she and only she had insight into the real man behind the cool mask of power and assurance.

But was she really the only one privileged to see that?

That sudden disconcerting thought came like a fast ball out of nowhere and hit her for six—but already he was edging her legs apart and the thought was disappearing as quickly as it had come.

He drove into her and she cried out with pleasure. When he withdrew to ram into her with yet more force, sinking his shaft to the very hilt, she crooked her legs over his back and was carried away on a tide of shockingly erotic ecstasy as he kept thrusting, pushing her back on the sofa, pinching her nipples as she arched up to heighten the wild sensations.

She was carried away with primitive, elemental lust. It emptied her head of all thought, swept aside the dimensions of space and time…

Only afterwards, when they had both surfaced from their lovemaking, did the questions begin again, nibbling away at the back of her mind with sharp little rat's teeth.

He was sprawled on the sofa, the very picture of the Lord of the Manor whose needs had been met, and Lucy pushed herself up to clamber over him.

'Where are you going?' Gabriel asked with lazy amusement. He propped himself up on his elbow and savoured her nudity. 'Good luck locating all your clothes. I think if you follow the trail you'll probably get to the first item we discarded when we walked through the front door.'

He reluctantly followed her out of the room, watching as she scooped up underwear in one place, her jeans somewhere else, all the way until she was clutching the last item and heading up the stairs. He thought that she moved like a dancer, lithe and graceful.

Lucy was screamingly aware of his eyes on her behind, and she hurried up the stairs—only to spin round at the top and ask in a rush, 'So…I never asked…how was *your* week?'

The question took him by surprise. 'My week was fine—and yours?' He dealt her a smile of pure amusement.

'You know how my week was. You telephoned and I told you all about it.'

'The business with the plant order…that illustration that's giving you trouble…Martha the landscape gardener who's having an affair with John the other landscape gardener on the team… Oh, yes—so you did…'

'It's all very boring, isn't it?' Lucy sniped back.

Now she felt ashamed that she had flung herself into bed with him when she had all these ugly doubts at the back of her mind. Had she no pride? Could it be undone so easily with a few caresses? She was desperate not to let those pictures get to her, to give him the benefit of the doubt, but was that because she really and truly believed that he would never cheat on her? Or because the thought of having to deal with something that might end up in a place she didn't want scared the living daylights out of her?

'What's got into you?'

Lucy didn't trust herself to answer. She spun round and flew down the marble corridor, with its silk rugs and the perfectly positioned chaise longue, towards his bedroom, where she proceeded to fling her holdall into the bathroom and slam the door behind her, making sure to lock it. Many a time, her bath had been interrupted by him, and they had ended up doing things to each other that would have made her hair curl six months ago. Right now, she just wanted to *think*.

She ran a bath and let her body relax in the bubbles. So she had gone and fallen in love with him, she thought bitterly. Well, she was on a learning curve now, and the first thing she would have to master was the art of not melting the second he laid a finger on her. He would surely be able to talk his way out of the sexy brunette, and he would probably be telling the truth, but from now on she would have to start pulling back. The longer she remained with him, floating in this vacuum where any future together was a subject that was strictly off-limits, the more she would be hurt when they inevitably broke up.

He was clothed and on the bed when she emerged into the bedroom, his dark eyes watchful.

'I'm listening,' Gabriel said bluntly.

'I just think we need to talk.'

'We talk a lot.'

'*I* talk a lot. I tell you all about my dull life at the garden centre. Since when are you *really* interested in plants and flowers and landscape gardeners having flings?' She paced the room, only pausing to throw him a frowning look from under her lashes. She could have added that he wasn't interested in her family...that he had practically banned any talk about that...

'I'm interested because you're interested,' Gabriel said shortly.

'Not good enough, Gabriel. And I don't want to talk to you here.' She hesitated when he continued to look at her coolly, without moving a muscle. He would be hating this—but tough. 'There's something I want to show you.'

'Just tell me where this is leading, Lucy, and spare me the dramatics.'

'I'm not being dramatic.' She felt like a piece of elastic, stretched to breaking point, and it was really hard looking at him because she was so aware of how weak she was in his company. She went to her holdall, in which she had stuck the glossy magazine, and pulled it out. The backs of her eyes stung with unshed tears as she smoothed out the centre spread and walked over to the bed with it.

'What's this?' Gabriel slung his legs over the side of the bed and walked over to the window with the magazine.

She was fighting to hold back tears. He could see that. There was nothing he disliked more than a weeping woman, and he fought off the unusual temptation to pull her to him and let her cry. He realised that he didn't like thinking of her unhappy. She so seldom was. He glanced down at the coloured pictures and then stopped to look a little more carefully at the pictures of him, taken by one of the snap-happy photographers who had been milling at that art gallery like parasites.

'Well?' Lucy was stunned when he casually stretched out his hand to return the magazine to her. 'Aren't you going to say anything?'

'What's there to say?' He threw the magazine onto the chair when she failed to take it and strode towards her. 'Since when have you started reading rubbish like that? I'm disappointed. I thought you had better taste.'

'It's not a matter of taste, Gabriel. You're missing the point!'

'And what *is* the point?'

'You never mentioned a word about any art gallery opening! You never said a thing about going there with some…some…woman…'

'I didn't think I had to give you a minute-by-minute explanation of what I do during the week!'

'That's not what I'm saying at all!'

'No? It sounds that way to me,' Gabriel said coolly. He had never tolerated having his movements questioned and he wasn't about to start now. 'Look how worked up you are! Let's go downstairs—get some food, have something to drink. You're making a mountain out of a molehill.' As conciliatory gestures went that was as good as it got—and it was considerably more than he had ever offered any other woman.

Lucy's heart was beating furiously as they went back down the stairs. He hadn't even seen fit to explain those pictures and she was tormented by what his silence on the subject meant. A part of her wished that she had never mentioned anything at all, and she had to will herself into acknowledging that it never paid to duck reality.

She accepted a glass of wine and listened to him in dull silence as he ordered food in from his caterers.

'How am I making a mountain out of a molehill?' she asked shakily. 'Who was that woman? Are you involved with her?'

'That's an outrageous question!'

'No, it's not.' Lucy dug in her heels and stared down at the kitchen counter. She was grasping the stem of her wine glass so tightly that it might shatter. 'It's a perfectly normal question, Gabriel, and you're blind if you don't see that.'

She raised troubled deep-green eyes to him and he was skewered to the spot. How *dare* she question his integrity? He absolutely refused to be buttonholed into an explanation about nothing!

'We're supposed to be going out together…' Lucy forged ahead in the face of his ominous silence. 'And yet you can't even tell me who that woman is—or else you won't…'

'I refuse to explain myself and that's the end of the matter.'

'Does that mean that you'd prefer not to have an exclusive relationship?'

'No comment.'

'In other words you wouldn't mind if *I* decided to see someone on the side? You wouldn't mind if you discovered that I'd been seeing someone on the side all along? While we've been sleeping together? You'd think that was perfectly all right?'

'Are you?' Gabriel asked in a dangerously soft voice. He was not prepared to yield on this matter even though he was well aware of his double standards—because if he *ever* found out that she had been playing around behind his back…

'If you can't be open and honest and straightforward

with me, then why should I be open and honest and straightforward with you?'

'You knew the kind of man I was before we got into this.' Gabriel raked his fingers through his hair and glowered darkly at her. 'No ties—and that includes not having to justify what I do or don't do. That said, I'm prepared to tell you that the woman in the pictures is just someone I met there. She decided to follow me around, which I found frankly irritating.'

Lucy released a long sigh of relief. But now her thoughts had started moving in another direction, and once embarked on that course they were running wildly out of control.

So he didn't know that woman, and they hadn't slept together. But for him nothing had changed from that very first time they had made love. Emotionally, he had progressed no further—while she had fallen hopelessly in love with him. Seeing him in those shots had brought that home to her very clearly indeed. No ties, no silly dreams. She'd known what she was getting into. With those words he had intended to make it obvious where he stood on her getting any more ideas about questioning his movements.

'So, are we all done with this?'

Lucy shrugged even while she continued to labour the point furiously in her head.

'And I'm taking it that all that nonsense about other men was just your emotions talking…?'

'Yes. I suppose so.'

Gabriel looked at her narrowly. *I suppose so? What the hell did that mean?* Truthfully, though, he knew that she would never fool around behind his back, and he was reluctant to prolong the conversation now that the flashpoint had been averted. In future he would try to be a bit more revealing about what he did from one day to the next. It was a small thing, and it would stop this sort of situation arising again.

'So…dinner in?'

He was back to normal, but Lucy had little appetite for the fabulous meal that was delivered to the door forty-five minutes later. She picked at her sea bass and asked him about the art show—what he had seen, who had been there.

'Next time come with me.' Gabriel had noted her lack of appetite and was prepared to make more concessions. 'You can discover first-hand how deadly some of these things can be.'

'Not my thing. Besides, getting time off work would be difficult.'

'They never give you holidays?' He idly wondered whether it might be a good idea to take her somewhere on holiday. Somewhere hot. Maybe over the Christmas period.

They never spoke about her parents. He had issued a blanket ban on that thorny subject, which could only lead to pointless disagreement, but was she close to them? Would she want to spend Christmas with them? Was that possible? Surely not… After all, what sort of parents gave their daughter the go-ahead to sleep with a man for the sake of a bail-out? Not that he was complaining. She had exceeded expectations when it came to pleasing him. Time was passing and so far the usual stirrings of restlessness that afflicted all his relationships with women were noticeably absent. That said something.

'I would never fit in to those sorts of things, Gabriel. I'm not interested in networking with celebrities and important people I don't know. Life is much safer with my plants.'

'Safer doesn't necessarily mean better.' Gabriel was irritated by her contrary stance. She was usually so obliging, but she had obviously got a bee in her bonnet over the whole art show debacle and was taking her time to regain her easy humour.

Safer means better for me...

That realisation filled her with hot dismay. Not so long ago, when she had kidded herself that she was as nonchalant about their relationship as he was, she had been eager to throw herself into the exciting, dangerous world of being Gabriel Diaz's mistress. She had felt as though for the first time she was really *living*.

Now she was slowly realising that, like some of those wildly beautiful and exotic flowers in the hothouse, Gabriel came with thorns—and his were deadly.

For once she wasn't on red-hot alert for bed. She couldn't face following that train of thought down to its inevitable conclusion so she kept the conversation going, finding more and more things to talk about, until Gabriel looked at her wryly and asked her if she thought she might run out of steam any time soon.

'I can't do this any longer, Gabriel.' She was so shocked at what she had said that she put her hand over her mouth and felt her skin crawl with discomfort.

'Do what? Carry on talking? Then let's go to bed.' He knew it was not what she meant, but he deliberately pretended to misunderstand as an antidote to the sudden flare of panic that had left him feeling a little sick.

'I think we should call it a day.'

'Because of a bloody art show? I told you—I don't even know who that woman was. Was it *my* fault that I couldn't shake her?' When she failed to respond he stood up and began pacing the kitchen. 'You don't mean this.' He leaned over her, caging her in. 'I know you don't. I can see it in your eyes. I could take you right here, right now, if I put my mind to it.'

'I'm sure you could,' Lucy said shakily, 'because I just

lose control when I'm around you. But it wouldn't mean that I'd change my mind. You're not good for me.'

'I've been faithful. I haven't once thought of another woman!'

'I'm really tired.'

'You're blowing one lousy art show out of all proportion!'

'Maybe, but I just want to go to sleep—and not with you. I'd rather sleep in one of the spare rooms.' She suddenly knew that if he was next to her she would just give in again, because she was like an addict—weak. And what he offered was too powerful, too irresistible.

Gabriel thought quickly. She was so rarely emotional. If she needed to sleep on her own—well, he would give her space. She would be fine in the morning. Forcing her to concede now how crazy she was being would most probably backfire on him, whereas she would wake up refreshed in the morning, they would make love, and things would be back on track.

'Your choice.' He hated the thought of it, and even giving in to her request was like swallowing acid.

'I'm sorry.'

'Just get a good night's sleep,' he said quickly, to dispel the finality he heard in her voice. 'Things always look better in the morning, and you'll realise that this is all nonsense. You have nothing to worry about. You're the only woman I want.'

He had to stop himself from physically barring her way as she walked towards the door. He had to tell himself firmly that he was way too disciplined to chase her—and besides, there was no need, because everything would be back to normal in the morning.

CHAPTER SEVEN

GABRIEL STARED OUT of his office window. He was unaware of what was happening outside. There could have been a carnival parade in the streets below for all he cared. Nor was he any more focused on what was happening in his own office. He was aware that he was functioning below par—that he had delegated too many meetings to his directors, had been mentally absent at those meetings he *had* attended.

But the past four days had been tough.

He still couldn't believe that he had been dumped. Yes, Lucy had gone to sleep in a separate room and, yes, she hadn't been in the best of moods, but it had still come as a sickening shock when the following morning, at a little after eight-thirty, he had opened the door to the guest room to find that she and her holdall were no longer in residence.

He should have gone in earlier. It wasn't as though he hadn't been up. He shouldn't have killed time having that shower, giving her a bit more space before he took back control of the situation. In fact, he shouldn't have let her sleep in that guest room at all. If she had been at his side, in his bed where she belonged, she would never have walked out on him!

Hard on the heels of all those frustrating thoughts came the bracing conviction that it was all for the best. All those

questions about what he had been up to and with whom…
they'd indicated a neediness he despised. He wasn't in
the market for being tied down! She had overstepped the
boundaries. It was *good* that she was no longer around!
He'd had a narrow escape from a woman who had become
too demanding. He could move on now. The world was
full of women!

He buzzed Nicolette in and she entered with a distinctly
wary expression.

'I'll be out for the rest of the day,' Gabriel informed her
as he began putting on the coat he had slung over his chair.

'Any instructions?'

'Yes—make sure I'm not disturbed.'

'And what about your meeting with the lawyers from
Martins?'

Gabriel looked at her impassively. 'Rearrange. Just
make sure I get no calls. If some of these guys can't handle emergencies in my absence then they don't deserve
the ludicrously over-inflated salaries they're being paid.'

'When will you be back?' Nicolette hoped that he would
take as long as he saw fit and return in less of a foul mood.
Walking on eggshells was beginning to get trying.

'I'll be back when I'm back. I'll pick up my voicemail
and my emails but I'm counting on you to make sure no
one gets through to me.'

For the first time in four days Gabriel was beginning to
feel good. Hell, he was well rid of any woman who started
trying to tie him down, but damn if she was going to get
away with leaving without an explanation that made sense!
He'd treated her fairly, hadn't he? More than fairly, in fact,
and no one could deny that she had come with a price on
her very pretty head. Had he forced her into a deal against
her will? No. The second she had told him that she was a
virgin he had been the perfect gentleman and had backed

off, *still* sticking to his half of the bargain and bailing out her thieving father.

It incensed him to think that his magnanimity had been repaid with her walking out on him without even so much as the courtesy of a note!

It made complete sense that he should want to drive down to Somerset and demand a full explanation face-to-face...the explanation that she had obviously been too cowardly to provide when she had chosen to slink out of his house, *out of his life*, without a backward glance!

There was a bounce in his step as he left the building half an hour later, and he was positively relaxed once in his car, with the radio on, his mobile switched off and his driver given the day off to do whatever he liked to do. Experiment with food, if Gabriel's memory served him right.

He had no intention of taking Lucy back, even if she begged. No, he would just demand an explanation for her irrational behaviour, give her a robust piece of his mind and then he would leave—although the thought of her begging was distinctly satisfying, and it pleasurably occupied his mind for a great deal of the journey.

Lucy locked her front door behind her with a sinking heart. She had dragged out her chores for as long as she possibly could, including walking Freddy. She had also cooked a dessert to take to her parents, and wasted time decorating it with pointless swirls of cream that she knew they would both scrape away for health reasons.

But now she couldn't put off the moment any longer. They had asked her over to dinner and there were things that needed to be said. Including...

She glanced down at her finger, where the tawdry engagement ring she had purchased the weekend before gleamed accusingly in the darkness.

It was only right and proper that a situation that had commenced in a welter of little white lies should end the same way.

Her parents had been pleased when she had begun seeing Gabriel. It hadn't crossed their minds that their relationship was one that was travelling down a one-way street, and she had been loath to break it to them. Why destroy their illusions? she had asked herself guiltily. Now, in retrospect, she could see that she had been nurturing a little seed of hope that had whispered *Who knows? Maybe something will come of it...*

But over the past few weeks they had begun to express curiosity as to where it was all going. They had tactfully skirted round the acknowledgement that she was sleeping with him, but had suggested, with an equal amount of tact, that surely a decent, honourable man who was sleeping with their precious daughter would by now be showing some concrete sign that he was serious about the relationship....

So she had got herself engaged.

Lucy dithered in the cold and then took a deep breath as she began walking towards her car.

Why had she told her parents that she was engaged? It had been just another crazy decision in a long line of crazy decisions that had begun the moment Gabriel Diaz had entered her life. But it had calmed their anxieties and that had been good—because Lucy lived with the constant unspoken dread that her mother might end back up in hospital if she became too stressed or anxious.

Well, now she had to unengage herself, and she wasn't looking forward to the process.

She was about to climb into the driver's seat when a car came pelting down the lane that led to her cottage.

She could hardly make out the shape of it because the

lane was quite unlit. It screeched to a halt, blocking her in, and her mouth fell open just as she was about to lay into whatever maniac was behind the wheel.

Even in the dark it was impossible to miss Gabriel's long, lean silhouette as he slung himself out of his sports car and strode towards her. He was danger personified and Lucy fell back, her mouth still inelegantly open in shock.

'What are you doing here?' she whispered as he neared her.

She had spent the past few days hoping and praying that he would chase her, and then hoping and praying that he wouldn't, and now that he was actually here, standing in front of her like a dark, avenging angel, her bones felt as though they had turned to water.

'You walked out on me.' Five words spoken with grim, merciless accusation.

'That was *days* ago….' Except, having blurted that out, Lucy now realised how plaintive it sounded—as though she had been expecting him to be in touch sooner. 'And… and I don't want you here…I'm…just about to go out, as you can see…'

'You're not going anywhere till we've talked.' He glanced across to his car. 'Unless, of course, you can walk to your destination. In which case, you'll have me for company all the way.'

'You can't do that! And there's nothing to talk about. I said everything I had to say.'

'Why did you run away? Couldn't you face me?' He strolled up to the front door and waited for her.

She couldn't get anywhere—not unless she could work a minor miracle with her car and three-point turns.

Lucy had broken out in a fine film of nervous perspiration. How could she explain that she hadn't been able to face him because he had such a powerful hold over her?

That in her heart she suspected that he could talk her into doing whatever he wanted, however strong her objections? That she had to protect herself because she had been stupid enough to fall in love with him?

'I have to make a call,' she muttered, her nerves jumping all over the place as she pushed open the front door and hurriedly made a hushed call to her mother, telling her that she might be a little late for dinner.

'Something's come up,' she whispered *sotto voce*, while Gabriel breathed down her neck. She concluded the call before her mother could launch into a series of worried questions.

'You bet something's come up,' Gabriel ground out as he followed her into the sitting room. 'Who were you on the phone to?'

'No one.' She spun round to face him. She did her utmost to take a determined stance, but the second her eyes fell on that magnificently, darkly brooding face all her determination seemed to turn to dust and her mouth went dry.

Gabriel picked up on her every emotion with the accuracy of a jungle cat sensing its prey. He shoved his hands into his pockets and strolled towards her, noting the way she had frozen to the spot, the way her pupils were dilated, the pallor of her face that made that little line of freckles across the bridge of her nose really stand out.

She had flown out of his house under cover of darkness but he could still take her right here, right now, if he wanted to. It was something he just *knew*.

Did he want that, though? Hadn't he driven down here for the explanation he deemed justified? Wasn't that the only reason? He certainly wasn't into chasing women who dumped him—not that it had ever been known to happen before.

'Interesting,' Gabriel drawled. 'And do you often make hushed phone calls to *no one*?'

'I haven't got time to stand here and listen to you being sarcastic, Gabriel.'

Her hand was shaking as she lifted it to brush her fingers through her hair. Which was when he saw the ring. Although, because it was the last thing he expected to see, it took a few seconds for the image to compute and for the information to be transmitted to his brain.

And then every nerve in his body froze. His very clever, always fast-functioning mind, seemed to shut down. His skin crawled with a growing onslaught of ugly suspicion that coalesced into white-hot fury.

A lifetime's worth of discipline slammed into place. He reached out and caught her fluttering hand in his.

'What's this?'

'Nothing!' She hadn't even thought about the wretched fake engagement ring. She had been so busy trying not to fall apart at the seams that she had completely forgotten about it, but now she stared down at it, scarcely able to breathe.

'Speaking to no one on the telephone and wearing nothing on your finger? Incredible.'

'Gabriel, let me explain…'

'Why bother? I already know what's going on. The last thing I need is a bunch of nasty little lies from you.'

'What do you mean?'

'You've played me for a fool, and no one does that.'

'How? How have I played you for a fool?' Lucy's eyes were round with incomprehension.

'How long has it been going on?'

'Gabriel, I don't know what you're talking about!'

'When did you decide that it would be an idea to use *me* to get the sexual experience you were lacking? That boyfriend of yours walked out on you because you wouldn't go the final distance with him…'

Lucy stared at him in horror. She was mesmerised as much by the seething fury in his black-as-midnight eyes as by the incredible ability of his agile brain to jump to all the wrong conclusions.

Belatedly she realised that the fictitious boyfriend was yet again rising to the surface—which just proved how one small, innocently spoken fib could end up landing you in a lot of trouble.

'You don't understa—'

'Did you think that you could use me as a practice run for…' his voice was wintry cold as he lifted her hand with its gleaming fake engagement ring '…boyfriend number two? It makes sense now, why the virginal maiden didn't take the escape route I offered and chose instead to jump into the sack with me….'

'You've got it all wrong!'

'Was the other man on the scene then? Or did he appear later on? When you had all the confidence you needed to go out into the big, bad world and hook some other poor sap?'

'How dare you?' Shock was giving way to anger. 'Do you know how insulting you're being, Gabriel? Do you *really* think that I'm the kind of girl who could have two men at the same time?'

'How the hell do I know who you are? Did I think that you were the sort of girl to walk out without bothering to leave a note? No. So let's just say that I got it all wrong when it came to sussing you out!'

Where had his cool gone? And how dare she look at him with those big, accusing green eyes as though *he* was the one in the wrong? And how dare his body, his *disci-*

plined body, react to those big green eyes with a disobedient surge of uncontrollable *craving*?

'Was I worth it?' he ground out hoarsely. 'I must have been if you've managed to bag an engagement ring!'

'Oh, why don't you take a closer look at this stupid ring?' Lucy cried.

This wasn't what Gabriel had been expecting. Insincere excuses, out-and-out lies, maybe a robust defence and some heated counter-attack—but why on earth would she be asking him to look at the damned ring?

'Come again?'

'Take a close look at the ring, Gabriel! And tell me what you think!'

Gabriel caught her hand and frowned at the glitzy bauble on her finger.

'I think you could have done better,' he growled.

He flung her hand away and walked to the French doors, through which he stared at the darkened shadows in the garden. He was dimly aware of a dog yapping merrily away from the direction of what he assumed was the kitchen.

'Surely,' he said, turning to look at her coldly, 'I primed you for more than some cheapskate guy who can't even run to a real diamond?'

He could breathe now that she wasn't right there in front of him, close enough for him to give in to the tawdry temptation to reach out and pull her to him and demand whether his competition was better in the sack than he was.

'Are you going to tell me who he is?' Gabriel thought that the second he was in possession of a name he would make sure to hunt the guy out and physically teach him a thing or two. 'Does he know about us?'

'How can you be so *thick*…?' Tears shimmered on her eyelashes and she chewed her lip to hold them back from spilling. 'And what sort of opinion do you *have* of me?'

She glared at him angrily. How could a guy who was so smart be so *stupid*? 'I thought you might know me well enough by now! I'm not *bloody* engaged to someone else! And I *haven't* been sleeping with anyone behind your back! How could you think that I would ever *use* you as...as practice...?'

She walked on unsteady legs towards him. She was distantly aware of Freddy yapping from where she had shut him in the kitchen. She was also aware of her telephone ringing and knew that it would be her parents.

'I bought this...this...*idiotic* ring for myself!'

'What? I'm not following you.'

In any other situation Lucy would have burst out laughing, because she had wrong-footed him and it showed in the uncustomary bewilderment on his face.

'I'm engaged to *you*!'

'Don't be ridiculous!'

'Before you start panicking, it's not a *real* engagement. I know that! It's a stupid, *stupid* phoney engagement—just like this stupid, *stupid* phoney ring!' She twisted it round and round on her finger.

Gabriel shook his head and raked his fingers through his hair. He wasn't getting this. On the other hand, he was strangely relieved that there was no other guy on the scene. The relief, indeed, was far greater than the new conundrum facing him.

'I was about to go and have dinner with my parents when you showed up,' Lucy continued grudgingly. 'To tell them that the engagement's off. So you'll have to leave. If I'm not with Mum and Dad in the next half an hour they'll probably fly over here to find out if I'm still alive. They're like that.'

'I'm not going anywhere until I know what the hell is going on, Lucy.'

'Gabriel, *please*…'

'Why would you lie to your parents? Is deception something that runs in your family?'

'Oh, shut up!' She turned away. Her eyes were blurred with tears. She just couldn't speak. Everything was so *wrong*. She felt as helpless as if she had suddenly been caught in a riptide without warning and without a life belt.

Gabriel found that the sight of her crying was the equivalent of having a shard of glass driven through his chest. He loathed the feeling.

'So you're going to see your parents? Fine. I'll come with you. You can explain on the way. And we'll take my car. I don't like the look of that pile of rusting tin in your drive.'

'You *can't* come with me!' Lucy clenched her fists by her sides and glared up fiercely at him. 'Didn't you hear a *word* I've just been telling you? I'm going over there to tell them that it's all over between us! That the engagement's off! You can't just show up with me!'

'As the wounded party, I have every right.' He began moving towards the door. He still didn't know what the hell was going on, but one thing he *did* know. The questions in his head needed answering, and he had no intention of leaving until they were all answered.

Lucy stared at him and hated the familiar stirrings in her body. 'I hate you right now,' she breathed.

'We're wasting time. You don't want your mum and dad racing over here, do you? Far better for us to drive there and talk on the way.…' He reached for his car keys and tossed them casually in his hand.

Any qualms he might have had about embarking on this trip—and there had been very few—had all been neatly laid to rest. In fact, he was congratulating himself on a decision well made. Whatever transpired, he would certainly be returning to London without that unsettling shadow lurking over his life, making it impossible for him to function.

'What about the dog?' he asked as she followed him out of the house and slammed the door behind her.

'I stick him in the kitchen when I'm going out,' Lucy replied. 'He's got plenty of food and water and not much he can chew on.'

'So...' Car started, engine purring, Gabriel turned to her, cool as a cucumber. 'I'm all ears...'

Lucy stared stonily ahead of her, but continuing silence wasn't going to work. Gabriel was as persistent as a dog with a bone. He wasn't going to give up until he had squeezed every ounce of her miserable story out of her and she just refused to care any longer.

Maybe it would be a good thing if he met her parents anyway. Maybe he would see, then, that her father *wasn't* a dedicated criminal who had escaped the hands of justice by the skin of his teeth. And maybe her parents would be able to see *why* she and Gabriel, sadly but inevitably, had had to break off their 'engagement'! They had asked so many times to meet the lucky guy dating their daughter. Now they would see just how far apart she and the 'lucky guy' really were. They would understand *first hand* how two people from two different planets could never make a relationship work!

'My parents are very old-fashioned people...' she began wearily.

Gabriel stifled a hoot of derisive laughter. If she wanted to introduce her story via a sob story that no one in their right mind would believe, then so be it.

'I never told them about...that you had *blackmailed* me into a deal...that you wanted *sex* for money...'

'Just as well,' Gabriel inserted smoothly, 'because you

would likewise have had to confess that you threw yourself at me even when I was prepared to fulfil my side of the bargain and release you from your dirty deal—no sex, just lovely money....'

Lucy blushed furiously, but there was no denying the truth behind that infuriatingly barbed statement of fact.

'I gave them the impression that we were...dating. After a while they began asking questions. They wanted to meet you.'

'They must have been over the moon at the development,' Gabriel murmured mildly. 'The king of bail-outs sleeping with their daughter. I bet they thought that their boat had really docked...'

'You make me so angry, Gabriel. You think you know everything.'

'I've always been good at judging human nature. But, hey, let's not get sidetracked. I'm curious to see where all this is leading.'

'They wanted to know if what we had was going anywhere. I could have told them that it wasn't...' Lucy thought she might expand on this point, just in case he got it into his arrogant head that she had nurtured dreams beyond her reach. She didn't think she could bear the humiliation of him thinking that she had done just that. 'Which would have been the truth. But my mother's health isn't brilliant. She suffered a massive stroke a while back and she's been left with heart problems ever since. Dad and I have done all we can to protect her from stress, and I knew it would stress her out if she thought that we were sleeping together but weren't in any kind of serious relationship...'

'So you decided that you'd better have us engaged and on the road to a happy-ever-after wedding?' He marvelled that she could make her parents sound like two characters from a Disney movie. 'How long have we been engaged?'

'Not long. A week.'

'And now you're about to call the whole thing off…' He was following her directions to her parents' house on autopilot. As tales went, this was the most far-fetched one he had ever heard in his life.

'I just couldn't carry on with us any longer, Gabriel. I'm sorry I didn't leave you a letter, or something, but I honestly didn't see what difference it would make. I'd made my mind up and I didn't think you'd really mind anyway… I know you have a casual approach to relationships…'

'Are we going to hark back to the non-existent sex I was supposed to have with a random stranger who followed me around an art exhibition I didn't want to go to?'

'No,' Lucy interjected hurriedly. 'I'm just saying that I have to break off the fake engagement because I won't be travelling to London every weekend….'

The absence of those visits swamped her. She was staring into a deep, black, bottomless void with no sign of light. It was a suffocating feeling. Maybe if Gabriel wasn't sitting right next to her she would be taking the first steps to recovery, but his presence was overwhelming—a horrible reminder of the empty future awaiting her.

'So what are you going to tell them?' Gabriel asked with interest. He slid his eyes across to her profile. She was the most unpredictable person he had ever known. Maybe that had been part of her fascination. 'I won't be amused if I'm painted as the bad guy.'

'I intend to tell them that we're poles apart and that it's an amicable separation. Take the next left and then the first right and we're there. You don't have to come in with me.' She turned to him impulsively. Forget about her parents meeting him first-hand. Lucy just couldn't envisage Gabriel in her parents' little detached cottage, judging them, believing her father to be a crook despite what she might tell him to the contrary. 'In fact, I'd rather you didn't. You could just drop me at the end of the street and I can make my way there….'

'Won't it be difficult to explain why you've walked to their house? At night? Down these remarkably unlit side roads?'

Lucy leaned back and closed her eyes. She felt thoroughly defeated. How had life become so complicated? The good old days of the garden centre, gossip with her friends, the occasional cinema trip and absolutely *no Gabriel* on the scene seemed like a lifetime ago.

'So you're going to come in, are you?' She looked at him and her breath caught in her throat. He was just so beautiful. *Beautiful*, she reminded herself, and *dangerous*.

'I feel I should, don't you? Considering I'm part of this ongoing drama. Even though I didn't apply for the position.' He slowed the car right down and pulled over, leaving the engine to idle.

'What are you doing?' She was suddenly inexplicably panicked.

'You're as jumpy as a cat on a hot tin roof. Is that because you're scared at how your parents are going to take the bad news?'

Lucy could have told him that next to his being in the car here the *drama* with her parents and her concern over how they would take the news ran a very poor second. The minute Gabriel was around everything and everyone faded into the background, and it was no different now, even though she had broken up with him. Developing a tough shell to protect herself felt as hopelessly out of reach as a trip to the moon.

'Of course I am!' she agreed quickly. 'You would be too if you knew them. They're not what you think they are.

But I don't know why I'm bothering to tell you this when I know you won't listen to a word I have to say anyway.'

'Well, soon I'll find out for myself what they're like, won't I?'

The house he pulled up in front of moments later was a comfortable detached bungalow, not in the least flashy—but then the man had been caught before he'd had had time to really dip his hands in the till.

This was a slice of Lucy's life he had deliberately sealed off into a closed compartment. She had attempted on several occasions to open up a dialogue on the subject of her father and he had very quickly terminated the conversation. He had felt no necessity to remind himself of her highly questionable background. After a while she had given up. Now, he felt as though the missing bits of her were quietly slotting into place to form a complete picture. Did he want that? Well, he certainly didn't have much of a choice, because he wasn't about to drive off into the distant horizon, which was what *she* wanted.

Gabriel killed the engine and turned as he felt her small hand lightly rest on his arm.

'This was such bad timing,' Lucy murmured. 'One day later and you would never have known about…any of this….'

'True…but then perhaps fate decreed that I shouldn't miss my own engagement….'

'Promise me you won't say anything?' Lucy pleaded in an urgent undertone. 'I mean, just take the lead from me. I'll get us out of this, and then you can get back to London and forget any of this ever happened.'

Gabriel refrained from saying that that seemed a very tall order.

'And please try and…be kind to my dad….'

Gabriel wouldn't dream of being *kind* to anyone who

had stolen from him. He looked at her anxious face and shrugged. 'What your father did is history, and I have no intention of dredging up the past. Besides…' he shot her a slow smile that made her suddenly breathless '…I'd be the first to admit that I got more than my money's worth….'

Lucy knew that he was going to kiss her. It was as if somewhere deep inside her she could connect to him on an unspoken, elemental level. She gave a soft little moan of protest and surrender and was ashamed to find herself clinging to him as his lips covered hers savagely, fiercely demanding. She was leaning over to him and the familiar heat was making her giddy….

She pulled back when sanity reasserted itself and he looked at her sardonically.

'Okay,' Lucy blurted out before he could say anything, 'so you're an attractive man…' She could hardly breathe, and every bit of her body wanted this forbidden experience to carry on. 'But it still doesn't work for me. I…let's just get this over with and then you can leave and we can both get on with our lives….'

CHAPTER EIGHT

NICHOLAS AND CELIA ROBINS opened the door on the first ring of the bell and Lucy beamed so broadly at them that her jaw began to ache. She would be calm, relaxed, in control and cheerful at this amicable end to a relationship that wasn't meant to be. She had instructed Gabriel to lurk to one side, out of sight, to give her an opportunity to announce his entrance.

She was still smarting from his kiss. Her lips felt swollen. She prayed that her parents wouldn't spot that when, very shortly, she would be breaking the sad news that their dreams of marrying her off were at an end. The demise of an engagement was never preceded by the fiancé kissing his woman until her skin burned.

'We've been worried!' Her mother's thin face still wore signs of anxiety.

'Mum, I'm an hour late. Not even that!'

'You know what your mother's like, pet. If you're five seconds late she's wondering if you've had an accident and complaining about the state of your car.'

As usual they were both formally dressed, her mother in a pair of slacks and a pink jumper, her father in grey trousers, a blue jumper and a tie. She had frequently tried to introduce them both to the concept of comfortable jogging pants and sweaters but had never been able to make much headway. They were both in their sixties and old habits, as they always smilingly told her, died hard. Now they were ushering her in, already beginning to tell her an anecdote about a fox that had taken a liking to their garden, asking her opinion on whether it was a pest or a pal of sorts. She stopped them.

'I...I...er...there's someone I'd like you to meet... Gabriel's here....' It all came out in an embarrassed rush and she winced at the pleasure that spread across her mother's face.

She had no idea how to proceed. The fact that Gabriel was around changed everything. She'd had her little speech planned, had worked out what she intended to say. Did she trust him to follow her lead, as she had instructed? Did Gabriel Diaz *ever* listen to instructions or follow leads?

While she frantically debated all possible scenarios he was already edging himself through the door behind her, and all of a sudden she was swept along into an impromptu situation where he was being pulled inside and led to the sitting room and she loitered behind like a spare part.

She hardly dared cast her eyes in his direction. What was he thinking? That he had stepped into his worst nightmare? Being forced to meet the man who had defrauded his company? Father of the woman who had ditched him? How much worse could it get for him?

She traipsed into the sitting room in a daze, to find him seated and with a drink being pressed into his hand.

The bungalow, whilst spacious for two, and certainly having benefits from its one floor because her mother had no need to tackle stairs while she was still recovering from her stroke, was small. Lucy thought that the entire bungalow would fit into the downstairs of Gabriel's massive London townhouse.

She knew that if she didn't get a grip very soon the conversation would run away and it would be difficult to rein it back. She had told Gabriel to follow her lead. She fancied he must be cringing at the ongoing assumption that they were an engaged couple. But before she could launch into explanations and apologies her mother was tugging her towards the kitchen and whispering that they should *'leave the boys alone for a little while...your father would like a quiet word with Gabriel...'*

'You should have warned us that Gabriel would be coming!' was the first thing her mother said once they were in the kitchen and out of earshot. 'I've only done something simple for us. Beef pie. I know it's your favourite, but it's really not fancy at all. Plus there's no champagne in the house!'

'Mum, please stop fussing,' Lucy said awkwardly. 'Um...champagne won't be necessary anyway...' Once again she bitterly regretted the lies that had thrown her into this situation.

'Of *course* champagne's necessary, darling. Not only to celebrate, but because we're both so grateful for Gabriel's generosity... Not many employers would have looked so kindly on your father's situation. In fact, I think that's what they're talking about now. Your dad contemplated writing him a letter, but I told him it would be so much better to thank Gabriel face-to-face. He would have gone up to London to see him personally, but when you two started dating he thought he would wait until he visited. Neither of us guessed for a minute that he would be visiting as our future son-in-law!'

'Well, here's the thing, Mum...'

But Celia Robins was in full flow. She ordered her daughter to peel more carrots and to fetch a recipe book, because she could remember seeing a recipe with carrots that would elevate them from boiled with butter to something a little fancier—and what about the crockery? Should they get their best out or stick to casual?

'I'm as nervous as anything,' she confided at one point, 'but I can tell that he's a wonderful person. Kind-hearted. And good-looking, too!'

Lucy had to stop herself from bursting into laughter. The truth was that her mission seemed to be fraying miserably at the edges and her mother had taken up her pen and asked where to sign to become a full-time member of the Gabriel Diaz fan club!

'Look, Mum…there's really no need to go out of your way. In fact, maybe you'd like to sit down for what I have to tell you…'

'Sit? *Now?* When I'm in the middle of these carrots?' She sat. 'You're not pregnant, are you, darling?' Celia Robins went a deep shade of pink. 'These things happen. Of course they do. I just want to say that your dad and I will be here for you.…'

'Mum! Of course I'm not pregnant! Look…I know you're very excited about this…um…engagement thing… but I've taken a step back in the past few days and, well… I've had to be realistic…'

She couldn't quite meet her mother's eyes. Instead she sought inspiration from the kitchen clock, the old-fashioned range cooker, the pine table, the little row of spices in bottles neatly lined up on the shelf her father had put up only a year ago.

'There are loads of differences between me and Gabriel.…'

'Opposites attract,' her mother said promptly. 'It's a cliché, but it also happens to be true.'

'Yes, well…' Lucy cleared her throat and looked at her mother with what she hoped was an expression of sincere regret. 'It's not just that we come from two completely different worlds...'

'Are you talking about...*money*?'

'There's that,' Lucy said cautiously. 'I mean, Mum, you should see his house. It's huge. It's full of silk rugs and expensive paintings...'

'I didn't raise you to be concerned about things like that,' Celia admonished her daughter gently.

'And I'm not! But it's all symptomatic of the bigger differences between us.' Lucy sighed. 'I mean, he's a sophisticated, wealthy man. He's good-looking, clever, urbane... In comparison I'm just a simple country girl who has problems when it comes to menus in foreign languages...'

'I've told you that you should never be concerned about that!'

Lucy and her mother both looked up in surprise to see Gabriel lounging in the doorway, dwarfing the kitchen and filling it with his indefinable *presence*.

He strolled forward and placed his hands firmly on Lucy's shoulders. She smiled weakly, rested one hand over his and gave it an over-firm squeeze to remind him that *she* was supposed to be in charge of the break-up conversation with her parents.

'Your daughter seems to think that there's something shameful in asking a waiter to translate a menu, even though I've told her often enough that it's their job,' he said, and bent to feather a kiss on her neck.

Lucy stiffened in confusion but maintained the rictus grin on her face.

'It's flattering to know that you think so highly of me... you should say it more often. A man likes to hear these things...'

He moved round so that he was looking at her. With all four of them now piled into the kitchen Lucy was beginning to feel claustrophobic. She knew she was perspiring. She desperately wanted to know what was going on—but now the meal was being brought to the table and everyone was chatting…

Exhausted from the effort, she finally threw in the towel and announced that she was tired.

'Long week,' she muttered vaguely. 'All sorts of heavy-duty lifting at the garden centre because Pete and Jake are both on holiday.'

Only when they were safely out of the house and in his car did she turn to Gabriel—but he spoke before she could open her mouth.

'I feel I owe you something of an apology.' He started the engine and the powerful sports car slowly pulled away from the drive and into the street outside.

'Sorry?' Like a helpless moth drawn to a flame she stared at him in the darkness, drinking in the hard angles of his face.

'It's possible that I may have jumped to certain conclusions regarding your father's character. Don't get me wrong, in no way do I condone theft of any kind, but that said, your father was…er…somewhat emotional about what he did and why he did it.'

'Oh?'

'In fact, tearful might be a more accurate description…'

'You hate tears.'

'That's perfectly true, but it was obvious that his regret is sincere. He explained about your mother's illness at the time, and his desperation.'

'He wasn't thinking straight. I could have told you all that if you had given me half a chance, Gabriel.'

'It's not in my nature to give credence to sob stories. I've learnt from experience that anyone can rustle up a heart-warming tale of woe if they think there's a pot of gold to be gained at the end of it.'

'You are so cynical.'

'And yet open-minded when it comes to admitting that I may have made a mistake.' Gabriel glanced across at her. She was as rigid as a plank of wood.

Lucy grudgingly admitted to herself that there was an element of truth to that. In the time she had known him she had come to realise that underneath the ruthless demeanour was a fair-minded guy who did all sorts of things no one would ever have guessed just by looking at him. He was a generous contributor to charity, and respected by all the people who worked for him—Nicolette included. She had told Lucy in passing that the profit-related bonuses awarded to his employees, from the bottom up, were second to none in the City. He made generous donations to a dogs' home because, he had confided in one of the rare moments when his vulnerability had made her love him all the more, he had always wanted to have a dog. Of course he had never had the chance as a boy, and now he just travelled too much for the responsibility.

'Well, I'm really happy that you've heard Dad's side of the story…but that's not what I wanted to talk to you about.'

'No?'

'You said that you'd let me take the lead in this whole business….'

'You mean the phoney engagement that's encouraged your mother to start talking with the vicar and buying bridal magazines for tips on how to hold the perfect reception?'

'She hasn't?' Lucy blanched. 'But I only told her this… this…'

'Outrageous lie…?'

'…a week ago!'

'Excited parents can be fast movers. Your father confided that he had seen a formal black suit on sale in the local department store…he was tempted to buy it… My thoughts here are that this engagement is just a formality, with the marriage due any second now—at least as far as your parents are concerned…'

'You're making this stuff up!'

—'No, I leave the fabrications to you.' But he was strangely lacking in fury at this unexpected development. He decided that the creative way to play it would be simply to go along for the ride and see where it led him.

'This is *terrible*.' Lucy's voice wobbled. 'I never thought…'

'Hoist by your own petard, is the expression that springs to mind…'

'Well, you didn't make things any easier,' Lucy was constrained to point out. 'I told you to leave all the talking to me. I was going to break it to Mum in the kitchen that it was all over…'

'Because you're just a simple country girl and I'm such a devilishly good-looking, sexy, sophisticated man of the world…well-versed in the art of reading complicated menus…'

He could see her cottage approaching. For the first time he wondered what she must think of his townhouse, with its *über*-expensive furnishings and its ultra-modern feel. Less than impressed, he surmised. So different from all the women he had ever gone out with. Sure, she had oohed and aahed in all the right places, but this country cottage was what she was unashamedly all about. He thought he might like to see that garden centre of hers, meet those people she worked with. She had told him enough about them over the months.

'You realise that I'm going to have to stay the night with you?' Gabriel said gravely as he pulled up outside the cottage. He swung round to face her. 'We still have a conversation to finish, and it's far too late for me to contemplate driving all the way back to London....'

'Yes, well...' she stammered.

'But...' Gabriel held up one hand to interrupt her, '...you needn't fear that I'm going to make a nuisance of myself. You can point me in the direction of the spare room....'

'It's called the sofa in the living room, and you might have Freddy for company. If he knows that you're in the house and sleeping in the living room he'll make sure he informs you that the kitchen isn't good enough for him.'

'I like dogs. You know that.'

Freddy, released from the kitchen, bounded out like a bat out of hell. After a few seconds of astonishment at seeing a new face, he proceeded to demonstrate all the ways he had of enlisting Gabriel as a new friend. Gabriel, returning the favour, didn't seem to care about getting his hands and face licked. Nor did he care about the paw prints all over his expensive designer clothes.

From the sidelines, Lucy watched—hating him for being there and sending her into disarray, and loving him for being there because, as always, he was a sight for sore eyes.

He looked up when she offered to get him a cup of coffee, but it was a while before Freddy calmed down and reluctantly agreed to take his favourite spot in front of the fire, where he was asleep within minutes.

'Your father went into some detail about your mother's health.' Gabriel relaxed back on the sofa and glanced at his surroundings for the first time since he had entered the cottage. There was a higgledy-piggledy charm to the room, with photos in frames, lots of plants and flowers in rustic pots and vases, three small prints of old movie posters, and a big basket by the open fireplace, in which wood had been placed in readiness for when the weather turned cold. The furniture was dated, but comfortable.

'She's never fully recovered,' Lucy admitted. She had taken up position in the comfy chair by the fire, legs tucked under her—a good vantage point from which to observe Gabriel, who now sprawled on the sofa, one arm stretched out along the back, legs crossed ankle on knee, a man at home in his surroundings. It seemed to be a talent he had. He had looked equally at home in her parents' house, even though his own surroundings were so wildly different.

'When you told me that they were old-fashioned I have to admit that I had trouble swallowing it. It didn't quite tally with the embezzler scenario. But I'm seeing your point of view now. And I'm seeing why you plumped for fabrication when your parents started asking questions about us. You thought there would be no harm in taking the path of least resistance.'

'And it was a big mistake. I know that. Now you've been dragged in. I'm very glad that you haven't exploded, but I'm going to set this whole thing straight.'

'And risk your mother going into a meltdown?'

'She won't. I think she's stronger than Dad and I have given her credit for. It's just been so easy to worry... She might be disappointed, but she won't go into a meltdown.'

'And the vicar and the bridal magazines?'

'Why are you *doing* this?' Lucy cried.

In front of the fire Freddy shifted, opened one drowsy eye, and promptly decided that sleep was a better option.

She leapt to her feet and began pacing the room, feverishly trying to keep calm.

'If you want to take the decision to spill the beans and

damn the consequences then go ahead, but I won't be part of that decision. I don't intend to have anyone's hospitalisation on my head,' he said.

'And yet you would have slept like a baby with Dad's incarceration on your head!'

'Different set of circumstances—as you're all too well aware.'

'So what are you saying?'

Gabriel shrugged. 'We could always let this one play out for a little while.'

'Play out for a little while?'

'I looked at your mother over dinner. She's jumpy, anxious, she worries about you, but when she talks about this engagement she lights up like a Christmas tree. I'll be frank: I remember my own mother only in snatches. She wasn't around long enough…and my various stepmothers never left much of a mark. I don't want to be the one who interferes with the relationship you have with her. It's obviously a good one. You're the golden child they had when they were old enough to have given up hoping…'

'Stop trying to make me feel guilty…' But her voice was not quite as convinced as it had been half an hour before.

Was he right? *Had* this engagement given her mother something positive to hold on to? Lucy thought that the vicar and the bridal magazines might be a worrying indication that she had underestimated the value her mother might place on the announcement. And her father had been checking out a *suit*? All that in the space of *a week*? Lucy was appalled.

'Not my intention.'

'We broke up.'

'So we did. Because you overreacted to a picture in a trashy magazine.'

'That's not true!'

'Would you have decided to call it a day if you *hadn't* come across that picture?'

He looked steadily at her and Lucy was suddenly thrown into confusion. Would she? Had seeing that photo been a blessing or a curse? She wanted to ask him why he couldn't just respect her decision. Now he had shown up on her doorstep in a moment of impeccable bad timing and found himself drawn into a drama he hadn't initiated. Could she lay into him because he wasn't reacting the way she had told him to? Because he happened to be in possession of a conscience?

'You should never have shown up here,' she countered weakly. 'I don't even know why you came.'

'I had unanswered questions.'

Dented masculine pride. The same reason he had offered her that deal all those months ago. He didn't love her, and he hadn't charged down to Somerset like a knight in shining armour to try and persuade her to come back. He had come down because, in the end, he just had to win. He had to have the last word.

'If you break off this phoney engagement after a week there's a chance your mother will be more affected than if you leave it a bit longer.'

'I have no idea how you work *that* one out.'

'Leave it longer and it gives you more time to ease her into the notion that we're just not suited.' He shrugged eloquently. 'Of course, having never been in this situation before, I'm only throwing out ideas. Far be it from me to tell you what you should or shouldn't do.'

Lucy looked at him narrowly. Since when had Gabriel ever shied away from telling people what they could or couldn't do? When it came to voicing his opinions he was anything but the shrinking violet.

'People don't suddenly stop being suited to each other in

the space of a few days and hard on the heels of cementing their engagement with a ring.' He eyed her finger with a jaundiced expression. 'And I'd like to say that if that *were* a genuine engagement ring from me it wouldn't look like something straight out of a Christmas cracker.'

'Believe it or not, I didn't put a lot of thought into it. It was the cheapest thing on offer. I was going to try and return it for a refund.'

Gabriel flushed, because that slice of cynicism didn't sit well on her and he knew she had arrived at that place because of him. On the plus side, it never paid to live in cloud cuckoo land. He had done her a favour.

'Sleep on it.' He stood up and stretched. 'It's been a long drive for me. Where can I find some linen?'

Lucy sprang up. So he wasn't going to try anything. Well, *good*! At least her message on that front had been received loud and clear.

She disappeared, to return moments later with an armful of linen. All the stuff she kept for when any of her friends happened to sleep over, if they had had too much to drink and needed a bed for the night.

Once upstairs, she feverishly tried to view the situation from every angle, and from every angle it seemed to be a mess. She was also horribly aware of Gabriel downstairs on the sofa. Grudgingly, she had to admit to herself that he had been pretty sanguine about the whole thing. He had also been generous in his forgiveness of her father's upsetting theft from his company—a complete U-turn from his stance of not wanting to hear a thing about a situation he had condemned as morally inexcusable.

He had made no waves over dinner. He had also given her no opportunity to jump in and announce that their so-called engagement was over, but now, thinking about it, perhaps he was right. One week didn't seem like a long time in which to have decided that their relationship was dead and buried. Leave it a bit longer and she could begin to work on her parents. Disappointment was easier to swallow if it was offered up in stages. A rueful sigh here, a mournful turn of phrase there... Maybe she could even send Gabriel overseas! Perhaps turn him into a world-traveller who couldn't possibly sustain a marriage because he was never in the country!

Her parents would have to agree that she couldn't possibly marry a man who practically lived in Australia! She could even send him to New Zealand, where he could become neighbours with her fictitious boyfriend and his fictitious wife and baby....

Reluctantly she had to concede that she had concocted too many half-truths. Throwing any more into the cauldron would certainly spell disaster.

It was a restless night, and when she awoke the following morning and, having changed into her work clothes, tentatively ventured downstairs, it was to find the house empty. Both Gabriel and Freddy were missing. But her peace was short-lived. No sooner had she buttered her slice of toast than there was the sound of the front door slamming shut and Freddy's excited yelps.

'Hope you don't mind....' Gabriel had clearly not brought a change of clothes, and he was now wet from the fine, grey drizzle outside. 'Thought I'd put in a couple of hours' work and take your mutt for a walk.'

'Shouldn't you be getting back to London?'

'In due course.' He made himself at home in the kitchen, fixing them both coffee and seemingly knowing where everything was to be found.

Lucy followed his movements compulsively. Too well could she recall those weekends at his place, having breakfast together, planning what they would do over the days that had always seemed way too short. Often the breakfast would only be half eaten, because they couldn't keep their hands off one another. On one memorable occasion they had actually made love in the kitchen—fast, hard love that had left her limp and blissfully happy.

Guiltily she averted her eyes, because it no longer seemed appropriate to be staring at him. She had forfeited that right when she had walked away, and she had walked away because she had been stupid enough to fall in love and smart enough to realise that leaving was her only protection.

Except look where she was now!

'You're dressed for work. Why are you dressed for work?' he asked.

'Because that's where I'm going.'

'I'll come with you.'

'Why?'

'I'd like to meet your friends there.' He was already slinging on his coat, giving Freddy one last pat.

'Freddy comes with me. And why do you want to meet my friends?'

'Just showing a natural curiosity about my fiancée's life.'

'I am *not* your fiancée and they don't even know that I'm…we're…'

Gabriel feigned shock. 'So the storyline is purely for the benefit of your parents?'

'That was the plan.'

'You weren't thinking straight when you concocted it, in that case. If the vicar knows, half the village probably does as well. Won't your work friends feel hurt that you didn't share the good tidings with them?'

'This is crazy…' Lucy found herself being gently led

out of the house with Freddy running round in mad circles behind her.

'Crazy in a not very well-thought-out way…' Gabriel murmured.

'You're wet,' Lucy replied inanely.

'Which is why, as soon as we break the good news to your gardening pals, I'm going to get myself down to the nearest shops and buy some clothes.…'

'No!' She spun round to face him and felt a little giddy. 'This is all getting completely out of hand.'

'You should have thought of that when you embarked on your well-intentioned charade. You should have realised that your parents weren't to know that they had to keep this engagement a deep, dark secret. Maybe you should have told them that…but I suppose that wouldn't have tallied with true love and romance…'

Lucy fancied she could hear amusement and sarcasm in his voice and she stiffened. 'No. It wouldn't,' she told him shortly. 'They would have found it really hard to understand us falling into bed just for the fun of it. They wouldn't have got it. I'm not your type and you're definitely not mine. I'm not going in your car, Gabriel. I need to take Freddy, and he won't fit in a sports car.'

'In which case, I'll follow you.'

'You don't have to *do* that!' Lucy exploded. 'I suppose I'll have to mention *something*, if Mum's been telling everyone in the village, but if they see you, then they're going to know that it's all a sham!'

'Because…?'

'Because they *know* me, and they *know* that I'd never go for you. At least not as far as getting engaged!'

She stormed over to her car and yanked open the door. She was shaking like a leaf. She hated herself for knowing that, deep down, she would have loved nothing better than to be wearing a *real* ring on her finger, to be secure in a *real* engagement and looking forward to a *real* wedding. She hated *him* for being able to carry on with a farcical engagement because it really didn't trouble him one way or another. He was not emotionally invested. He could afford to look at the bigger picture and have a conscience about the situation. Maybe he felt guilty that he hadn't listened to her in the first place when she had tried to explain about her father. Maybe he felt compassion because he had not had a mother for most of his life and, as he said, he didn't want to be responsible for damaging *hers*. He could *afford* to be as cool as a cucumber while she was a seething mass of conflicting emotions.

Freddy leapt into the back of the beaten-up Land Rover and leaned over the passenger seat, for all the world as if he was truly interested in the scene being played out by the driver's door.

'And something else…' She pulled up the hood of her cardigan and glared at him. She had a driving need to get under his skin. He was just *so* stunning and *so* controlled. He had been a bad choice, but all she could remember when she looked at him was how wonderfully happy he had made her. 'I bet you haven't even thought about the practicalities of what happens if this stupid phoney engagement continues!'

'Explain.' Her eyes were the colour of stormy seas, enormous in her small heart-shaped face. He just had to look at her and his libido went into overdrive. He had stopped trying to find an explanation for that phenomenon. No longer would he beat himself up with the fact that he could still get turned on by a woman who had managed to go against every rule and regulation he had always made sure to lay down about relationships with the opposite sex.

A phoney engagement? This was the stuff of pure horror movies, as far as Gabriel was concerned, and yet, staring down into those sea-green eyes, he could still feel his manhood rising magnificently and inappropriately to the occasion.

'What am I supposed to do at the weekends? Where am I supposed to go?'

'London.' Gabriel shrugged. 'Your visits can taper off in due course.'

'London?' Lucy practically shrieked. 'And what am I supposed to *do* when I'm hiding out in London? Where am I supposed to stay?'

'I'm your so-called fiancée,' Gabriel remarked drily. 'Join the dots.'

'Stay with *you*?'

'Unless,' he murmured, 'you think that I might overstep the mark?'

'I'm not saying that.' Of *course* he wouldn't overstep the mark. His mocking voice was reminder enough that he was over her, that he was simply rolling with the punches.

She resented the fact that she should be grateful to him for not laying his cards on the table when he had visited her parents. He could have told them that it had all been a ridiculous lie—could have left her parents distraught and mistrustful of her for ever.

'Then what other reason could there be not to accept the most obvious solution?'

'So I'd stay with you…?'

'It makes more sense than hiding under your kitchen table and praying that no one comes to the door. I don't *have* to do this, Lucy. Consider it a friendly gesture in recognition of the time we spent together.'

'A friendly gesture…?' Why didn't she like that terminology?

Gabriel spread his hands wide and shot her a slow, toe-curling smile. 'What else? As you've been at pains to point out, we're not each other's type…so there won't be any risk of either of us straying outside the boundaries, will there?'

CHAPTER NINE

THE NEXT FEW WEEKS saw a change in their relationship. Lucy had reluctantly agreed to continue her weekend visits to London, but if she had expected those visits to be awkward and argumentative then she found that she had been mistaken.

Gabriel had moved from being the perfect lover to the perfect host. They went sightseeing. London was explored with the methodical precision of a military campaign. Maps and guidebooks were brought out and consulted. Art galleries were visited. In the evenings—Friday and Saturday—they would eat out in expensive formal restaurants.

Every weekend the guest room awaited her, with the bed neatly made and towels freshly laid out in the adjoining bathroom. They would return from their meals and the second they were in his house he would remove himself to his office. She would be left to contemplate the indifference of the empty bed and the fresh towels.

Gone was any hint of flirtation. Just like that. It was as though they had never slept together. At least insofar as he was concerned. For Lucy, being in his presence and not being able to touch him was agonising. Her fingers seemed poised to stroke his face or rest lightly on his arm, her lips were primed to kiss him, her whole body yearned for the feel of his. She longed for the easy laughter and the teasing. The absence of any physical contact was a continuing wake-up call to the role she had really played in his life. He might have made love to her with consummate passion, but in the end he could detach from all of that as though it had never happened.

He always spoke to her during the week, and she had become accustomed to receiving his calls. They were a guilty pleasure even though there was nothing in them that could be construed as intimate or, as he had said weeks ago, overstepping the boundaries.

After that first flush of realising that she was in love with him, and knowing that her only salvation lay in escape before she could be sucked deeper into the hopeless situation in which she had found herself, Lucy knew that she was sinking fast into a routine that was equally destructive. Buying time before she told her parents that the engagement was off was just a handy excuse. Deep down she knew that what she really needed to do was cut all ties with Gabriel and suffer the withdrawal symptoms, however long it took.

They were no longer lovers, and she gave herself long, scornful lectures on how transitory any feelings he had for her had been, but she still found herself in a state of excitement as Friday rolled round and her trip to London was underway.

He usually sent his driver for her, but today, as she walked out of the station, her heart gave a treacherous little lurch at the sight of him leaning against the car, coolly elegant in a charcoal-grey hand-tailored suit. He must have come directly from work. Her mouth was dry as she walked towards him, shading her eyes from the cold winter glare of the sun.

'What are you doing here?' Lucy asked, surprised.

'Now, now—is that any way to greet your fiancé?'

Dark eyes gave her the once-over, taking in the soft full mouth, the slender body underneath the swinging coat, her very blond, very long hair that trailed over her shoulders and down her back underneath the navy blue woollen hat pulled low to her eyes. He could never get enough of looking at her.

She flushed. This was one of those rare times when she could detect that lazy teasing in his voice that still had the power to make her feel self-conscious.

'Tell me how your trip was,' he encouraged as they settled into the back seat and his driver slowly pulled away from the kerb. 'And tell me what's happening with your friends at the garden centre….'

Lucy sighed. It was way too easy to talk to him. 'They're all fine. The same. I've… I've begun to sow some seeds of doubt, Gabriel…you know… It's been a few weeks, and people are beginning to ask questions…wanting to know when the big day is going to be….' She sneaked a sideways glance at him but couldn't read anything from his expression. 'I've been doing the same with Mum and Dad,' she continued reluctantly. 'They're away this weekend. They left last night and won't be back until Sunday evening. I'm hoping that they'll think about the stuff I said.'

'Which was what, exactly?'

'Oh, just that we hadn't been getting along lately. You know—I harped on about how different we were…. I mean, I didn't lay it on too thick. I just think that it's time for us to really start…ending this. Mum showed me those magazines and tried to drag me along to see the vicar, which I managed to avoid, but it's getting a little tricky and I'm fed up having to pretend. I…I just want to move on with the rest of my life, and I know you want that, too…so…'

'What makes you think that you know what I want?'

'I feel like I'm standing still, and I don't like having to skirt around uncomfortable questions. I don't want to have to see that little pile of bridal magazines in the basket by the television at my parents' house. I don't like the person I've become… I've always been honest. Sometimes I don't even recognise myself.'

'So, we've suddenly stopped getting along and things are tricky between us…?'

'With any luck this might be the last weekend I come to London.' She stared out of the window without blinking. 'I think when I get back home I'll just break it to them that it's over.' She turned to him and threw him a faint smile. 'I shall have to make sure I keep Mum away from the trashy weeklies. I wouldn't want her to see a picture of you in a week's time and think how fast you've recovered from your so-called engagement.'

Her voice was steady but her breathing was laboured. She'd always known that things would have to be dealt with sooner rather than later, but every word she'd spoken had still come as a surprise. It was as though someone else had decided to take charge, so that the words emerged as shocking as though they had been spoken by a third party.

She didn't dare look at Gabriel. She didn't want to see his expression of relief.

'I take it that *you'll* put in a suitable time of mourning before you move on…?'

Lucy hated that polite voice. It was the voice that told her that they were just friends. She felt she might hit him if he suggested that they keep in touch…as *friends*….

'Mum and Dad will understand. They know that not everything works out according to plan, and I've learnt a lot from this.'

'Enlighten me.'

'Well, for a start, it's made me see that one small white lie can snowball,' she told him truthfully.

Her mouth was talking and making sense, but all she could see was the void opening up in front of her. Their last weekend. The ring of finality made her feel sick.

'When I meet the man of my dreams I'm not going to play any games or tell any little white lies.'

'The man of your dreams...?'

'There's someone out there for me. A soulmate.'

'So romance is alive and kicking still?'

'I have to believe in it or else what's the point? I know you'd never understand, Gabriel. We come from different planets as far as that is concerned. Who knows? Maybe there's someone out there for you, too.'

Her heart squeezed, but she was proud of her control and of the way she was handling a horrible conversation. She wondered what this mystery woman would look like. A sexy brunette who wore the kind of clothes he liked and enjoyed all the presents he would give her. He had notice-ably stopped offering to buy *her* things. Clothes, bits of jewellery, sexy underwear. All of that had become inap-propriate, but she had discovered she missed the relent-lessness of his offers.

'Who knows...?' Gabriel murmured. 'But in the mean-time I have something of a surprise in store for you.'

'Oh? What is it?' She'd been enjoying working herself into a lather and was disgruntled at his interruption.

'Brace yourself. I've had a phone call from your mother.'

'What?' Lucy looked at him in consternation. 'Why on earth would my mother phone you?'

'Because I'm the other half of this crumbling relation-ship.'

'I'm not following you.' In her head she was frantically trying to slot in this new development. Just when she'd thought she would be stepping off the rollercoaster ride, allowing herself time to get used to being back on firm ground, it picked up speed.

'Your hints and insinuations did their job. Your mother thought she would phone me for clarification.'

'She *what*?' Lucy stared at him in dismay. 'This is your fault! You…if you hadn't been so charming… I didn't even know she had your number! Did you back me up?'

'Apparently I'm about to embark on a considerable amount of travelling…?'

Lucy flushed. She had meant to steer clear of that particular excuse, but she had somehow found herself in a tight spot and had blurted out the first thing that came to her head.

'I had no idea I was supposed to run with that one,' Gabriel was saying. 'For starters, where do you intend to ship me off to?'

'You *do* travel a lot with your job….'

'But relatively little compared to the amount now looming on the horizon, apparently….' In fact, his overseas travel had become remarkably curtailed. He had discovered that ruthless delegation had its benefits.

'What did you tell her?' Lucy asked in a small voice.

'I told her that it was a conversation best had on a face-to-face basis.'

'Okay. Right.' She sighed and leaned back with her eyes closed. 'It'll all be fine once I've explained that we're no longer an item.'

'Because I'm the creep who wants you to change for him, and on top of that I won't even be around to see you because my job will be taking me to all four corners of the globe for most of the year? I'm not surprised all the lying is beginning to get to you. For someone who has always been honest, I must say you show immense talent for being creative with the truth.'

'I never said anything about you being a creep,' Lucy told him defensively, still keeping her eyes closed as a sense of weariness settled over her.

'You didn't have to. It's implicit.'

'Please let's not argue over this, Gabriel. We both know that there isn't a choice. It would have been better if I had just told the truth when you came to visit and met them for the first time. If I had told them the truth then, they would have been over it by now.'

'And you would have embarked on your glittering new life? You have a point. Maybe that was a misjudgement. But what's the use crying over it now?'

'So is that the surprise? That my mother phoned?'

'They're in London.'

'What?' Lucy sat up, her heart beating very fast.

'I asked them up.'

'What on earth *for*?'

'I felt that if I was about to be shot down in flames for being a bastard then I should be around to have some input.'

'Why? What for? You won't be seeing any of us ever again!'

'Call me egotistical,' Gabriel gritted in a hard voice, 'but I don't care for the thought of my reputation being dragged through the mud with your parents.'.

'Until recently you wouldn't have cared less!'

'We've already been over that old ground, Lucy. Let's move on from there. Your mother wanted to know what was going on.'

'Was she upset?'

'Bewildered. Apparently everything was fine and dandy last weekend, and then suddenly there were problems—

insurmountable problems. Your timing has been less than spectacular.'

'How can you just…*sit there* and be so calm about this? Why didn't they tell me that they were coming to London?'

'I expect they thought you'd try and talk them out of it—or maybe they just wanted to talk to me without you around, throwing them your side of the woeful story,' Gabriel said drily.

'So what do we do now?' Lucy threw him an accusing look from under her lashes. 'Where are they staying? Where are they now? Are they at your house?'

'No, they're not….'

Lucy looked at him, perplexed. 'Well, where *are* they? No, don't answer that—just tell me what you've said to them….'

'You mean so that we can get our stories straight?'

Lucy flushed. He had moaned about the person she had become, and now he had contrived, in that one sentence, to bring on a heady rush of guilt. 'You should have told me that they would be here,' she ploughed on valiantly. 'I know it's horrible to be sneaking around, pretending to be something we're not, but we both agreed that we had no choice at the time….'

'However, let's not forget that *you* were the one who generated the situation in the first place….'

'Yes, well…'

'I've told them that we definitely come from different worlds….'

Lucy breathed a sigh of heartfelt relief. 'You have so much…I could never adjust to your lifestyle—plus I'm not materialistic. I would never completely understand how someone can spend their whole lives motivated by money….'

'Just for reference—and apologies for dragging you

down from your moral high ground—if you'd been raised by someone whose finances were a source of constant change you might be a little closer to understanding….'

Disconcerted by that personal remark, Lucy stared at him.

'Thank goodness for the unchanging face of boarding school.' Gabriel, still leaning indolently against the car door, returned her stare lazily. 'Always nice to have a solid point of reference in a changing world, don't you agree?'

'Why do I think that you don't really mean that?' Lucy ventured uncertainly.

After weeks of amicable politeness, this detour into a more personal conversation dangled in front of her as tempting as a carrot being waved in front of a hungry rabbit. Helpless, she marvelled at how easy it was for him to draw her in. Was that what love was all about? An inability to keep her distance even when her head was telling her that it was imperative? She had the giddy sensation of walking into a trap.

'For an eleven-year-old boy, boarding school in a foreign country isn't always the most pleasant of experiences.'

'Why are you telling me this?' Lucy asked, in an attempt to regain control.

Gabriel inclined his head to one side. 'You want to paint me as morally suspect because I make a lot of money.'

'Not *morally suspect*. I *know* you're a pretty moral guy. I mean, you didn't *have* to bail my father out when our… our…deal fell through because I was a…a virgin….'

Gabriel drew in a sharp, long breath. Did she have any idea how sexually charged that innocent statement was? It brought back a host of memories that were as vibrant and as powerful as if he had just slept with her for the first time yesterday. He had to shift to ease the painful throb of his sudden erection, bulging and pressing against the zipper of his trousers.

'It must have been hard for you....' Lucy couldn't help the flare of sympathy she felt for a boy without a mother, stuck in a boarding school where presumably he had had to grapple with the language, while his father lurched from one failed marriage to another.

Gabriel swept past that wobbly interruption. 'So you see making money isn't necessarily the sign of a monster, but of the desire to have financial stability. If you're going to paint me as someone who is incapable of drawing lines, then I feel I need to be there to set the record straight.... But, getting back to the surprise I have in store for you... it has nothing to do with your parents being in London....'

'It hasn't?' Torn between lingering over that image of Gabriel as a young boy and the dawning realisation that *setting the record straight* was just going to muddy the already muddy waters, Lucy looked at him in surprise.

'Look around. Does this route seem familiar?'

Lucy obediently looked out of the window. Since stepping into the car she had not paid any heed to her surroundings. She was now accustomed to the drive through London to his house. It was always trafficky. The pavements were always swarming with pedestrians. Even in the peaceful oasis of his road, where his house stood in opulent splendour, she still always felt vaguely claustrophobic. As though the rush of people and cars, although not evident in the expensive road, thrummed under the pavements as a constant reminder that peace was only an illusion.

'I can't tell,' she said doubtfully. 'It's getting dark, and anyway, I've never really taken in where we were driving.'

'I get that,' Gabriel murmured softly. 'There were always more pressing things on your mind. On both our minds...'

He was still watching her in that closed, brooding manner that made her shiver with awareness and plunged her into nervous confusion. Could she be mistaken about the sexy undertones behind that mildly spoken reminder? She wouldn't have thought that he had a nostalgic bone in his body as far as women were concerned. He had certainly staged a terrific show of indifference towards her over the past few weeks—had complied with her demand to be left alone without any sign of hardship on his part at her decision… But was there some residual nostalgia there? Now that he knew that the farce was about to come to an end? She hated herself for so weakly wanting to explore that option.

'So where are we going?' She changed the subject, although her heart was jumping all over the place and prickles of tension were making her perspire.

Despite the fact that she had always laughingly turned down offers of presents from him, and although she had striven to ignore his teasing about her choice of clothes, her wardrobe had altered subtly over time. She had ditched her uniform of jeans and dungarees, and even though the weather had turned considerably colder she was now in a skirt and a soft, fleecy jumper. Images of him pushing his hand underneath her skirt, wriggling his fingers beneath the constricting tights and undies to find that part of her that was now growing damp, made her want to faint.

'Will Mum and Dad be there?' she pressed anxiously. She felt a twinge of treacherous resentment that if she broke the bad news to them as soon as she saw them then she wouldn't even be left with the memory of a last weekend with Gabriel. Why had he asked them to London? Why couldn't he just have phoned her, told her about her mother's concerns, left *her* to deal with it all?

Gabriel flicked back a pristine white cuff to consult his

watch. 'They've gone to the theatre. Matinee performance with a meal out afterwards. On the house, so to speak.'

'Thanks,' Lucy told him tightly.

Gabriel shrugged. 'Apparently, the last time they went to the theatre was over a decade ago.'

'That's not what I was thanking you for. I was being *sarcastic*, Gabriel. You're doing all this stuff...building yourself up to be the perfect...perfect...'

'Son-in-law that never was...?'

'We're supposed to be at each other's throats....'

'It's fair to say that you can be argumentative.'

Lucy flushed because there it was again—that soft, lazy drawl that brought her out in goosebumps.

'I expect the entertainment to be over by ten. It will give us time to visit a little property I've recently acquired.'

At a loss, Lucy stared at him without saying anything. 'I don't understand,' she said eventually. 'Why would I want to see a house you've bought? Why have you bought a house? Are you tired of living where you do? It *is* very big for one person,' she conceded, 'and of course, it's not a very friendly area—but then I didn't think that sort of thing mattered to you....'

'I like space, and I've never cared who my neighbours were,' Gabriel conceded, breaking eye contact. 'In fact, the less I know about the people who live around me the better. Nothing worse than nosy neighbours. Anyway, this house is just an addition to my property portfolio. It occurred to me a while ago that if this engagement continued any longer it might be more to your liking if we stayed there than at my townhouse.'

He flushed darkly. He couldn't believe he was actually saying this. In fact, he couldn't believe that he had bought a house he didn't need for the sake of a woman who had set him up in a phoney engagement, openly stated that he wasn't her type of guy and now, purchase complete and house decorated, had informed him that this was to be their last weekend.

He had been the model of good behaviour over the past few weeks. He had blithely assumed that she would be unable to resist what she thought she couldn't get. He had been willing to bide his time with her. Where he should have been enraged that a woman—any woman—had put him in such an awkward position, he had chosen to accept it because he had stopped fighting the curious reality that he wanted her at all costs.

Except she hadn't given in, and her obstinacy had made his desire to repossess her even more urgent.

'You bought a *house* because I was silly enough to condemn us to more weekends together for the sake of my parents?' Even for him, Lucy thought that sounded excessive, but then she reminded herself that whatever mansion he had bought would be an investment. Gabriel never did anything that wasn't fully anchored in firm logic and reason.

'I buy a lot of property.' Gabriel's lips thinned. He loathed the lack of control that prevented him from walking away from her. He knew he should have walked away a long time ago. In fact, he should never have made love to her in the first place. Any woman who was a virgin at twenty-four promised to be difficult in one way or another. He hated difficulties on the emotional front. He liked keeping things as uncomplicated as possible in that particular area.

'I thought you would have been more interested in places in the city centre.' Lucy was beginning to realise that they were no longer in the busy, fashionable part of London beloved by people who enjoyed showing the world how much money they had. 'Actually, I'm sure you once told me that you only invested in commercial property, and that most of it was outside the UK....'

'A change is as good as a rest,' Gabriel muttered.

The car pulled down a side street and finally drew up in front of a small detached house with a white fence, against which was pressed lots of foliage. In the dark, Lucy couldn't quite make out the individual species of plants.

'This is *it*?'

'There's no need to sound so shocked,' Gabriel said irritably. 'I'm not a completely urban animal.' His sports car was parked in the small drive.

'Yes, you are, Gabriel,' she teased cautiously. It felt good to break away from the guarded politeness of the past few weeks. 'Open spaces and too much green make you nervous.'

'You're so literal when it comes to interpreting what I say.'

He unlocked the front door and Lucy stepped into a picture-perfect house—except it was nothing like his sprawling mansion in Kensington. In fact, in some ways it reminded her of her own cottage in Somerset, although this had obviously been done up to a much higher standard. The flagstone tiles in the hall gleamed, the walls were newly painted and, glancing sideways, she could see a cheerful sitting room with an open fire. Only the presence of expensive silk rugs, similar to those in his other house, reminded her that this little gem carried a mighty price tag.

'What do you think?' Gabriel hadn't moved from the closed front door, against which he was now leaning with his hands shoved in his trouser pockets.

'I can't believe you would invest money in a house like this,' Lucy said truthfully. 'But then I suppose you have a team of people working for you who do stuff like this...

source rentable properties…make sure you're not throwing money away on something that isn't going to pay off….'

'You have such talent for seeing the worst in me,' Gabriel murmured.

Lucy pinkened but remained silent. The truth was that she loved him so much she could only see the best in him—past all those traits she once considered faults.

'Explore,' he urged, pushing himself away from the door.

Lucy almost didn't want to. Already she liked what she saw and it was painful to concede that she would be destined to have no more than one weekend in it. She noticed that he still couldn't bring himself to come close to her, and was ashamed to realise that if he reached out and touched her she would fling herself back at him without a thought for the consequences.

Very much aware of him behind her, she made her way through the downstairs of the house, which was bigger than it looked from the outside. His other house was a testimony to open space, clean lines and minimum clutter, but this was a honeycomb of exciting nooks and crannies. The kitchen, at the back, even had a bottle-green range, and she stroked it, loving the feel of the warmth under her fingers.

'There's a garden,' Gabriel said awkwardly. He sidestepped her to the conservatory leading off from the kitchen and stepped through the French doors, letting in a waft of chill air.

'Wow! It's big, isn't it?' She strolled outside, hugging herself against the cold. Fairy lights illuminated a perfectly landscaped garden, complete with a bench under a weeping willow.

'If this so-called engagement was going to continue, I figured it would be a good idea to have somewhere you could bring the mutt….'

Lucy spun round to look at him. 'Really?'

'Made sense,' Gabriel told her with a shrug. 'My house wouldn't work, and you made the point on more than one occasion that you didn't like leaving Freddy behind….'

'So are you saying that you *specifically* picked this place out with me in mind?'

In a heartbeat Gabriel realised that there was no room for prevarication, and that his usual automatic cool withdrawal from any question designed to pin him down wasn't going to work. He was a man who could handle any competition in the business world, who could face down anybody rash enough to think that they could take him on, but right now he was powerless against the earnest enquiry in those big green eyes. The woman had managed to worm her way through the dense walls of his self-imposed fortress, changing all the rules.

'Something like that, I suppose,' he conceded grudgingly. 'Of course places like these can be rented in a second….' he was compelled to point out. 'Have a look around the rest of the house. Upstairs. Your parents are in one of the guest rooms.'

'I can't believe they never mentioned a word of this to me…. What did they do last night? Did they talk to you about…about…?'

'No, they didn't,' Gabriel said shortly. 'I wasn't about to engage in a long conversation in your absence. Besides, I'd already gathered that I'd been painted into a corner. Problem was, I didn't know what the corner was supposed to look like. There seemed no point fabricating stories about trips to China if I was supposed to be setting sail for the New World.'

Lucy nodded and followed him back into the house. She was still reeling from the thought that he'd had personal input into the property—that he had bought it with

her in mind. Did that indicate that perhaps he actually
wanted their relationship to develop? He hadn't touched
her, or even come close to touching her recently, but then
again he hadn't run screaming into the distance either....
Surely for a commitment-phobe like Gabriel an engagement foisted upon him would have been the final straw,
however great the sex between them was, but he had stuck
around. What did that mean?

She opened doors to three bedrooms—one with angled
old timber beams—and a generous-sized bathroom, before finally walking into the master bedroom, where she
stopped dead at the bed of her dreams. A king-sized four-
poster, the last word in romantic luxury. Eyes shining,
Lucy spun round to look at Gabriel.

'You chose this especially for me?' she breathed in wonder. Hope pushed through the layers of disappointment.

'It's not a big deal. You once said you liked four-poster
beds. In fact, more than once. Several hundred times.'

'So what does this mean?' she demanded as she looked
at him searchingly.

'What are you talking about?'

'If you got this…for me…for us…'

'It's a four-poster bed, Lucy. Not a marriage proposal.'

Hope was extinguished as rapidly as it had taken root.
What on earth had she been thinking? That a wildly extravagant show of thoughtfulness indicated a deliberate
act of commitment? Had she lost her senses? Beds were
about sex. He didn't want to see where they were going! He
hadn't become a convert to the possibility of long-lasting
relationships that led to the altar! He had stuck around,
keeping a careful distance, because he still wanted her
and his intention was to get her back into bed.

'A four-poster bed for me?'

'A four-poster bed for *us*.' Already he was picturing

her in it, her long blond hair splayed out around her, her small, perfect breasts pouting up at him, her slender body waiting for his attention. She was made for a four-poster bed. 'I chose it myself.'

'You haven't come near me for weeks….' Lucy was cold inside and getting colder by the second.

'You wanted me to back off,' Gabriel said softly. 'I did.'

'Did you think that I wouldn't be able to last? That I would crack?' She thought how often she had come close to doing just that and thanked her lucky stars that she hadn't. 'And, when I didn't, did you think that you could tempt me back into bed by buying this house and furnishing it with a great big four-poster bed? Just the kind of bed you knew I would like?'

Gabriel frowned. 'I've never had this much personal input into anything I've bought for a woman.'

'And you don't get any brownie points for doing it *this* time!' Lucy shouted. 'I'm not going to be your mistress until you get sick of me just because you bought a house and a four-poster bed and chose it all yourself!'

'Since when is it a crime to do something I think you'd like!' Frustrated, Gabriel raked his fingers through his hair. 'You've kept me at arm's length, and I've respected that. But keeping each other at arm's length is something neither of us wants. So you want to start hunting down your soulmate. Specifically where do you intend to pin him down? And why be a martyr in the meanwhile? Okay, so the whole phoney engagement thing adds a complicated dimension, but there's still chemistry between us. You can't deny it. Why don't you accept my gesture for what it is and enjoy it?'

'It's not what I *want*!' She could have flung something at him. One of the cushions on the bed. He wasn't a man for *cushions*! How had he dared to think that he could

entice her back between the sheets by throwing a couple
on a bed? 'As soon as Mum and Dad get back I'm going
to tell them that it's over between us. Tomorrow morning
we're going to leave first thing, and I never, *ever* want to
see you again!'

CHAPTER TEN

IT WAS A MONTH before Lucy was forced to admit to herself
that her mantra of never wanting to set eyes on Gabriel
again was a sham.

True to her word, she had left with her parents early the
following morning after her stormy argument with him.
The house had been empty. Gabriel had left even before
her parents had returned from their theatre expedition and
he had failed to reappear.

As soon as they had returned to Somerset she had sat
her parents down and haltingly told them the truth. What
had started as a fling had been turned into an engagement
because she hadn't wanted to stress them out or, if truth
be told, face their disappointment. They had old-fashioned
beliefs and she had never given them cause to question
that she didn't share those beliefs. Had she been more of a
rebel, she thought to herself, she might have had that fling
without a conscience—but that was a passing thought that
didn't have the substance to take root. The truth was that
she would still have fallen in love with him, despite their
inauspicious beginnings, and she would still have wanted
more than he could ever give her.

Her parents had listened and accepted her explanation
without passing judgement. On the surface things had returned to normality. Her routine was back in place. Things

were busy at the garden centre. Christmas was just around the corner. There should have been little time to dwell on the emptiness that engulfed her, stifling her usual upbeat nature like creeping poisonous ivy.

Unfortunately, questions had begun to push themselves to the surface, and it didn't seem to matter how hard she tried to shove them back down, they still kept rising up until she could barely function.

He might not have had the vocabulary to tell her that he wanted a proper relationship with her, but hadn't he, effectively, *bought her a house*? Who did something like that if he was completely detached? And he had chosen everything inside it. Or at least some of the things inside it. Definitely the bed. The four-poster bed he had known she would adore. He had made sure that the house had a garden—somewhere for Freddy. If actions spoke louder than words, then hadn't he been trying to tell her *something*?

She hated herself for not being strong enough to make the right decision and stick to it. Or to make *any* decision and stick to it! She resented the fact that she just couldn't help trying to analyse a way out of the paralysis that had overtaken her. She couldn't sleep at night. Sometimes, during the day, she found herself drifting off into all sorts of imaginary scenarios as she tried to wrestle with the unwanted questions that kept bobbing up to the surface.

She decided that she wouldn't tell anyone when she finally made up her mind to go to London and see him. She could barely credit to herself that she was going to do it, never mind broadcast it! And she certainly wouldn't breathe a word to her parents. Things still felt a little weird with them, even though his name never passed their lips. She had the feeling that they were *concerned* for her, and their concern lay between them like a big black cloud. She had a sneaking suspicion that the smile she always made sure to wear wasn't fooling them.

She left one of her friends to look after Freddy, and it was a freezing, blustery Saturday afternoon when she boarded the familiar train to London.

She hadn't thought through what she would say to Gabriel. She didn't even know whether he would be in or not. But she didn't want to lose the element of surprise by getting in touch with him. She was firmly convinced that he wouldn't want to have anything to do with her, but she couldn't spend the rest of her life with nagging doubts as to whether she had made the right decision or not.

If she showed up and he chucked her out, then at least she could retreat as the wounded party and have some sort of closure.

Her heart was beating like a jackhammer when, hours later, she was standing in front of his house. It was a little after six-thirty and already so dark that the street lights were on.

She pressed the doorbell before she could talk herself out of it. She had passed the train ride telling herself that this was a win-win situation. Either he would hear her out, and then they could do what she knew she wanted, which was simply to enjoy each other, no questions asked, or else he would slam the door in her face, in which case, she would at least have tried.

She couldn't recall why she had been so sanctimonious. It just felt important to see him.

She was so busy trying to predict his reaction should he be in, and should that front door open, that she was temporarily caught unawares when the door was indeed opened and he was standing in front of her.

Her mouth went dry. Her fevered thoughts flew out of her head. She found that she was clutching her bag in a vice-like grip. How could she have forgotten just how beautiful he was? The few pictures she had taken of him on her phone, which she had guiltily looked at on a daily basis, didn't begin to scrape the surface of his compelling good looks.

'I…I guess you're surprised to see me….' Lucy croaked in a rush. She was riveted by the striking lines of his face, and only belatedly noticed that he was dressed to go out. Dark grey tailored trousers emphasised his long, muscular legs, and he wore a grey-and-white pinstriped shirt, one sleeve rolled to the elbow, the other in the process of being rolled down.

'I'm—I'm sorry,' she stammered, beetroot-red. 'You're going out…'

'What the hell are *you* doing here?'

He towered over her and she instinctively took a small step back. It had been a terrible mistake making this trip. She didn't know what she had been thinking. Her thoughts were all over the place when she heard a woman's voice calling from behind him—and then the owner of the voice sashayed into view.

In all the scenarios that had flashed through her head during the weeks since she had walked out of that house she had carelessly and conveniently chosen to ignore the most obvious one. That he had simply forgotten about her and moved on. She was starkly reminded of that now as a sultry brunette, clad in a skintight red dress that clung to every voluptuous curve, moved to stand next to him.

'Gabriel, darling, who on earth is this?'

Dark, heavily made-up eyes swept contemptuously over her and Lucy wanted the ground to open up and swallow her whole.

'No one,' she whispered in a desperate little voice. 'I'm no one…. I think I may have come…to the wrong house.

In fact...' She moved to turn away and felt a hand descend on her arm.

'Not so fast,' Gabriel growled, while next to him the brunette released an exasperated string of protests.

'Whoever the hell you are,' she said, resting a hand possessively on Gabriel's arm so that the three of them were connected through him in a oddly staged tableau, 'we're on our way to the opera! Gabriel, darling, can't this wait?'

Lucy raised reluctant eyes to the brunette, who was now pouting at him. She felt faint when she tried to think about what Gabriel would say should she come between him and his hot date. Did he feel that he had no choice but to invite her in because she had come such a long way to see him?

'I'll go....' she volunteered feebly. 'Actually, I was just passing through....'

'Isabella,' Gabriel said softly, without taking his eyes off Lucy's flushed face, 'time for you to leave.'

'But...'

'Apologies. My driver will deliver you back to your place. He's already outside.'

'We have tickets for the opera!'

'Feel free to use them. And don't forget your coat on your way out.'

Lucy looked longingly at the front door as it shut behind the brunette, and then her eyes slid to the floor. 'I'm so sorry,' she whispered. 'I've ruined your evening. I didn't think...' She reluctantly looked up and nervously took in his shuttered expression. 'You had a date....'

'You haven't said why you've shown up here.' He spun around, heading for the kitchen and rolling his sleeve back up as he did so.

Lucy traipsed behind him. This couldn't have been a worse outcome. When he offered her a drink she accepted with alacrity, and sat at one of the bar stools by the granite-topped kitchen counter.

'Was that your girlfriend?' she heard herself ask.

'Not relevant.' He circled her expressionlessly, forcing her into the awkward position of having to swivel round on the stool until she was looking at him where he sat on one of the chairs at the kitchen table.

'It *is* relevant,' Lucy whispered tightly.

'Because…?'

'Because…' She took a deep breath and stared down into her glass of wine. 'Because I came here to tell you that I'm sorry… I made a mistake… I've… I've missed you…' She drained her glass and braced her shoulders. 'There. I've said it. Now I'm going to leave and you can get on with the rest of your evening.'

'Isabella has been dispatched,' Gabriel drawled. 'Believe it or not, *you* have now become the rest of my evening. So you made a mistake…so you've missed me… Where is this heading? I'm curious.'

'No, you're not,' Lucy breathed on an indrawn breath, 'you're getting a kick out of this!'

She made to move past him but again he reached for her, this time pulling her back hard against him so that she half stumbled into his solid frame. She rested her free hand against his chest and could feel the rapid beating of his heart. Her mouth parted. She wanted him so badly that it physically hurt, but there was no way she would put herself forward as competition with the woman who had clearly already stepped into her shoes. She turned away, but he tilted her chin towards him so that once again their eyes were locked.

'You've moved on.' She heard the forlorn note in her voice and didn't care. Her eyes were drawn to the beating pulse in his neck. 'She's very attractive. I'm glad for you.'

'Are you? Even though you came back here to seduce me into bed with you? And there's no point denying it. I can *feel* it.'

'I'd never seduce anybody who has a girlfriend!' Her absence of any denial of his assumption was answer enough to his question, but she didn't care about that either. She was hurting everywhere inside. She could only think that once she got back on that train matters would finally be sorted.

'Isabella isn't a girlfriend,' Gabriel told her abruptly, and just as abruptly released her to pour himself another drink. Two in quick succession. Never had he needed them more.

'But you were on a date...'

'The third in three weeks.'

'Thank you for that, Gabriel.' This time she met his eyes without flinching. 'That's *just* what I needed to hear. That I was so forgettable.'

'Forgettable? No. Never that.'

'I should leave.'

'You were going to seduce me. Would you feel free to put that into action if I told you that the three women I dated, I dated once, and I wasn't tempted into bed by any of them?'

'Is that true?'

'What happened to those principles of yours? What happened to Mr Right lurking round the corner?'

'I don't care if you don't want a relationship with me.' Lucy had nothing to lose by finally being honest. After all the little deceptions along the way it was a cleansing feeling. 'I don't care if we have some fun for a day or a week or a month. There's no longer any cloud of a phoney engagement. I guess, *yes*, I came here to offer you the no-strings situation you wanted....'

'I think,' Gabriel held her eyes with his, 'it may be a little too late for that.'

'So you *did* sleep with one of those women...you *are* involved with someone else....' Ice-cold resignation pooled inside her and she couldn't get past it to convince herself that at least they were well and truly finished.

'I told you,' Gabriel said huskily, 'I didn't. If you must know, I couldn't...'

'What do you mean?'

'A kitchen isn't the place for this type of conversation.' He drained his glass and debated whether to go for the kill and have a third, but dumped the idea to make his way to the sitting area. Lucy followed, bewildered.

'So?' she asked.

'I need you to sit by me.'

'Why?'

'Because I don't feel comfortable shouting halfway across the room that my libido disappeared the day you walked out of my life.'

In a daze, Lucy teetered across to the sofa and subsided next to him. She badly wanted his arm around her but he sat forward, his hands resting loosely on his thighs, and when he spoke he addressed the ground, so that she had to lean towards him to catch what he was saying.

'I didn't expect you to come,' he threw at her, 'and I wouldn't have chased you. Hell, I figured that, with your exit, my life would get back to normal. So you wanted to hunt down your soulmate. Well, good luck to you! But nothing got back to normal, and now here you are....' He inclined his head to one side so that he was looking at her askance.

'Except the no-strings-attached relationship I'm offering is no longer on the cards,' Lucy intoned dully, and he gave her a crooked smile that had her craven pulses racing. 'I blew it.'

'Let me explain how I never wanted any kind of committed relationship with a woman. Hadn't even contemplated such a possibility. But then *you* happened, and I'm telling you now that a relationship with all the strings you can find attached is the only relationship I'm willing to accept from you.'

'Sorry?'

'You want me… Well, you'll have to get your head round the idea that I'm the guy in your life. I'm the main event. You take me on and your search for Mr Right is down the drain, because I'm going to tie you down for the rest of your life. There won't be anyone else and there's no compromise, no deal to be done.'

'I don't understand. Why would you want that?'

'Why do you think?' He gave a low, dry laugh. 'I'm in love with you, woman. I should have known as much the second I started thinking about you and houses, picturing you on that four-poster bed, getting stressed over whether you would like the garden, whether it would be big enough for the mutt…. And then keeping my hands off you…trying to prove to you that I could be the one… I didn't even know at the time just how important it was to me that you realised that, but I was going to give it a damn good go.'

'You're in love with me…?'

'I could have gone out with a hundred different women when you left and the net result would have been the same. They would have bored me to death. I've spent the past few weeks thinking about you and telling myself that there was no way I was going to show up on your doorstep and open myself up for being knocked back.'

'You love me…. You're in love with me….' She reached out and laced her fingers into his hair. Her heart melted at the searching, open look he gave her. 'I fell in love with you ages ago,' she confessed in a husky undertone, 'and it scared the living daylights out of me because I knew you weren't into commitment. When I went to that little house you'd bought I started to think that maybe you felt there was something more between us than just a fling....'

'And I told you that it was just a house...'

'And not a marriage proposal...'

'I still hadn't come round to the fact that life without you wasn't worth living. I wanted to stop you from leaving, but I didn't know how. And then you walked out and I found that I could barely function.' He straightened, pulled her into him and buried his head in her sweetly scented hair. 'You'll be pleased to hear that I'm functioning just fine right now....'

He took her hand and placed it on his zipper. She shivered to feel the telltale impressive bulge of his erection.

'Remember what I said about the house not being a marriage proposal?' he murmured as he swept her off her feet and began carrying her up to his bedroom. 'Would you do me the favour of ignoring that bloody stupid statement?'

He deposited her gently on the bed. It was where she belonged. It sickened him to think of her anywhere else, and it sickened him even more to think what might have happened if she hadn't shown up on his doorstep.

Would he have sought her out despite what he had said? Where she was concerned his pride was practically non-existent. Hell, he would have. The excuse would have been flimsy, but he wouldn't have been able to bear her absence.

He began removing his clothes, his dark, lustrous eyes pinned to her expressive face, which was now looking at him questioningly.

When he was fully naked he moved to stand by the bed. His big body shuddered as she propped herself up so that she could take his throbbing erection into her mouth and slowly pay it just the sort of exquisite attention that had him rearing back and groaning as his fingers tightened in her hair.

'I need you to marry me,' he told her with the driving urgency that was so much part and parcel of his personality.

He sank onto the bed alongside her and began undressing her with shaking hands. He would never have guessed how good it felt to lose his self-control like this.

'Yes!' Lucy was laughing as she wriggled out of her clothes. 'Yes, yes, *yes*!' She captured his beautiful face between her hands and looked at him seriously. 'You are the most amazing thing that has ever happened in my life. You entered it and changed it and I love you so much it hurts. It was horrible coming to London and doing stuff with you and not having you touch me.'

'It can't have been as hard for you as it was for me, but you wanted space and I was so damn scared that if I made a move you'd take to the hills.'

They hadn't seen each other in weeks and they made love hungrily, greedily, touching each other as though frantic to make up for lost time.

She was ready for him as he thrust powerfully into her, not bothering as he always had in the past with precautions. Lucy didn't even notice until she was lying pleasurably sated next to him. When, suddenly alarmed, she pointed out his omission, he laughed softly and stroked her hair away from her face.

'Would you believe last week I caught myself thinking that if I had got you pregnant you wouldn't have run out on me? So if you *do* get pregnant...' He smoothed his hand over her flat stomach. 'You won't hear me complaining....

In fact, I'm thinking that it might be an idea to start trying right away....'

'I see what you mean about those strings tying us down....' But she was flooded with joyful warmth, as though the sun had begun to shine inside her.

'And by the way—the engagement ring? You know that tasteless bauble has to hit the bin, don't you...?'

'The shop wouldn't have it back. It's in one of the kitchen drawers. I might just hang on to it as a souvenir of a very strange affair.'

'Twists and turns, my darling. Thank God we ended up in the right place. And, while we're on the subject, I'll just tell you that I *would* have hounded you—not that I don't prefer it this way. There's nothing a guy likes more than knowing his woman would cross deserts for him.... On a different subject, I know you don't like accepting gifts from me, but there's no way you're wearing anything but the best on your finger.'

He nudged his leg between hers and grinned as she wriggled against him until she was perfectly positioned.

'You're going to be engaged in style—although it's going to be a very short engagement. In fact, you might find me encouraging that trip to the vicar when we go and break the good news to your parents tomorrow.'

He lifted her hair to nuzzle the nape of her neck while his hand strayed to tease the stiffened bud of her nipple. He flipped her onto him and circled her narrow waist with his big hands.

'Better—much better. I want all my seed in you. Don't forget that we're trying for a baby now....'

Lucy laughed and eased him into her with a groan of pure satisfaction.

'You're moving fast!' She feathered kisses on his face, loving the feel of his rock-hard shaft inside her.

'I'm not one to let the grass grow under my feet,' Gabriel said roughly. 'I have you, and I want to get all those strings as fast as I can and tie you up with them. Figuratively, of course. Although I wouldn't be averse to exploring that concept in the literal sense....'

'Hmm...ruthless...' There was a smile in her voice and her heart was singing with joy.

'You bet. It's just one of those adorable character traits you can spend your life finding out about. Now, enough talking...we have a baby to make....'

* * * * *

THE TRUTH BEHIND
HIS TOUCH

BY
CATHY WILLIAMS

CHAPTER ONE

CAROLINE fanned herself wearily with the guide book which she had been clutching like a talisman ever since she had disembarked from the plane at Malpensa airport in Milan, and took the time to look around her. Somewhere, nestled amongst these ancient, historic buildings and wide, elegant *piazzas*, lay her quarry. She knew that she should be heading directly there, bypassing all temptations of a cold drink and something sweet, sticky, chocolatey and deliciously fattening, but she was hot, she was exhausted and she was ravenous.

'It will take you no time at all!' Alberto had said encouragingly. 'One short flight, Caroline. And a taxi... Maybe a little walking to find his offices, but what sights you'll see. The Duomo. You will never have laid eyes on anything so spectacular. *Palazzos.* More than you can shake a stick at. And the shops. Well, it is many, many years since I have been to Milan, but I can still recall the splendour of the Vittorio Gallery.'

Caroline had looked at him with raised, sceptical eyebrows and the old man had had the grace to flush sheepishly, because this trip to Milan was hardly a sightseeing tour. In fact, she was expected back within forty-eight hours and her heart clenched anxiously at the expectations sitting heavily on her shoulders.

She was to locate Giancarlo de Vito, run him to ground and somehow return to Lake Como with him.

'I would go myself, my dear,' Alberto had murmured, 'but my health does not permit it. The doctor said that I have to rest as much as possible—the strain on my heart… I am not a well man, you understand…'

Caroline wondered, not for the first time, how she had managed to let herself get talked into this mission but there seemed little point dwelling on that. She was here now, surrounded by a million people, perspiring in soaring July temperatures, and it was just too late in the day to have a sudden attack of nerves.

The truth was that the success or failure of this trip was really not her concern. She was the messenger. Alberto, yes, *he* would be affected, but she was really just his personal assistant who happened to be performing a slightly bizarre duty.

Someone bumped into her from behind and she hastily consulted her map and began walking towards the small street which she had highlighted in bold orange.

She had dressed inappropriately for the trip, but it had been cooler by the lake. Here, it was sweltering and her cream trousers stuck to her legs like glue. The plain yellow blouse with its three-quarter-length sleeves had looked suitably smart when she had commenced her journey but now she wished that she had worn something without sleeves, and she should have done something clever with her hair. Put it up into some kind of bun, perhaps. Yes; she had managed to twist it into a long braid of sorts but it kept unravelling and somehow getting itself plastered around her neck.

Caught up in her own physical discomfort and the awkwardness of what lay ahead, she barely noticed the old mellow beauty of the cathedral with its impressive buttresses, spires and statues as she hurried past it, dragging her suitcase which behaved like a recalcitrant child, stopping and swerving and doing its best to misbehave.

Anyone with a less cheerful and equable temperament might have been tempted to curse the elderly employer who had sent them on this impossible mission, which was frankly way beyond the scope of their duties. But Caroline, tired, hot and hungry as she was, was optimistic that she could do what was expected of her. She had enormous faith in human nature. Alberto, on the other hand, was the world's most confirmed pessimist.

She very nearly missed the building. Not knowing what exactly to expect, she had imagined something along the lines of an office in London. Bland, uninspiring, with perhaps too much glass and too little imagination.

Retracing her steps, she looked down at the address which she had carefully printed on an index card, and then up at the ancient exterior of stone and soft, aged pinks, no more than three storeys tall, adorned with exquisite carvings and fronted by two stone columns.

How difficult could Giancarlo be if he worked in this wonderful place? Caroline mused, heart lightening.

'I cannot tell you anything of Giancarlo,' Alberto had said mournfully when she had tried to press him for details of what she would be letting herself in for. 'It is many, many years since I have seen him. I could show you some pictures, but they are so out of date. He would have changed in all these years... If I had a computer... But an old man like me... How could I ever learn now to work one of those things?'

'I could go and get my laptop from upstairs,' she had offered instantly, but he had waved her down.

'No, no. I don't care for those gadgets. Televisions and telephones are as far as I am prepared to go when it comes to technology.'

Privately, Caroline agreed with him. She used her computer to email but that was all, and it was nigh on impossible trying to access the Internet in the house anyway.

So she had few details on which to go. She suspected, however, that Giancarlo was rich, because Alberto had told her in passing that he had 'made something of himself'. Her suspicion crystallised when she stepped into the cool, uber-modern, marbled portico of Giancarlo's offices. If the façade of the building looked as though it had stepped out of an architectural guide to mediaeval buildings, inside the twenty-first century had made its mark.

Only the cool, pale marble underfoot and the scattering of old masterpieces on the walls hinted at the age of the building.

Of course, she wasn't expected. Surprise, apparently, was of the utmost importance, 'or else he will just refuse to see you, I am convinced of it!'.

It took her over thirty-five minutes to try to persuade the elegant receptionist positioned like a guard dog behind her wood-and-marble counter, who spoke far too quickly for Caroline to follow, that she shouldn't be chucked out.

'What is your business here?'

'Ah…'

'Are you expected?'

'Not *exactly…*'

'Are you aware that Signore de Vito is an extremely important man?'

'Er…' Then she had practised her haltering Italian and explained the connection to Giancarlo, produced several documents which had been pored over in silence and the wheels of machinery had finally begun to move.

But still she would have to wait.

Three floors up, Giancarlo, in the middle of a meeting with three corporate financiers, was interrupted by his secretary, who whispered something in his ear that made him still and brought the shutters down on his dark, cold eyes.

'Are you sure?' he asked in a clipped voice. Elena Carli seldom made mistakes; it was why she had worked for him so successfully for the past five-and-a-half years. She did her job with breathtaking efficiency, obeyed orders without question and *seldom* made mistakes. When she nodded firmly, he immediately got to his feet, made his excuses—though not profusely, because these financiers needed him far more than he needed them—and then, meeting dismissed, he walked across to the window to stare down at the paved, private courtyard onto which his offices backed.

So the past he thought to have left behind was returning. Good sense counselled him to turn his back on this unexpected intrusion in his life, but he was curious and what harm would there be in indulging his curiosity? In his life of unimaginable wealth and vast power, curiosity was a rare visitor, after all.

Giancarlo de Vito had been ferociously single-minded and ruthlessly ambitious to get where he was now. He had had no choice. His mother had needed to be kept and after a series of unfortunate lovers the only person left to keep her had been him. He had finished his university career with a first and had launched himself into the world of high finance with such dazzling expertise that it hadn't been long before doors began to open. Within three years of finishing university, he'd been able to pick and choose his employer. Within five years, he'd no longer needed an employer because he had become the powerhouse who did the employing. Now, at just over thirty, he had become a billionaire, diversifying with gratifying success, branching out and stealing the march on competitors with every successive merger and acquisition and in the process building himself a reputation that rendered him virtually untouchable.

His mother had seen only the tip of his enormous success, as she had died six years previously—perhaps, fittingly, in the passenger seat of her young lover's fast car—a victim, as he had seen it, of a life gone wrong. As her only offspring, Giancarlo knew he should have been more heartbroken than he actually was, but his mother had been a temperamental and difficult woman, fond of spending money and easily dissatisfied. He had found her flitting from lover to lover rather distasteful, but never had he once criticized her. At the end of the day, hadn't she been through enough?

Unaccustomed to taking these trips down memory lane, Giancarlo shook himself out of his introspection with a certain amount of impatience. Presumably the woman who had come to see him and who was currently sitting in the grand marble foyer was to blame for his lapse in self-control. With his thoughts back in order and back where they belonged, he buzzed her up.

'You may go up now.' The receptionist beckoned to Caroline, who could have stayed sitting in the air-conditioned foyer quite happily for another few hours. Her feet were killing her and she had finally begun cooling down after the hours spent in the suffocating heat. 'Signora Carli will meet you up at the top of the elevator and show you to Signore De Vito's office. If you like, you may leave your…case here.'

Caroline thought that the last thing the receptionist seemed to want was her battered pull-along being left anywhere in the foyer. At any rate, she needed it with her.

And, now that she was finally here, she felt a little twist of nervousness at the prospect of what lay ahead. She wouldn't want to return to the lake house empty-handed. Alberto had suffered a heart attack several weeks previously. His health was not good and, his doctor had confided in her, the less stress the better.

With a determined lift of her head, Caroline followed the personal assistant in silence, passing offices which seemed abnormally silent, staffed with lots of hard-working executives who barely looked up as they walked past.

Everyone seemed very well-groomed. The women were all thin, good-looking and severe, with their hair scraped back and their suits shrieking of money well spent.

In comparison, Caroline felt overweight, short and dishevelled. She had never been skinny, even as a child. When she sucked her breath in and looked at herself sideways through narrowed eyes, she could almost convince herself that she was curvy and voluptuous, but the illusion was always destroyed the second she took a harder look at her reflection. Nor was her hair of the manageable variety. It rarely did as it was told; it flowed in wild abandon down her back and was only ever remotely obedient when it was wet. Right now the heat had added more curl than normal and she knew that tendrils were flying wildly out of their impromptu braid. She had to keep blowing them off her face.

After trailing along behind Elena—who had introduced herself briefly and then seen fit to say absolutely nothing else on the way up—a door was opened into an office so exquisite that for a few seconds Caroline wasn't even aware that she had been deposited like an unwanted parcel, nor did she notice the man by the window turning slowly around to look at her.

All she could see was the expanse of splendid, antique Persian rug on the marble floor; the soft, silk wallpaper on the walls; the smooth, dark patina of a bookshelf that half-filled an entire wall; the warm, old paintings on the walls—not paintings of silly lines and shapes that no one could ever decipher, but paintings of beautiful landscapes, heavy with trees and rivers.

'Wow,' she breathed, deeply impressed as she continued to look around her with shameless awe.

At long last her eyes rested on the man staring at her and she was overcome with a suffocating, giddy sensation as she absorbed the wild, impossible beauty of his face. Black hair, combed back and ever so slightly too long, framed a face of stunning perfection. His features were classically perfect and invested with a raw sensuality that brought a heated flush to her cheeks. His eyes were dark and unreadable. Expensive, lovingly hand-tailored charcoal-grey trousers sheathed long legs and the crisp white shirt rolled to the elbows revealed strong, bronzed forearms with a sprinkling of dark hair. In the space of a few seconds, Caroline realised that she was staring at the most spectacular-looking man she had ever clapped eyes on in her life. She also belatedly realised that she was gaping, mouth inelegantly open, and she cleared her throat in an attempt to get a hold of herself.

The silence stretched to breaking point and then at last the man spoke and introduced himself, inviting her to take a seat, which she was only too happy to do because her legs felt like jelly. His voice matched his appearance. It was deep, dark, smooth and velvety. It was also icy cold, and a trickle of doubt began creeping in, because this was not a man who looked as though he could be persuaded into doing anything he didn't want to do.

'So…' Giancarlo sat down, pushing himself away from his desk so that he could cross his long legs, and stared at her. 'What makes you think that you can just barge into my offices, Miss…?'

'Rossi. Caroline.'

'I was in the middle of a meeting.'

'I'm so sorry.' She stumbled over the apology. 'I didn't mean to interrupt anything. I would have been happy to wait until you were finished…' Her naturally sunny personality rose to the surface and she offered him a small smile. 'In fact, it was so wonderfully cool in your foyer and I was just so grateful to rest my legs. I've been on the go for absolutely ages and it's as hot as a furnace out there...' In receipt of his continuing and unwelcoming silence, her voice faded away and she licked her lips nervously.

Giancarlo was quite happy to let her stew in her own discomfiture.

'This is a fantastic building, by the way.'

'Let's do away with the pleasantries, Miss Rossi. What are you doing here?'

'Your father sent me.'

'So I gather. Which is why you're sitting in my office. My question is *why*? I haven't had any contact with my father in over fifteen years, so I'm curious as to why he should suddenly decide to send a henchman to get in touch with me.'

Caroline felt an uncustomary warming anger flood through her as she tried to marry up this cold, dark stranger with the old man of whom she was so deeply fond, but getting angry wasn't going to get her anywhere.

'And who *are* you anyway? My father is hardly a spring chicken. Don't tell me that he's managed to find himself a young wife to nurse him faithfully through his old age?' He leaned back in his chair and steepled his fingers together. 'Nothing too beautiful, of course,' he murmured, casting insolent, assessing eyes over her. 'Devotion in the form of a young, beautiful, nubile wife is never a good idea for an old man, even a rich old man...'

'How dare you?'

Giancarlo laughed coldly. 'You show up here, unannounced, with a message from a father who was written out of my life a long time ago... Frankly, I have every right to dare.'

'I am *not* married to your father!'

'Well, now the alternative is even more distasteful, not to mention downright stupid. Why involve yourself with someone three times your age unless you're in it for the financial gain? Don't tell me the sex is breathtaking?'

'I can't believe you're saying these things!' She wondered how she could have been so bowled over by the way he looked when he was obviously a loathsome individual, just the sort of cold, unfeeling, sneering sort she hated. 'I'm not involved with your father in any way other than professionally, *signore*!'

'No? Then what is a young girl like you doing in a rambling old house by a lake with only an old man for company?'

Caroline glared at him. She was still smarting at the way his eyes had roamed over her and dismissed her as 'nothing too beautiful'. She knew she wasn't beautiful but to hear it casually emerge from the mouth of someone she didn't know was beyond rude. Especially from the mouth of someone as physically compelling as the man sitting in front of her. Why hadn't she done what most other people would have in similar circumstances and found herself an Internet café so that she could do some background research on the man she had been told to ferret out? At least then she might have been prepared!

She had to grit her teeth together and fight the irresistible urge to grab her suitcase and jump ship.

'Well? I'm all ears.'

'There's no need to be horrible to me, *signore*. I'm sorry if I've ruined your meeting, or…or whatever you were doing, but I didn't *volunteer* to come here.'

Giancarlo almost didn't believe his ears. People never accused him of being *horrible*. Granted, they might sometimes think that, but it was vaguely shocking to actually *hear* someone come right out and say it. Especially a woman. He was accustomed to women doing everything within their power to please him. He looked narrowly at his uninvited visitor. She was certainly not the sort of rake-thin beauty eulogised in the pages of magazines. She was trying hard to conceal her expression but it was transparently clear that the last place she wanted to be was in his office, being interrogated.

Too bad.

'I take it my father manipulated you into doing what he wanted. Are you his housekeeper? Why would he employ an English housekeeper?'

'I'm his personal assistant,' Caroline admitted reluctantly. 'He used to know my father once upon a time. Your father had a one-year posting in England lecturing at a university and my father was one of his students. He was my father's mentor and they kept in touch after your father returned to Italy. My father is Italian. I think he enjoyed having someone he could speak to in Italian.

'Anyway, I didn't go to university, but my parents thought it would be nice for me to learn Italian, seeing that it's my father's native tongue, and he asked Alberto if he could help me find a posting over here for a few months. So I'm helping your father with his memoirs and also pretty much taking care of all the admin—stuff like that. Don't you want to know…um…how he is? You haven't seen him in such a long time.'

'If I had wanted to see my father, don't you think I would have contacted him before now?'

'Yes, well, pride can sometimes get in the way of us doing what we want to do.'

'If your aim is to play amateur psychologist, then the door is right behind you. Avail yourself of it.'

'I'm not playing amateur psychologist,' Caroline per-

sisted stubbornly. 'I just think, well, I know that it probably wasn't ideal when your parents got divorced. Alberto
doesn't talk much about it, but I know that when your
mother walked out and took you with her you were only
twelve...'

'I don't believe I'm hearing this!' Intensely private,
Giancarlo could scarcely credit that he was listening to
someone drag his past out of the closet in which it had been
very firmly shut.

'How else am I supposed to deal with this situation?'
Caroline asked, bewildered and dismayed.

'I am not in the habit of discussing my past!'

'Yes, well, that's not *my* fault.' She felt herself soften.
'Don't you think that it's a good thing to talk about the
things that bother us? Don't you *ever* think about your dad?'

His internal line buzzed and he spoke in rapid Italian,
telling his secretary to hold all further calls until he ad-
vised her otherwise. Suddenly, filled with a restless energy
he couldn't seem to contain, he pushed himself away from
the desk and moved across to the window to look briefly
outside before turning around and staring at the girl on the
chair who had swivelled to face him.

She looked as though butter wouldn't melt in her
mouth—very young, very innocent and with a face as transparent as a pane of glass. Right now, he seemed to be an
object of pity, and he tightened his mouth with a sense of
furious outrage.

'He's had a heart attack,' Caroline told him abruptly, her
eyes beginning to well up because she was so very fond
of him. Having him rushed into hospital, dealing with the
horror of it all on her own had been almost more than she
could take. 'A very serious one. In fact, for a while it was
touch and go.' She opened her satchel, rummaged around

for a tissue and found a pristine white handkerchief pressed into her hand.

'Sorry,' she whispered shakily. 'But I don't know how you can just stand there like a statue and not feel a thing.'

Big brown eyes looked accusingly at him and Giancarlo flushed, annoyed with himself because there was no reason why he should feel guilty on that score. He had no relationship with his father. Indeed, his memories of life in the big house by the lake were a nightmare of parental warfare. Alberto had married his very young and very pretty blonde wife when he had been in his late forties, nearly twenty-five years older than Adriana, and was already a cantankerous and confirmed bachelor.

It had been a marriage that had struggled on against all odds and had been, to all accounts, hellishly difficult for his demanding young wife.

His mother had not held back from telling him everything that had been so horrifically wrong with the relationship, as soon as he had been old enough to appreciate the gory detail. Alberto had been selfish, cold, mean, dismissive, contemptuous and probably, his mother had maintained viciously, would have had other women had he not lacked even basic social skills when it came to the opposite sex. He had, Adriana had wept on more than one occasion, thrown them out without a penny—so was it any wonder that she sometimes needed a little alcohol and a few substances to help her get by?

So many things for which Giancarlo had never forgiven his father...

He had stood on the sidelines and watched his delicate, spoilt mother—without any qualifications to speak of, always reliant on her beauty—demean herself by taking lover after lover, searching for the one who might want her enough to stick around. By the time she had died she had been a pathetic shadow of her former self.

'You have no idea of what my life was like, or what my mother's life was like,' Giancarlo framed icily. 'Perhaps my father has mellowed. Ill health has a habit of making servants of us all. However, I'm not interested in building bridges. Is that why he sent you here—because he's now an old man and he wants my forgiveness before he shuffles off this mortal coil?' He gave a bark of cynical, contemptuous laughter. 'I don't think so.'

She had continued playing with the handkerchief, twisting it between her fingers. Giancarlo thought that when it came to messengers, his father could not have been more calculating in his choice. The woman was a picture of teary-eyed incomprehension. Anyone would be forgiven for thinking that she worked for a saint, instead of for the man who had made his mother's life a living hell.

His sharp eyes narrowed and focused, taking in the details of her appearance. Her clothes were a fashion disaster—trousers and a blouse in a strange, sickly shade of yellow, both of which would have been better suited to someone twice her age. Her hair seemed to be escaping from a sort of makeshift braid, and it was long—really long. Not at all like the snappy bobs he was accustomed to seeing on women. And it was curly. She was free of make-up and he was suddenly conscious of the fact that her skin was very smooth, satin smooth, and she had an amazing mouth—full, well-defined lips, slightly parted now to reveal pearly-white teeth as she continued to stare at him with disappointment and incredulity.

'I'm sorry you're still so bitter about the past,' she murmured quietly. 'But he would really like to see you. Why is it too late to mend bridges? It would mean the world to him.'

'So have you managed to see anything of our beautiful city?'

'What? No. No, I've come directly here. Look, is there anything I can do or say to convince you to...to come back with me?'

'You have got to be kidding, haven't you? I mean, even if I were suddenly infused with a burning desire to become a prodigal son, do you really imagine that I would be able to drop everything, pack a bag and hop on the nearest train for Lake Como? Surprise, surprise—I have an empire to run.'

'Yes, but...'

'I'm a very busy man, Miss Rossi, and I have already allotted you a great deal of my very valuable time. Now, you could keep trying to convince me that I'm being a monster in not clapping my hands for joy that my father has suddenly decided to get in touch with me thanks to a bout of ill health...'

'You make it sound as though he's had a mild attack of flu! He's suffered a very serious *heart attack*.'

'For which I am truly sorry.' Giancarlo extended his arms wide in a gesture of such phoney sympathy that Caroline had to clench her fists to stop herself from smacking him. 'As I would be on learning of any stranger's brush with death. But, alas, you're going to have to go back empty-handed.'

Defeated, Caroline stood up and reached down for her suitcase.

'Where are you staying?' Giancarlo asked with scrupulous politeness as he watched the slump of her shoulders. God, had the old man really thought that there would be no consequences to pay for the destructive way he had treated his wife? He was as rich as they came and yet, according to Adriana, he had employed the best lawyers in the land to ensure that she received the barest of settlements, accessed through a trustee who had made sure the basics, the *absolute* basics, were paid for, and a meagre allowance handed over to her, like a child being given pocket money, scarcely enough to provide any standard of living. He had often wondered, over the years, whether his mother would have been as desperate to find love if she had been left sufficient money to meet her requirements.

Caroline wearily told him, although she knew full well that he didn't give a damn where she was staying. He just wanted her out of his office. She would be returning having failed. Of course, Alberto would be far too proud to do anything other than shrug his shoulders and say something about having tried, but she would know the truth. She would know that he would be gutted.

'Well, you make sure you try the food market at the Rinascente. You'll enjoy it. Tremendous views. And, of course, the shopping there is good as well.'

'I hate shopping.' Caroline came to a stop in front of the office door and turned around to find that he was virtually on top of her, towering a good eight or nine inches above her and even more intimidating this close up than he had been sitting safely behind his desk or lounging by the window.

The sun glinted from behind, picking out the striking angles of his face and rendering them more scarily beautiful. He had the most amazing eyelashes, long, lush and dark, the sort of eyelashes that most women could only ever have achieved with the help of tons of mascara.

She felt a sickening jolt somewhere in the region of her stomach and was suddenly and uncomfortably aware of her breasts, too big for her height, now sensitive, tingly and weighty as he stared down at her. Her hands wanted to flutter to the neckline of her blouse and draw the lapels tightly together. She flushed with embarrassment; how could she have forgotten that she was the ugly duckling?

'And I don't want to be having this polite conversation with you,' she breathed in a husky, defiant undertone.

'Come again?'

'I'm sorry your parents got divorced, and I'm really sorry that it left such a mark on you, but I think it's horrible that you won't give your father another chance. How do you know exactly what happened between your parents? You were only a child. Your father's ill and you'd rather carry on holding a grudge than try and make the most of the time you have left of him. He might die tomorrow, for all we know!'

That short speech took a lot out of her. She wasn't usually defiant, but this man set her teeth on edge. 'How can you say that, even if you were interested in meeting him, you couldn't possibly get away because you're too important?'

'I said that I have an empire to run.'

'It's the same thing!' She was shaking all over, like a leaf, but she looked up at him with unflinching determination, chin jutting out, her brown eyes, normally mild, flashing fire. 'Okay, I'm not going to see you again…' Caroline drew in a deep breath and impatiently swept her disobedient hair from away her face. 'So I can be really honest with you.'

Giancarlo moved to lounge against the door, arms folded, an expression of lively curiosity on his face. Her cheeks were flushed and her eyes glittered. She was a woman in a rage and he was getting the impression that this was a woman who didn't *do* rages. God, wasn't this turning into one hell of a day?

'I don't suppose *anyone* is really ever honest with you, are they?' She looked around the office, with its mega-expensive fittings, ancient rug, worn bookshelves, the painting on the wall—the only modern one she had glimpsed, which looked vaguely familiar. Who was really ever that honest with someone as wealthy as he appeared to be, as good-looking as he was? He had the arrogance of a man who always got exactly what he wanted.

'It's useful when my man who handles my stocks and shares tells me what he thinks. Although, in fairness, I usually know more than he does. I should get rid of him but—' he shrugged with typical Italian nonchalance '—we go back a long way.'

He shot her a smile that was so unconsciously charming that Caroline was nearly knocked backwards by the force of it. It was like being in a dark room only to be suddenly dazzled by a ray of blistering sunshine. Which didn't distract her from the fact that he refused to see his father, a sick and possibly dying old man. Refused to bury the hatchet, whatever the consequences. Charming smiles counted for nothing when it came to the bigger picture!

'I'm glad you think that this is a big joke,' she said tightly. 'I'm glad that you can laugh about it, but you know what? I feel *sorry* for you! You might think that the only thing that matters is all…all *this*…but none of this counts when it comes to relationships and family. I think you're… you're *arrogant* and *high-handed* and making a huge mistake!'

Outburst over, Caroline yanked open the office door to a surprised Elena, who glanced at her with consternation before looking behind to where her boss, the man who never lost his steely grip on his emotions, was staring at the small, departing brunette with the incredulous expression of someone who has been successfully tackled when least expecting it.

'Stop staring,' Giancarlo said. He shook his head, dazed, and then offered his secretary a wry grin. 'We all lose our cool sometimes.'

CHAPTER TWO

MILAN was a diverse and beautiful city. There were sufficient museums, galleries, basilicas and churches to keep any tourist busy. The Galleria Vittorio was a splendid and elegant arcade, stuffed with cafés and shops. Caroline knew all this because the following day—her last day before she returned to Alberto, when she would have to admit failure—she made sure to read all the literature on a city which she might not visit again. It was tarnished with the miserable experience of having met Giancarlo De Vito.

The more Caroline thought about him, the more arrogant and unbearable he seemed. She just couldn't find a single charitable thing to credit him with. Alberto would be waiting for her, expecting to see her arrive with his son and, failing that, he would be curious for details. Would she be honest and admit to him that she had found his sinfully beautiful son loathsome and overbearing? Would any parent, even an estranged parent, be grateful for information like that?

She looked down to where her ice-cold glass of lemonade was slowly turning warm in the searing heat. She had dutifully spent two hours walking around the Duomo, admiring the stained-glass windows, the impressive statues of saints and the extravagant carvings. But her heart hadn't been in it, and now here she was, in one of the little cafés, which outside on a hot summer day was packed to the rafters with tourists sitting and lazily people-watching.

Her thoughts were in turmoil. With an impatient sigh, she glanced down at her watch, wondering how she would fill the remainder of her day, and was unaware of the shadow looming over her until she heard Giancarlo's velvety, familiar voice which had become embedded in her head like an irritating burr.

'You lied to me.'

Caroline looked up, shading her eyes from the glare of the sun, at about the same time as a wad of papers landed on the small circular table in front of her.

She was so shocked to see him towering over her, blocking out the sun like a dark avenging angel, that she half-spilled her drink in her confusion.

'What are you doing here? And how did you find me?' Belatedly she noticed the papers on the table. 'And what's all that stuff?'

'We need to have a little chat and this place isn't doing it for me.'

Caroline felt her heart lift a little. Maybe he was reconsidering his original stance. Maybe, just maybe, he had seen the light and was now prepared to let bygones be bygones. She temporarily forgot his ominous opening words and the mysterious stack of papers in front of her.

'Of course!' She smiled brightly and then cleared her throat when there was no reciprocal smile. 'I… You haven't said how you managed to find me. Where are we going? Am I supposed to bring all this stuff with me?'

Presumably, yes, as he spun round on his heels and was scouring the *piazza* through narrowed eyes. Did he notice the interested stares he was garnering from the tourists, particularly the women? Or was he immune to that sort of attention?

Caroline grabbed the papers and scrambled to follow him as he strode away from the café through a series of small roads, leaving the crush of tourists behind.

Today, she had worn the only other outfit she had brought with her, a summer dress with small buttons down the front. Because it left her shoulders bare, and because she was so acutely conscious of her generous breasts, she had a thin pink cardigan slung loosely over her—which wasn't exactly practical, given the weather, but without it she felt too exposed and self-conscious.

With the ease of someone who lived in the city, he weaved his way through the busier areas until they were finally at a small café tucked away from the tourist hotspots, although even here the ancient architecture, the charming square with its sixteenth-century well, the engravings on some of the façades, were all photo opportunities.

She dithered behind him, feeling a bit like a spare part as he spoke in rapid Italian to a short, plump man whom she took to be the owner of the café. Then he motioned her inside where it was blessedly cool and relatively empty.

'You can sit,' Giancarlo said irritably when she continued to hover by the table. What did his father see in the woman? He barely remembered Alberto, but one thing he *did* remember was that he had not been the most docile person in the world. If his mother had been a difficult woman, then she had found her match in her much older husband. What changes had the years wrought, if Alberto was happy to work with someone who had to be the most background woman he had ever met? And once again she was in an outfit that would have been more suitable on a woman twice her age. Truly the English hadn't got a clue when it came to fashion.

He found himself appraising her body and then, surprisingly, lingering on her full breasts pushing against the thin cotton dress, very much in evidence despite the washed-out cardigan she had draped over her shoulders.

'You never said how you managed to find me,' Caroline repeated a little breathlessly as she slid into the chair opposite him.

She shook away the giddy, drowning feeling she had when she looked too hard at him. Something about his animal sex-appeal was horribly unsettling, too hard to ignore and not quite what she was used to.

'You told me where you were staying. I went there first thing this morning and was told by the receptionist that you'd left for the Duomo. It was just a question of time before you followed the herd to one of the cafés outside.'

'So…have you had a rethink?' Caroline asked hopefully. She wondered how it was that he could look so cool and urbane in his cream trousers and white shirt while the rest of the population seemed to be slowly dissolving under the summer sun.

'Have a look at the papers in front of you.'

Caroline dutifully flicked through them. 'I'm sorry, I have no idea what these are—and I'm not very good with numbers.' She had wisely tied her hair back today but still some curling strands found their way to her cheeks and she absent-mindedly tucked them behind her ears while she continued to frown at the pages and pages of bewildering columns and numbers in front of her, finally giving up.

'After I saw you I decided to run a little check on Alberto's company accounts. You're looking at my findings.'

'I don't understand why you've shown me this. I don't know anything about Alberto's financial affairs. He doesn't talk about that at all.'

'Funny, but I never thought him particularly shy when

it came to money. In fact, I would say that he's always had his finger on the button in that area.'

'How would you know, when you haven't seen him for over a decade?'

Giancarlo thought of the way Alberto had short changed his mother and his lips curled cynically. 'Let's move away from that contentious area, shall we? And let's focus on one or two interesting things I unearthed.' He sat back as cold drinks were placed in front of them, along with a plate of delicate little *tortas* and pastries. 'By the way, help yourself…' He gestured to the dish of pastries and cakes and was momentarily sidetracked when she pulled her side plate in front of her and piled a polite mound, but a mound nevertheless, of the delicacies on it.

'You're actually going to eat all of those?' he heard himself ask, fascinated against his will.

'I know, I shouldn't really. But I'm starving.' Caroline sighed at the diet which she had been planning for ages and which had yet to get underway. 'You don't mind, do you? I mean…they're not just here for *show*, are they?'

'No, *di niente*.' He sat back and watched as she nibbled her way through the pastries, politely leaving one, licking the sweet crumbs off her fingers with enjoyment. A rare sight. The stick-thin women he dated pushed food round their plates and would have recoiled in horror at the thought of eating anything as fattening as a pastry.

Of course, he should be getting on with what he wanted to say, but he had been thrown off course and he still was when she shot him an apologetic smile. There was an errant crumb at the side of her mouth and just for an instant he had an overwhelming urge to brush it off. Instead, he gestured to her mouth with his hand.

'I always have big plans for going on a diet.' Caroline blushed. 'Once or twice I actually did, but diets are deadly.

Have you ever been on one? No, I bet you haven't. Well, salads are all well and good, but just try making them interesting. I guess I just really love food.'

'That's...unusual. In a woman. Most of the women I meet do their best to avoid the whole eating experience.'

Of course he would be the type who only associated with model types, Caroline thought sourly. Thin, leggy women who weighed nothing. She wished she hadn't indulged her sweet tooth. Not that it mattered because, although he might be good-looking—well, staggering, really—he wasn't the sort of man she would ever go for. So what did it matter if he thought that she was overweight and greedy into the bargain?

'You were saying something about Alberto's financial affairs?' She glanced down at her watch, because why on earth should he have the monopoly on precious time? 'It's just that I leave tomorrow morning and I want to make sure that I get through as much as possible before I go.'

Giancarlo was, for once in his life, virtually lost for words. Was she *hurrying him along*?

'I think,' he asserted without inflection, 'that your plans will have to take a back seat until I'm finished.'

'You haven't told me whether you've decided to put the past behind you and accompany me back to Lake Como.' She didn't know why she was bothering to ask the question because it was obvious that he had no such intention.

'So you came here to see me for the sole purpose of masterminding a jolly reunion...'

'It wasn't *my* idea.'

'Immaterial. Getting back to the matter in hand, the fact is that Alberto's company accounts show a big, gaping black hole.'

Caroline frowned because she genuinely had no idea what he was talking about.

'*Si,*' Giancarlo imparted without a shade of regret as he continued to watch her so carefully that she could feel the colour mounting in her cheeks. 'He has been leaking money for the past ten years but recently it's become something more akin to a haemorrhage...'

Caroline gasped and stared at him in sudden consternation. 'Oh my goodness... Do you think that that's why he had the heart attack?'

'I beg your pardon?'

'I didn't think he took an active interest in what happened in the company. I mean, he's been pretty much a recluse since I came to live with him.'

'Which would be how long ago?'

'Several months. Originally, I only intended to come for a few weeks, but we got along so well and there were so many things he wanted me to do that I found myself staying on.' She fixed anxious brown eyes on Giancarlo, who seemed sublimely immune to an ounce of compassion at the news he had casually delivered.

'Are you...are you sure you've got your facts right?'

'I'm never wrong,' he said drily. 'It's possible that Alberto hasn't played an active part in running his company for some time now. It's more than possible that he's been merrily living off the dividends and foolishly imagining that his investments are paying off.'

'And what if he only recently found out?' Caroline cried, determined not to become too over-emotional in front of a man who, she knew, would see emotion in a woman as repellent. Besides, she had cried on him yesterday. She still had the handkerchief to prove it. Once had been bad enough but twice would be unforgivable.

'Do you think that that might have contributed to his heart attack? Do you think that he became so stressed that it affected his health?' Horribly rattled at that thought, she distractedly helped herself to the last pastry lying uneaten on her plate.

'No one can ever accuse me of being a gullible man, Signorina Rossi.' Giancarlo was determined to stick to the script. 'One lesson I've learnt in life is that, when it comes to money, there will always be people around who are more than happy to scheme their way into getting their hands on some of it.'

'Yes. Yes, I suppose so. Whatever. Poor Alberto. He never mentioned a word and yet he must have been so worried. Imagine having to deal with that on your own.'

'Yes. Poor Alberto. Still, whilst poring over these findings, it occurred to me that your mission here might very well have been twofold…'

'The doctor said that stress can cause all sorts of health problems.'

'Focus, signorina!'

Caroline fell silent and looked at him. The sun wafting through the pane of glass made his hair look all the more glossy. She vaguely noticed the way it curled at the collar of his shirt. Somehow, it made him look very exotic and very European.

'Now are you with me?'

'There's no need to talk down to me!'

'There's every need. You have the most wandering mind of anyone I've ever met.'

Caroline shot him a look of simmering resentment and added 'rude' to the increasingly long list of things she didn't like about him.

'And you are the *rudest* person I've ever met in my entire life!'

Giancarlo couldn't remember the last time anyone had ever dared to insult him to his face. He didn't think it had ever happened. Rather than be sidetracked, however, he chose to overlook her offensive remark.

'It occurred to me that my father's health, if your story about his heart attack is to be believed, might not be the primary reason for your visit to Milan.'

'If my story is to be believed?' She shook her head with a puzzled frown. 'Why would I lie about something like that?'

'I'll answer a question with a question—why would my father suddenly choose *now* to seek me out? He had more than one opportunity to get in touch. He never bothered. So why now? Shall I put forward a theory? He's wised up to the fact that his wealth has disappeared down the pro- verbial tubes and has sent you to check out the situation. Perhaps he told you that, if I seemed amenable to the idea of meeting up, you might mention the possibility of a loan?'

Shocked and disturbed by Giancarlo's freewheeling as- sumptions and cynical, half-baked misunderstandings, Caroline didn't know where to begin. She just stared at him as the colour drained away from her face. She wasn't normally given to anger, but right now she had to stop her- self from picking her plate up and smashing it over his ar- rogant head.

'So maybe I wasn't entirely accurate when I accused you of lying to me. Maybe it would be more accurate to say that you were conveniently economical with the full truth...'

'I can't believe I'm hearing you say these things! How could you accuse your own father of trying to squeeze money out of you?'

Giancarlo flushed darkly under her steady, clear-eyed, incredulous gaze. 'Like I said, money has a nasty habit of bringing out the worst in people. Do you know that it's a given fact that the second someone wins a lottery, they suddenly discover that they have a hell of a lot more close friends and relatives than they ever imagined?'

'Alberto hasn't sent me here on a mission to get money out of you or…or to ask you for a loan!'

'Are you telling me that he had no idea that I was now a wealthy man?'

'That's not the point.' She remembered Alberto's statement that Giancarlo had made something of himself.

'No? You're telling me that there's no link between one semi-bankrupt father who hasn't been on the scene in nearly two decades and his sudden, inexplicable desire to meet the rich son he was happy to kick out of his house once upon a time?'

'Yes!'

'Well, if you really believe that, if you're not in cahoots with Alberto, then you must be incredibly naïve.'

'I feel very sorry for you, Signor De Vito.'

'Call me Giancarlo. I feel as though we almost know each other. Certainly no one can compete with you when it comes to delivering offensive remarks. You are in a league of your own.'

Caroline flushed because she was not given to being offensive. She was placid and easy-going by nature. However, she was certainly not going to apologise for speaking her mind to Giancarlo.

'You are pretty offensive as well,' she retaliated quietly. 'You've just accused me of being a liar. Maybe in *your* world you can never trust anyone…'

'I think it's fair to say that trust is a much over-rated virtue. I have a great deal of money. I've learnt to protect myself, simple as that.' He gave an elegant shrug, dismissing the topic. But Caroline wasn't quite ready to let the matter drop, to allow him to continue believing, unchallenged, that he had somehow been targeted by Alberto. She wouldn't let him walk away thinking the worst of either of them.

'I don't think that trust is an over-rated virtue. I told you that I feel sorry for you and I really do.' She had to steel herself to meet and hold the dark, forbidding depths of his icy eyes. 'I think it's sad to live in a world where you can never allow yourself to believe the best in other people. How can you ever be happy if you're always thinking that the people around you are out to take advantage of you? How can you ever be happy if you don't have faith in the people who are close to you?'

Giancarlo very nearly burst out laughing at that. What planet was this woman from? It was a cutthroat world out there and it became even more cutthroat when money and finances were involved. You had to keep your friends close and your enemies a whole lot closer in order to avoid the risk of being knifed in the back.

'Don't go getting evangelical on me,' he murmured drily and he noted the pink colour rise to her cheeks. 'You're blushing,' he surprised himself by saying.

'Because I'm angry!' But she put her hands to her face and glared at him. 'You're so...so *superior*! What sort of people do you mix with that you would suspect them of trying to use you for what you can give them? I didn't know anything about you when I agreed to come here. I didn't know that you had lots of money. I just knew that Alberto was ill and he wanted to make his peace with you.'

The oddest thing seemed to be happening. Giancarlo could feel himself getting distracted. Was it because of the way those tendrils of curly hair were wisping against her face? Or was it because her anger made her almond-shaped eyes gleam like a furious spitting cat's? Or maybe it was the fact that, when she leant forward like that, the weight and abundance of her breasts brushing against the small table acted like a magnet to his wandering eyes.

It was a strange sensation to experience this slight loss of self-control because it never happened in his dealings with women. And he was a connoisseur when it came to the opposite sex. Without a trace of vanity, he knew that he possessed a combination of looks, power and influence that most women found an irresistible aphrodisiac. Right now, he had only recently broken off a six-month relationship with a model whose stunning looks had graced the covers of a number of magazines. She had begun to make noises about 'taking things further'; had started mentioning friends and relatives who were thinking of tying the knot; had begun to show an unhealthy interest in the engagement-ring section of expensive jewellery shops.

Giancarlo had no interest in going down the matrimonial path. There were two vital lessons he felt he had taken away from his parents: the first was that there was no such thing as a happy-ever-after. The second was that it was very easy for a woman to turn from angel to shrew. The loving woman who was happy to accommodate on every level quickly became the demanding, needy harridan who needed reassurance and attention round the clock.

He had watched his mother contrive to play the perfect partner on so many occasions that he had lost count. He had watched her perform her magic with whatever man happened to be the flavour of the day for a while, had watched her bat her eyelashes and flutter her eyes—but then, when things began winding down, he had seen how she had changed from eager to desperate, from hard-to-get to clingy and dependent. The older she had got, the more pitiful a sight she had made.

Of course, he was a red-blooded man with an extremely healthy libido, but as far as Giancarlo was concerned work was a far better bet when it came to reliability. Women, enjoyable as they might be, became instantly expendable the second they began thinking that they could change him.

He had never let any woman get under his skin and he was surprised now to find his thoughts drifting ever so slightly from the matter at hand.

He had confronted her, having done some background research, simply to have his suspicions confirmed. It had been a simple exercise in proving to her—and via her to Alberto—that he wasn't a mug who could be taken for a ride. At which point, his plan had been to walk away, warning guns sounding just in case they were tempted to try a second approach.

From the very second Caroline had shown up unannounced in his office, he had not allowed a shred of sentiment to colour his judgement. Bitter memories of the stories handed down to him from his mother still cast a long shadow. The truth he had seen with his very own eyes—the way her lack of any kind of robust financial settlement from a man who would have been very wealthy at the time had influenced her behaviour patterns—could not be overlooked.

'You must get bored out there,' Giancarlo heard himself remark when he should have really been thinking of concluding their conversation so that he could return to the various meetings waiting for him back at the office. Without taking his eyes off her, he flicked a finger and more cold drinks were brought to their table.

Caroline could no more follow this change in the conversation than she could have dealt with a snarling crocodile suddenly deciding to smile and offer her a cup of tea. She looked at him warily and wondered whether this was a roundabout lead-up to another scathing attack.

'Why are you interested?' she asked cautiously.

'Why not? It's not every day that a complete stranger waltzes into my office with a bombshell. Even if it turns out to be a bombshell that's easy to defuse. Also—and I'll be completely honest on this score—you don't strike me as the sort of person capable of dealing with the man I remember as being my father.'

Caroline was drawn into the conversation against her will. 'What do you remember?' she asked hesitantly. With another cold drink in front of her, the sight of those remaining pastries was awfully tempting. As though reading her mind, Giancarlo ordered a few more, different ones this time, smiling as they were placed in front of her.

He was amused to watch the struggle on her face as she looked down at them.

'What do I remember of my father? Now, let's think about this. Domineering. Frequently ill-tempered. Controlling. In short, not the easiest person in the world.'

'Like you, in other words.'

Giancarlo's mouth tightened because this was an angle that had never occurred to him and he wasn't about to give it house-room now.

'Sorry. I shouldn't have said that.'

'No, you shouldn't, but I'm already getting used to the idea that you speak before you think. Something else I imagine Alberto would have found unacceptable.'

'I really don't like you *at all*,' Caroline said through gritted teeth. 'And I take back what I said. You're *nothing* like Alberto.'

'I'm thrilled to hear that. So, enlighten me.' He felt a twinge of intense curiosity about this man who had been so thoroughly demonised by his ex-wife.

'Well.' Caroline smiled slowly and Giancarlo was amazed at how that slow, reluctant, suspicious smile altered the contours of her face, turning her into someone strangely beautiful in a lush, ripe way that was even more erotic, given the innocence of everything else about her. It put all sorts of crazy thoughts in his head, although the thoughts lasted only an instant, disappearing fast under the mental discipline that was so much part and parcel of his personality.

'He can be grumpy. He's very grumpy now because he hates being told what he can and can't eat and what time he has to go to bed. He hates me helping him physically, so he's employed a local woman, a nurse from the hospital, to help him instead, and I'm constantly having to tell him that he's got to be less bossy and critical of her.

'He was very polite when I first arrived. I think he knew that he was doing my dad a favour, but he figured that he would only have to be on good behaviour for a few weeks. I don't think he knew what to do with me, to start with. He's not been used to company. He wasn't comfortable making eye contact, but none of that lasted too long. We discovered that we shared so many interests—books, old movies, the garden. In fact, the garden has been invaluable now that Alberto is recovering. Every day we go down to the pond just beyond the walled rose-garden. We sit in the folly, read a bit, chat a bit. He likes me to read to him even though he's forever telling me that I need to put more expression in my voice... I guess all that's going to have to go...'

Giancarlo, who hadn't thought of what he had left behind for a very long time, had a vivid memory of that pond and of the folly, a weird gazebo-style creation with a very comfortable bench inside where he likewise had enjoyed whiling away his time during the long summer months when he had been on holiday. He shook away the memory as if clearing cobwebs from a cupboard that hadn't been opened for a long time.

'What do you mean that you guess that's all "going to have to go"?'

Caroline settled worried eyes on his face. For someone who was clearly so intelligent, she was surprised that he didn't seem to follow her. Then she realised that she couldn't very well explain without risking another attack on Alberto's scruples.

'Nothing,' she mumbled when his questioning silence threatened to become too uncomfortable.

'Tut tut. Are you going to get tongue-tied on me?'

The implication being that she talked far too much, Caroline concluded, hurt.

'What do you mean? And don't bother trying to be coy. It doesn't suit you.'

Caroline didn't think she could feel more loathing for another human being if she tried.

'Well, if Alberto has run into financial difficulties, then he's not going to be able to maintain the house, is he? I mean, it's enormous. Right now, a lot of it isn't used, but he would still have to sell it. And please don't tell me that this is a ploy to try and get money out of you. It isn't.' She sighed in weary resignation. 'I don't know why I'm telling you that. You won't believe me anyway.' Suddenly, she was anxious to leave, to get back to the house on the lake, although she had no idea what she was going to do once she got there. Confront Alberto with his problems? Risk jeopardising his fragile health by piling more stress on his shoulders?

'I'm not even sure your father knows the truth of the situation,' she said miserably. 'I'm certain he would have mentioned something to me.'

'Why would he? You've been around for five seconds. I suggest the first person on his list of confidants would probably have been his accountant.'

'Maybe he's told Father Rafferty. I could go and see him at the church and find out if he knows about any of this. That would be the best thing, because Father Rafferty would be able to put everything into perspective. He's very practical and upbeat.'

'Father Rafferty…?'

'Alberto attends mass at the local church every Sunday. Has done for a long time, I gather. He and Father Rafferty have become close friends. I think your father likes Father Rafferty's Irish sense of humour—and the odd glass of whisky. I should go. All of this…'

'Is probably very unsettling, and probably not what you contemplated when you first decided to come over to Italy.'

'I don't mind!' Caroline was quick to reply. She bit back the temptation to tell him that *someone* had to be there for Alberto.

Giancarlo was realising that his original assumption, which had made perfect sense at the time, had been perhaps a little too hasty. The woman was either an excellent, Oscar-winning actress or else she had been telling the truth all along: her visit had not been instigated for financial purposes.

Now his brain was engaged on a different path; he sat back and looked at her as he stroked his chin thoughtfully with one long, brown finger.

'I expect this nurse he's hired is a private nurse?'

Caroline hadn't given that a second's thought, but now she blanched. How much would that be costing? And didn't it prove that Alberto had no idea of the state of his finances? Why, if he did know, would he be spending money on hiring a private nurse who would be costing him an arm and a leg?

'And naturally he must be paying *you*,' Giancarlo continued remorselessly. 'How much?' He named a figure that was so ridiculously high that Caroline burst out laughing. She laughed until she felt tears come to her eyes. It was as though she had found a sudden outlet for her stressful, frantic thoughts and her body was reacting of its own volition, even though Giancarlo was now looking at her with the perplexed expression of someone dealing with a complete idiot.

'Sorry.' She hiccupped her way back to some level of seriousness, although she could still feel her mirth lurking close to the surface. 'You've got to be kidding. Take that figure and maybe divide it by four.'

'Don't be ridiculous. No one could survive on that.'

'But I never came here for the money,' Caroline explained patiently. 'I came here to improve my Italian. Alberto was doing me a favour by taking me in. I don't have to pay for food and I don't pay rent. When I return to England, the fact that I will be able to communicate in another language will be a great help to me when it comes to getting a job. Why are you staring at me like that?'

'So it doesn't bother you that you wouldn't be able to have much of a life given that you're paid next to nothing?' *Cheap labour,* Giancarlo thought. *Now, why am I not surprised?* A specialised nurse would hardly donate her services through the goodness of her heart, but a young, clearly inexperienced girl? Why not take advantage? Oh, the old man knew the state of his finances, all right, whatever she exclaimed to the contrary.

'I don't mind. I've never been fussed about money.'

'Guess what?' Giancarlo signalled to the waiter for the bill. When Caroline looked at her watch, it was to find that the time had galloped by. She hadn't even been aware of it passing, even though, disliking him as she did, she should have been counting every agonising minute.

'What?'

'Consider your little mission a success. I think it's time, after all, to return home…'

CHAPTER THREE

GIANCARLO'S last view of his father's house, as he had twisted around in the back of the car, while in the front his mother had sat in stony silence without a backward glance, was of lush gardens and the vast stone edifice which comprised the back of the house. The front of the house sat grandly on the western shores of the lake, perfect positioning for a view of deep blue water, as still as a sheet of glass, that was breathtakingly beautiful.

It was unsettling to be returning now, exactly one week after Caroline had left, seemingly transported with excitement at the fact that she had managed to persuade him to accept the supposed olive-branch that had been extended.

If she was of the opinion that all was joyful in the land of reconciliation, then Giancarlo was equally and coldly reserved about sharing any such optimism. He was under no illusions when it came to human nature. The severity of Alberto's heart attack was open to debate and Giancarlo, for one, was coolly prepared for a man in fairly robust health who may or may not have persuaded a very gullible Caroline otherwise to suit his own purposes. His memories of his father were of a towering man, greatly into discipline and without an emotional bone in his body. He couldn't conceive of him being diminished by ill health, although rapidly disappearing funds might well have played a part in lowering his spirits.

The super-fast sports car had eaten up the miles of motorway and only now, as he slowed to drive through the picturesque towns and villages on the way to his father's house, were vague recollections beginning to surface.

He had forgotten how charming this area was. Lake Como, the third largest and the deepest of the Italian lakes, was picture-postcard perfect, a lush, wealthy area with elegant villas, manicured gardens, towns and villages with cobbled streets and *piazzas* dotted with Romanesque churches and very expensive hotels and restaurants which attracted the more discerning tourist.

He felt a pleasing sense of satisfaction.

This was a homecoming on *his* terms, just the way he liked it. A more in-depth perusal of Alberto's finances had shown a company torn apart by the ravaging effects of an unprecedented economic recession, mismanagement and an unwillingness to move with the times and invest in new markets.

Giancarlo smiled grimly to himself. He had never considered himself a vengeful person but the realisation that he could take over his father's company, rescue the old man and thereby level the scales of justice was a pleasing one. Really, what more bitter pill could his father ever swallow than know that he was indebted, literally, to the son he had turned his back on?

He hadn't mentioned a word of this to Caroline when they had parted company. For a few minutes, Giancarlo found himself distracted by thoughts of the diminutive brunette. She was flaky as hell; unbelievably emotional and prone to tears at the drop of a hat; jaw-droppingly forthright and, frankly, left him speechless. But, as he got closer and closer to the place he had once called his home, he realised that she had managed to get under his skin in a way that was uniquely irritating. In fact, he had never devoted this much time to thinking about any one woman, but that, he reasoned sensibly, was because this particular woman had entered his life in a singularly weird way.

Never again would he rule out the unexpected. Just when you thought you had everything in control, something came along to pull the rug from under your feet.

In this instance, it wasn't all bad. He fiddled with the radio, got to a station he liked and relaxed to enjoy the scenery and the pleasing prospect of what lay ahead.

He gave no house room to nerves. He was on a high, in fact, fuelled by the self-righteous notion of the wheel having turned full circle. Yes, he was curious to reacquaint himself with Alberto, but over the years he had heard so many things about him that he almost felt as though there was nothing left to know. The steady drip, drip, drip of information from a young age had eroded his natural inclination to question.

If anything, he liked to think that Alberto would be the one consumed by nerves. His business was failing and sooner or later, ill health or no ill health, Giancarlo was certain that his father would turn the conversation around to money. Maybe he would try and entice him into some kind of investment. Maybe he would just ditch his pride and ask outright for a loan of some sort. Either approach was possible. Giancarlo relished the prospect of being able to confirm that money would indeed be forthcoming. Wasn't he magnanimous even though, all things considered, he had no reason to be? But a price would have to be paid. He would make his father's company his own. He would take it over lock, stock and barrel. Yes, his father's financial security would rest on the generosity of his disowned son.

He intended to stay at the villa just long enough to convey that message. A couple of days at most. Thereafter it would be enough to know that he had done what he had to do.

He didn't anticipate having anything to say of interest to the old man. Why should he? They would be two strangers, relieved to part company once the nitty-gritty had been sorted out.

He was so wrapped up in his thoughts that he very nearly missed the turning to the villa. This side of the lake was famous for its magnificent villas, most of them eighteenth-century extravaganzas, a few of which had been turned into hotels over the years.

His father's villa was by no means the largest but it was still an impressive old place, approached through forbidding iron gates and a long drive which was surrounded on both sides by magnificent gardens.

He remembered the layout of these glorious spreading lawns more than he had anticipated. To the right, there was the bank of trees in which he had used to play as a child. To the left, the stone wall was barely visible behind rows upon rows of rhododendrons and azaleas, a vibrant wash of colour as bright and as dramatic as a child's painting.

He slowed the car in the circular courtyard, killed the engine and popped the boot, which was just about big enough to fit his small leather overnight case—and, of course, his computer bag in which resided all the necessary documents he would need so that he could begin the takeover process he had in mind for his father's company.

He was an imposing sight. From her bedroom window, which overlooked the courtyard, Caroline felt a sudden sick flutter of nerves.

Over the past seven days, she had done her best to play down the impact he had made on her. He wasn't *that* tall, *that* good-looking or *that* arrogant, she convinced herself.

She had been rattled when she had finally located him and her nerves had thrown everything out of perspective.

Unfortunately, staring down at Giancarlo as he emerged from his sports car, wearing dark sunglasses and walking round to swing two cases out of the miniscule boot of his car, she realised that he really *was* as unbelievably forbidding as she had remembered.

She literally flew down the corridor, took the staircase two steps at a time and reached the sitting-room at the back of the house, breathless.

'He's here!'

Alberto was sitting in a chair by the big bay window that had a charming view of the gardens stretching down to the lake, which was dotted with little boats.

'Anyone would think the Pope was paying a visit. Calm down, girl! Your colour's up.'

'You're going to be nice, aren't you, Alberto?'

'I'm always nice. You just fuss too much, get yourself worked up over small things—it's not good for you. Now, off you go and let the boy in before he climbs back into his car and drives away. And on your way you can tell that nurse of yours that I'm having a glass of whisky before dinner. Whether she likes it or not!'

'I'll do no such thing, Alberto De Vito. If you want to disobey doctor's orders, then you can tell Tessa yourself— and I would love to see how she takes that.' She grinned fondly at the old man, who was backlit by the evening sun glinting through the window. Having met Giancarlo, she found the similarities between them striking. Both had the same proud, aristocratic features and the long, lean lines of natural athletes. Of course, Alberto was elderly now, but it was easy to see that he must have been as striking as his son in his youth.

'Oh, stop that endless chattering, woman, and run along.'

He waved her off and Caroline, steadying her nerves, got to the front door just as the doorbell chimed.

She smoothed nervous hands along her skirt, a black maxi in stretch cotton which she wore with a loose-fitting top and, of course, the ubiquitous cardigan, although at least here it was more appropriate thanks to the cooling breeze that blew off the lake.

She pulled open the door and her mouth went dry. In a snug-fitting cream polo-necked shirt and a pair of tan trousers with very expensive-looking loafers, he was every inch the impeccably dressed Italian. He looked as though he had come straight from a fashion shoot until he raised one sardonic eyebrow and said coolly, 'Were you waiting by the window?'

Remembering that she *had*, actually, been at her window when his car had pulled into the courtyard, Caroline straightened her spine and cleared her throat.

'Of course I wasn't! Although I *was* tempted, just in case you didn't show up.' She stood aside; Giancarlo took a step through the front door and confronted the house in which he had spent the first twelve years of his life. It had changed remarkably little. The hall was a vast expanse of marble, in the centre of which a double staircase spiralled in opposing directions to meet on the impressive galleried landing above. On either side of the hall, a network of rooms radiated like tentacles on an octopus.

Now that he was back, he could place every room in his head: the various reception rooms; the imposing study from which he had always been banned; the dining-room in which portraits of deceased family members glared down at the assembled diners; the gallery in which were hung paintings of great value, another room from which he had been banned.

'Why wouldn't I show up?' Giancarlo turned to face her.

She looked more at home here, less ill at ease, which was hardly surprising, he supposed. Her hair which she had attempted to tie back in Milan was loose, and it flowed over her shoulders and down her back in a tangle of curls, dark brown streaked with caramel where the sun had lightened it.

'You might have had a change of heart,' Caroline admitted in a harried voice, because yet again those dark, cloaked eyes on her were doing weird things to her tummy. 'I mean, you were so adamant that you didn't want to see your father and then all of a sudden you announced that you'd changed your mind. It didn't make sense. So I thought that maybe you might have changed your mind again.'

'Where are the staff?'

'I told you, most of the house is shut off. We have Tessa, the nurse who looks after Alberto. She lives on the premises, and two young girls take care of cleaning the house, but they live in the village. I'm glad you decided to come after all. Shall we go and meet your father? I guess you'll want to be with him on your own.'

'So that we can catch up? Exchange fond memories of the good old days?'

Caroline looked at him in dismay. There was no attempt to disguise the bitterness in his voice. Alberto rarely mentioned the past, and his memoirs, which had taken a back seat over the past few weeks, had mostly got to the state of fond reminiscing about his university days and the places he had travelled as a young man. But she could imagine that Alberto had not been the easiest of fathers. When Giancarlo had agreed to visit, she had naïvely assumed that he had been willing, finally, to overlook whatever mishaps had drastically torn them apart. Now, looking at him, she was uneasily aware that her simple conclusions might have been a little off the mark.

'Or even just agree to put the past behind you and move on,' Caroline offered helpfully.

Giancarlo sighed. Should he let her in to what he had planned? he wondered.

'Why don't you give me a little tour of the house before I meet my father?' he suggested. 'I want to get a feel of the old place. And there are a couple of things I want to talk to you about.'

'Things? What things?'

'If you don't fancy the full tour, you can show me to my bedroom. What I have to say won't take long.'

'I'll show you to your room,' she said stiffly. 'But first I'll go and tell Alberto where we are, so he doesn't worry.'

'Why would he worry?'

'He's been looking forward to seeing you.'

'I'm thinking I will be in my old room,' Giancarlo murmured. 'Left wing. Overlooking the side gardens?'

'The left wing's not really used now.' Making her mind up, she eyed his lack of luggage and began heading up the stairs. 'I'll take you up to where you'll be staying. If we're quick, I'm sure your father won't get too anxious. And you can tell me whatever it is you have to tell me.'

She could feel her heart beating like a sledgehammer inside her as she preceded him up the grand staircase, turning left along the equally grand corridor, which was broad enough to house a *chaise longue* and various highly polished tables on which sat bowls of fresh flowers. Caroline had added that touch soon after she had come to live with Alberto and he had grumpily acquiesced, but not before informing her that flowers inside a house were a waste of time. Why bother when they would die within the week?

'Ah, the Green Room.' Giancarlo looked around him and saw the signs of disrepair. The room looked tired, the wallpaper still elegant but badly faded. The curtains he dimly remembered, although this was one of the many guest rooms into which he had seldom ventured. Nothing had been changed in over two decades. He dumped his overnight bag on the bed and walked across to the window to briefly look down at the exquisite walled garden, before turning to her.

'I feel I ought to tell you that my decision to come here wasn't entirely altruistic,' he told her bluntly. 'I wouldn't want you having any misplaced notions of emotional reunions, because if you have, then you're in for a crashing disappointment.'

'Not entirely altruistic?'

'Alberto's rocky financial situation has—how shall I put it?—delivered me the perfect opportunity to finally redress certain injustices.'

'What injustices?'

'Nothing you need concern yourself with. Suffice to say that Alberto will not have to fear that the banks are going to repossess this house and all its contents.'

'This house was going to be repossessed?'

'Sooner or later.' Giancarlo shrugged. 'It happens. Debts accumulate. Shareholders get the jitters. Redundancies have to be made. It's a short step until the liquidators start converging like vultures, and when that happens possessions get seized to pay off disgruntled creditors who are out of pocket.'

Caroline's eyes were like saucers as she imagined this worst-case scenario.

'That would devastate Alberto,' she whispered. She sidled towards the bed and sat down. 'Are you sure about all this? No. Forget I asked that. I forgot that you never make mistakes.'

Giancarlo looked at the forlorn figure on the bed and clicked his tongue impatiently. 'Isn't it a good thing that he'll be spared all of that? No bailiffs showing up at the door, demanding the paintings and the hangings? No bank clamouring for the house to be put on the market to the highest bidder, even if the price is way below its worth?'

'Yes.' She looked at him dubiously.

'So you can wipe that pitiful look from your face immediately!'

'You said that you were going to…what, exactly? Give him the money? Won't that be an awful lot of money? Are you *that* rich?'

'I have enough,' Giancarlo stated drily, amused by her question.

'How much is enough?'

'Enough to ensure that Alberto's house and company don't end up in the hands of the receivers. Of course, there's no such thing as a free lunch.'

'What do you mean?'

'I mean…' He pushed himself away from the window and strolled through the bedroom, taking in all those little signs of neglect that were almost impossible to spot unless you were looking for them. God only knew, the house was ancient. It was probably riddled with all manner of damp, dry rot, termites in the woodwork. Having grown up in a house that dated back centuries, Giancarlo had made sure that his own place was unashamedly modern. Dry rot, damp and termites would never be able to get a foothold.

'I *mean* that what is now my father's will inevitably become mine. I will take over his company and return it to its once-thriving state and naturally I will do the same with this villa. It's in dire need of repair anyway. I'll wager that those rooms that have been closed off will be in the process of falling to pieces.'

'And you won't be doing any of that because you care about Alberto,' Caroline spoke her thoughts aloud while

Giancarlo looked at her through narrowed eyes, marvelling at the way every thought running through her head was reflected in the changing nuances of her expressions.

'In fact,' she carried on slowly, her thoughts rearranging themselves in her head to form a complete picture of what was really going on, 'you're not interested in reconciling with your father at all, are you?'

Giancarlo wasn't about to encourage any kind of conversation on what she considered the rights and wrongs of his reasons for coming to the lake, so he maintained a steady silence—although the resigned disappointment in her voice managed to pierce through his rigid self-control in a way that was infuriating. Her huge, accusing eyes were doing the same thing as well and he frowned impatiently.

'It's impossible to reconcile with someone you can barely recall,' he said in a flatly dismissive voice. 'I don't know Alberto.'

'You know him enough to want to hurt him for what you think he did to you.'

'That's a ridiculous assumption!'

'Is it? You said yourself that you were going to buy him out because it would give you the chance to redress injustices.'

Giancarlo was fiercely protective of his private life. He never discussed his past with anyone and many women had tried. They had seen it as a stepping stone to getting to know him better, had mistakenly thought that, with the right amount of encouragement, he would open up and pour his heart out. It was always a fatal flaw.

'Alberto divorced my mother and did everything legally possible to ensure that, whilst the essentials were paid, she was left with the minimum, just enough to get by. From *this*—' he gestured in a sweeping arc to encompass the villa and its fabulous surroundings '—she was reduced to living in a small modern box in the outskirts of Milan. You can see that I carry a certain amount of bitterness towards my father.

'However, it has to be said that, were I a truly vengeful person, I would not have returned here and I certainly would not be contemplating a lucrative buy-out. Lucrative from Alberto's point of view, that is. A lot less lucrative from where I'm standing, because his company will need a great deal of money pouring into it to get it off the starters' gate. Face it, I could have read those financial reports, turned my back, walked away. Waited until I read about the demise of his company in the financial section of the newspapers. Believe me, I seriously considered that option, but then… Let's just say that I opted for the personal touch. So much more satisfying.'

Caroline was finding it impossible to tally up Giancarlo's version of his father with her own experiences of Alberto. Yes, he was undoubtedly difficult and had probably been a thousand times more so when he had been younger, but he wasn't stingy. She just couldn't imagine him being vindictive towards his ex-wife, although how could she know for sure?

One thing she *did* know now was that Giancarlo might justify his actions as redressing a balance but it was revenge of a hands-on variety and no part of her could condone that. He would rescue his father in the certain knowledge that guilt would be Alberto's lifelong companion from then onwards. He would attack Alberto's most vulnerable part: his pride.

She stood up, hands on her hips, and looked at him with blazing eyes.

'I don't care how you put it, that's absolutely *rotten*!'

'*Rotten*, to step in and bail him out?' Giancarlo shook his head grimly and took a couple of steps towards her.

He had his hands in the pockets of his trousers and his movements were leisurely and unhurried, but there was an element of threat in every step he took that brought him closer and Caroline fought to stay her ground. She couldn't wrench her eyes away from him. He had the allure of a dangerous but spectacularly beautiful predator.

Looking down at her, Giancarlo's dark eyes skimmed the hectic flush in her cheeks, her rapid, angry breathing.

'You're a spitfire, aren't you…?' he murmured lazily, which thoroughly disconcerted Caroline. She wasn't used to dealing with men like this. Her experience of the opposite sex was strictly confined to the two men she had dated in the past, both of whom were gentle souls with whom she still shared a comfortable friendship, and work colleagues after she had left school.

'No, I'm not! I never argue. I don't like arguing.'

'You could have fooled me.'

'You do this to me,' she breathed, only belatedly realising that somehow that didn't sound quite right. 'I mean…'

'I get you worked up?'

'Yes! No…'

'Yes? No? Which is it?'

'Stop laughing at me. None of this is funny.' She drew her cardigan tightly around her in a defensive gesture that wasn't lost on him.

'For a young woman, your choice of clothes is very old-fashioned. Cardigans are for women over forty.'

'I don't see what my clothes have to do with anything.' But she stumbled over her words. Was he trying to throw her? He was succeeding. Now, along with anger was a creeping sense of embarrassment.

'Are you self-conscious about your body?' This was the sort of question Giancarlo never asked any woman. He had never been a big fan of soul-searching conversations. He had always preferred to keep it light, and yet he found that he was really curious about the hell cat who claimed not to be a hell cat. Except when in his presence.

Caroline broke the connection and walked towards the door but she was shaking like a leaf.

She stood in the doorway, half-in, half-out of the bedroom, which suddenly seemed as confining as a prison cell when he was towering above her.

'And when do you intend to tell Alberto everything?'

'I should imagine that he will probably be the one who brings up the subject,' Giancarlo said, still looking at her, almost regretful that the conversation was back on a level footing. 'You seem to have a lot of faith in human nature. Take it from me, it's misplaced.'

'I don't want you upsetting him. His doctor says that he's to be as stress-free as possible in order to make a full recovery.'

'Okay. Here's the deal. I won't open the conversation with a casual query about the state of his failing company.'

'You really don't care about anyone but yourself, do you?' Caroline asked in a voice tinged with genuine wonder.

'You have a special knack for saying all the wrong things to me,' Giancarlo muttered with a frown.

'What you mean is that I say things you don't want to hear.' She stepped quickly out into the corridor as he walked towards her. She was beginning to understand that being too close to him physically was like standing too close to an electric field. 'We should go downstairs. Alberto will be wondering where we've got to. He tires easily now, so we'll be having an early supper.'

'And tell me, who does the cooking? The same two girls who come in to clean?' He fell into step alongside her, but even though the conversation had moved on to a more neutral topic he was keenly aware of her still clutching the cardigan around her. His first impression had been of someone very background. Now, he was starting to review that initial impression. Underneath the straightforward personality there seemed to be someone very fiery and not easily intimidated. She had taken a deep breath and stood up to him in a way that not very many people did.

'Sometimes. Now that Alberto is on a restricted diet, Tessa tends to prepare his meals, and I cook for myself and Tessa. It's a daily fight to get Alberto to eat bland food. He's fond of saying that there's no life worth living without salt.'

Giancarlo heard the smile in her voice. For his sins, his father had found himself a very devoted companion.

For the first time he wondered what it would have been like to have had Alberto as a father. The man had clearly mellowed over time. Would they have had that connection? How much had he suffered because of his constant warfare with his wife?

Irritated with himself for being drawn back into a past he could not change, Giancarlo focused on sustaining the conversation with a number of innocuous questions as they walked back down the grand staircase, Caroline leading the way towards the smallest of the sitting-rooms at the back of the house.

Even with the majority of the rooms seemingly closed off, there was still a lot of ground to cover. Yet again he found himself wondering what the appeal was for a young woman. Terrific house, great grounds, pleasing views and interesting walks—but take those things out of the equation and boredom would gradually set in, surely?

How bored had his mother been, surrounded by all this ostentatious wealth, trapped like a bird in a gilded cage?

Alberto had met her on one of his many conferences. She

had been a sparkling, pretty waitress at the only fancy restaurant in a small town on the Amalfi coast where he had gone to grab a couple of days of rest before the remainder of his business trip. She had been plucked from obscurity and catapulted into wealth, but nothing, she had repeatedly complained to her son over the years following her divorce, could compensate for the horror of living with a man who treated her no better than a servant. She had done her very best, but time and again her efforts had been met with a brick wall. Alberto, she had said with bitterness, had turned out to be little more than a difficult, unyielding and unforgiving man, years too old for her, who had thwarted all her attempts at having fun.

Giancarlo had been conditioned to loathe the man whom his mother had held responsible for all her misfortunes.

Except now he was prey to a disturbing sensation of doubt as he heard Caroline chatter on about his father. How disagreeable could the man be if she was so attached to him? Was it possible for a leopard to change its spots to that extreme extent?

Before they reached the sitting-room, she paused to rest one small hand lightly on his arm.

'Do you promise that you won't upset him?'

'I'm not big into making promises.'

'Why is it so hard to get through to you?'

'Believe it or not, most people don't have a problem. In our case, we might just as well be from different planets, occupying different time zones. I told you I won't greet him with an enquiry about the health of his finances, and I won't. Beyond that, I promise nothing.'

'Just try to get to know him,' Caroline pleaded, her huge brown eyes welded to his as she dithered with her hand still on his arm. 'I just can't believe you know the real Alberto.'

Giancarlo's mouth thinned and he stared down pointedly at her hand before looking down at her, his dark eyes as cold and frozen as the lake in winter.

'Don't presume to tell me what I know or don't know,' he said with ice in his voice, and Caroline removed her hand quickly as though she had been burnt suddenly. 'I've come here for a purpose and, whether you like it or not, I will ensure that things are wrapped up before I leave.'

'And how long are you intending to stay? I never asked, but you really haven't come with very much luggage, have you? I mean, one small bag...'

'Put it this way, there will be no need to go shopping for food on my account. I plan on being here no longer than two days. Three at the very most.'

Caroline's heart sank further. This was a business visit, however you dressed it up and tried to call it something else. Two days? Just long enough for Giancarlo to levy his charge for Alberto's past wrongdoings, whatever those might have been, with interest.

She didn't think that he was even prepared to get to know his father. The only thing that interested him, his only motivation for coming to the villa, was to dole out his version of revenge, whether he chose to call it that or not.

'Now, any more questions?' Giancarlo drawled and Caroline shook her head miserably, not trusting herself to speak. Once again, he felt a twinge of uninvited and unwelcome doubt. 'I'm surprised at your level of attachment to Alberto,' he commented brusquely, annoyed at himself, because would her answer change anything? No.

'Why?' Her eyes were wide and clear when she looked at him. 'I didn't have a load of prejudices when I came here. I came with an open mind. I found a lonely old man with a kind heart and a generous nature. Yes, he might be prickly, but it's what's inside that counts. At least, that's how it works for me.'

He really shouldn't have been diverted into encouraging her opinion. He should have known that whatever chirpy, homespun answer she came out with would get on his nerves. He was very tempted to inform her that he was the least prejudiced person on the face of the earth, that if on this single occasion he was prey to a very natural inclination towards one or two preconceived ideas about Alberto, then no one could lay the blame for that at his door. He cut short the infuriating desire to be sidetracked.

'Well, I'm very pleased that he has you around,' Giancarlo said neutrally. Caroline bristled because she could just *sense* that he was being patronising.

'No, you aren't. You're still so mad at him that you probably would much rather have preferred it if he was still on his own in this big, rambling house with no one to talk to. And, if there *was* someone around, then I'm sure you'd rather it wasn't me, because you don't like me at all!'

'What gives you that idea?'

Caroline ignored that question. The promise of what was to come felt like a hangman's noose around her neck. She was fit to explode. 'Well, I don't like you either,' she declared with vehemence. 'And I hope you choke on your plans to ruin Alberto's life.' She spun away from him so that he couldn't witness the tears stinging her eyes. 'He's waiting for you,' she muttered in a driven voice. 'Why don't you go in now and get it over with?'

CHAPTER FOUR

GIANCARLO entered a room that was familiar to him. The smallest of the sitting-rooms at the back of the house had always been the least ornate and hence the cosiest. Out of nowhere came the memory of doing his homework in this very room, always resisting the urge to sneak outside, down to the lake. French doors led out to the sprawling garden that descended to the lake via a series of landscaped staircases. Alberto sat in a chair by one of the bay windows with a plaid rug over his legs even though it was warm in the room.

'So, my boy, you've come.'

Giancarlo looked at his father with a shuttered expression. He wondered if his memory was playing tricks on him, because Alberto looked diminished. In his head, he realised that he had held on to a memory that was nearly two decades old and clearly out of date.

'Father…'

'Caroline. You're gaping. Why don't you offer a drink to our guest? And I will have a whisky while you're about it.'

'You'll have no such thing.' Back on familiar ground, Caroline moved past Giancarlo to adopt a protective stance by her employer, who made feeble attempts to flap her away. Looking at their interaction, Giancarlo could see that it was a game with which they were both comfortable and familiar.

Just for a few seconds, he was the outsider looking in, then that peculiar feeling was gone as the tableau shifted. Caroline walked across to a cupboard which had been re-configured to house a small fridge, various snacks and cartons of juice.

He was aware of her chattering nervously, something about it being time efficient to have stuff at hand for Alberto because this was his favourite room in the house and he just wasn't as yet strong enough to continually make long trips to the kitchen if he needed something to drink.

'Of course, it's all supervised,' she babbled away, while the tension stretched silent and invisible in the room. 'No whisky here. Tessa and I know that that's Alberto's Achilles' heel so we have wine. I put some in earlier, would that be okay?' She kept her eyes firmly averted from the uncomfortable sight of father and son, but in her head she was picturing them circling one another, making their individual, quiet assessments.

Given half a chance, she would have run for cover to another part of the house, but her instinct to protect Alberto kept her rooted to the spot.

When she finally turned around, with drinks and snacks on a little tray, it was to find that Giancarlo had taken up position on one of the chairs. If he was in any way uncomfortable, he wasn't showing it.

'Well, Father, I have been told that you've suffered a heart attack—'

'How was the drive here, Giancarlo? Still too many cars in the villages?'

They both broke into speech at the same time. Caroline drank too much far too quickly to calm her nerves and lapsed into an awkward silence as ultra-polite questions were fielded with ultra-polite answers. She wondered if they were aware that many of their mannerisms were identical—the way they both shifted and leaned forward when a remark was made; the way they idly held their glasses, slightly stroking the rim with their fingers. They should have bonded without question. Instead, Giancarlo's cool, courteous conversation was the equivalent of a door being shut.

He was here. He was talking. But he was not conversing.

At least he had kept his word and nothing, so far, had been mentioned about the state of Alberto's finances, although she knew that her employer must surely be curious to know why his son had bothered to make the trip out to Lake Como when he displayed so little enthusiasm for the end result.

Dinner was a light soup, followed by fish. One of the local girls had been brought in, along with the two regular housekeepers, to take care of the cooking and the clearing away. So, instead of eating in the kitchen, they dined in the formal dining-room, which proved to be a mistake.

The long table and the austere surroundings were not conducive to light-hearted conversation. Tessa had volunteered to have her meal in the small sitting-room adjoining her bedroom, in order to give them all some space to chat without her hovering over Alberto, checking to make sure he stuck to his diet. Caroline heartily wished she could have joined her, because the atmosphere was thick with tension.

By the time they had finished their starters and made adequately polite noises about it, several topics of conversation had been started and quickly abandoned. The changes in the weather patterns had been discussed, as had the number of tourists at the lakes, the lack of snow the previous winter and, of course, Alberto asked Giancarlo about his work, to which he received such brief replies that that too was a subject quickly shelved.

By the time the main course was brought to them—and Alberto had bemoaned the fact that they were to dine on fish rather than something altogether heartier like a slab of red meat—Caroline had frankly had enough of the painfully stilted conversation.

If they didn't want to have any kind of meaningful conversation together, then she would fill in the gaps. She talked about her childhood, growing up in Devon. Her parents were both teachers, very much into being 'green'. She laughed at memories of the chickens they had kept that laid so many eggs at times that her mother would bake cakes a family of three had no possibility of eating just to get rid of some of them. She would contribute them to the church every Sunday and one year was actually awarded a special prize for her efforts.

She talked about exchange students, some of whom had been most peculiar, and joked about her mother's experiments in the kitchen with home-grown produce from their small garden. In the end, she and her father had staged a low-level rebellion until normal food was reintroduced. Alberto chuckled but he was not relaxed. It was there in the nervous flickering of his eyes and his subdued, downturned mouth. The son he had desperately wanted to see didn't want to see him and he wasn't even bothering to try to hide the fact.

All the while she could feel Giancarlo's dark eyes restively looking at her and she found that she just couldn't look at him. What was it about him that brought her out in goose bumps and made her feel as though she just wasn't comfortable in her own skin? The timbre of his low, husky voice sent shivers down her spine, and when he turned to look at her she was aware of her body in such miniscule detail that she burned with discomfort.

By the time they adjourned for coffee back in the small sitting-room, Caroline was exhausted and she could see that Alberto was flagging. Giancarlo, on the other hand, was as coldly composed as he had been at the start of the evening.

'How long do you plan on staying, my boy? You should get yourself out on the lake. Beautiful weather. And you were always fond of your sailing. Of course, we no longer have the sailboat. What was the point? After, well, after...'

'After what, Father?'

'I think it's time you went to bed, Alberto,' Caroline interjected desperately as the conversation finally threatened to explode. 'You're flagging and you know the doctor said that you really need to take it easy. I'll get hold of Tessa and—'

'After you and your mother left.'

'Ah, so finally you've decided to acknowledge that you ever had a wife. One could be forgiven for thinking that you had erased her from your memory completely.' No mention had been made of Adriana. Not one single word. They had tiptoed around all mention of the past, as though it had never existed. Alberto had been on his best behaviour. Now Giancarlo expected to see his real father, the cold, unforgiving one, the one who, from memory, had never shied away from arguing.

'I've done no such thing, my son,' Alberto surprised Giancarlo by saying quietly.

'It's time you went to bed, Alberto.' Caroline stood up and looked pointedly at Giancarlo. 'I will not allow you to tire your father out any longer,' she said, and in truth Alberto was showing signs of strain around his eyes. 'He's been very ill and this conversation is *not* going to help anything at all.'

'Oh, do stop fussing, Caroline.' But his pocket handkerchief was in his hand and he was patting his forehead wearily.

'*You—*' she jabbed a finger at Giancarlo '*—*are going to wait *right here* for me while I go to fetch Tessa because I intend to have a little chat with you.'

'The boy wants to talk about his past, Caroline. It's why he's come.'

Caroline snorted without taking her eyes away from Giancarlo's beautiful face. If only Alberto knew!

She spun back around to look at her employer. 'I'm going to fetch Tessa and tomorrow you won't have your routine disrupted. Your son is going to be here for a few days. There will be time enough to take a trip down memory lane.'

'*A few days?*' They both said the same thing at the same time. Giancarlo was appalled and enraged while Alberto was hesitantly hopeful. Caroline decided to favour Giancarlo with a confirming nod.

'Maybe even as long as a week,' she threw at him, because wasn't it better to be hanged for a sheep than a lamb? 'I believe that's what you said to me?' She wondered where on earth this fierce determination was coming from. She always shied away from confrontation!

'So tomorrow,' she continued to both men, 'there will be no need for you to worry about entertaining your son, Alberto. He will be sailing on the lake.'

'I'll be *sailing on the lake*?'

'Correct. With me.' This in case he decided to argue the rules she was confidently laying down, with a silent prayer in her head that he wasn't going to launch into an outraged argument which would devastate Alberto, especially after the gruesome evening they had just spent together.

'I thought you couldn't sail, Caroline,' Alberto murmured and she drew herself up to her unimpressive height of a little over five-three.

'But I've been counting down the days I could start learning.'

'You told me that you had a morbid fear of open water.'

'It's something I've been told I can only overcome by facing it…on open water. It's a well-known fact that, er, that you have to confront your fears to overcome them…'

She backed out of the room before Alberto could pin her down and flew to Tessa's room. She could picture the awkward conversation taking place between Giancarlo and Alberto in her absence, and that was a best-case scenario. The worst-case scenario involved them both taking that trip down memory lane, the one she had temporarily managed to divert. It was a trip that could only lead to the sort of heated argument that would do no good to Alberto's fragile recovery. With that in mind, she ran back to the sitting-room like a bat out of hell and was breathless by the time she reappeared ten minutes later.

It was to discover that Giancarlo had disappeared.

'The boy has work to do,' Alberto told her.

'At this hour?'

'I remember when I was a young man, I used to work all the hours God made. Boy's built like me, which might not be such a good thing. Hard work is fine but the important thing is to know when to stop. He's a fine-looking lad, don't you think?'

'I suppose there might be some who like that sort of look,' Caroline said dismissively. With relief, she heard Tessa approaching. Alberto drew no limits when it came to asking whatever difficult questions he had in his head. It was, he had proclaimed, one of the benefits of being an old bore. The last thing she wanted was to have an in-depth question-and-answer session on what she thought of his son.

'Bright, too.'

Caroline wondered how he could be so clearly generous in his praise for someone who had made scant effort to meet him halfway. She made an inarticulate noise under her breath and tried not to scowl.

'Said he'd meet you by his car at nine tomorrow morning,' Alberto told her, while simultaneously trying to convince Tessa, who had entered the room at a brisk pace, that he didn't need to be treated like a child all the time. 'Think he'll enjoy a spot of sailing. It'll relax him. He seems tense. Of course, I totally understand that, given the circumstances. So don't you mind me, my dear. Think I'll rise and shine, but not with the larks, and the old bat here can take me for my constitutional walk.'

Tessa winked at Caroline and grinned behind Alberto's back as she helped him up.

'Anyone would think he wasn't a complete poppet when I settle him at night,' she said, unfazed.

Having issued her dictate to Giancarlo for 'a chat', Caroline realised that chatting was the last thing she wanted to do with him. All her bravado had seeped out of her. The prospect of a morning in his company now seemed like an uphill climb. Would he listen to her? He hadn't as yet revealed to Alberto the real reason for his visit but he would the following day; she knew it. Just as he would declare that his visit was not going to last beyond forty-eight hours, despite what she had optimistically announced to Alberto.

There was no way that she would be able to persuade Giancarlo into doing anything he didn't want to do and the past few hours had shown her that grasping the olive branch was definitely not on his agenda.

* * *

She had a restless night. The villa was beautiful but no modernisation had taken place for a very long time. Air-conditioning was unheard of and the air was still and sluggish.

She barely felt rested when she opened her eyes the following morning at eight-thirty. It took her a few seconds to remember that her normal routine was out of sync. She wouldn't be having a leisurely breakfast with Alberto before taking him for a walk, then after lunch settling into sifting through some of his first-edition books which, in addition to his memoirs, was one of her jobs for him: sorting them into order so that he could decide which ones might be left to the local museum and which would be kept. He had all manner of historical information about the district, a great deal of which was contained in the various letters and journals of his ancestors. It was a laborious but enjoyable task which she would be missing in favour of a sailing trip with Giancarlo.

She dressed quickly: a pair of trousers, a striped tee shirt and, of course, her cardigan, a blue one this time; covered shoes. She didn't know anything at all about being on a boat, but she knew enough to suspect that a skirt and sandals would not be the required get-up. Impatiently, she tied her hair back in a long braid for the purpose of practicality.

There was no time for breakfast and she walked from one wing of the villa to the other, emerging outside into a blissfully sunny day with cloudless skies, bright turquoise shot through with milk. Giancarlo was standing by his car, sunglasses on, talking into his mobile phone. For a few seconds she stared at him, her heart thudding. He might have severed all ties with his aristocratic background, but he couldn't erase it from the contours of his face. Even in tattered clothes and barefoot he would still look the ultimate sophisticate.

He glanced across, registered her presence and snapped shut his phone to lounge indolently against the car as she walked towards him.

'So,' he drawled, staring down at her when she was finally in front of him. 'I'm apparently here on a one-week vacation.' He removed the sunglasses to dangle them idly between his fingers while he continued to look at her until she felt herself blush to the roots of her hair.

'Yes, well…'

'Maybe you could tell me how I had this week planned out? Bearing in mind that you seemed to have arranged it.'

'You *could* make just a little polite conversation before you start laying into me.'

'Was I doing that?' He pushed himself off the car and swung round to open the door for her, slamming it shut as she clambered into the passenger seat. 'I distinctly recall having told you that the most I would be staying would be a matter of two days. Tell me how you saw fit to extend that into a week?' He had bent down, propping himself against the car with both hands so that he could question her through her open window. He felt so close up and personal that she found herself taking deep breaths and gasping for air.

'Yes, I realise that,' Caroline muttered mutinously when he showed no signs of backing off. 'But you made me mad.'

'I—made—you—mad?'

Caroline nodded mutely and stared straight ahead, keenly aware of his hawk-like eyes boring into her averted profile. She visibly sagged when he strode round to get into the car.

'And how,' he asked softly, 'do you think I felt when you backed me into a corner?'

'Yes, well, you deserved it!'

'Do you know, I can't believe you.' He exited the gravelled courtyard with a screeching of angry tyres and she clenched her fists so tightly that she could feel her nails biting into the palms of her hands. 'I didn't come here for relaxation!'

'I know! Don't you think you made that pretty obvious last night?'

'I gave you my word that I wouldn't introduce the contentious issue of money on day one. I kept my word.'

'*Just about.* You didn't make the slightest effort with Alberto. You just sat there *sneering*, and okay, so maybe I was wrong to imply that you were staying a tiny bit longer than you had planned.'

'You are the master of understatement!'

'But when you mentioned your mother, well, I just wanted to avert an argument, so possibly I said the first thing that came into my head. Look, I'm sorry. I guess you could always tell Alberto that I made a mistake, that I got the dates wrong. I know you have lots of important things to do and probably can't spare a week off, whatever the reason, but just then I didn't think I had a choice. I had to take the sting out of the evening, give Alberto something to hang on to.'

'What a shame you couldn't use your brain and think things through before you jumped in feet first! I take it the little *chat* you had in mind last night has now been covered?'

'It was an awkward evening. Alberto really tried to make conversation. Do you know, after you disappeared to work he actually seemed to understand? It was almost as though he wasn't prepared to see anything wrong in his son coming to see him for the first time in years, barely making an effort and then vanishing to work!'

Giancarlo flushed darkly. The evening had not gone quite as he had envisaged, and now he wasn't entirely sure

what he had envisaged. He just knew that the argumentative man—the one who had loomed larger than life in his
head thanks to Adriana's continuing bitterness; the one who
would have made it so easy for him to treat with the patronising contempt he had always assumed would be richly
deserved—had not lived up to expectations.

For starters, it was clear that Alberto's ill health was
every bit as grave as Caroline had stated, and even more
surprising, instead of a conversation spiked with the sort of
malice and bitterness to which he had become accustomed
with his mother over the years, there had been no mention made of a regrettable past and a miserable marriage.
Alberto had been so wildly different from the picture in
his head that Giancarlo had spent the time when he should
have been working trying to figure out the discrepancies.

Naturally, the question of money, the *raison d'être* for
his presence at the villa, would rear its ugly head in due
course. He might have been weirdly taken aback at the man
he had found, but sooner or later the inevitable begging
bowl would emerge. However, not even that certainty could
still the uneasy doubt that had crept stealthily through him
after he had vacated the sitting-room.

'Perhaps,' he said, glancing around at scenery that felt
more familiar with every passing second, 'a few days away
from Milan might not be such a terrible idea.' The very second he said it, Giancarlo knew that he had made the right
decision.

'Sorry?'

'I wouldn't call it a holiday, but it is certainly more restful here than it is in Milan.' He looked sideways at Caroline.
Through the open window, the breeze was wreaking havoc
with her attempts at a neat, sensible hair-style, flinging it
into disarray.

'I guess you don't really do holidays,' she said tentatively.

Even if his intention was still to consume his father's house and company, a few days spent with Alberto might render him a little less black and white in his judgement, might invest him with sufficient tact so that Alberto wasn't humiliated.

'Time is money.'

'There's more to life than money.'

'Agreed. Unfortunately, it usually takes money to enjoy those things.'

'Why have you decided to stay on? Just a short while ago you were really angry that I had put you in a difficult position.'

'But put me in it you did, and I'm a man who thinks on his feet and adjusts to situations. So I might be here for a bit longer than I had anticipated. It could only work to my advantage when it comes to constructing the sort of business proposal my father will understand. I'll confess that Alberto isn't the man I had expected. I initially thought that talk of his ill health might have been exaggerated.'

His eyes slid across to her face. Predictably, her expression was one of tight-lipped anger. 'Now I see for myself that he is not a well man, which would no doubt explain his unnaturally docile manner. I am not a monster. I had intended to confront him with his financial predicament without bothering with the tedious process of beating around the bush. Now I accept that I might have to tiptoe towards the conclusion I want.'

The scenery rushing past him, the feeling of open space and translucent light, was breathtaking. He was behind the wheel of a car, he was driving through clear open spaces with a view of glittering blue water ahead, and for the first time in years he felt light-headed with a rushing sense of freedom.

'Besides,' he mused lazily, 'I haven't been to this part of the world for a long time.'

He was following signs to one of the many sailing jetties scattered around the lake and now he swerved off the main road, heading down towards the glittering water.

Caroline forgot all her misgivings about Giancarlo's mission. She forgot how angry and upset she was at the thought of Alberto being on the receiving end of a son who had only agreed to see him out of a misplaced desire for revenge.

'I don't think I can go through with this,' she muttered as the car slowed to a stop.

Giancarlo killed the engine and turned to face her. 'Wasn't this whole sailing trip *your* idea?'

'It was supposed to be *your* sailing trip.' There were tourists milling around and the sailing boats bobbed like colourful playthings on the calm water. Out on the lake many more of them skirted over the aquamarine surface. At any given moment, one might very well sink, and where would that leave those happy, smiling tourists on board? She blanched and licked her lips nervously.

'You're white as a sheet.'

'Yes, well…'

'You're seriously scared of water?'

'Of *open* water. Anything could happen. Especially on something as flimsy as a sailboat.'

'Anything could happen to anyone, anywhere. Driving here was probably more of a risk than that boat out there.' He opened his door and swung his long body out, moving round to open the passenger door for her. 'You were right when you said that you can't kill an irrational fear unless you confront it.' He held out one hand and, heart beating fast, Caroline took it. The feel of his fingers as they curled around hers was warm and comforting.

'How would you know?' she asked in a shaky voice as

she eased herself out of the car and half-eyed the lake the way a minnow might eye a patch of shark-infested water. 'I bet you've never been scared of anything in your life.'

'I'll take that as a compliment.' He kept his fingers interlinked with hers as he led her down towards the jetty.

Hell, he never thought he'd live to see the day when there were no thoughts of work, deals to be done or lawyers to meet impinging on his mind. His mother's uncertain finances—the details of which he had never been spared, even when he had been too young to fully understand them—had bred a man to whom the acquisition of money was akin to a primal urge. The fact that he was very, very good at it had only served to strengthen his rampant ambition. Women had come and gone, and would continue to come and go, for his parents were a sad indictment of the institution of marriage, but the challenge of work would always be a constant.

Except, now, it appeared to have taken a back seat.

And he barely recognised the boyish feeling inside him as her fingers tightly squeezed his the closer they got to the jetty.

'Hey, trust me,' he told her. 'It'll be worth it. There's nothing like the freedom of being out on the lake and it's not like being on the sea. The edge of the lake is always visible. You'll always be able to orienteer yourself by the horizon.'

'How deep is it?'

'Don't think about that. Tell me why you're so scared.'

Caroline hesitated. She disapproved of everything about this man and yet his invitation to confide was irresistible. *And* her fingers were still entwined with his. Suddenly conscious of that, she wriggled them, which encouraged him to grasp them slightly harder.

'Well?'

'I fell in a river when I was a child.' She sighed and glanced up at him sheepishly. 'I must have been about seven, just learning how to swim. There were four of us and it was the summer holidays. Our parents had all arranged this picnic in the woods.'

'Sounds idyllic.'

'It was, until the four of us kids went off to do a bit of exploring. We were crossing a bridge, just messing around. Looking back now, the river must not have been more than a metre deep and the bridge was just a low, rickety thing. We were playing that game, the one where you send a twig from one side of the bridge and race to the other side to see it float out. Anyway, I fell, headlong into the river. It was terrifying. Although I could swim enough to get out, it was as though my mind had blanked that out. All I could taste was the water and I could feel floating weeds on my face. I thought I was going to drown. Everyone was screaming. The adults were with us within seconds and there was no harm done, but ever since then I've hated the thought of open water.'

'And when I was fourteen, I tried my hand at horse riding and came off at the first hurdle. Ever since then I've had an irrational fear of horses.'

'No, you haven't.' But she grinned up at him, shading her eyes from the glare of the sun with one hand.

'You're right. I haven't. But it's a possibility. I've never been near a horse in my life. I can ski down any black run but I suspect a horse would have me crying with terror.'

Caroline laughed. She was relaxing, barely noticing that the sailboat was being rented, because Giancarlo had continued to talk to her in the soothing voice of someone intent on calming a skittish animal, describing silly scenarios that made her smile. He was certain that he would have a fear of horses. Spiders brought him out in a sweat. Birds brought to mind certain horror movies. He knew that he would definitely have had a phobia of small aircraft had he not managed to successfully bypass that by owning his own helicopter.

Giancarlo hadn't put this much effort into a woman in a long time. It was baffling, because had someone told him a week ago that he would be held to account by a woman who didn't know the meaning of tact, he would have laughed out loud. And had that someone then said that he would find himself holed up at his father's villa for a week, courtesy of the same woman who didn't know the meaning of tact, he would have called out the little men with strait-jackets because the idea was beyond ridiculous.

Yet here he was: reaching out to help a woman with unruly brown hair streaked with caramel, who didn't seem to give a damn about all the other nonsense other women cared about, onto a sailboat. And enjoying the fact that he had managed to distract her from her fear of water by making her laugh.

Obeying an instinctive need to rationalise his actions, Giancarlo easily justified his uncharacteristic behaviour by assuming that this was simply his creative way of dealing with a situation. So what would have been the point in tearing her off a strip for having coerced him into staying at the villa longer than he had planned? He would still do what he had come to do, and anyway it made a relaxing change to interact with a woman in whom he had no sexual interest. He went for tall, thin blondes with a penchant for high-end designer clothes. So take away the sometimes-tedious game of chase and catch with a woman and it seemed that he was left with something really quite enjoyable.

Caroline was on the sailboat before she really realised what had happened. One minute she was laughing, enjoying his silly remarks with the sun on her face and the breeze running its balmy fingers through her hair and gradually undoing her loose plait—the next minute, terra firma was no longer beneath her feet and the swaying of the boat was forcibly reminding her of everything she feared about being out at sea, or in this case out on the lake.

Did he even know how to handle this thing? Wasn't he supposed to have had a little pep talk from the guys in charge of the rentals—a refresher course in how to make sure this insignificant piece of plywood with a bit of cloth didn't blow over when they were in the middle of the lake?

Giancarlo saw her stricken face, the panicked way she looked over her shoulder at the safety of a shoreline from which they were drifting.

He reacted on pure gut impulse.

He kissed her. He curled his long fingers into her tangle of dark hair and with one hand pulled her towards him. The taste of her full lips was like nectar. He felt her soft, lush body curve into him, felt her full breasts squash softly against his chest. He had taken her utterly by surprise and there was no resistance as the kiss grew deeper and more intimately exploring, tasting every part of her sweet mouth. God, he wanted to do more! His arousal was fast and hard and his fabled self-control disappeared so quickly that he was at the mercy of his senses for the first time in his life.

He wanted to strip off her shirt, tear off her bra, which wouldn't be one of those lacy slips of nothing the women he dated wore but something plainly, resolutely and impossibly sexy. He wanted to lose himself in her generous breasts until he stopped thinking altogether.

Caroline was in the grip of something so intensely powerful that she could barely breathe.

She had never felt like this in her life before. She could feel her body melting, could feel her nipples tightening and straining against her bra, knew that she was hot and wet between her legs…

Her body was behaving in a way it had never behaved before and it thrilled and terrified her at the same time.

When he eventually broke free, she literally felt lost.

'You kissed me,' she breathed, still clutching him by the shirt and looking up at him with huge, searching eyes. She wanted to know *why*. She knew why *she* had responded! Underneath her disapproval for everything he had done and said, there was a strong, irresistible current of pure physical attraction. She had been swept along by it and nothing she had ever experienced in her life before had prepared her for its ferocity. Lust was just something she had read about. Now she knew, firsthand, how powerful it could be. Was he feeling the same thing? Did he want to carry on kissing her as much as she wanted him to?

She gradually became aware of their surroundings and of the fact that, with one hand, he had expertly guided the small sailboat away from shore and out into the open lake. They had become one of the small bright toys she had glimpsed from land.

'You kissed me. Was that to distract me from the fact that we were heading away from land?'

Hell, how did *he* know? He just knew that he had been blown away, had lost all shreds of self-control. It was not something of which he was proud, nor could he understand it. Rallying quickly, he recovered his shattered equilibrium and took a couple of steps back, but then had to look away briefly because her flushed cheeks and parted mouth were continuing to play havoc with his libido.

'It worked, didn't it?' He nodded towards the shore, still not trusting himself to look at her properly. 'You're on the water now and, face it, you're no longer scared.'

CHAPTER FIVE

CAROLINE remained positioned in the centre of the small boat for the next hour. She made sure not to look out to the water, which made her instantly conjure up drowning scenarios in her head. Instead, she looked at Giancarlo. It was blissfully easy to devote all her attention to him. He might not have sailed for a long time but whatever he had learnt as a boy had returned to him with ease.

'It's like riding a bike,' he explained, doing something clever with the rudder. 'Once learnt, never forgotten.'

Caroline found herself staring at his muscular brown legs, sprinkled with dark hair. Having brought just enough clothes to cover a one-night stay, he had, he had admitted when asked, pulled strings and arranged for one of the local shops to open up early for him. At eight that morning, he had taken his car to the nearest small town and bought himself a collection of everyday wear. The khaki shorts and loose-fitting shirt, virtually unbuttoned all the way down, were part of that wardrobe and they offered her an incredible view of his highly toned body. Every time he moved, she could see the ripple of his muscles.

Now he was explaining to her how he had managed to acquire his expertise in a boat. He had always been drawn to the water. He had had his first sailing lesson at the age of five and by the age of ten had been adept enough to sail on his own, although he had not been allowed. By the time he had left the lake for good, he could have crewed his own sailboat, had he been of legal age.

Caroline nodded, murmured and thought about *that kiss*. She had been kissed before but never like that. Neither of the two boyfriends she'd had had ever made her feel as though the ground was spinning and freewheeling under her feet; neither had ever made her feel as if the rules of time and space had altered, throwing her into a wildly different dimension. With an eye for detail she never knew she possessed, she marvelled at how a face so coldly, exquisitely beautiful could inspire such craven weakness deep inside her when she had never previously been drawn to men because of how they looked. She wondered at the way she had fallen headlong into that kiss, never wanting it to stop when she barely liked the guy she had been kissing.

'Hello? Calling Planet Earth…'

'Huh?' Caroline blinked and realised that the sailboat was now practically at a standstill. The sound of the water lapping gently against the sides was mesmeric.

'If you stay in that position any longer, your joints will seize up,' Giancarlo informed her drily. 'Stand up. Walk about.'

'What if I topple the boat over and fall in?'

'Then I'll rescue you. But you'll be easier to rescue if you stripped off to your swimsuit. You *are* wearing a swimsuit underneath those clothes, aren't you?'

'Of course I am!'

'Then, off you go.' To show the way, he dispensed with his shirt, which was damp from his exertions, and laid it flat to dry.

Caroline felt her breath catch painfully in her throat as all her misbehaving senses went into immediate overdrive. Her lips felt swollen and her breasts were tender. She wanted to tell him to look away but knew that that would have been childish. She gave herself a stern little lecture—how many times had she worn this swimsuit? Hundreds! In summer, she would often go down to the beach with her friends. She never went in the water but she lazed and tanned and had never, not once, felt remotely self-conscious.

With a mental shrug, she quickly peeled off her clothes, folding them neatly and accepting the soft towel which Giancarlo had packed in a waterproof bag, then she stood up and took a few tentative steps towards the side of the boat. In truth, she felt much, much calmer than when she had first stepped on the small vessel. There were far too many other things on her mind to focus on her fears.

Watching her, Giancarlo felt a sudden, unexpected rush of pure sexual awareness. She was staring out to sea, her profile to him, offering him a view of the most voluptuous body he had ever laid eyes on, even though her one-piece black swimsuit was the last word in old-fashioned and strove to conceal as much as possible. She had the perfect hourglass figure that would drive most men mad. With the breeze making a nonsense of her plait, she had finally unravelled it and her hair fell in curls almost to her waist. He found that his breathing had become shallow, and his arousal was so prominent and painful that he inhaled sharply and began busying himself with the other towel which he had packed.

A youth spent on water had primed him for certain necessities: towels, drinks, something to snack on and, of course, sun-tan lotion.

He had taken up a safer position, sitting on his towel, when she turned to him with a little frown. He was tempted to tell her to cover herself up as he looked through half-closed eyes at her luscious breasts, which not even her sensible swimsuit could downplay.

'I never even asked,' Caroline said abruptly. 'Are you married?' Proud of herself for having ventured into the unknown and terrifying realms of standing at the side of the boat, she now made her way to where he was sitting and spread her towel alongside his to sit.

'Do I look like a married man?'

Caroline considered her father. 'No,' she admitted. 'And I know that you're not wearing a wedding ring, but lots of married men don't like jewellery of any kind. My dad doesn't.'

'Not married. No intention of ever getting married. You're staring at me as though I've just announced a ban on Christmas Day. Have I shocked you?'

'I just don't understand how you can be so certain of something.'

Giancarlo remained silent for such a long time that she wondered whether he was going to answer. He was now lying down on the towel, his hands folded behind his head, a brooding, dangerous Adonis in repose.

'I don't talk about my private life.'

'I'm not asking you to bare your soul. I was just curious.' She hitched her legs up and wrapped her arms around them. 'You're so… uptight.'

'Me—*uptight*?' Giancarlo looked at her with incredulity.

'It's as though you're scared of ever really letting go.'

'Scared? *Uptight*?'

'I don't mean to be offensive.'

'I never knew I had such a boundless capacity for patience,' Giancarlo confessed in a staggered voice. 'Do you ever think before you speak?'

'I wouldn't have said those things if you had just answered my question but it doesn't matter now.'

Giancarlo sighed heavily and raked his fingers through

his hair in sheer frustration as Caroline stubbornly lay down, closed her eyes and enjoyed the sunshine.

'I've seen firsthand how unreliable the institution of marriage is,' he admitted gruffly. 'And I'm not just talking about the wonderful example set by my parents. The statistics prove conclusively that only an idiot would fall for that fairy-tale nonsense.'

Caroline opened her eyes, propped herself up on one elbow and looked at him with disbelief.

'I'm one of those so-called idiots.'

'Now, I wonder why I'm not entirely surprised?'

'What right do you have to say that?'

Giancarlo held both hands up in surrender. 'I don't want to get into an argument with you, Caroline. The weather's glorious, I haven't been out on a sailboat for the longest while. In fact, this is pretty much the first unscheduled vacation I've had in years. I don't want to spoil it.' He waited for a few seconds and then raised his eyebrows with amusement. 'You mean you aren't going to argue with me?' He shot her a crooked grin that made her go bright red.

'I hate arguing.'

'You could have fooled me.'

But he was still grinning lazily at her. She felt all hot and flustered just looking at him, although she couldn't drag her eyes away. It was impossibly still out here, with just the sound of gentle water and the far-away laughter of people on the nearest sailboat, which was still a good distance away. Suddenly, and for no reason, Caroline felt as though they were a million miles from civilisation, caged in their own intensely private moment. Right now, she wanted nothing more than to be kissed by him again, and that decadent yearning was so shocking that her mouth fell half-open and she found that she was holding her breath.

'Okay, but you have to admit that you give me lots to argue about.'

'I absolutely have to admit that, do I?'

The soft, teasing amusement in his voice made her blush even harder. Suddenly it seemed very important that she remind herself of all the various reasons she had for disliking Giancarlo. She loathed arguing and had never been very good at it, but right now arguing seemed the safest solution to the slow, burning, treacly feeling threatening to send her mind and body off on some weird, scary tangent.

'So, what about girlfriends?' she threw recklessly at him.

'What about *girlfriends*?' Giancarlo couldn't quite believe that she was continuing a conversation which he had deemed to be already closed. She had propped herself up on one elbow so that she was now lying on her side, like a figure from some kind of crazily erotic masterpiece. The most tantalizing thing about her was that he was absolutely convinced that she had no idea of her sensational pulling power.

'Well, I mean, is there someone special in your life at the moment?'

'Why do you ask?'

'I… I just don't want to talk about Alberto…' Caroline clutched at that explanation. In truth, the murky business between Giancarlo and his father seemed a very distant problem as they bobbed on the sailboat, surrounded by the azure blue of the placid lake.

'And nosing where you don't belong is the next best thing?' He should have been outraged at the cavalier way with which she was overstepping his boundaries, but he didn't appear to be. He shrugged. 'No. There's no one special in my life, as you call it, at the moment. The last special woman in my life was two months ago.'

'What was she like?'

'Compliant and undemanding for the first two months. Less so until I called it a day two months later. It happens.'

'I guess most women want more than just a casual fling. Most women like to imagine that things are going to go somewhere after a while.'

'I know. It's a critical mistake.' Giancarlo never made it a habit to enquire about women's pasts. The present was all that interested him. The past was another country, the future a place in which the less interest shown, the better.

Breaking all his own self-imposed restrictions, he asked, with idle curiosity, 'And what about you? Now that we've decided to shelve our arguments over Alberto for a while, you never told me how it is that someone of your age could be tempted to while away an indefinite amount of time in the middle of nowhere with only an old man for company. And forget all that nonsense about enjoying walks in the garden and burying yourself in old books. Did you come to Italy because you were running away from something?'

'Running away from what?' Caroline asked in genuine bewilderment.

'Who knows? Maybe the country idyll proved too much, maybe you got involved with someone who didn't quite fit the image, was that it? Was there some guy lurking in paradise who broke your heart? Was that why you escaped to Italy? Why you're content to hide away in a big, decaying villa? Makes sense. Only child…lots of expectations there…doting parents. Did you decide to rebel? Find yourself the wrong type of man?'

'That's crazy.' She flushed and looked away from those too-penetrating, fabulous bitter-chocolate eyes.

'Is it? Why am I getting a different impression here?'

'I didn't get involved with the wrong type of guy.' Caroline scoffed nervously. 'I'm not attracted to… This is a silly conversation.'

'Okay, maybe you weren't escaping an ill-judged, torrid affair with a married man, but what then? Were the chickens and the sheep and the village-hall dances every Friday night all a little too much?'

Caroline looked at him resentfully from under her lashes and then hurriedly looked away. How had he managed to turn this conversation on its head?

'Well?' Giancarlo asked softly, intrigued. 'You can't make the rules to only suit yourself. Two can play at this little game of going where you don't belong...'

'Oh, for goodness' sake! I *may* have become just a little bored, but so what?' She fidgeted with the edge of the towel and glared at him, because she felt like a traitor to her parents with that admission, and it was *his* fault. 'Italy seemed like a brilliant idea,' she admitted, sliding a sideways look at him, realising that he wasn't smirking as she might have expected. 'London was just too expensive. You need to have a well-paid job to go there and actually be able to afford somewhere to rent, and I didn't want to go to any of the other big cities. When Dad suggested that he get in touch with Alberto, that brushing up on my Italian would be a helpful addition to my CV, I guess I jumped at the chance. And, once I got here, Alberto and I just seemed to click.'

'So why the guilty look when I asked?'

'I think Mum and Dad always expected that I'd stay in the country, live the rural idyll just round the corner from them, maybe get married to one of the local lads...'

'They said so?'

'No, but...'

'They would have wanted you to fly the nest.'

'They wouldn't. We're very close.'

'If they wanted to keep you tied to them, they would never have suggested a move as dramatic as Italy,' Giancarlo told her drily. 'Trust me, they aren't fools. This would have been their gentle way of helping you to find your own space. Shame, though.'

'What do you mean?'

'I was really beginning to warm to the idea of the unsuitable lover.'

Caroline's breath caught sharply in her throat because she was registering how close they were to one another, and lying on her side, she felt even more vulnerable to his watchful dark eyes. Conscious of her every movement, she awkwardly sat up and half-wrapped the towel over her legs.

'I… I'm not attracted to unsuitable men,' she croaked, because he appeared to be waiting for a reply to his murmured statement, head slightly inclined.

'Define *unsuitable*…' He lazily reached over to the cooler bag which he had brought with him, and which she had barely noticed in her panic over the dreaded sailing trip, and pulled out two cold drinks, one of which he handed to her.

Held hostage to a conversation that was running wildly out of control, Caroline could only stare at him in dazed confusion. She pressed the cold can to her heated cheeks.

'Well?' Giancarlo tipped his head back to drink and she found that she couldn't tear her eyes away from him, from the motion of his throat as he swallowed and the play of muscles in his raised arm.

'I like kind, thoughtful, sensitive men,' she breathed.

'Sounds boring.'

'It's not boring to like *good guys*, guys who won't let you down.'

'In which case, where are these guys who don't let you down?'

'I'm not in a relationship at the moment, if that's what

you're asking,' Caroline told him primly, hoping that he wouldn't detect the flustered catch in her voice.

'No. Good guys can be a crashing disappointment, I should imagine.'

'I'm sure some of your past girlfriends wouldn't agree with that!' Bright patches of colour had appeared on her cheeks, and her eyes were locked to his in a way that was invasive and thrilling at the same time. Had he leant closer to her? Or had she somehow managed to shorten the distance between them?

'I've never had any complaints in that department,' Giancarlo murmured. 'Sure, some of them have mistakenly got it into their heads that they could persuade me to be in it for the long term. Sure, they were disappointed when I had to set them straight on that, but complaints? In the sex department? No. In fact—'

'I'm not interested,' Caroline interrupted shrilly.

Giancarlo dealt her a slashing smile tinged with a healthy dose of disbelief.

'I guess you haven't met a lot of Italian studs out here,' he said, shamelessly fishing and enjoying himself in a way that had become alien to him. His high-pressured, high-octane, high-stressed, driven everyday life had been left behind on the shores of Lake Como. He was playing truant now and loving every second of it. His dark eyes drifted down to her full, heaving breasts. She might have modestly half-covered her bare legs with the towel but she couldn't hide what remained on display, nor could he seem to stop himself from appreciating it.

'I didn't come here to meet anyone! That wasn't the point.'

'No, but it might have been a pleasant bonus—unless, of course, you've left someone behind? Is there a local lad waiting for you in the wings? Someone your parents approve heartily of? Maybe a farmer?'

Caroline wondered why he would have picked a *farmer*, of all people. Was it because he considered her the outdoor kind of girl, robust and healthy with pink cheeks and a hearty appetite? The kind of girl he would nevei have kissed unless he had been obliged to, as a distraction from the embarrassment of having the girl in question make a fool of herself and of him by having a panic attack at the thought of getting into a boat? She sucked her stomach in, gave up the losing battle to look skinny and stood up to move to the side of the boat, where she held the railings and looked out to the lake.

The shore was a distant strip but she wasn't scared. Just like that, her irrational fear of water seemed to have subsided. There wasn't enough room for that silly phobia when Giancarlo was doing crazy things to her senses. And, much as he got under her skin, his presence was weirdly reassuring. How did *that* work?

She was aware that he had moved to stand behind her and in one swift movement she turned around, her back to the waist-high railing. 'It's so peaceful and beautiful here.' She looked at him steadily and tried hard to focus just on his face rather than on his brown, hard torso and its generous sprinkling of dark hair that seemed horribly, unashamedly masculine. 'Do you miss it? I know Milan is very busy and very commercial, but you grew up here. Don't you sometimes long for the tranquillity of the open spaces?'

'I think you're confusing me with one of those sensitive types you claim to like,' Giancarlo murmured. He clasped the railing on either side of her, bracing himself and locking her into a suffocating, non-physical embrace, his lean body only inches away from her. 'I don't do nostalgia. Not, I might add, that I have much to be nostalgic about.'

The smile he shot her sent a heat wave rushing through her body. She was barefoot and her toes curled against the smooth wooden planks of the sailboat. God, she could scarcely breathe! Their eyes tangled and Caroline felt giddy under the shimmering intensity of his midnight-dark eyes.

She could barely remember what they had been talking about. The quiet sounds of the water had receded and she thought she could hear the whoosh of blood rushing through her veins and the frantic pounding of her heart.

She wasn't aware of her eyes half closing, or of her mouth parting on a question that was never asked.

Giancarlo was more than aware of both those things. The powerful scent of lust made his nostrils flare. He realised that this was exactly what he wanted. Her lush, sexy body combined with her wide-eyed innocence had set up a chain reaction in him that he hadn't been able to control.

'And as for getting away from it all…' Some of her long hair blew across his face. She smelled of sun and warmth. 'I have a place on the coast.' From nowhere sprang such a strange notion that he barely registered it. He would like to take her there. He had never had any such inclination with any woman in the past. That was purely his domain, his private getaway from the hassle of everyday life, always maintained, waiting and ready for those very rare occasions when he felt the need to make use of it.

'You have the most amazing hair.' He captured some of it, sank his fingers into its untamed length. 'You should never have it cut.'

Caroline knew that he was going to kiss her and she strained up towards him with a sigh of abandon. She never knew that she could want something so much in her life.

She lifted her hand and trembled as her fingers raked through his fine, dark, silky hair.

With a stifled groan, Giancarlo angled down and lost himself in a kiss that was hungry and exploring. His questing tongue melded with hers and, as the kiss deepened, he spanned her rib cage with urgent, impatient hands. They were out in the open but visible to no one. Other boats, dotted on the sparkling, still water, were too far away to witness his lack of control.

The push of her breasts as she curved her body up to him was explosive to his libido and he hooked his fingers under the straps of her swimsuit. He couldn't pull them down fast enough, and as her breasts spilled out in their glorious abundance he had to control the savage reaction of his throbbing arousal.

'God, you're beautiful,' he growled hoarsely.

'Beautiful' had never been one of those things Caroline had ever considered herself. Friendly, yes. Reasonably attractive, perhaps. But *beautiful*?

Right now, however, as she looked at him with a fevered, slumberous gaze, she believed him and she was infused with a heady, wanton feeling of total recklessness. She wanted to bask in his open admiration. It was a huge turn-on. He looked down and her nipples tightened and ached in immediate response. Her ability to think and to reason had been scattered to the four winds and she moaned and arched her back as his big hands covered her breasts, massaging them, pushing them up so that her swollen nipples were offered up to his scorching inspection. The sun on her half-naked body was beautifully warm. She closed her eyes, hands outstretched on the railing on either side of her.

It was a snapshot of an erotic, abundant goddess with her hair streaming back, and Giancarlo lowered his head to close his mouth over the pulsating pink disc of a surrendered nipple.

Reaching down, Caroline curled her fingers into his hair. She felt like a rag doll and had to stop herself from sinking to the floor of the boat as he plundered her breasts, first one then the other, suckling on her nipple, drawing it into his mouth so that he could tease the distended tip with his tongue. She felt powerful and submissive at the same time as he feasted on her, licking, nipping, sucking, driving her crazy with his mouth.

When his hand clasped her thigh, she nearly fainted. The swimsuit was pulled lower and he trailed kisses over each inch of flesh that was gradually exposed. The paleness of her stomach was a sharp contrast to the golden colour she had acquired over the summer months.

Giancarlo found that he liked that. It was a *real* body, the body of a living, breathing, fulsome woman, unlike the statue-perfect, all-over-bronzed bodies of the stick insects he was accustomed to. He rose to his feet and pushed his leg between her thighs, moving it slowly and insistently which made the boat rock ever so slightly. Caroline, with her phobia of water, barely noticed. She was on a different planet and experiencing sensations that were all new and wonderful.

She only surfaced, abruptly and rudely, when the sound of an outboard motor broke through her blurry, cotton-wool haze. She gasped, shocked at her state of undress and mortified at her rebellious body, which had disobeyed every law of self-preservation to flirt perilously with a situation that instinctively screamed danger.

Struggling to free herself, she felt the boat sway and rock under her and she stumbled to rebalance herself.

'What the hell are you doing? You're going to capsize this thing. Stay still!'

He tried to hold her arms as she frantically endeavoured to pull up her swimsuit and hide the shameful spectacle of her nudity.

'How *could* you?' Caroline was shaking like a leaf as she cautiously made her way back to the centre of the boat. Her huge brown eyes were wide with accusation, and Giancarlo, who had never in living memory experienced any form of rejection from a woman, raked his hand impatiently through his hair.

'How could I *what*?'

'You *know* what!'

He took a couple of steps towards her and was outraged when she shrank back. Did she find him *threatening*?

'What I *know*—' his voice was a whiplash, leaving her no leeway to nurse fanciful notions of being seduced against her will '—is that you *wanted* it, and it's no good huddling there like a virtuous maiden whose virginity has been sullied. Snap out of it, Caroline. You practically threw yourself at me.'

'I did no such *thing*,' Caroline whispered, distraught, because she had, she really *had*, and she couldn't for the life of her understand why.

Giancarlo shook his head with such rampant incredulity that she was forced to look away. When she next sneaked a glance at him, it was to see him preparing to sail back to shore. His face was dark with anger.

With agonising honesty, Caroline licked her lips and cleared her throat. It was no good letting this thing fester in simmering silence. She had had a terrible moment of horrifying misjudgement and she would just have to say something.

'I'm sorry,' she said bravely, addressing his profile, which offered nothing by way of encouragement. 'I know I was partly to blame…'

Giancarlo glanced over to her with a brooding scowl. 'How kind of you to rethink your accusation that I was intent on taking advantage of you.'

'I know you weren't! I never meant to imply that. Look…' With urgent consternation, Caroline leaned towards him. 'I don't know what happened. I don't even *like* you! I disapprove of everything about you.'

'*Everything*, Caroline? Let's not labour that statement too much. You might find that you need to retract it.' Not only was Giancarlo furious at her inexplicable withdrawal, when it had been plain to see that she had been as hot and ready for him as he had been for her, but he was more furious with himself for not being able to look at her for fear of his libido going haywire all over again.

'You took me by surprise.'

'Oh, we're back to that old chestnut, are we? I'm the arch-seducer and you're the shrinking violet!'

'It's the heat,' she countered with increasing desperation. 'And the situation. I've never been on the water like this before. Everything must have just been too much.' She continued to look at him earnestly. 'It's *impossible* for me to be attracted to you.' She sought to impose an explanation for her wildly out-of-character behaviour. 'We don't get along at *all* and I disapprove of why you decided to come here to see Alberto. I don't care about money and I've never been impressed by people who think that making money is the most important thing in the world. And, furthermore, I just don't get it with guys who are scared of commitment. I have no respect for them. So…so…'

'So, despite all of that, you still couldn't resist me. What do you think that says?'

'That's what I'm trying to tell you. It doesn't say *anything*!'

Giancarlo detected the horror in her voice and he didn't

quite know how to deal with it. He would have made love to her right there, on the boat, and he certainly couldn't think of any other woman who wouldn't have relished the experience. The fact that this woman was intent on treating it as something she had to remove herself from as quickly as possible was frankly an insult of the highest order.

Caroline felt that she was finally in possession of her senses once again. 'I think you'll agree that that unfortunate episode is something we'd best put right behind us. Pretend it never happened.'

'You're attracted to me, Caroline.'

'I'm not. Haven't you listened to a word I've just been saying? I got carried away because I'm here, on a boat, out of my comfort zone. I don't go for men like you. I know you probably find that horribly insulting but it happens to be the truth.'

'You're attracted to me, and the faster you face that the better off you'll be.'

'And how do you figure that out, Giancarlo? How?'

'You've spent your life thinking that the local lad who enjoys the barn dance on a Saturday and whose greatest ambition is to have three kids and buy a semi-detached house on the street next to where your parents live is your ideal man. Just as you tried to kid yourself that never leaving the countryside was what you wanted out of life. Wrong on both counts. Your head's telling you what you should want, but here I am, a real man, and you just can't help yourself. Don't worry. Amazingly, it's mutual.'

Caroline went white at his brutal summary of everything she didn't want to face. Her behaviour made no sense to her. She didn't approve of him one bit, yet she had succumbed faster than she could ever have dreamt possible.

It was lust, pure and simple, and he wanted to drag that shameful admission out of her because he had an ego the size of a liner and he didn't care for the fact that she had rejected him. Had he thought that he was complimenting her when he told her that, *amazingly*, he found her attractive? Did he seriously think that it felt good to be somebody's novelty for five minutes before he returned to the sort of woman he usually liked?

Warning bells were ringing so loudly in her head that she would have been a complete idiot not to listen to them. She found that she was gripping the sides of the salty plank of wood sufficiently hard for her knuckles to whiten.

Glancing across at her, Giancarlo could see the slow, painful realisation of the truth sinking in. He had never thought himself the kind of loser who tolerated a woman who blew hot and then blew cold. Women like that were a little too much like hard work. But this woman…

'Okay.' Caroline's words tumbled over one another and she kept her eyes firmly fixed on the fast-approaching shoreline. 'So I find you attractive. You're right. Satisfied? But I'm glad you've dragged that out of me because it's only lust and lust doesn't mean anything. Not to me, anyway. So there. Now it's out in the open and we can both forget about it.'

CHAPTER SIX

It was after five by the time they were finally back at the villa. The outing on the lake had taken much longer than she had thought and then, despite its dramatic conclusion, Giancarlo had insisted on stopping somewhere for them to have a very late lunch.

To add insult to injury, he had proceeded to talk to her as naturally as though nothing had happened between them. He pointed out various interesting landmarks; he gave her an informative lecture on the Vezio Castle, asking her whether she had been there. She hadn't. He seemed to know the history of a lot of the grand mansions, monuments to the rich and famous, and was a fount of information on all the local gossip surrounding the illustrious families.

Caroline just wanted to go home. She was bewildered, confused and in a state of sickening inner turmoil. As he had talked, gesticulating in a way that was peculiarly Italian, she had watched those hands and felt giddy at the thought of where they had been—on her naked body, touching and caressing her in a way that made her breathing quicken and brought a flush of hectic colour to her cheeks. She looked at his sensual mouth as he spoke and remembered in graphic detail the feel of his lips on her breasts, suckling her nipples until she had wanted to scream with pleasure.

How was she supposed to laugh and chat as though none of that had happened?

And yet, wasn't that precisely what she wanted, what she had told him to do—pretend that nothing had happened? Sweep it all under the carpet and forget about it?

She hated the way he could still manage to penetrate her tight-lipped silence to make her smile at something he said. Obviously, *she* was the only one affected by what had happened out there on the lake.

'Thank you for today,' she told him politely as she opened the car door almost before he had had time to kill the engine.

'Which bit of it are you thanking me for?' Giancarlo rested glittering eyes on her and raised his eyebrows in a telling question that made her blush even more ferociously. She was the perfect portrait of a woman who couldn't wait to flee his company. In fact, she had withstood his polite onslaught over an unnecessarily prolonged lunch with the stoicism of someone obliged to endure a cruel and unusual punishment and, perversely, the fiercer her long-suffering expression, the more he had become intent on obliterating it. Now and again he had succeeded, making her laugh even though he could see that she was fighting the impulse.

Giancarlo didn't understand where his reaction to her was coming from.

She had made a great production of telling him just why she couldn't possibly be attracted to a man like him—all lies, of course, as he had proceeded to prove. But she had had a valid point. Where was the common ground between them? She was gauche, unsophisticated and completely lacking in feminine wiles. In short, nothing like the sort of women he went out with. But, hell, she turned him on. She had even managed to turn him on when she had been sitting there, at the little trattoria, paying attention to everyone around them and only reluctantly looking at him when she'd had no choice.

What was that about? Was his ego so inflated that he couldn't abide the thought of wanting a woman and not having instant and willing gratification? It was not in his nature to dwell on anything, to be remotely introspective, so he quickly shelved that thorny slice of self-examination.

Instead, he chose to focus on the reality of the situation. He was here, dragged back to his past by circumstances he could never have foreseen. Although he had a mission to complete, one that had been handed to him on a plate, it was, he would now concede, a mission that would have to be accomplished with a certain amount of subtlety.

In the meantime, reluctant prisoner though he might be, he found himself in the company of a woman who seemed to possess the knack of wreaking havoc with his self-control. What was he to do about it? Like an itch that had to be scratched, Giancarlo found himself in the awkward and novel position of wanting her beyond reason and knowing that he was prepared to go beyond the call of duty to get her. It was frustrating that he knew she wanted him too and was yet reluctant to dip her toes in the water. Heck, they were both adults, weren't they?

Now, faced with a direct question, she stared at him in mute, embarrassed silence.

'I haven't seen as much of the countryside around here as I would have liked,' Caroline returned politely, averting her eyes to stare just behind his shoulder. 'I have a driving licence, and of course Alberto said that I was more than welcome to use the car, but I haven't been brave enough to do much more than potter into the nearest town. Before he fell ill, we did take a couple of drives out for lunch, but there's still so much left to explore.'

Giancarlo smiled back at her through gritted teeth. He

wanted to turn her face to him and *make* her look him in the eyes. It got on his nerves the way she hovered, as if waiting for permission to be dismissed.

He also hated the way he could feel himself stirring into unwelcome arousal, getting hard at the sight of her, her soft, ultra-feminine curves and her stubborn, pouting full mouth. He wanted to snatch her to him and kiss her into submission, kiss her until she was begging him to have his way with her. He almost laughed at his sudden caveman-like departure from his normal polished behaviour.

'Any time,' he said shortly and she reluctantly looked at him.

'Oh, thanks very much, but I doubt the occasion will arise again. After all, you're not here for much longer and I'll be returning to my usual routine with Alberto from to-morrow. Do you need a hand taking anything in? It's just that I'm really hot and sticky and dying to have a shower...'

'In that case, off you go. I think I can manage a couple of towels and a cool bag.'

Caroline fled. She intended on ducking into the safety of her room, which would give her time to gather herself. Instead, she opened the front door to be confronted with a freshly laundered Alberto emerging from the kitchens, with Tessa in tow.

He paused in the middle of a testy row, which Tessa was enduring with a broad smile, to look shrewdly at Caroline from under beetling brows.

'Been a long time out there, my girl. What have you been getting up to, eh? You look tousled.'

'Leave the poor woman alone, Alberto. It's none of your business *what* she's been getting up to!'

'I haven't been getting up to *anything*!' Caroline ad-dressed both of them in a high voice. 'I mean, it's been a lovely day out...'

'Sailing? I take it my son managed to cure your fear of water?'

'I…I… Turns out I wasn't as scared of the water as I'd thought. You know how it is…childhood trauma…long story. Anyway, I'm awfully hot and sticky. Are you going to be in the sitting-room, Alberto? Shall I join you there as soon as I've had my shower?'

'Where's Giancarlo?'

'Oh, he's just taking some stuff out of the car.' The devil worked on idle hands, and a day spent lazing around had made Alberto frisky. Caroline could spot that devilish glint in his eyes a mile away and she eyed the staircase behind him with longing.

'So you two got along, then, did you? Wasn't sure if you would, as you seem very different characters, but you know what they say about opposites attracting…' Inquisitive eyes twinkled at her as a tide of colour rose into her face. Next to him, Tessa was rolling her eyes to the ceiling and shooting her a look that said, 'Just ignore him—he's in one of his playful moods.'

'I'm not in the *slightest* attracted to your son!' Caroline felt compelled to set the record straight. 'You're one-hundred percent right. We're completely different, *total* opposites. In fact, I'm *surprised* that I managed to put up with him for such a long time. I suppose I must have been so *engrossed* with the whole sailing business that *I barely noticed* him at all.' By the time she had finished that ringing declaration, her voice was shrill and slightly hoarse. She was unaware of Giancarlo behind her and when he spoke it sent shivers of awareness racing up and down her spine, giving her goose bumps.

'Now, now,' he drawled softly. 'It wasn't as bad as all that, was it, Caroline?'

The way he spoke her name was like a caress. Alberto

was looking at them with unconcealed, lively interest. She had to put a stop to this nonsense straight away.

'I never said it was bad. I had a lovely day. Now, if you'll all excuse me…' As an afterthought, she said to Tessa, 'You'll be joining us tonight for dinner, won't you?' But, as luck would have it, Tessa was going to visit her sister and would be back later, in time to make sure that Alberto took his medication—which at least diverted the conversation away from her. She left them to it, with Alberto informing Tessa that he was feeling better and better every day, and he would be in touch with the consultant to see whether he could stop the tablets.

'And then, my dearest harridan, you'll be back to the daily grind at the hospital, tormenting some other poor, innocent soul. You'll miss me, of course, but don't think for a moment that I'll be missing you.' Caroline left him crowing as she hurried towards the staircase.

She took her time having a long, luxurious bath and then carefully choosing what she would wear. Everything, even the most boring and innocuous garments, seemed to be flagrantly revealing. Her tee shirts stretched tautly across her breasts; her jeans clung too tightly to her legs; her blouses were all too low-cut and her skirts made her think how easy it would be for his hand to reach under to the bare skin of her thighs.

In the end she settled for a pair of leggings and a casual black top that screamed 'matronly'.

She found them in the sitting-room where a tense silence greeted her arrival.

Alberto was in his usual position by the window and Giancarlo, on one of the upright chairs, was nursing what looked like a glass of whisky.

Caught off-guard by an atmosphere that was thick and

uncomfortable, Caroline hovered by the door until Alberto waved her impatiently in.

'I can't face the dining-room tonight,' he declared, waving at a platter of snacks on the sideboard. 'I got the girl to bring something light for us to nibble on here. For God's sake, woman, stop standing there like a spectre at the feast and help yourself to something to drink. You know where it all is.'

Caroline slid her eyes across to Giancarlo. His long legs were stretched out, lightly crossed at the ankles. For all the world he looked like a man who was completely relaxed, but there was a threatening stillness about him that made her nervous.

She became even more nervous when Alberto said, with a barb to his voice, 'My son and I were just discussing the state of the world. And, more specifically, the state of *my* world, as evidenced in my business interests.'

Giancarlo watched for her reaction with brooding, lazy interest. So the elephant in the room had been brought out into the open. Why not? If the dancing had to begin, why not be the one to start the music instead of waiting? So much easier to be the one in control and, of course, control was a weapon he had always wielded with ruthless efficiency.

'Your colour's up, Alberto,' Caroline said worriedly. She glared at Giancarlo, who returned her stare evenly. 'Perhaps this isn't the right time to…'

'There is no right time or wrong time when it comes to talking about money, my girl. But maybe we should carry on with our little *discussion* later, eh, my boy?' He impatiently gestured for Caroline to bring him the tray of snacks but his sharp eyes were on Giancarlo.

So he'd done it, Caroline thought in a daze, he'd *actually* gone and done it. She could feel it in her bones. Giancarlo had tired of dancing around the purpose for his visit to the villa. Maybe her rejection had hastened thoughts of departure and he had decided that this would be as good a time as any to finally achieve what he had intended to achieve from the very start. Perhaps Alberto's declarations of improving health had persuaded Giancarlo that there was no longer any need to beat around the bush. At any rate, Alberto's flushed face and Giancarlo's cool, guarded silence were saying it all.

Caroline felt crushed by the weight of bitter disappointment. She realised that there had been a part of her that had really hoped that Giancarlo would ditch his stupid desire for revenge and move on, underneath the posturing. She had glimpsed the three-dimensional, complex man behind the façade and had dared to expect more. God, she'd been a fool.

She sank into the deepest, most comfortable chair by the sprawling stone fireplace. From there, she was able to witness, in ever-increasing dismay, the awkwardness between father and son. The subject of money was avoided, but it lay unspoken in the air between them, like a Pandora's box waiting for the lid to be opened.

They talked about the sailing trip. Alberto politely asked what it felt like to be back on the water. Giancarlo replied that, of course, it was an unaccustomed pleasure bearing in mind that life in Milan as a boy had not included such luxuries as sailing trips, not when money had been carefully rationed. In a scrupulously polite voice, he asked Alberto about the villa and then gave a little lecture on the necessity for maintenance of an old property because old properties had a nasty habit of falling apart if left unattended for too long. But of course, he added blandly, old places *did* take money… Had he ever thought of leaving or was possession of one of the area's most picturesque properties just too big a feather in his cap?

After an hour and a half, during which time Ella had removed the snacks and replaced them with a pot of steaming coffee, Caroline was no longer able to bear the crushing discomfort of being caught between two people, one of whom had declared war. She stood up, said something polite about Tessa being back soon and yawned; she would be off to bed. With a forced smile, she parroted something to Alberto about making sure he didn't stay up much longer, that he was to call her on her mobile if Tessa was not back within the hour so that she could help him upstairs. She couldn't look at Giancarlo. His brooding silence frightened her.

'You should maybe come up with me.' She gave it her last best shot to avert the inevitable, but Alberto shook his head briskly.

'My son and I have matters to discuss. I can't pretend there aren't one or two things that need sorting out, and might as well sort them out now. I've never been one to run from the truth!' He was addressing Caroline but staring at Giancarlo. 'It's much better to get the truth out than let things fester.'

Caroline imagined the showdown—well, in Giancarlo's eyes, it was a showdown that had been brewing for the best part of his life and he had come prepared to win it at all costs. She was being dismissed but still she hesitated, searching valiantly for some miracle she could produce from nowhere, like a magician pulling a rabbit from a hat. But there was no miracle and she retreated upstairs. The villa was so extensive that there was no way she could possibly pick up the sound of raised voices, nor could she even hear whether Tessa had returned or not to rescue Alberto from his own son.

She fell into a fitful sleep and awoke with a start to the moon slanting silver light through the window. She had been reading and her book had dropped to the side of the bed. It took a few seconds for her eyes to adjust to the darkness and a few more seconds for her to remember what had been worrying her before she had nodded off: Alberto and Giancarlo. The unbearable tension, like a storm brewing in the distance, waiting to erupt with devastating consequences.

Groaning, she heaved herself out of the four-poster bed, slipped on her dressing gown and headed downstairs, although she wasn't quite sure what she expected to find.

Alberto's suite of rooms lay at the far end of the long corridor, beyond the staircase. Hesitating at the top of the winding staircase, Caroline was tempted to check on him, but first she would go downstairs, make sure that the two of them weren't still locked in a battle to the bitter end. Truth, as Alberto had declared, was something that could take hours to hammer out—and in this case the outcome would be certain defeat for Alberto. He would finally have to bow to Giancarlo and put his destiny in his hands. With financial collapse at his door, what other alternative would there be?

She arrived at the sitting-room to see a slither of light under the shut door. Although she couldn't hear any voices, what else could that light mean except that they were both still in the room? She pushed open the door before she could do what she really wanted to do, which was to run away.

The light came from one of the tall standard lamps that dotted the large room. Sprawled on the chair with his head flung back, eyes closed and a drink cradled loosely in one hand, Giancarlo looked heart-stoppingly handsome and, for once, did not appear to be a man at the top of his game. His hair was tousled, as though he had raked his fingers through it too many times, and he looked ashen and exhausted.

She barely made a sound, but he opened his eyes immediately, although it seemed to take him a few seconds before he could focus on her, and when he did he remained where he was, slumped in the chair.

'Where is Alberto?'

Giancarlo swirled the liquid in his glass without answering and then swallowed back the lot without taking his eyes from her face.

'How much have you *drunk*, Giancarlo?' Galvanised into sudden action, Caroline walked briskly towards him. 'You look terrible.'

'I love a woman who tells it like it is.'

'And you haven't told me where Alberto is.'

'I assure you, he isn't hiding anywhere in this room. You have just me for the pleasure of your company.'

Caroline managed to extract the glass from him. 'You need sobering up.'

'Why? Is there some kind of archaic house rule that prohibits the consumption of alcohol after a certain time?'

'Wait right here. I'm going to go and make a pot of coffee.'

'You have my word. I have no intention of going anywhere, any time soon.'

For once, Caroline failed to be awed by the size and grandeur of the villa. For once, she wished that the kitchens didn't involve a five-minute hike through winding corridors and stately reception rooms. She could barely contain her nerves as she anxiously waited for the kettle to boil, and by the time she made it back to the sitting-room, burdened with a tray on which was piled a mound of buttered toast and a very large pot of black, strong coffee, she half-expected to find that Giancarlo had disappeared.

He hadn't. He had managed to refill his glass and she gently but firmly removed it from him, brought the tray over to place it on the oval table by his chair and then pulled one of the upright, velvet-covered stools towards him.

'What are you doing here, anyway? Did you come down to make sure that the duel at dawn hadn't begun?'

'You should eat something, Giancarlo.' She urged a slice of toast on him and he twirled it thoughtfully between his fingers, examining it as though he had never seen anything like it before.

'You are a very caring person, Caroline Rossi, but I expect you've been told that before. I can't imagine too many women preparing me toast and coffee because they were worried that I'd drunk too much. Although…' He half-leaned towards her, steadying himself on the arm of his chair. 'I've never drunk too much—least of all when in the company of a woman.' He bit into the toast with apparent relish and settled his lustrous dark eyes on her.

'So, what happened? I don't mean to pry…'

'Of course you mean to pry.' He half-closed his eyes, shifted a little in the chair, indicated that he wanted more toast and drank some of the very strong coffee. 'You have my father's welfare at heart.'

'We can talk in the morning, when you're feeling a little less, um, worse for wear.'

'It would take more than half a bottle of whisky to make me feel worse for wear. I've the constitution of an ox. I made a mistake.'

'I know. Well. That's what people always say after they've drunk too much. They also say that they'll never do it again.'

'You're not following me. I made a *mistake*. I screwed up.'

'Giancarlo, I don't know what you're talking about.'

'Of course you don't. Why should you? To summarise—you were right and I was wrong.' He rubbed his eyes, sighed heavily, thought about standing up and discovered that he couldn't be bothered. 'I came here hell-bent on setting the record straight. There were debts to be settled. I was going to be the debt collector. Well, here's one for the book—the invincible Giancarlo didn't get his facts straight.'

'What do you mean?'

'I was always led to believe that Alberto was a bitter ex-husband who had ensured that my mother got as little as possible in her divorce settlement. I was led to believe that he was a monster who had walked away from a difficult situation, having made sure that my mother suffered for the temerity of having a mind of her own. I was drip-fed a series of half-truths! I think another glass of whisky might help the situation.'

'It won't.'

'You told me that there might be another side to the story.'

'There always is.' Her heart constricted in sympathy. Unused to dealing with any kind of emotional doubt, Giancarlo had steadily tried to drink his way out of it. More than anything in the world, Caroline wanted to reach out and smooth away the lines of bitter self-recrimination from his beautiful face.

'My mother had been having affairs. By the time the marriage dissolved, she was involved with a man who turned out to be a con artist. There was a massive settlement. My mother failed to do anything with it. Instead, she handed it over to a certain Bertoldo Monti who persuaded her that he could treble what she'd had. He took the lot and disappeared. Alberto showed me all the documents, the letters my mother wrote begging for more money. Well, he carried on supporting her, and in return she refused to let him see me. She informed him that I was settled, that I didn't want contact. Letters he sent me were returned unopened. He kept them all.'

Giancarlo's voice was raw with emotion. Caroline could feel tears begin to gather at the back of her eyes and she blinked them away, for the last thing a man as proud as Giancarlo would want would be any show of sympathy. Not now, not when his eyes had been ripped open to truths he had never expected.

'I expect that the only reason I received the top education that I did was because the money was paid directly to the school. It was one of those *basics* that Alberto made sure were covered because, certainly, there seems little question that my mother would have spent it or given it away to one of her many lovers, had she had it in her possession.'

'I'm sure, in her own way, she never thought that what she was doing was bad.'

'Ever the cheerful optimist, aren't you?' He laughed harshly, but when he looked at her, his eyes were wearily amused. 'So, it would seem, is my father. Do you know, I used to wonder what you had in common with Alberto. He was a bitter and twisted old man with no time for anyone but himself. You were young and innocent. Seems you two have more in common than I ever imagined. He, too, told me the same thing—my mother was unhappy. He worked too hard. She was bored. He blamed himself for not being around sufficiently to build up a relationship with me and she took advantage of that. She took advantage of his pride, threatened to air all their dirty linen in public if he tried to pursue custody, convinced him that he had failed as a father and that visits would be pointless and disruptive. I was her trump card and she used me to get back at him.

'God, do you know that when she died, Alberto requested to see me via a lawyer and I knocked him back?

She behaved badly, she warped my attitudes, but the truth
is she was a simple waitress who was plucked from obscurity and deposited into a lifestyle with which she was unfamiliar and ill at ease. The whole thing was a mess. *Is* still a
mess. Alberto didn't know the extent of his financial losses.
He's relied on his trusted accountant for the past ten years
and he's been kept pretty much in the dark about the true
nature of the company accounts. Of course, like a bull in
a china shop, that was one of my choice opening observa-
tions.'

'Stop blaming yourself, Giancarlo. You were a child
when you left here. You weren't to know that things weren't
as they seemed. Was…was Alberto okay when he heard? I
guess in a way it's quite a good thing that you came along
to tell him, because if you hadn't none of these secrets
would have ever emerged. He's old. How good is it for the
two of you that all these truths have come out? How much
better for you both to have reached a place where new beginnings can start, even though the price you've both paid
has been so high?'

This time Giancarlo offered her a crooked smile. 'I suppose that's one upbeat way of looking at it.'

'And I know the situation between you hasn't been *ideal*,
but when it comes to Alberto and the money, how much
worse for him to have been called into an impersonal office somewhere, told that everything he'd spent your life
working for had been washed down the tubes?'

'As things turn out.' He closed his eyes briefly, giving
her some stolen moments to savour the harsh, stunning
contours of his face. Seeing him like this, vulnerable and
flawed but brutally, fiercely honest with himself, did something strange inside her. A part of her seemed to connect
with him in a way that was scary and thrilling.

'As things turn out?' she prompted, while her mind

drifted to things going on in her head that made her heart beat faster and her pulses race. Could she be *falling* for the guy? Surely not? She would be crazy to do something like that, and she wasn't crazy. But he made her feel *alive*, took her to a different level where all her emotions and senses were amplified in a way that was new and dangerous but also wonderful.

'As things turn out, reparation is long overdue. I don't blame my mother for the things she did. She was who she was, and I have to accept my own portion of responsibility for failing to question when I was old enough to do so.' He held his hand up as though to forestall an argument, although the last thing Caroline was about to do was argue with him. First and foremost, she wanted to get her thoughts in order. She looked at him with a slightly glazed expression.

'Right,' she said slowly, blinking and nodding her head thoughtfully. She noticed that, even having been at the bottle, he was still in control of all his faculties, still able to rationalise his thoughts in a way that many sober people couldn't. He might be ruthless with others who didn't meet his high standards, but he was also ruthless with himself, and that was an indication of his tremendous honesty and fairness. Throw killer looks into the mix, and was it any wonder that her silly, inexperienced head had been well and truly turned? Surely that natural reaction could not be confused with love.

'The least I can do—' he murmured in such a low voice that she had to strain to hear him '—and I have told Alberto this—is to get people in to sort out the company. Old friends and stalwarts are all well and good, but it appears that they have allowed time to do its worst. Whatever it takes, it will be restored to its former glory and an injection of new blood will ensure that it remains there. And there will be no transfer of title. My father will continue to own his company, along with his villa, which I intend to similarly restore.'

Caroline smiled without reservation. 'I'm so glad to hear that, Giancarlo.'

'You mean, you aren't going say "I told you so", even though you did?'

'I would never say anything like that.'

'Do you know, I'm inclined to believe you.'

'I'm really glad I came downstairs,' she confessed honestly. 'It took me ages to fall asleep and then I woke up and wanted to know that everything was all right, but I wasn't sure what to do.'

'Would you believe me if I told you that I'm glad you came downstairs too?'

Caroline found that she was holding her breath. He was staring at her with brooding intensity and she couldn't drag her fascinated eyes away from his face. Without realising it, she was leaning forwards, every nerve in her body straining towards him, like a flower reaching towards a source of heat and light.

'Really?'

'Really,' Giancarlo said wryly. 'I'm not the sort of man who thinks there's anything to be gained by soul searching but you appear to have a talent for listening.'

'And, also, drink lowers inhibitions,' Caroline felt compelled to add, although she was flushed with pleasure.

'This is true.'

'So what happens next?' Caroline asked breathlessly. She envisaged him heading off to sort out companies and a bottomless void seemed to open up at her feet. 'I mean, are you going to be leaving soon?' she heard herself ask.

'For once, work is going to be put on hold.' Giancarlo looked at her lazily. 'I have a house on the coast.'

'So you said.'

'A change of scenery might well work wonders with Alberto and it would give us time to truly put an uncomfortable past behind us.'

'And would I stay here to look after the villa?'

'Would that be what you wanted?'

'No! I…I need to be with Alberto. It's part of my job, you know, to make sure that he's okay.' Silence descended. Into it, memories of that passing passion on the boat dropped until her head was filled with images of them together. Her pupils dilated and she couldn't say a word. She was dimly aware that she was shamelessly staring at him, way beyond the point of politeness.

She was having an out-of-body experience. At least, that was what it seemed like and so it felt perfectly natural to reach out, just extend her hand a little and trace the outline of his face.

'Don't touch, Caroline.' He continued to look at her with driving intensity. 'Unless you're prepared for the consequences. Are you?'

CHAPTER SEVEN

CAROLINE propped herself up on one elbow and stared at Giancarlo. He was dozing. Due to the throes of love-making, the sheets had become a wildly crumpled silken mass that was draped half-on, half-off the bed, and in the silvery moonlight, his long, muscular limbs in repose were like the silhouettes of a perfectly carved fallen statue. She itched to touch them. Indeed, she could feel the tell-tale throb between her legs and the steady build-up of damp-ness that longed for the touch of his mouth, his hands, his exploring fingers.

He had asked her, nearly a fortnight ago, whether she was prepared for the consequences. Yes! Caroline hadn't thought twice. Of course, that first time—and, heck, it seemed like a million years ago—they hadn't made love. Not properly. He was scrupulous when it came to con-traception. No, they had touched each other and she had never known that touching could be so mind-blowing. He had licked every inch of her body, had teased her with his tongue, invaded every private inch of her until she had wanted to pass out.

For Caroline, there had been no turning back.

The few days originally planned by Giancarlo for his visit had extended into two weeks and counting, for he had taken it upon himself to personally oversee the ground changes that needed to be made to Alberto's company. With the authority of command, he had snapped his fingers and in had marched an army of his loyal workforce, who had been released into the company like ants, to work their magic. They stayed at one of the top hotels in the nearby town while Giancarlo remained at the villa, taking his time to try and rebuild a relationship that had been obliterated over time. He would vanish for much of the day, returning early evening, where a routine of sorts had settled into place.

Alberto would always be found in his usual favourite chair in the sitting-room, where Giancarlo would join him for a drink, while upstairs Caroline would ready herself with pounding heart for that first glimpse of Giancarlo of the day.

Alberto didn't suspect a thing. It was in Caroline's nature to be open and honest, and she was guiltily aware that what she was enjoying was anything but a straightforward relationship. The fact that she and Giancarlo had met under very strange circumstances and that, were it not for those strange circumstances, their paths would never have been destined to cross, was an uneasy truth always playing at the back of her mind. She preferred not to dwell on that, however. What was the point? From that very moment when she had closed her eyes and offered her lips to him, there had been no going back.

So late at night, with Alberto safely asleep, she would creep into Giancarlo's bedroom, or he would come to her, and they would talk softly, make love and then make love all over again like randy teenagers who couldn't get enough of one another.

'You're staring at me.' Giancarlo had always found it irritating when women stared at him, as though he was some kind of poster-boy pin-up, the equivalent of the brainless blonde bimbo. He had found, though, that he could quite happily bask in Caroline's openly appreciative gaze. When they were with Alberto and he felt her eyes slide surreptitiously over him, it was a positive turn-on. On more than one occasion he had had to fight the desire to drag her from the room and make love to her wherever happened to be convenient, even if it was a broom cupboard under the stairs. Not that such a place existed in the villa.

'Was I?'

'I like it. Shall I give you a bit more to stare at?' Lazily, he shrugged off the sheet so that his nakedness was fully exposed and Caroline sighed softly and shuddered.

With a groan of rampant appreciation, Giancarlo reached out for her and felt her willingly fall into his arms. He opened his eyes, pulled her on top of him and ground her against him so that she could feel the rock-hard urgency of his erection. As she propped herself up on his chest, her long hair tumbled in a curtain around her heart-shaped face. Roving eyes took in the full pout of her mouth, the sultry passion in her eyes, the soft swing of her generous breasts hanging down, big nipples almost touching his chest.

What was it about this woman's body that drove him to distraction?

They had made love only an hour before and he was ready to go again; incredible. He pulled her down to him so that he could kiss her, and now she no longer needed any prompting to move her body in just the right way so that he felt himself holding on by a slither.

'You're a witch,' he growled, tumbling her under him in one easy move, and Caroline smiled with satisfaction, like the cat that not only had got the cream but had managed to work out where there was an unlimited supply.

He pushed her hair back so that he could sweep kisses along her neck while she squirmed under him.

The thrill of anticipation was running through her like a shot of adrenaline. She couldn't seem to get enough of his mouth on her, and as he closed his lips around one nipple she moaned softly and fell back, arms outstretched, to receive the ministrations of his tongue playing against the erect bud of her nipple. She arched back and curled her fingers in his hair as he sucked and suckled, teasing and nipping until the dampness between her legs became pleasurably painful.

She wrapped her legs around him and as he began moving against her she gave a little cry of satisfaction.

They had arrived at his house on the coast only two days previously, and although it wasn't nearly as big as the villa it was still big enough to ensure perfect privacy when it came to being noisy. Alberto and Tessa were in one wing of the house, she and Giancarlo in the other. It was an arrangement that Caroline had been quick to explain, pointing out in too much detail that it was far more convenient for Tessa to be readily at hand, and the layout of the villa predicated those sleeping arrangements. She had been surprised when Alberto had failed to put up the expected argument, simply shrugging his shoulders and waving her lengthy explanation away.

'Not so fast, my sexy little witch.' Giancarlo paused in his ministrations to stare down at her bare breasts, which never failed to rouse a level of pure primal lust he had hitherto not experienced with any other woman. The circular discs of her nipples were large and dark and he could see the paleness of her skin where the sun hadn't reached. It was incredibly sexy. He leant down and licked the underside of her breasts, enjoying the feel of their weight against his face, then he traced a path down her flat stomach to circle her belly button with his tongue. She was salty with perspiration, as he was, even though it was a cool night and the background whirr of the fan was efficiently circulating the air.

Caroline breathed in sharply, anticipating and thrilling to what was to come, then releasing her breath in one long moan as his tongue flicked along the pulsating sensitised tip of her clitoris, endlessly repeating the motion until she wanted to scream.

In a mindless daze, she looked down at the dark head buried between her thighs and the eroticism of the image was so powerful that she shuddered.

She could barely endure the agony of waiting as, finally, he slipped on protection and entered her in a forceful thrust that sent waves of blissful sensation crashing through her. His hands were under her buttocks as he continued to drive into her, his motions deep and rhythmic. The wave of sensation peaked, and she stiffened and whimpered, her eyes fluttering shut as she was carried away to eventually sag, pleasurably sated, on the bed next to him.

Similarly spent, Giancarlo rolled off her and lay flat, one arm splayed wide, the other clasped around her.

Not for the first time, Caroline was tempted to ask him where they were going, what lay around the corner for the two of them. Surely something that was as good as this wasn't destined to end?

And just as quickly she bit back the temptation. She had long given up on the convenient delusion that what she felt for Giancarlo was nothing more than a spot of healthy lust. Yes, it was lust, but it was lust that was wrapped up in love—and instinctively she knew that love, insofar as it applied to Giancarlo, was a dangerous emotion, best not mentioned.

All she could do was hope that day by day she was becoming an indispensable part of his life.

Certainly, they enjoyed each other's company. He made

her laugh and he had told her countless times that she was unique. Unique and beautiful. Surely that meant something?

She steered clear of perilous thoughts to say drowsily, 'I've got to get back to my room. It's late and I'm really, really tired…'

'Too tired for a bath?'

Caroline giggled and shifted in little movements so that she was curled against him. 'Your baths are not good for a girl who needs to get to sleep.'

'Now, what would make you say that?' But he grinned at her as she delicately hid a yawn.

'Not many women fall asleep on me,' he said sternly and she smiled up at him.

'Is that because you tell them that they're not allowed to?'

'It's because they never get the chance. I've never been a great fan of post-coital situations.'

'Why is that?' Thin ice stretched out in front of her because she knew that she could easily edge towards a conversation that might be off-limits with him. 'Is that because too much conversation equals too much involvement?'

'What's brought this on?'

Caroline shrugged and flopped back against the pillows. 'I just want to know if I'm another in a long line of women you sleep with but aren't really involved with.'

'I'm not about to get embroiled in a debate on this. Naturally, I've conversed with the women I've dated. Over dinner. After dinner. On social occasions. But my time after we've made love has been for me. I've never encouraged lazing around between the sheets chatting about nothing in particular.'

'Why not? And don't tell me that I ask too many questions. I'm just curious, that's all.'

'Remember what they say about curiosity and cats…'

'Oh, forget it!' Caroline suddenly exploded. 'It was just a simple question. You get so defensive if someone asks you something you don't want to hear.'

Giancarlo discovered that his gut instinct wasn't to ditch the conversation, even though he didn't like where it was going. What did she expect him to say?

'Maybe I've never found the woman I wanted to have chats with in bed...' he murmured softly, drawing her back to him and feeling her relent in his arms. 'Let's not argue,' he said persuasively. 'This riviera is waiting to be explored.'

'Are you sure you can take all that time off work?'

'Surprisingly, I'm beginning to realise the considerable benefits of the World Wide Web. My father may be a dinosaur when it comes to anything technological, but it's working wonders for me. Almost as good as being at an office but with the added advantage of having a sexy woman I can turn to whenever I want.' He smoothed his big hands along her waist then up to gently caress the softness of one of her breasts.

'*And* you're teaching him.' Caroline was glad to put that moment of discomfort behind them. Questions might be jostling for room in her head but she didn't want to argue. She didn't want to explore the outcome of any arguments. 'He's really enjoying those lessons,' she confided, running her hand along his shoulder and liking the hard feel of muscle and sinew. 'I think he finds the whole experience of having a son rather wonderful. In fact, I know *you* feel maybe a bit guilty that you lived with a past that wasn't quite what you thought it was, but he feels guilty too.'

'He's told you that?'

'He called himself a proud old fool the other day when we were out in the garden, which is his way of regretting that he never got in touch with you over the years.' She glanced behind Giancarlo to where the clock on the ornate bedside table was informing her that it was nearly two in the morning. Her eyelids felt heavy. Should she just grab fifteen minutes of sleep before she trudged back to her bedroom? The warmth of Giancarlo's body next to her dulled her senses but she began edging her way out of the bed.

'Stay,' he urged, pulling her back to him.

'Don't be silly.' Caroline yawned.

'Alberto doesn't get up until at least eight in the morning and by the time he gets his act together it's more like nine-thirty before he makes an appearance in the breakfast room. You can be up at seven and back in your room by five past.' He grinned wolfishly at her. 'And isn't the thought of early-morning sex tempting…?' The suggestion had come from nowhere. If he didn't encourage after-sex chat, he'd never encouraged any woman to stay the night. In fact, no one ever had.

He was playing truant from his real life. At least, that was what it felt like, and why shouldn't he enjoy the time out, at least for a little while? Having been driven all his adult life, having poured all his energies into the business of making money, which had been an ambition silently foisted onto him by his mother, why the hell shouldn't he now take time out under these extraordinary circumstances?

Neither he nor his father had been inclined to indulge in lengthy, analytical conversations about the past. In time and at leisure, they could begin to fill in the gaps, and Giancarlo was looking forward to that. For the moment, Alberto had explained what needed to be explained, and his scattered reminiscences had built a picture of sorts for Giancarlo, a more balanced picture than the one he had been given as a child growing up, but the blame game hadn't been played. After an initial surge of anger at his mother and at himself, Giancarlo was now more accepting of the truth that the past couldn't be changed and so why beat himself up over the unchangeable?

However, he could afford to withdraw from the race for a few weeks, and he wanted to. If Alberto had lost his only child for all those years, then Giancarlo had likewise been deprived of his father and it was a space he was keen to fill. Slowly, gradually, with them both treading the same path of discovery and heading in the same direction.

His thoughts turned to Caroline, so much a part of the complex tableau…

Acting out of character by asking her to spend the night with him was just part and parcel of his time out.

He could feel her sleepily deliberating his proposal. To help her along with her decision, he curved one big hand over her breast and softly massaged the generous swell. Tired she might very well be, and spent after their urgent, hungry love-making, but still her nipple began to swell and pulse as he gently rolled his thumb over the tip.

'Not fair,' Caroline murmured.

'Since when would you expect me to play fair?'

'You can't always get what you want.'

'Why not? Don't you want to wake up in the morning with me touching you like this? Or like this?' He slid his hand down to the damp patch between her legs and slowly stroked her, on and on until she felt her breathing begin to quicken.

Giancarlo watched her face as he continued to pleasure her, enjoyed her heightened colour and then, a whole lot more, enjoyed her as she moved against his fingers, her body gently grinding until she came with a soft, startled gasp.

There seemed to be no end to his enjoyment of her body and he had ceased to question the strange pull she had over him. He just knew that he wanted her here with him in his bed because he wanted to wake up next to her.

'Okay. You win and I lose.' Caroline sighed. She shouldn't. She knew that. She was just adding to the house of cards she had fabricated around herself. She loved him and it was just so easy to overlook the fact that the word *love* had never crossed his lips. It shamed her to think how glad she was to have him, whatever the price she would have to pay later.

He kissed her eyelids shut; she was *so* tired…

The next time Caroline opened her eyes, it was to sunshine pouring through the open slats of the wooden shutters. She swam up to full consciousness and to the weight of Giancarlo's arm sprawled possessively over her breasts. Their tangled nakedness galvanised her into immediate action and she leapt out of the bed as he groggily came to and tried to tug her back down to him.

'Giancarlo!' she said with dismay. 'It's after seven! I have to go!'

Fully awake, Giancarlo slung his long legs over the side of the bed and killed the instinct to drag her back to him, to hell with the consequences. She was anxiously scouring the ground for her clothes and he sat for a while on the side of the bed to watch her.

'Are you looking for these, by any chance?' He held up her bra, a very unsexy cotton contraption which led him to think that he would quite like to buy her an entirely new set of lingerie, stuff that he would personally choose, sexy, lacy stuff that would look great on her fabulously lush body.

Caroline tried to swipe them and missed as he whipped them just out of reach.

'You'll have to pay a small penalty charge if you want your bra,' he chided. Sitting on the edge of the bed with her standing in front of him put her at just the perfect height for him to nuzzle her breast.

'We haven't got time!' She tried to slap him away and grab her bra, but put up next to no struggle when he yanked her on top of him and rolled her back on the bed.

'I'll shock you at how fast I can be.'

Fast and just as blissfully, sinfully satisfying. It was past seven-thirty as Caroline quietly opened the bedroom door.

She knew that she was unnecessarily cautious because Giancarlo was right when he had pointed out that his father was a late riser. Very early on in her stay, Alberto had told her that he saw no point in rushing in the morning.

'Lying in bed for as long as you want in the morning,' he had chuckled, 'is the happy prerogative of the teenager and the old man like myself. It's just about the only time I feel like a boy again!'

So the very last thing she expected as she opened the door and let herself very quietly out of Giancarlo's bedroom was to hear Alberto say from behind her, 'And what do we have *here*, my dear?'

Caroline froze and then turned around. She could feel the hot sting of guilt redden her cheeks. Alberto, walking stick in hand, was looking at her with intense curiosity.

'Correct me if I'm wrong, but isn't that my *son's* bedroom?'

He invested the word *bedroom* with such heavy significance that Caroline was lost for words.

'I thought you would still be asleep,' was all she could manage to dredge from her befuddled mind. He raised his bushy eyebrows inquisitively.

'Do you mean that you *hoped* I would still be asleep?'

'Alberto, I can explain…'

As she racked her brains to try and come up with an ex-

planation, she was not aware of Giancarlo quietly opening the bedroom door she had previously shut behind her.

'No point. My father wasn't born yesterday. I'm sure he
can jump to all the right conclusions.'

As if to underline his words, Caroline spun round to find
that Giancarlo hadn't even bothered to get dressed. He had
stuck on his dressing gown, a black silk affair which was
only loosely belted at the waist. Was he wearing anything
at all underneath? she wondered, subduing a frantic temptation to laugh like a maniac. Or would some slight shift
expose him in all his wonderful naked glory? Surely not.

The temptation to laugh gave way to the temptation to
groan out loud and bash her head against the wall.

Alberto was looking between them. 'I'm not sure how
to deal with this shock,' he said weakly, glancing around
him for support and finally settling on the dado rail. 'This
is not what I expected from either of you!'

'I'm so sorry.' Caroline's voice was thin and pleading.
She was suddenly very ashamed of herself. She was in her
twenties and yet she felt like a teenager being reprimanded.

'Son, I'll be honest with you—I'm very disappointed.'
He shook his head sadly on a heavy sigh and Giancarlo and
Caroline remained where they were, stunned. Giancarlo,
however, was the first to snap out of it. He took two long
strides down the corridor, where a balmy early-morning
breeze rustled against the louvres and made the pale voile
covering them billow provocatively.

'Papa…'

Alberto, who had turned away, stopped in his unsteady
progress back to his wing of the house and tilted his head
to one side.

Giancarlo too temporarily paused. It was the first time he
had used that word, the first time he had called him 'Papa'
as opposed to Alberto.

'Look, I know what you're probably thinking.' Giancarlo raked his fingers through his bed-tousled hair and shook his head in frustration.

'I very much doubt you do, son,' Alberto said mournfully. 'I know I'm a little old-fashioned when it comes to these things, and I do realise that this is your house and you are a grown man fully capable of making his own rules under his own roof, but just tell me this—how long? How long has this been going on? Were you two misbehaving while you were in the villa?'

'*Misbehaving* is not exactly what I would term it,' Giancarlo said roughly, his face darkly flushed, but Alberto was looking past him to where Caroline was dithering on legs that felt like jelly by the louvred window.

'When your parents sent you over to Italy, I very much think that this is not the sort of thing they would have expected,' he told her heavily, which brought on another tidal wave of excruciating guilt in her. 'They entrusted your well-being to me, and by that I'm sure they were not simply referring to your nutritional well-being.'

'Papa, enough.' Giancarlo plunged his hands into the deep pockets of his dressing gown. 'Caroline's well-being is perfectly safe with me. We are both consenting adults and…'

'Pah!' Alberto waved his hand impatiently.

'We're not idiots who haven't stopped to consider the consequences.' Giancarlo's voice was firm and steady and Alberto narrowed his eyes on his son.

'Carry on.'

Caroline was mesmerised. She had inched her way forwards, although Giancarlo's back was still to her, a barrier against the full force of Alberto's disappointment.

'I may have been guilty in the past of fairly random relationships…' Just one confidence shared with his father after several drinks. 'But Caroline and I…er…have something different.' He glanced over his shoulder towards her. 'Don't we?'

'Um?'

'In fact, only yesterday we were discussing where we were going with what we have here…'

'Ah. You mean that you're serious? Well, that's a completely different thing. Caroline, I feel I know you well enough to suspect that you're the marrying kind of girl. I'm taking it that marriage no less is what we're talking about here?' He beamed at them, while a few feet away Caroline's jaw dropped open and she literally goggled like a goldfish.

'Marriage changes everything. I might be old but I'm not unaware of the fact that young people are, shall we say, a little more experimental before marriage than they were in my day. I can't believe you two never breathed a word of this to me.'

He chose to give them no scope for interruption. 'But I have eyes in my head, my boy! Could tell from the way you're relaxed here, a changed man, not to put too fine a point on it. And, as for Caroline, well, she's so skittish when she's around you. All the signs were there. I can't tell you what this means to me, after my brush with the grim reaper!'

'Er, Alberto…'

'You get to my age and you need to have something to hold on to, especially after my heart attack. In fact, I think I might need to rest just now after all this excitement. I wish you'd told me instead of letting me find out for myself, not that the end result isn't the same!'

'We didn't say anything because we didn't want to unduly excite you.' Giancarlo strolled back to her and proceeded to sling his arm over her shoulder, dislodging the robe under which he was thankfully decently clad in some silk boxers. 'It's been a peculiar time, why muddy the waters unnecessarily?'

'Yes, I see that!' Alberto proclaimed with an air of satisfaction. 'I'm thrilled. You must know by now, Giancarlo, that I think the world of your fiancée. Can I call you that now, my dear?'

Fiancée? Engaged? Getting married? Had she been transported into some kind of freaky parallel universe?

'We were going to break it to you over dinner tonight,' Giancarlo announced with such confidence that Caroline could only marvel at his capacity for acting. How much deeper was he going to dig this hole? she wondered.

'Of course, you two will want to have some time off to do the traditional thing—buy a ring. I could come with you,' Alberto tacked on hopefully. 'I know it's a private and personal thing, but I can't think of a single thing that would fill me with more of a sense of hope and optimism, a reason for *going on*.'

'A reason for going on where?' Tessa demanded, striding up towards them. 'You're worse than a puppy off a leash, Alberto! I told you to wait for me and I would help you down to the breakfast room.'

'Do I look as though I need help, woman?' He waggled his cane at her. 'Another week and I won't even need this damnable piece of tomfoolery to get around! And, not that it's part of your job description to be nosing around, but these two love birds are going to be married!'

'When?' Tessa asked excitedly, while she did something with Alberto's shirt, tried to rearrange the collar; predictably he attempted to shoo her away.

'Good question, my shrewish nurse. Have you two set a date yet?'

Finally, Caroline's tongue unglued itself from the roof of her mouth. She stepped out of Giancarlo's embrace and folded her arms. 'No, we certainly haven't, Alberto. And I think we should stop talking about this. It's…um…still in the planning stage.'

'You're right. We'll talk later, perhaps over a dinner, something special.' Alberto glowered at Tessa, who smiled serenely back at him. 'Get in a couple of bottles of the finest champagne, woman, and don't even think of giving me your "demon drink" lecture. Tonight we celebrate and I fully intend to have a glass with something drinkable in it when we make a toast!'

'Okay,' Giancarlo said, once his father and Tessa had safely disappeared down the stairs and out towards the stunning patio that overlooked the crystal-clear blue of the sea from its advantageous perch on the side of the hill. 'So what else was I supposed to do? I feel like I'm meeting my father for the first time. How could I jeopardise his health, ruin his excitement? You heard him, this gives him something to cling to.'

Caroline felt as though she had done several stomach-churning loops on a roller-coaster which had slackened speed, but only temporarily, with the threat of more to come over the horizon.

'What else were you *supposed to do*?' she parroted incredulously. Engagement? Marriage? All the stuff that was so important to her, stuff that she took really seriously, was for Giancarlo no more than a handy way of getting himself out of an awkward situation.

'My mother slept around,' Giancarlo told her abruptly, flushing darkly. 'I knew she wasn't the most virtuous person on the face of the earth. She was never afraid of introducing her lovers to me but she was single, destroyed after a bad marriage, desperate for love and affection. Little did I know at the time that her capacity for sleeping around had started long before her divorce. She was very beautiful and very flighty. My father refrained from using the word *amoral*, but I'm guessing that that's what he thought.

'Here I am now. The estranged son back on the scene. I'm trying to build something out of nothing because I want a relationship with my father. Finding out that we're sleeping together, him thinking that it's nothing but a fly-by-night romance, well, how high do you think his opinion is going to be of me? How soon before he begins drawing parallels between me and my mother?'

'That's silly,' Caroline said gently. 'Alberto's not like that.' But how far had Giancarlo come? It wasn't that long ago that he had agreed to see Alberto purely for the purpose of revenge. He felt himself on fragile ground now. His plans had unravelled on all sides, truths had been exposed and a past rewritten. She could begin to see why he would do anything within his power not to jeopardise the delicate balance.

But at what price?

She had idiotically flung herself into something that had no future and when she should be doing all she could to redress the situation—when, in short, she should be pulling back—here she now was, even more deeply embedded and through no fault of her own.

The smell of him still clinging to her was a forceful reminder of how dangerous he could prove to be emotionally.

'If I dragged you into something you didn't court, then I apologise, but I acted on the spur of the moment.'

'That's all well and good, Giancarlo,' Caroline traded with spirit. 'But it's a *crazy* situation. Alberto believes we're *engaged*! What on earth is he going to do when he finds out that it was all a sham? Did you hear what he said about this giving him something to *carry on for*?'

'I heard,' Giancarlo admitted heavily. 'So the situation

is not ideal. I realise it's a big favour, but I'm asking you to play along with it for a while.'

'Yes, but for how long?' A pretend engagement was a mocking, cruel reminder of what she truly wanted—which, shamefully, was a real engagement, excited plans for the future with the man she loved, *real* plans for a *real* future.

'How long is a piece of string? I'm not asking you to put your life on hold, but to just go with the flow for this window in time—after all, many engagements end in nothing.' Giancarlo propped himself up against the wall and glanced distractedly out towards breathtaking scenery, just snatches of it he could glimpse through the open shutters. 'In the meantime, anything could happen.' Why, he marvelled to himself, was this sitting so comfortably with him?

'You mean Alberto will come to accept that you're nothing like your mother, even though it's in your nature to have flings with women and then chuck them when you get bored?'

'Yet again your special talent for getting right to the heart of the matter,' Giancarlo gritted.

'But it's true, isn't it? Oh, I guess you could soft-soap him with something about us drifting apart, not really being suited to one another.'

'Breaking news—people *do* drift apart, people *do* end up in relationships only to find that they weren't suited to each other in the first place.'

'But you're different.' Caroline stubbornly stood her ground. 'You don't give people a chance. Relationships with you never get to the point where you drift apart because they're rigged to explode long before then!'

'Is this your way of telling me that you have no intention of going along with this? That, although we've been sleeping together, you don't approve of me?'

'That's not what I'm saying!'

'Then explain. Because if you want me to tell Alberto the truth, that we're just having a bit of fun, then I will do that right now and we will both live with the consequences.'

And the consequences would be twofold: the fledgling relationship Giancarlo was building with his father would be damaged—not terminally, although Giancarlo could very well predetermine an outcome he might gloomily predict. And, of course, Alberto would be disappointed in her as well.

'I feel boxed in,' Caroline confessed. 'But I guess it won't be for long.' Would she have been able to sail through the pretence if her heart hadn't been at stake? She would have thought so, but if she felt vulnerable then it was something she would have to put up with, and who else was to blame if not herself? Had she ever thought that what she had with Giancarlo qualified for a happy-ever-after ending? 'I feel awful about deceiving your father, though.'

'Everyone deserves the truth, but sometimes a little white lie is a lot less harmful.'

'But it's not really *little*, is it?'

Giancarlo maintained a steady silence. It was beginning to dawn on him that he didn't know her as well as he had imagined. Or maybe he had arrogantly assumed that their very satisfying physical relationship would have guaranteed her willingness to fall in with what he wanted.

'Nor is it really a lie,' he pointed out softly. 'What we have *is* more than just a bit of fun.'

With all her heart, Caroline wanted to believe him, but caution allied with a keen sense of self-preservation prevented her from exploring that tantalising observation. How much *more* than just a bit of fun? she wanted to ask. How much did he *really* feel for her? Enough to one day love her?

She felt hopelessly vulnerable just thinking like that; she

felt as though he might be able to see straight into her head and pluck out her most shameful, private thoughts and desires. She wondered whether he had not dangled that provocative statement to win her over. Giancarlo would not be averse to a little healthy manipulation if he thought it might suit his own ends. But he needn't have bothered trying to butter her up, she thought gloomily. There was no way that she could ever conceive of jeopardising what had been a truly remarkable turnaround between father and son. She would have had to be downright heartless to have done so.

'Okay,' she agreed reluctantly. 'But not for long, Giancarlo.'

Lush lashes lowered over his eyes, shielding his expression. 'No,' he murmured. 'We'll take it one day at a time.'

CHAPTER EIGHT

CAROLINE wished desperately that this new and artificial dimension to their relationship would somehow wake her up to the fact that they weren't an item. A week ago, when they had launched themselves into this charade, she had tried to get her brain to overrule her rebellious heart and pull back from Giancarlo, but within hours of Alberto's crazy misconceptions all her plans had nosedived in the face of one unavoidable truth.

They were supposedly a couple, madly in love, with the clamour of wedding bells chiming madly in the distance, so gestures of open physical affection were suddenly *de rigeur*. Giancarlo seemed to fling himself into the role of besotted lover with an enthusiasm that struck her as beyond the call of duty.

'How on earth are we ever going to find the right time to break it to your father that we're *drifting apart*, when you keep touching me every time we're together? We're not giving the impression of two people who have made a terrible mistake!' she had cried, three days previously after a lazy day spent by his infinity pool. Those slight brushes against her, the way he had held her in the water under Alberto's watchful gaze, were just brilliant at breaking down all her miserable defences. In fact, she was fast realising that she had no defences left. Now and again, she reminded herself to mutter something pointed to Giancarlo under her breath, but she was slowly succumbing to the myth they had fabricated around themselves.

'One day at a time,' he had reminded her gently.

He was beautifully, staggeringly, wonderfully irresistible and, although she *knew* that it was all a fiction which would of course backfire and injure her, she was lulled with each passing hour deeper and deeper into a feeling of treacherous happiness.

Alberto made no mention of their sleeping arrangements. Ideally, Caroline knew that she and Giancarlo should no longer be sleeping together. Ideally, she should be putting him at a distance, and sleeping with him was just the opposite of that. But every time that little voice of reason popped up, another more strident voice would take charge of the proceedings and tell her that she no longer had anything left to lose. She was with Giancarlo on borrowed time so why not just enjoy herself?

Besides, whether he was aware of it or not, he was burying all her noble intentions with his humour, his intelligence, his charm. Instead of feeling angry with him for putting her in an unenviable position with Alberto, she felt increasingly more vulnerable. With Alberto and Tessa, they explored the coastline, stopping to have lunch at any one of the little towns that clung valiantly to the hilltop from which they could overlook the limpid blue sea. Giancarlo was relaxed and lazily, heart-stoppingly attentive. Just walking hand in hand with him made her toes curl and her heart beat faster.

And now they were going to Milan for three days. The last time she had gone to Milan, her purpose for the visit had been entirely different. Today she was going because Giancarlo had stuff to do that needed his physical presence.

'I think I should stay behind,' she had suggested weakly,

watching while he had unbuttoned her top and vaguely thinking that her protestations were getting weaker with every button undone.

'You're my beloved fiancée.' Giancarlo had given her a slashing smile that brooked no argument. 'You should *want* to see where I work and where I live.'

'Your *pretend* fiancée.'

'Let's not get embroiled in semantics.'

By which time he had completely undone her blouse, rendering her instantly defenceless as he stared with brazen hunger at her abundant, bra-less breasts. As he closed his eyes, spread his hands over her shoulders and took one pouting nipple into his mouth, she completely forgot what she had been saying.

By the time they made it to Milan, Caroline had had ample opportunity to see Giancarlo in work mode. They had taken the train, because Giancarlo found it more relaxing, and also because he wanted the undisturbed time to focus and prepare for the series of meetings awaiting him in Milan. An entire first-class carriage had been reserved for them and they were waited on with the reverential subservience reserved for the very wealthy and the very powerful.

This was no longer the Giancarlo who wore low-slung shorts and loafers without socks and laughed when she tried to keep up with him in the swimming pool. This was a completely different Giancarlo, as evidenced in his smart suit, a charcoal-grey, pin-striped, hand-tailored affair, the jacket of which he had tossed on one of the seats. In front of his laptop computer—frowning as he scrolled down pages and pages of reports; engaging in conference calls which he conducted in a mixture of French, English and Italian, moving fluently between the languages as he spoke with one person then another—he was a different person.

Caroline attempted to appreciate the passing scenery but time and again her eyes were drawn back to him, fascinated at this aspect to the man she loved.

'I'm just going to get in your way,' she said at one point, and he looked up at her with a slow smile.

'I hope so. Especially at night. In my bed. I definitely want you in my way then.'

It was late by the time they made it to Milan. Meetings would start in the morning, which was fine, because there was so much she wanted to see in the city that she had not found the time for on her previous visit. While Giancarlo worked, she would explore the city, and she had brought a number of guide books with her for that purpose.

Right now, as they were ushered into the chauffeur-driven car waiting for them at the station, she was just keen to see where he actually lived.

After the splendid seclusion of his villa on the coast and the peaceful tranquility of the view over the sea, the hectic frenzy of Milan, tourists and workers peopling the streets and pavements like ants on a mission, was an assault on all the senses. But it was temporary, for his apartment was in one of the small winding streets with its stunning eighteenth-century paving with a view of elegant gardens. Caroline didn't need an estate agent to tell her that she was in one of the most prestigious postcodes in the city.

The building in front of which the air-conditioned car finally stopped was the last word in elegance. A historic palace, it had clearly been converted into apartments for the ultra-wealthy and was accessed via wrought-iron gates, as intricate as lace, which led into a beautiful courtyard.

She openly goggled as Giancarlo led the way through the courtyard into the ancient building and up to his penthouse which straddled the top two floors.

He barely seemed to notice the unparalleled, secluded

luxury of his surroundings. In a vibrant city, the financial beating heart of Italy, this was an oasis.

His apartment was not at all what she had expected. Where his villa on the coast was cool and airy, with louvred windows and voile curtains that let the breeze in but kept the ferocity of the sun out, this was all dark, gleaming wooden floors, rich drapes, exquisite furniture and deep, vibrant Persian rugs.

'This is amazing,' she breathed, standing still in one spot and slowly turning round in a circle so that she could take in the full entirety of the vast room into which she had been ushered.

Much more dramatically than ever before, she was struck by the huge, gaping chasm between them. Yes, they were lovers, and yes, he enjoyed her, lusted after her, desired her, couldn't keep his hands off her, but really and truly they inhabited two completely different worlds. Her parents' house was a tiny box compared to this apartment. In fact, the entire ground floor could probably have slotted neatly into the entrance hall in which she was now standing.

'I'm glad you approve.' He moved to stand behind her and wrapped his arms around her, burying his face in her long hair, breathing in the clean smell of her shampoo. She was wearing a flimsy cotton dress, with thin spaghetti straps and he slowly pulled these down, and from behind began unfastening the tiny pearl poppers. She wasn't wearing a bra and he liked that. He had long disbanded any notion of her in fine lingerie. If he had his way, she would never wear any at all.

'Show me the rest of the apartment.' She began doing up the poppers he had undone but it was a wasted mission because as fast as she buttoned them up he proceeded to unbutton them all over again.

'I'm hungry for you. I've had a long train trip with far

too many people hovering in the background, making it impossible for me to touch you.'

Caroline laughed with the familiar pleasure of hearing him say things like that, things that made her feel womanly, desirable, heady and powerful all at the same time.

'Why is sex so important to you?' she murmured with a catch in her voice as he began playing with her breasts, his big body behind her so that she could lean against him, as weak as a kitten as his fingers teased the tips of her nipples into tight little buds.

'Why do you always initiate deep and meaningful conversations when you know that talking is the last thing on my mind?' But he chuckled softly. 'I should be making inroads into my reports but I can't stop wanting you for long enough,' he murmured roughly.

'I'm not sure that's a good thing.' She had arched back and was breathing quickly and unsteadily, eyes fluttering closed as he rolled the sensitised tips of her nipples between gentle fingers.

'I think it's a *very* good thing. Would you like to see my bedroom?'

'I'd like to see the *whole* apartment, Giancarlo.'

He gave an elaborate sigh and released her with grudging reluctance. He had long abandoned the urge to get to the bottom of her appeal. He just knew that, the second he was in her presence, he couldn't seem to keep his hands off her. Hell, even when she wasn't around she somehow still managed to infiltrate his brain so that images of her were never very far away. It was one reason he hadn't hesitated to ask her to accompany him to Milan. He just couldn't quite conceive not having her there when he wanted her. He also couldn't believe how much time he had taken off work. He wondered whether his body had finally caught up with him after years of being chained to the work place.

'Okay.' He stepped back, watched with his hands in his pockets as she primly and regrettably did up all those annoying little pearl buttons that ran the length of her dress. 'Guided tour of the apartment.'

While he was inclined to hurry over the details, Caroline took her time, stopping to admire every small fixture; gasping at the open fireplace in the sitting-room; stroking the soft velvet of the deep burgundy drapes; marvelling at the cunning way the modern appliances in the kitchen sat so comfortably alongside the old hand-painted Italian tiles on the wall and the exquisite kitchen table with its mosaic border and age-worn surface.

His office, likewise, was of the highest specification, geared for a man who was connected to the rest of the working world twenty-four-seven. Yet the desk that dominated the room looked to be centuries old and on the built-in mahogany shelves spanning two of the walls, first-edition books on the history of Italy nestled against law manuals and hardbacks on corporate tax.

Up a small series of squat stairs, four enormous bedrooms shared the upstairs space with a sitting-room in which resided the only television in the apartment.

'Not that I use it much,' Giancarlo commented when he saw her looking at the plasma screen. 'Business news. That's about it.'

'Oh, you're so boring, Giancarlo. *Business news!* Don't you get enough business in your daily life without having to spend your leisure time watching more of it on the telly?'

Giancarlo threw back his head and laughed, looking at her with rich appreciation. 'I don't think anyone's ever called me *boring* before. You're good for me, do you know that?'

'Like a tonic, you mean?' She smiled. 'Well, I don't think anyone has ever told me that before.'

'Come into my bedroom,' he urged her along, restlessly waiting as she poked her head into all of the bedrooms and emitted little cries of delight at something or other, details which he barely noticed from one day to the next. Yes, the tapestry on that wall behind that bed was certainly vibrant in colour; of course that tiffany lamp was beautiful and, sure, those narrow strips of stained glass on either side of the window were amazing. He couldn't wait to get her to his bedroom. He was tormented at the prospect of touching her and feeling her smooth, soft, rounded body under his hands. His loss of self-control whenever she was around still managed to astound him.

'Your mother must have been really proud of you, Giancarlo, to have seen you scale these heights.'

'Mercenary as I now discover she really was?' He shot her a crooked smile and Caroline frowned. 'How long have you been storing up that question?'

'You're so contained and I didn't want to bring up an uncomfortable subject. Not when things have been going so well between you and Alberto, yet I can't help but think that you must be upset at finding out that things weren't as you thought.'

'Less than I might have imagined,' Giancarlo confessed, linking his fingers with hers and leading her away from where she was heading towards one of the windows through which she would certainly exclaim at the view outside. It was one which still managed to impress him, and he was accustomed to it. 'Hell, I should be livid at the fact that my mother rewrote the past and determined my future to suit the rules of her own game, but...'

But he wasn't, because Caroline seemed to cushion him, seemed to be the soothing hand that was making acceptance easier. She was the softly spoken voice that blurred the edges of a bitterness that failed to surface. It made his head spin when he thought about it.

'I'm old enough to be able to put things in perspective. When I was younger, I wasn't. My youth helped determine my hardline attitude to my father but now that I'm older I see that my mother never really grew up. In a funny way, I think she would have been happier if Alberto really had been the guy she portrayed him as being. She would have found toughness easier to handle than understanding. He actually kept supporting her even when she had shown him that she was irresponsible with money, and would have taken everything and thrown it all away had Alberto not had the good sense to lock most of it up. He had bank statements going back for well over a decade.'

He hesitated. 'Three years after we left, she made an attempt to get back with my father. He turned her down. I think that was when she decided that she could punish him by making sure he never saw me.'

'How awful.' Caroline's eyes stung with sympathy but Giancarlo gave an expressive, philosophical shrug.

'It's in the past, and don't feel sorry for me. Adriana might have had dubious motivations for her behaviour— she certainly did her best to screw up whatever relationship I might have had with my father—but she could also be great fun and something of an adventurer. It wasn't all bad. She just spoke without thinking, acted without foreseeing consequences and was a little too gullible when it came to the opposite sex. In the end she was as much a victim of her own bitterness as I was.'

They had reached his bedroom and he pushed open the door, gazing with boyish satisfaction at her look of pleasure as she tentatively stepped into the vast space.

One wall was entirely dominated by a massive arched window that offered a bird's-eye view of Milan. She walked towards it, looked out and then turned round to find him watching her with a smile.

'I know you think I'm gauche.' She blushed.

'Don't worry about it. I happen to like that.'

'Everything's so *grand* in this apartment.'

'I know. I never thought it would be my style. Maybe I find it restful, considering the remainder of my life is so hectic.' He walked slowly towards her and Caroline felt that small frisson of anticipated pleasure as he held her gaze. 'It's easy to forget that the rest of the world exists outside this apartment.' He curved one hand around her waist. With the other, he unhooked the heavy taupe drape from a cord, instantly shrouding the room in semi-darkness.

He gathered her into his arms and they made love slowly. He lingered on her body, drawing every last breath of pleasure out of her, and in turn she lingered over his so that the chocolate-brown sheets and covers on the bed became twisted under their bodies as they repositioned themselves to enjoy one another.

It was dark by the time they eventually surfaced. A single phone call ensured that food was brought to them so that they could eat in the apartment, although Caroline was laughingly appalled at the fact that his fridge was bare of all but the essentials.

Despite the opulence of the decor, this was strictly a bachelor's apartment. Lazing around barefoot in one of his tee shirts, she teased him about his craziness in stocking the finest cheeses in his fridge but lacking eggs; having the best wines and yet no milk; and she pointed to all the shiny, gleaming gadgets and made him list which he was capable of using and which were never touched.

She let herself enjoy the seductive domesticity of being in his space. After a delicious dinner, they washed the dishes together—because he frankly hadn't a clue how to operate the dishwasher—and then she curled into him on the huge sofa in the sitting-room, reading while he flicked through papers with his arm lazily around her.

It all felt so right that it was easy to push away the notion that her love was making a nonsense of her pride and her common sense.

'Wake me up before you leave in the morning,' she made him promise, turning to him in bed and sliding her body against his. She had always covered herself from head to toe whenever she had gone to bed but he had changed all that. Now she slept naked and she loved the feel of his hard body against hers. When she covered his thigh with hers, the pleasure was almost unbearable.

Giancarlo grinned and kissed the corner of her mouth as she tried to disguise a delicate yawn.

'Have I worn you out?'

'You're insatiable, Giancarlo.'

'Only for you, *mi amore*, only for you.'

Caroline fell asleep clutching those words to herself, safeguarding them so that she could pull them out later and examine them for content and meaning.

When she next opened her eyes, it was to bright sunshine trying to force its way through the thick drapes. Next to her the bed was empty and a sleepy examination of the apartment revealed that Giancarlo had left. She wondered what time he had gone, and tried to squash the niggling fear that he might be going off her. Was he? Or was she reading too much in the fact that he had left without saying goodbye? It was hardly nine yet. In the kitchen, prominently displayed on the granite counter, were six eggs, a loaf of bread, some milk and a note informing her that he could be as twenty-first-century as any other man when it came to stocking his larder.

Caroline smiled. It was hardly an outpouring of emotion, but there was something weirdly pleasing about that admission, an admission of change whether he saw it as such or not. She made herself some toast and scrambled eggs, finally headed out with her guide books at a little after ten and, pleasantly exhausted after several hours doing all those touristy things she had missed out on first time around, returned with the warming expectation of seeing him later that evening.

'I might be late,' he had warned her the night before. 'But no later than eight-thirty.'

It gave her oodles of time to have a long, luxurious bath and then to inspect herself in the mirror in the new outfit she had bought that morning. It was a short flared skirt that felt lovely and silky against her bare skin and a matching vest with three tiny buttons down the front. When she left the buttons undone, as she now did, her cleavage was exposed and she knew that without a bra he would be able to see the swing of her heavy breasts and the outline of her nipples against the thin fabric.

Of course she would never go bra-less in public, not in something as thin and flimsy as this top was, but she imagined the flare in his dark eyes when he saw her and felt a lovely shiver of anticipation.

With at least another couple of hours to go, she was thrilled to hear the doorbell ring.

She was smiling as she pulled open the door. Very quickly, her smile disappeared and confusion took over.

'Who are you?'

The towering, leggy blonde with hair falling in a straight sheet to her waist spoke before Caroline had time to marshal her scattered thoughts.

'What are you doing here? Does Giancarlo know that you're here? Are you the maid? Because, if you are, then your dress code is inappropriate. Let me in. Immediately.'

She pushed back the door and Caroline stepped aside in complete bewilderment. She hadn't had time to get a single word in, and now the impossibly beautiful blonde in the elegant short silk shift with the designer bag and the high, high heels that elevated her to over six feet, was in the apartment and staring around her through narrowed, suspicious eyes which finally came to rest once more on Caroline's red, flustered face.

'So.' The blonde folded her arms and looked at Caroline imperiously. 'Explain!'

'Who *are* you?' She had to crane her neck upwards to meet the other woman's eyes. 'Giancarlo didn't tell me that he was expecting anyone.'

'*Giancarlo?* Since when is the maid on first-name terms with her employer? Wait until he hears about this.'

'I'm *not* the maid. I'm…I'm…' There was no way that he would want her to say anything along the lines of 'fiancée', not when it was a relationship fabricated for Alberto's benefit, not when it meant nothing. 'We're…involved.'

The blonde's mouth curled into a smile that got wider and wider until she was laughing with genuine incredulity, while Caroline stood frozen to the spot. Her brain seemed to have shifted down several gears and was in danger of stalling completely. Next to such stupendous beauty, she felt like a complete fool.

'You have *got* to be joking!'

'I'm not, actually.' Caroline pulled herself up to her unimpressive height of a little over five-three. 'We've been seeing each other for a few weeks now.'

'He'd never go out with someone like you,' the blonde said in an exaggeratedly patient voice, the voice of someone trying to convey the obvious to a deluded lunatic.

'Sorry?' Caroline uttered huskily.

'I'm Lucia. Giancarlo and I were an item before I broke

it off a few months ago. Pressure of work. I'm a model, by the way. I hate to tell you this, but *I'm* the sort of woman Giancarlo dates.'

There was an appreciable pause during which Caroline deduced that she was to duly pay heed, take note and join the dots: Giancarlo dated models. He liked them long, leggy and blonde; short, round and brunette was not to his liking. She wished, uncharitably, that she was wearing an engagement ring, a large diamond cluster which she could thrust into the blonde's smirking face, but the trip to the jeweller's had not yet materialised despite Alberto's gentle prodding.

'Look, tell him I called, would you?'

Caroline watched as Lucia—elegant name for an elegant blonde—strutted towards the door.

'Tell him…' Lucia paused. Her cool blue eyes swept over Caroline in a dismissive once-over. 'That he was right. Crazy hours flying all over the world. Tell him that I've decided to take a rest for a while, so he can reach me whenever he wants.'

'Reach you to do *what*?' She forced the question out, although her mouth felt like cotton wool.

'What do you think?' Lucia raised her eyebrows knowingly. Despite her very blonde hair, her eyebrows were dark; a stunning contrast. 'Look, you must think I'm a bitch for saying this, but I'll say it anyway because it's for your own good. Giancarlo might be having a little fun with you because he's broken up about me, but that's all you are and it's not going to last. Do yourself a favour and get out while you can. *Ciao*, darling!'

Caroline remained where she was for a few minutes after Lucia had disappeared. Her brain felt sluggish. It was making connections and the process hurt.

This was Giancarlo's real life—beautiful women who suited his glamorous life. He had taken time out and had somehow ended up in bed with her and now she knew why. In extraordinary circumstances, he had behaved out of character, had fallen into bed with the sort of woman who under normal circumstances he would have overlooked, because she was the sort of woman he might employ as his maid.

Even more terrifying was the suspicion that she had just been *there*, a convenient link between himself and his father. She had bridged a gap that could have been torturously difficult to bridge, and by the way had leapt into bed with him as an added bonus. He had found himself in a win-win situation and, Giancarlo being Giancarlo, he had taken full advantage of the situation. The note she had found, which she had optimistically seen as the sign of someone learning to really share, now seemed casual and dismissive, a few scribbled lines paying lip service to someone who had made his life easier; a willing bed companion who gave him the privileges of a real relationship while conveniently having expectations of none.

Caroline hurt all over. She felt ridiculous in her stupid outfit and was angry and ashamed of having dressed for him. She was mortified at the ease with which she had allowed herself to be taken over body and soul until all her waking moments revolved around him. She had dared to think the impossible—that he would love her back.

She hurried to change. Off came the silly skirt and the even sillier top. She found that her hands were shaking as she rifled through her belongings, picking out a pair of jeans and a tee shirt. It was like stepping back into her old life and back into reality. She stuffed the new outfit—which only hours before had given her such pleasure as she had looked at her reflection in the changing room of the over-priced Italian boutique—into the front pocket of her suitcase which she usually kept for her shoes and dirty clothes.

She very much wanted to run away, but she made herself turn the telly on, and there she was when an hour and a half later she heard Giancarlo slot his key into the door.

She had a horrid image of herself in her silly outfit, scampering to the front door like a perfectly trained puppy greeting its master, and she forced herself to remain exactly where she was in front of the television until he walked into the sitting-room. As he strolled towards her, with that killer smile curving his mouth, he began loosening his tie and unbuttoning his shirt.

Bitter and disillusioned as she was, Caroline still couldn't contain her body's instinctive reaction, and she strove to quell the feverish race of her pulse and the familiar drag on her senses. She pulled up the image of the blonde and focused on that.

'You have no idea how much I've been looking forward to coming back...' Tie undone, he tossed it onto one of the sofas and walked towards her, leaning down over the chair into which she was huddled, his arms braced on either side, caging her in.

Caroline had trouble breathing.

'Really?'

'Really. You're very bad for me. Somehow trying to work out the logistics of due diligence is a lot less fun than thinking about you waiting for me back here.'

Like a faithful, mindless puppy.

'I left my chief in command at the meeting. The option of seeing you here, well, it wasn't a difficult choice.'

Seeing me here...in your bed...

'Food first? My man at the Capello can deliver within the hour.'

Because why would you take me out and cut into the time you can spend in bed with me? Before you get bored, because I'm nothing like the girls you want to date, girls

*who look good hanging on your arm... Long, leggy girls
with waist-length blonde hair and exotic, sexy names like
Lucia...*

'You're not talking.' Giancarlo vaulted upright and
strolled towards the closest chair, where he sat and then
leaned forwards, his arms on his thighs. 'I'm sorry I
couldn't go sightseeing with you today. Believe me, I would
have loved to have shown you my city. Were you bored?'

Caroline unfroze and rediscovered the power of speech.
'I had a very nice time. I visited the Duomo, the museum
and I had a very nice lunch in one of the *piazzas*.'

'I'm guessing that there's a 'but' tacked on to that description of your *very nice* day with the *very nice* lunch?'
Something was going on here. Giancarlo could feel it, although he was at a loss to explain it.

He had woken next to her at a ridiculously early hour
and had paused to look at her perfectly contented face as
she slept on her side, one arm flung up, her hands balled
into fists, the way a baby would sleep. She had looked incredibly young, and incredibly tempting. He had had to resist the urge to wake her at the ungodly hour of five-thirty
to make love. Instead he had taken a cold shower and had
spent most of the day counting down to when he would
walk through the front door. Never before could he remember having such a craving to return to his apartment.
'Wherever he laid his hat' had never been his definition of
home.

He frowned as a sudden thought occurred to him.

'Did something happen today?' he asked slowly. 'I take
no responsibility for my fellow Italians, but it's not unheard
of for some of them to be forward with tourists. Did you
get into some bother while you were sightseeing? Someone
follow you? Made a nuisance of himself?' He could feel
himself getting hot under the collar, and he clenched and

unclenched his fists at the distasteful thought of someone pestering her, making her day out a misery.

'Something *did* happen,' Caroline said quietly, her eyes sliding away from him because even the sight of him was enough to scramble her brains. 'But nothing like what you're saying. I didn't get into any bother when I was out. And, by the way, even if someone *had* made a nuisance of himself I'm not a complete idiot. I would have been able to handle the situation.'

'What, then?'

'I had a visit.' This time she rested her eyes steadily on his beautiful face. A person could drown in those dark, fathomless eyes, she thought. Hadn't *she*?

'A visit *here*?'

Caroline nodded. 'Tall. Leggy. Blonde. You might know who I mean. Her name was Lucia.'

CHAPTER NINE

GIANCARLO stilled.

'Lucia was *here*?' he asked tightly. The hard lines of his face reflected his displeasure. Lucia Fontana was history, one of his exes who had taken their break-up with a lot less grace than most. She was a supermodel at the height of her career, accustomed to men lusting after her, paying homage to her beauty, contriving to be in her presence. She was also, in varying degrees, annoying, superficial, vain, self-centred and lacking in anything that could be loosely termed *intelligence*. She had met him at a business function, an art exhibition which had been attended by the glitterati, and she had pursued him. His mistake had been lazily to go along for the ride. 'What the hell was she doing here?'

'Not expecting to find *me*,' Caroline imparted tonelessly. She toyed with the idea of telling him that the blonde had, at first, assumed that she was the maid, the hired help dressed inappropriately for the job of scrubbing floors and cleaning the toilets. She decided to keep that mortifying titbit to herself.

'I apologise for that. Don't worry. It won't happen again.'

Caroline shrugged. Did he expect her to be grateful for that heartening promise, just because she happened to be the flavour of the month, locked in a situation which neither of them could ever have foreseen? She felt an uncharacteristic temptation to snort with disgust.

'I expect there's probably a whole barrel-load of them lurking in the woodwork, waiting to crawl out at any minute.'

'What the hell are you talking about?'

'Women. Exes. Glamorous supermodels you threw over or, in the case of this one, a glamorous supermodel who threw *you* over.'

'Lucia? Did she tell you that she left me?' Giancarlo felt a surge of white-hot rage rip through him. He knew that he had badly dented her ego when he had dumped her, but the thought of her coming to his apartment and lying through her pearly-white teeth made him see red.

'Well, I guess it must have been difficult for her to conduct a relationship with someone when she was travelling all over the place, but she said that she's back now and you can contact her whenever you want. Pick up where you left off.'

No; he was not going to start explaining himself. No way. That was a road he had never been down and he wasn't about to go down it now. It just wasn't in his nature to justify his behaviour, not that he had anything *to* justify!

'And this is what you'll be expecting me to do, is it?' he asked coolly.

Caroline felt her heart breaking in two. She hadn't realised how much she had longed to hear him deny everything the other woman had said. His silence on the subject was telling. Okay, so maybe he wasn't going to race over to Lucia's apartment and fling himself at her feet, but surely if the other woman had been lying he would have denied her story?

'You've gone into a mood because, despite everything, you don't trust me.'

'I'm not in a mood!'

'That's not what my eyes are telling me. Lucia and I were finished months ago.'

'But did you end it or did *she*?'

'What difference does it make? You either trust me or you don't.'

'Why should I trust you, Giancarlo?' She had been determined not to lose her rag, but looking at his proud, aristocratic face she wanted to slap him. Her own crazy love for him, her stupidity in thinking that what they had meant something, rose up like bile to her throat.

'You wouldn't have looked twice at someone like me if we'd met under more normal circumstances, would you?'

'I refuse to get embroiled in a hypothetical discussion of what might or might not have happened. We met and you've had more than ample proof of how attracted I am to you.'

'But I'm not *your type*. I guess I knew that all along— deep down. But your girlfriend made it very clear that—'

'Lucia is *not* my girlfriend. Okay, if it means that much to you to know what happened between us, I'll tell you! I went out with the woman and it turned out to be a mistake. There's only room for one person in Lucia's life and that's Lucia. She's an airhead who can only talk about herself. No mirror is safe when she's around, and aside from that she's got a vicious tongue.'

'But she's beautiful.' Caroline found that she no longer cared about who had done the breaking up. What did it matter? Dig deep and the simple fact was that Lucia was more his type than *she* was. He liked them transient; playthings that wouldn't take up too much of his valuable time and wouldn't make demands of him.

'I dumped her and she took it badly.' He hadn't meant to explain himself but in the end he had been unable *not* to.

'Well, it doesn't matter.'

'It clearly does or you wouldn't be making such a big deal of this.'

Caroline thought that what was nothing to him was a very big deal for her, except there was no way that he would understand that because he hadn't dug himself into the same hole that she had. Every sign of hurt would be just another indication to him of how deeply embedded she had become in their so-called relationship.

What would he do if he discovered that she was in love with him? Laugh out loud? Run a mile? Both? She was determined that he wouldn't find out. At least then she would be able to extract herself with some measure of dignity instead of proving Lucia right, proving that she had made the fatal error of thinking that she meant more to Giancarlo than she did.

Unable to contain her agitation, she stood up and paced restlessly towards the window, peering outside in search of inspiration, then she perched on the broad ledge so that she was sitting on her hands. That way, they kept still.

'I was embarrassed,' Caroline told him. She swallowed back the tears of self-pity that were vying for prevalence over her self-control. 'I hadn't expected to open the door to one of your ex-girlfriends, although it's not your fault that she showed up here. I realise that. She said some pretty hurtful things and that's not your fault either.'

Considering that he was being exonerated of all blame from the sound of it, Giancarlo was disturbed to find that he didn't feel any better. And he didn't like the remote expression on her face. He preferred it when she had been angry, shouting at him, backing him into a corner.

'It *did* make me think, though, that what we're doing is… Well, we need to stop it.'

'Work that one through for me. One stupid woman turns

up uninvited on my doorstep and suddenly you've decided that what we have is a bad idea? We're adults, Caroline. We're attracted to one another.'

'We're deceiving an old man into thinking that this is something that it isn't, and I should have listened to my conscience from the start. It's not just about having fun, never mind the consequences.'

Giancarlo flushed darkly, for once lost for words. If Lucia had been in the room, he would have throttled her. It was unbelievable just how wrong the evening had gone. The worst of it was that he could feel Caroline slipping away from him and there was nothing he could do about it.

'The fact is, that woman was right. I'm not your type.' She couldn't help herself. She left a pause, a heartbeat of silence, something he could fill with a denial. 'You're not my type. We've been having fun, and in the process leading Alberto into thinking that there's more to what we have than there actually is.'

'It's crazy to come back to the hoary subject of *type*.' Even to his own ears he sounded like a man on the back foot, but any talk about the value of 'having fun', which seemed to have become dirty words, would land him even further in the quagmire. He raked frustrated fingers through his hair and glowered at her.

'Maybe if Alberto wasn't involved things might have been a bit different.'

'Isn't it a bit late in the day to start taking the moral high ground?'

'It's never too late in the day to do the right thing.'

'And a woman who meant nothing to me, who was an albatross around my neck after the first week of seeing her, has brought you to this conclusion?'

'I've woken up.' She felt as though she was swallowing

glass and her nerves went into frantic overdrive as he stood up to walk towards her.

Everything about him was achingly familiar, from the smell of him to the supple economy of his movements. Her imagination only had to travel a short distance to picture the feel of his muscular arms under his shirt.

She half-turned but her breathing was fast. More than anything else in the world, she didn't want him to touch her.

'I know it's late, but I really think I'd like to get back to the villa.'

'This is crazy!'

'I need to be—'

'Away from me? Because if you stay too close you're scared that your body might take over?' He muttered a low oath in the face of her continuing silence.

'I don't mind heading back tonight.'

'Forget it! You can leave in the morning, and I'll make sure that I'm not under your feet tonight. I'll instruct my driver to be here for you at nine. My private helicopter will take you back to the villa.' He turned away and began striding towards the bedroom. After a second's hesitation, Caroline followed him, galvanised into action and now terrified of the void opening up at her feet, even though she knew that there was no working her way around it.

'I know you're concerned about Alberto getting the wrong impression of you.'

She hovered by the door, desperate to maintain contact, although she knew that she had lost him. He was turning away, stripping off his shirt to hurl it on the antique chair that sat squarely under the window.

'I'll tell him that your meetings were so intensive that we thought it better for me to head back to the coast, to get out of the stifling heat in Milan.'

Giancarlo didn't answer. She found her feet taking her forwards until she was standing in front of him.

'Giancarlo, please. Don't be like this.'

He paused and looked at her with a shuttered expression. 'What do you want me to say, Caroline?'

She shrugged and stared mutely down at her feet.

'Where are you going to go? I mean, tonight? You said that you'll make sure that you aren't under my feet.' She placed one small hand on his arm and he looked down at it pointedly.

'If you want to touch, then you have to be prepared for the consequences.'

Caroline whipped her hand away and took a couple of unsteady steps back. He had said that before. Once. And back then, light-years ago, she had reached out and touched because she had wanted to fall into bed with him. Now she wanted to run as fast as she could away from him. How had she managed to breach the space between them? It was as if her body, in his presence, had a mind of its own and was drawn to him like a moth to a flame.

'This is your apartment. It's—it's silly for you to go somewhere else for the night,' she stammered.

'What are you suggesting? That I climb into bed next to you and we both go to sleep like chaste babes in the wood?'

'I could use one of the spare bedrooms.'

'I wouldn't trust me if I were you,' Giancarlo murmured, keen eyes watching her as she went a delicate shade of pink. 'You might just wake up to find me a little too close for comfort. Now, I'm going to have a shower. Do you want to continue this conversation in the bathroom?'

Her heart was still beating fast twenty minutes later when Giancarlo reappeared in his sitting-room, showered, changed and with a small overnight bag. He looked refreshed, calm and controlled. She, on the other hand, was perched on the edge of the sofa, her back erect, her hands primly resting on her knees. She looked at him warily.

'You do know,' he said, dropping his bag on one of the sprawling sofas and strolling towards the kitchen, where he proceeded to pour himself a drink, 'that I'll be heading back to the coast once this series of meetings is finished? So I need to know exactly what I'm going to be walking into.'

'Walking into?' She was riveted by the sight of him in a pair of faded jeans and a polo shirt in a similar colour, so different from the businessman who had walked through the door, and all over again she agonised as to whether she had made the right decision. Distressed and disconcerted by Lucia's appearance, had she overreacted? She loved Giancarlo! Had she blown whatever chance she had of somehow getting him to feel the way she felt? If they had continued seeing one another, would love eventually have replaced lust?

As soon as she started thinking like that, another scenario rushed up in her head. It was a scenario in which he became bored and disinterested, in which she became more and more needy and clingy. It was a scenario in which another Lucia clone came along, leggy, blonde and dim-witted, to lure him away from the challenge of someone who spoke too freely. He might find her frankness a novelty now, but it was not a trait he was used to—and did a leopard ever change its spots?

But the way he looked…

She swallowed and told herself just to *focus*.

'Now that you've seen the light, are you even planning on being there at the end of the week?'

'Of course I am! I told you that I'm prepared to go along with this for a short while longer, but we're going to have to show your father that we're drifting apart so that he won't be upset when we announce that it's over between us.'

'And any clues on how we should do that? Maybe we could stage a few arguments? Or you could play with the truth and tell him that you met one of my past girlfriends and you didn't like what you saw.'

Caroline thought of Lucia and she glanced hesitantly at Giancarlo. 'Were all your girlfriends like that?'

'Come again?'

'All your girlfriends, were they like Lucia?'

Giancarlo frowned, taken aback by the directness of the question and the gentle criticism he could detect underlying it.

'I know that Lucia might have annoyed you,' she continued. 'But were they all like her? Have you ever been out with someone who wasn't a model? Or an actress? I mean, do you just go out with women because of the way they look?'

'I don't see the relevance of the question.' Nor could he explain how it was that a beautiful, intellectually unchallenging woman could be less of a distraction than the other way around. But that was indeed the case as far as he was concerned. He had not been programmed for distraction. Somewhere along the line, that hard-wiring had just failed.

'No. It's not relevant.' She looked away from him and he was savagely tempted to force himself into her line of vision and bring her back to his presence.

Instead, he slung his holdall over his shoulder and began heading towards the front door.

Caroline forced herself to stay put, but it was hard because her disobedient feet wanted to fly behind him and cling, keep him there with a few more questions. She wanted to ask him what he ever saw in her. She wasn't beautiful, so was there something else that attracted him?

She wanted to prise anything favourable out of him but she bit back the words before they could tumble out of her mouth.

She thought of this so-called distancing that would have to take place and immediately missed the physical contact and the easy camaraderie. And the laughter. And everything else that had hooked her in.

She heard the quiet click of the front door shutting and the apartment suddenly felt very big and very, very empty.

With her mind in complete turmoil, she had no idea how she was ever going to get to sleep, but in actual fact she fell asleep easily and woke to thin grey light filtering through the crack in the heavy curtains. It took her a few seconds for the links in her mind to join up. Giancarlo wasn't there. The bed was empty. It hadn't been slept in. He was gone. For a few seconds more, she replayed events of the evening before. She was a spectator at a film, condemned to watch it even though she knew the ending and hated it.

The chauffeur was there promptly at nine, and Caroline was waiting for him, her bags packed. Right up until the last minute, she half-hoped to see Giancarlo appear. She guiltily allowed herself the fantasy of him appearing with a huge bouquet of flowers, red roses, full of apologies and possibly with a ring in a small box.

In the absence of any of that, she spent both the drive and the brief helicopter ride sickeningly scared at the very real possibility that he had left the apartment to seek solace in someone else's arms.

Would he do that? She didn't know. But then, how well did she know him, after all?

She had sworn that she had seen the complete man, but she had been living in a bubble. The Giancarlo she had known was not the same Giancarlo who dated supermodels because they were undemanding and because they looked good on his arm.

She felt a pang of agonising emptiness as finally, with both the drive and the helicopter ride behind her, the villa at last approached, cresting the top of the cliff like an imperious master ruling the waves beneath it.

What they had shared was over. She had been so busy dwelling on that that she had given scant thought as to what she would actually say to Alberto when she saw him.

Now, as she stepped out of the taxi which had taken her from the helipad close by to the house, her thoughts shifted into another gear.

They had as left the happy couple. How easy was it going to be to convince Alberto that in the space of only a few hours that had all begun unravelling?

As she frantically grappled with the prospect of yet more half-truths, and before she could slot the spare key which she had been given when they first arrived at the villa into the lock, the front door was pulled open and she was confronted with the sight of a fairly flabbergasted Alberto.

Caroline smiled weakly as he peered around her in search of Giancarlo.

'What's going on? Shouldn't you be in Milan on the roof terraces of the Duomo with the rest of the tourists, making a nuisance of yourself with your camera and your guide book and getting in the way of the locals?' He frowned keenly at her. 'Something you want to tell me?' He stood aside. 'I was just on my way out for a little stroll in the gardens, to take a breather from the harridan, but from the looks of it we need to talk...'

Giancarlo looked at his watch for the third time. He was battle-hardened when it came to meetings, but this particular one seemed to be dragging its feet. It was now nearly four in the afternoon and they had been at it since six-thirty that morning, a breakfast meeting where strong coffee had made sure all participants were raring to go. There was a hell of a lot to get through.

Unfortunately, his mind was almost entirely preoccupied with the woman he had left the previous evening.

He scowled at the memory and distractedly began tapping his pen on the conference table until all eyes were focused on him in anticipation of something very important being said. This was just the sort of awestruck respect to which he had become accustomed over time and which he now found a little irritating. Didn't any of these people have minds of their own? Was there a single one present who would dare risk contradicting anything he had to say? Or did he just have to tap a pen inadvertently to have them gape at him and fall silent?

He pushed his papers aside and stood up. Several half-rose and then resumed their seats.

Having spent the day in the grip of indecision, with his mind caught up in the last conversation he'd had with Caroline, Giancarlo had now reached a decision, and was already beginning to regain some of his usual self-assured buoyancy.

Step one was to announce to the assembled crew that he would be leaving, which was met with varying degrees of shock and surprise. Giancarlo walking out of a meeting was unheard of.

'Roberto.' He looked at the youngest member of the team, a promising lad who had no fear of long hours. 'This is your big chance for centre stage. You're well filled-in on the details of this deal. I will be contactable on my mobile, but I'm trusting you can handle the technicalities. Naturally, nothing will proceed without my final say-so.'

Which made at least one person extremely happy.

Step two involved a call to his secretary. Within minutes he was ready for the trip back to the coast. The helicopter was available but Giancarlo chose instead the longer option of the train. He needed to think.

Once on the train he checked his mobile for messages, stashed his computer bag away, because the last thing he needed was the distraction of work, and then gazed out of the window as the scenery flashed past him in an ever-changing riot of colour.

He was feeling better and better about his decision to leave Milan. Halfway through his trip, he reached the decision that he would start being more proactive in training up people who could stand in for him. Yes, he had a solid, dependable and capable network of employees, but he was still far too much the figurehead of the company, the one they all turned to for direction. Hell, he hadn't had time out for years!

It was dark by the time he arrived at the villa, and as he stood in front of it he paused to look at its perfect positioning and exquisite architectural detail. As getaways went, it was one that had seldom been used. He had just never seemed to find the down time. Getaways had been things for other people.

He let himself in and headed straight for the breezy patio at the front of the house. He knew the routine. His father would be outside, enjoying the fresh air, which he claimed to find more invigorating than the stuffiness of the lakes.

'Must be the salt!' he had declared authoritatively on day one, and Giancarlo had laughed and asked for medical proof to back up that sweeping statement.

It was a minute or two before Alberto was alerted to Giancarlo's shadowy figure approaching, and a few more seconds for Caroline to realise that they were no longer alone.

They had not switched on the bank of outside lights, preferring instead the soothing calm of the evening sky as the colours of the day faded into greys, reds and purples before being extinguished by black.

'Giancarlo!' Caroline was the first to break the silence. She stood up, shocked to see him silhouetted in front of her, tall and even more dramatically commanding because he was backlit, making it impossible for her to clearly see his face.

'We weren't expecting you.' Alberto looked shrewdly between them and waved Caroline back down. 'No need to stand, my girl. You're not in the presence of royalty.'

'What are you doing here?'

'Since when do I need a reason to come to my own house?'

'I just thought that in the light of what's happened you would remain in Milan.'

'In the light of what's happened?'

'I've told your father everything, Giancarlo. There's no need to pretend any longer.'

A thick silence greeted this flat statement and it stretched on and on until Caroline could feel herself begin to perspire with nervous tension. She wished he would move out to the patio. Anything but stand there like a sentinel, watching them both with a stillness that sent a shiver through her.

Caroline glanced over to Alberto for some assistance and was relieved when he rose to the occasion.

'Of course, I was deeply upset by this turn of events,' Alberto said sadly. 'I'm an old man with health problems, and perhaps I placed undue pressure on the both of you to feign something just for the purpose of keeping me happy. If that was the case, son, then it was inexcusable.'

'Aren't you being a little over-dramatic, Alberto?'

Giancarlo stepped out to the patio and shoved his hands in his pockets.

'There is nothing over-dramatic about admitting to being a misguided old fool, Giancarlo. I can only hope that my age and frailty excuse me.' He stood up and gripped the arm of the chair, steadying himself and flapping Caroline away when she rose to help him.

'I'm old, but I'm not dead yet,' he said with a return of his feisty spirit. 'Now I suppose you two should do some talking. Sort out arrangements. I believe you mentioned to me that you would be thinking of heading back to foreign shores, my girl?'

Caroline frantically tried to remember whether she had said any such thing. Had she? Perhaps she had voiced that thought out loud. It certainly hadn't been one playing on her mind. In fact, she hadn't really considered her next move at all, although now that the suggestion was out in the open didn't it make horrible sense? Why would she want to stick around when the guy who had broken her heart would always be there on the sidelines, popping in to see his father?

Besides, surely she had a life to lead?

'Er...'

'In fact, it might be appropriate for us to leave the coast, come to think of it. Head back to the lakes. We wouldn't want to take advantage of your hospitality, given the circumstances.'

'Papa, please. Sit down.'

'And I could have sworn that you two had chemistry. Just goes to show what a hopeful fool I was.'

'We got along fine.' Caroline waded in before Alberto could really put his foot in it. She had confessed everything to her employer, including how she felt about his son. Those were details with which he had been sworn to secrecy. 'We...we... We're just... I'm sure we'll remain friends.'

Giancarlo threw her a ferocious scowl and she wilted. So, not even friendship. It had been an impractical suggestion, anyway. There was no way she could remain friends with him. It would always hurt far too much.

'I'll toddle off now. Tessa will probably be fretting. Damn woman thinks I'm going off the rails if I'm not in bed by ten.'

Mesmerised by Giancarlo's unforgiving figure, Caroline was only dimly aware of Alberto making his way towards the sitting-room by the kitchen, where Tessa was watching her favourite soap on the television. Alberto would join her. Caroline was convinced that he was becoming hooked on it even though he had always been the first to decry anything as lightweight as a soap opera.

'So,' Giancarlo drawled, slowly covering the space between them until he was standing right in front of her.

'I know I said I wouldn't say anything to Alberto, but I got here and it all just poured out. I'm sorry. He was okay with it. We underestimated him. I don't understand why you came back, Giancarlo.'

'Disappointed, are you?' he asked fiercely. He stepped away from her and walked towards the wooden railing to lean heavily against it and stare out at the glittering silver ocean below.

He turned round to face her.

'Just surprised. I thought you had so much to do in Milan.'

'And if I hadn't shown up here tonight, would you have disappeared back to England without saying a word?'

'I don't know,' Caroline confessed truthfully. She bowed her head and stared down at her feet.

'Well, at least that's more honest than the last lot of assurances you gave me—when you said that you'd say nothing to my father. I can't talk to you here. I keep expecting

Alberto to pop out at any minute and join in the conversation.'

'What's there to talk about?'

'Walk with me on the beach. Please.'

'I'd rather not. Now that your father has no expectations of us getting married or anything of the sort, we need to put what we had behind us and move on.'

'Is that what you want?' Giancarlo asked roughly. 'If I recall, you said that, were it not for Alberto, you would consider us… Well, Alberto is now out of the picture.'

'There's more to it than that,' Caroline mumbled. The breeze lifted her hair, cooled her hot face. Beneath her, the sound of the waves crashing against rocks was as soothing as an orchestral beat, although she didn't feel in the least soothed.

'I need more than just a physical relationship, Giancarlo, and I suppose that was what I finally faced up to when your ex-girlfriend paid a visit to your apartment. She's reality. She's the life you lead. I was just a step out of time. When you decided, for whatever reason, to return to Lake Como to see your father, you were doing something totally out of the ordinary. I was just part and parcel of your time out. It was fun but I want more than to just be someone's temporary time-out girl.'

'Don't tell me we're not suited to one another. I can't accept that.'

'Because you just can't imagine someone turning you down? I believe you when you say that you dumped Lucia— and yet there she was, a woman who could snap her fingers and have anyone she wanted, ready to do whatever it took to get you back.'

'And now the boot's on the other foot,' Giancarlo said

in a husky undertone. 'Now I've found out what it's like to be that person who is willing to do whatever it takes to get someone back.'

CHATPER TEN

'You're just saying that,' Caroline whispered tautly. 'You just can't bear the thought of someone walking away from you.'

'I don't care who walks away from me. I just can't bear the thought that that person would be *you*.'

Caroline didn't want to give house room to any hope. One false move and it would begin taking over, like a pernicious weed, suffocating all her common sense and noble intentions. And then where would she be?

'Look, let's go down to the beach. It's private there.'

Caroline thought that that was exactly what she was scared of. Too much privacy with Giancarlo had always proved to be a disaster. On the other hand, what had he meant when he'd said that he would do whatever it took to get her back? Had she misheard?

'Okay,' she agreed, dragging that one word out with a pointed show of reluctance, just in case he got it into his head that he might have the upper hand. 'But I want to get to bed early. In the morning I think it would be best all round for us to leave, return to the lakes, and then I can start thinking about heading back to the U.K.' Her mind instantly went blank and she felt a sense of vague panic.

'I've already been in Italy far too long!' she babbled on

brightly. 'Mum's started asking when I plan to return. It's been a brilliant experience over here. I may not be incredibly fluent but I can hold my own now in Italian. I think it's going to be so much easier to get a really good job.'

'I'm not all that interested in your prospective CV.'

'I'm just saying that I have lots of stuff planned for when I return home and, now that Alberto is back on his feet and this silliness between us is over, there's no reason for me to stay on.'

'Do you really think that what we had could be termed *silly*?'

Caroline fell silent. When on a frustrated sigh Giancarlo began heading towards the lawns, to the side gate that opened onto a series of steps that had been carved into the hillside so that the cove beneath could be accessed, she followed him. It was dark, but the walk down was lit and the steps, in a graceful arch, were broad, shallow and easily manoeuvred thanks to iron railings on either side. She had no idea what the cove was like. The walk was a bit too challenging for Alberto and she had hesitated to go on her own. In Giancarlo's presence, her fear of open water was miraculously nonexistent. Without him around, she had been dubious at the prospect of the small beach on her own. What if the tide rushed up and took her away?

'The water is very shallow here,' Giancarlo said, reading her mind. 'And very calm.'

'I wasn't scared.'

He paused to turn around and look at her. 'No. Why would you be? I'm here.'

Her heart skipped a beat and she licked her lips nervously. Although it was after nine, it was still warm. In the distance, the sea beyond the protected cove glinted silver and black, constantly changing as the waves rose, fell, crashed against rocks and ebbed away. It was an atmosphere that was intimate and romantic but all she felt was trepidation and an incredible sadness that her last memories of Giancarlo would probably be of him right here, on his own private beach. Whatever he said about doing whatever it took, she would know what he meant: he didn't want to lose.

The cove was small and private. Giancarlo slipped off his shoes and he felt the sand under his feet with remembered delight. Then he walked to the water's edge and looked out to the black, barely visible horizon.

Behind him, Caroline was as still as the night. In fact, he could hardly hear her breathing. What was she talking about, leaving the country, returning to the U.K.? Uncertainty made him unusually hesitant. She had confessed everything to Alberto. For him, that said it all. He turned round to see her perched on a flat slab of rock, her knees drawn up, her arms wrapped around herself. She was staring out to sea but as he walked towards her she looked up at him warily.

'I don't want you to leave,' he said roughly, staring down at her. 'I came back here because I had to see you. I couldn't concentrate. Hell, that's never happened to me before.'

'I'm sorry.'

He sat next to her on the sand. 'Is that all you have to say? That you're sorry? What about the bit where I told you that I don't want you to leave?'

'Why don't you? Want me to leave, that is?'

'Isn't it obvious?'

'No. It's not.' Caroline shifted her gaze back to the inky sea. 'This is all about you being attracted to me,' she said in a low, even voice. 'I don't suppose you expected that to happen when you first came to see your father. In fact, I don't suppose you expected lots of things to happen.'

'If by that you mean that I didn't expect to reconcile with Alberto, then you're right.'

'I'm just part of an unexpected chain of events.'

'I have no idea what you're talking about.'

'That's the problem.' Caroline sighed. 'You don't know what I'm talking about.'

'Then why don't you enlighten me?'

Caroline wondered how she could phrase her deeply held fear that she had been no more than a novelty. How many times, as they had laughed and made love and laughed again, had he marvelled at the feeling of having taken time out of his ordinary life? Like someone going on holiday for the first time, he had picked her up and enjoyed a holiday romance with her, but had he ever mentioned anything permanent? Had he ever made plans for a future? Now that she had found the strength to walk away from him, he had come dashing back because she hadn't quite outstayed her welcome. But she would.

'I feel that my life's been on hold and now it's time for me to move on,' she said in a low voice. 'I never really meant to stay for this length of time in Italy in the first place, but Alberto and I got along so well together, and then when he fell ill I didn't want to leave him to on his own.'

'What does that have to do with us?' A cold chill was settling in the pit of his stomach. This had all the signs of a Dear John letter and he didn't like it. He refused to accept it.

'I don't want to just hang around here, living with Alberto, waiting for the occasional weekend when you decide to come down to visit until you get sick of me and go back to the sort of life you've always led.'

'What if I don't want to go back to the life I've always led?'

'What are you saying?'

'Maybe I've realised that the life I've always led isn't all that it's cracked up to be.'

Caroline gave him a smile of genuine amusement. 'So you've decided that you'll take to the lakes and become a sailing instructor?'

'You're so perfect for me. You never take me seriously.'

On the contrary, Caroline thought that she took him *far* too seriously.

'You swore to me that you weren't going to say a word to my father.'

How did they get back to this place? Caroline frowned her puzzlement but then she gave an imperceptible shrug. 'I hadn't planned to,' she confessed truthfully. 'But Alberto was at the front door when I got back. I think if I'd had time to get my thoughts in order—I don't know… But he opened the door to me and I took one look at him and I just knew that I couldn't carry on with the deception. He deserved the truth. It doesn't matter now, anyway.'

'It matters to me. I came here to try and persuade you that I didn't want us to break up. We're good for one another.'

For that, Caroline read 'we're good in bed together'. She looked at him sceptically.

'You don't believe me.'

'I believe that you've had a good time with me, and maybe you'd like the good time to continue a little bit longer, but it's crazy to confuse that with something else.'

'Something else like what?' he asked swiftly and Caroline was suddenly hot and flustered.

'Like a reason for not breaking up,' she muttered. 'Like a reason for trying to persuade me to stay on in Italy when I'm long overdue for my return trip. Like a reason for persuading me to think that it's okay to put my life on hold because we're good in bed together.'

'And let's just say that I want you in my life for longer than a few weeks? Or a few months? Or a few years? Let's just say that I want you in my life for ever?'

Caroline was so shocked that she held her breath and stared at him wide-eyed and unblinking.

'You're not the marrying sort. You don't even like women getting their feet through your front door.'

'You have an annoying habit of quoting me back to myself.' But he shot her a rueful grin and raked his fingers through his hair. 'You also have an annoying habit of making me feel nervous.'

'*I* make *you* feel nervous?' But her mind was still wrapped up with what he had said about wanting her in his life for ever. She desperately wanted to rewind so that she could dwell on that a bit longer. Well, a lot longer. What had he meant? Had she misheard or was that his way of proposing to her in a roundabout manner? Really proposing? Not just asking her to marry him as a pretence…?

Logically, there was no need for him to continue the farce of trying to pull the wool over Alberto's eyes. And Giancarlo was all about logic. Which meant…

Her brain failed to compute.

'I'm nervous now,' Giancarlo said roughly.

'Why?'

'Because there are things I want to say to you. No, things I *need* to say to you. Hell, have I mentioned that that's another annoying trait you have? You make me say things I never thought I would.'

'It's good to be open.'

'I love your homespun pearls of wisdom.' He held up one hand as though to prevent her from interrupting, although in truth she couldn't have interrupted if she had wanted to, not when that little word *love* had been uttered by him, albeit not exactly in the context she would have liked.

'I never knew how much I had been affected by my past until you came along,' he said in such a low voice that she had to lean forward in the darkness to follow him.

'Sure, I remembered my childhood, but it had been coloured by my mother and after a while her bitterness just became my reality. I accepted it. The financial insecurity was all my father's fault and my job was to know exactly where the blame lay and to make sure that I began rectifying the situation as soon as I was capable of doing that. I never questioned the rights or wrongs of being driven to climb to the top. It felt like my destiny, and anyway I enjoyed it. I was good at it. Making money came naturally to me and if I recognised my mother's inability to control her expenditures then I ignored it. The fact is, in the process, I forgot what it meant to just take each day at a time and learn to enjoy the little things that had nothing to do with making money.

'Am I boring you?' He smiled crookedly at her and Caroline's heart constricted.

'You could never do that,' she breathed huskily, not wanting to disturb the strange, thrilling atmosphere between them.

Giancarlo, who had never suffered a moment's hesitation in his life before, took comfort from that assertion.

'Ditto.' He badly wanted to reach out and touch her. It was an all-consuming craving that he had to fight to keep at bay.

'But you never got involved with anyone. Never had the urge to settle down?' It was a question she desperately needed answering. Yes, he might have been driven to make money—it might have been an ambition that had been planted in him from a young age, when he had been too young to question it and then too old to debate its value—

but that didn't mean that he couldn't have formed a lasting relationship somewhere along the way.

'My mother,' Giancarlo said wryly. 'Volatile, embittered, seduced by men who made empty promises and then vanished without a backward glance. I don't suppose she was the ideal role-model. Don't get me wrong, I accepted her and I loved her, but it never occurred to me that I would want someone like that in my life as a partner. I worked all the hours God made, and in a highly stressed environment the last thing I needed was a woman who was high maintenance and I was quietly certain that all women were. Until I met you.'

'I'm not sure that I should take that as a compliment.' But she was beaming. She could barely think straight and her heart was beating like a sledgehammer inside her. Take it as a compliment? She was on a high! She felt as though she had received the greatest compliment of her life! She had felt so inadequate thinking about the exciting, glamorous women he had dated. How could she ever hope to measure up? And yet here he was, reaching deep to find the true essence of her, and filling her with a heady sense of self-confidence that was frankly amazing.

'You're fishing.'

'Okay, you're right. I am. But can you blame me? I've spent weeks trying not to tell you how crazy I am about you.'

Giancarlo grinned and at last reached out and linked his fingers through hers. Warmth spread through him like treacle, heating every part of his body. He rubbed his thumb over hers.

'You're crazy about me,' he murmured with lazy satisfaction and Caroline blushed madly. Liberated from having to hold back what she would otherwise have confessed because she was so open by nature, she felt as though she was walking on cloud nine.

'Madly,' she admitted on a sigh, and when he pulled her towards him she relaxed against his hard body with a sensation of bliss and utter completion. 'I thought you were the most arrogant person on the face of the earth, to start with, but then I don't know what happened. You made me laugh and I began to see a side to you that was so wonderfully complex and fascinating.'

'Complex and fascinating. I like it. Carry on.'

She twisted to look up at him and smiled when he kissed her, his lips tracing hers gently at first, then with hungry urgency. Her breathing quickened and she moaned as he pushed up her top, quickly followed by her bra. He bent his legs slightly, supporting her so that she could lean back in a graceful arch as he began suckling on her nipples, pulling one then the other into his mouth, greedy to taste her.

She understood sufficient Italian now to know that his hoarse utterances were mind-blowingly erotic, although nothing was as erotic as when, temporarily sated, he looked down seriously at her flushed face to say with such fierce tenderness that her heart flipped over, 'I love you. I don't know when it started. I just knew when I was in Milan that I couldn't stand not being close to you. I missed everything about you.

'Meetings and conferences and lawyers and stockpiling wealth faded into insignificance. I was broken up by the way things had ended between us, and I had to get here as quickly as I could because I was so damned scared that I was on the verge of losing you. Damn it, I wondered whether I'd ever had you in the first place!'

It was unbearably touching to know that this big, strong man, so self-assured and controlled, had been uncertain.

'I love you so much,' she whispered.

'Enough to marry me? Nothing short of that will ever be enough.'

EPILOGUE

CAROLINE looked at the assembled guests with a smile. It wasn't a big wedding. Neither of them had wanted that, although they had had to restrain Alberto from his vigorous efforts to have a full-blown wedding of the century.

'Let's wake up these old bores in their big houses,' he had argued with devilish amusement. 'Give them something to talk about for the next ten years!'

They had chosen to be married in the small church close to where Alberto lived and where Giancarlo had grown up. It felt like home to Caroline, especially over the past two months, when the giddy swirl of having her parents over and planning the wedding had swept her off her feet.

She had never been happier. Giancarlo had proven himself to be a convert to the art of working from home and, along with all the marvellous renovations to the villa, had installed an office in one of the rooms from which he could work at his own chosen pace. Which included a great deal of down time with his bride to be.

Her gaze shifted to the man who was now her husband. Amongst the hundred or so guests—friends, family and neighbours who had delightedly enjoyed reconnecting with Alberto, who had become something of a recluse over the years—he stood head and shoulders above them all.

Right now, he was smiling, chatting to her parents,

doubtless charming them even more than they had already been charmed, she thought.

Unconsciously, she placed a hand on her stomach, and just at that instant their eyes connected. And this time his smile was all for her, locking her into that secret, loving world she shared with him and him alone.

As everyone began moving towards the formal dining-room, onto which a magnificent marquee had been cleverly attached so that the guests could all be seated comfortably for the five-course meal, he strode across to her, pulling her into the small sitting-room, now empty of guests.

'Have I told you how much I love you?' He curved his hand behind the nape of her neck and tilted her face to his.

'You have. But you need to remind me how much of this is down to Alberto.'

'The wily old fox.' Giancarlo grinned. 'To think that he knew exactly what he was doing when he decided that we were going to be married. Anyone would be forgiven for thinking, listening to his little speech in the drawing-room, that he had masterminded the whole thing.'

Caroline laughed and thought back affectionately to Alberto's smug declaration that anyone in need of match-making should seek him out.

'I know. Still, how can you do anything but smile when you see how thrilled he is that everything worked out according to his plans, if he's to be believed? I heard him telling Tessa the day before yesterday that there was no way he was going to allow us to go our separate ways because we were pig-headed. He would sooner have summoned the ambulance and threatened to jump in unless we came to our senses.'

'He now has a son and a daughter-in-law and you can bet that I'll be raising my glass to him during my after-dinner speech. He deserves it. You look spectacular tonight. Have I already mentioned that?'

'Yes, but I've always loved it when you repeat yourself.' Her eyes danced with amusement for he never tired of reminding her of his love.

'Have I also told you that I'm hard for you right now?' As if any proof were needed, he guided her hand to where his erection was pressing painfully against his zip. 'It's awkward having to constantly think of trivia to distract myself from the fact that I've spent the past four hours wanting to rip that dress off you.'

Caroline giggled and glanced down at her ivory dress, which was simple but elegant and had cost a small fortune. She was horrified at the thought of Giancarlo ripping it off her, and amazingly turned on by the image at the same time.

'But I guess I'll have to wait for a few more hours until I have you all to myself.' He curved his hand over her breast, gently massaged it just enough for her to feel that tell-tale moisture dampening between her legs, just enough for her eyelids to flutter drowsily and her pulses to begin their steady race.

He kissed the side of her mouth and then dipped his tongue inside to explore further until she was gasping, so tempted to pull him towards her, even though she knew that there was no way they could abandon their own reception even for the shortest of time.

But she wanted him to herself just for a few moments longer. Just long enough to tell him her news.

'I can't wait for us to be alone,' he murmured fervently, before she could speak. He relinquished his hold with evident regret and then primly smoothed the ruffled neckline of her dress. 'Talking and laughing, and making love and making babies, because in case you didn't know that cunning father of mine has already started making noises about wanting grandchildren while he still has the energy to play with them. And he's not above pulling any stunt he wants if it means he can get his way.'

'That seems to be a family trait but, now that you mention it…' Caroline couldn't contain her happiness a second longer. She smiled radiantly up at him and reached to stroke his cheek, allowing her hand to be captured by his. 'You might find that there's not much need to try on the making babies front.'

'What are you telling me?'

'I'm telling you that I'm a week late with my period, and I just couldn't hold off any longer so I did a pregnancy test this morning—and we're going to have a baby. Are you happy?'

Silly question. She knew that he would be. From the man who had made a habit of walking away from involvement, he had become a devoted partner; he would be a devoted husband and she couldn't think of anyone who would be a more devoted father.

The answer in his eyes confirmed everything she already knew.

'My darling,' he said brokenly. 'I am the happiest man on the face of the earth.' He took both her hands in his and kissed them tenderly. 'And my mission is to make sure that you never forget that.'

* * * * *

MILLS & BOON®
By Request

RELIVE THE ROMANCE WITH THE BEST OF THE BEST

0316/05

MILLS & BOON®

Helen Bianchin v Regency Collection!

MILLS & BOON®

Why not subscribe?

Never miss a title and save money too!

Here's what's available to you if you join the exclusive **Mills & Boon® Book Club** today:

✦ *Titles up to a month ahead of the shops*
✦ *Amazing discounts*
✦ *Free P&P*
✦ *Earn Bonus Book points that can be redeemed against other titles and gifts*
✦ *Choose from monthly or pre-paid plans*

Still want more?

Well, if you join today, we'll even give you
50% OFF your first parcel!

So visit **www.millsandboon.co.uk/subs**
to be a part of this exclusive Book Club!

MILLS & BOON®

Why shop at millsandboon.co.uk?

Each year, thousands of romance readers find their perfect read at millsandboon.co.uk. That's because we're passionate about bringing you the very best romantic fiction. Here are some of the advantages of shopping at www.millsandboon.co.uk:

* **Get new books first**—you'll be able to buy your favourite books one month before they hit the shops

* **Get exclusive discounts**—you'll also be able to buy our specially created monthly collections, with up to 50% off the RRP

* **Find your favourite authors**—latest news, interviews and new releases for all your favourite authors and series on our website, plus ideas for what to try next

* **Join in**—once you've bought your favourite books, don't forget to register with us to rate, review and join in the discussions

Visit **www.millsandboon.co.uk**
for all this and more today!